Pr
Carlton Mellick III

"Easily the craziest, weirdest, strangest, funniest, most obscene writer in America."
—*GOTHIC MAGAZINE*

"Carlton Mellick III has the craziest book titles... and the kinkiest fans!"
—CHRISTOPHER MOORE, author of *The Stupidest Angel*

"If you haven't read Mellick you're not nearly perverse enough for the twenty first century."
—JACK KETCHUM, author of *The Girl Next Door*

"Carlton Mellick III is one of bizarro fiction's most talented practitioners, a virtuoso of the surreal, science fictional tale."
—CORY DOCTOROW, author of *Little Brother*

"Bizarre, twisted, and emotionally raw—Carlton Mellick's fiction is the literary equivalent of putting your brain in a blender."
—BRIAN KEENE, author of *The Rising*

"Carlton Mellick III exemplifies the intelligence and wit that lurks between its lurid covers. In a genre where crude titles are an art in themselves, Mellick is a true artist."
—*THE GUARDIAN*

"Just as Pop had Andy Warhol and Dada Tristan Tzara, the bizarro movement has its very own P. T. Barnum-type practitioner. He's the mutton-chopped author of such books as *Electric Jesus Corpse* and *The Menstruating Mall*, the illustrator, editor, and instructor of all things bizarro, and his name is Carlton Mellick III."
—*DETAILS MAGAZINE*

Also by Carlton Mellick III

TUMOR FRUIT

CARLTON MELLICK III

ERASERHEAD PRESS
PORTLAND, OREGON

ERASERHEAD PRESS
205 NE BRYANT
PORTLAND, OR 97211

WWW.ERASERHEADPRESS.COM

ISBN: 1-62105-045-9

Copyright © 2012 by Carlton Mellick III

Cover art copyright © 2012 by Ed Mironiuk
www.edmironiuk.com

Printed in the USA.

AUTHOR'S NOTE

One day I plan to open up a Japanese toy store on a deserted island. Just a small building in the middle of the island, thousands of miles away from civilization. That way, when people get stranded on the island they'll eventually come across my store and wonder what the hell it's doing in the middle of nowhere. Then they'll see me sitting behind the counter with a welcoming smile on my face.

They'll say, "Thank God we found you. Got any food? Water?"

"No," I'll say. "Just toys and collectibles."

"Do you have a radio? A boat?"

I'd shake my head. "No, but I have a plushy Totoro."

If they asked me what the heck I was doing on the island or how I got there I'd just ignore their questions and try to sell them Hello Kitty backpacks or Naruto trading cards.

If they got too upset or didn't have any money I'd ask them to leave.

"Only paying customers are allowed in the store."

The castaways would return to their camp bewildered and confused. During the night, I would pack up my shop and take my private sailboat back home, leaving no trace I was ever there. When they returned the next day, there would be no sign of the Japanese toy store. Then they'd begin to wonder whether it was ever there in the first place.

Why would I go through the trouble of doing this? Well, because I think it would be hilarious. But more importantly it would make the castaways feel like they were a part of a mysterious island story. Like *Lost* or *Mysterious Island* or... *Lost*. And, if you ask me, nothing beats a good mysterious island story.

Ever since the Jules Verne novel published in 1874, there have been dozens to hundreds of movies and novels with a similar set up: people become stranded on a deserted island and soon learn there's something strange or supernatural about the island that makes their situation a lot more dangerous. Two of my favorites in recent years are the children's anime *Uninhabited Planet Survive* and the manga *Cage of Eden*. There's also the novella *Gargoyle Girls on Spider Island* by my friend and fellow bizarro author Cameron Pierce. It's one of my favorites by him and also fits well in the mysterious island genre.

Tumor Fruit is my mysterious island story. But with this story I wanted to focus more on the survival aspect and less on the supernatural. That's one thing that often gets lost in mysterious island stories. The characters tend to be so focused on solving mysteries and fighting strange monsters that they forget that their terrain is really the biggest danger they have to face. Surviving in the wild is not an easy thing to do. That giant crab monster coming after you is the least of your worries.

I've taken wilderness survival classes in the past and I can tell you that if you get stranded in the wild you're most likely completely screwed, unless you get rescued quickly or know exactly what you're doing. Most people these days would have an easier time surviving in the post-apocalypse than on a deserted island. Digging through rubble for cans of beans is a hell of a lot easier than digging for water in the middle of a desert.

But do you know what's a really hard place to survive in?

Outer space.

I'm not fucking with outer space.

I hope you enjoy reading Tumor Fruit as much as I enjoyed writing it. This one is filled with love. Oh, and pirates too!

—*Carlton Mellick III, 8/9/2012 5:44 am*

CHAPTER ONE
THE PIRATE AND THE TEDDY BEAR

"I'm a pirate!"

That's all Peter Boray said when the flight attendant asked him why he was wearing an eyepatch, pirate hat and fake hook for a hand.

"Why would a pirate go into outer space?" she said to him, pointing at the stars through the shuttlecraft window.

"Because I'm a space pirate, of course," Peter said, nodding his head proudly.

She placed a polite smile on her face. By the look she was giving him, it was obvious she assumed the 24-year-old man was mentally handicapped.

Peter just returned the smile and said, "Space pirates are obviously the ultimate pirates."

The flight attendant looked at the teddy bear buckled into the seat next to him. The stuffed animal wore a matching eyepatch and pirate clothes. A skull and crossbones centered the black bandana around its forehead.

"Who is sitting there?" she asked Peter.

He glanced down at the teddy bear.

"Oh, that's Captain Bearbeard," Peter said. "He's the space pirate leader."

"Is he yours?" she asked him.

"No, he belongs to my little brother, Louie," Peter said. "It was Lou's idea to be space pirates."

"Oh, I see," said the flight attendant. She sighed, suddenly feeling less awkward around Peter. "When he gets back from the bathroom, tell him to remain seated as we enter Barack's gravitational well."

"Yes, ma'am!" Peter said, saluting the flight attendant.

The smile did not leave his face even as she walked away from him to give pillows to an elderly woman a few rows back.

Sitting in the seat by the window, on the other side of the pirate teddy bear, a woman had her eyes locked on the odd little man.

"Are you high or something?" the woman asked.

Peter winked at her. "Of course I'm high. I'm in outer space!"

"Uh-huh," she said, throwing her long black hair over her shoulder. "So are the rest of us."

The excited pirate man pointed over the woman's shoulder and out the window. "Can you actually believe we're going to another planet? I never thought it'd be possible that any human being would get to do something like this for centuries, let alone me and Captain Bearbeard!"

When they lifted off in Texas, everyone on the shuttle was just as excited as Peter to be in space for the first time. Not a single eye was left dry after seeing Earth from orbit. Not a single face was absent of a giddy smile when the pilots turned off the artificial gravity and allowed the passengers to float through the cabin. But fourteen hours later—cramped in tiny seats with only a small window of stars to view—being in outer space had lost its appeal. That is, for everyone except Peter. He was just as exhilarated at that moment as he was on takeoff.

Although the woman sitting next to Peter had purposely avoided interaction with him the entire flight due to his hyperactive nature, boredom was setting in enough that she didn't know what else to do.

"Just wait until you see Barack," the woman said, her bright green eyes facing the window. "It's beautiful."

The woman said this so casually she sounded as if she were an expert on the planet.

"You've already seen it?" Peter said.

She nodded. "This is my third trip."

"Third? Third!" Peter nearly flew out of his seat. "How could you afford to go on so many flights? You must be rich!"

She smiled. "I had a shitload of money saved up. Originally, it was supposed to go toward college, but I decided I'm not really the college type. I'd rather visit Barack as many times as I can."

"You must live a glamorous lifestyle. Are you a movie star or something?"

"I'm a prostitute," she said.

Peter continued smiling at her, not at all fazed by her response.

"Not exactly what most people would call glamorous," she said. "But I'm good at my job and I like what I do."

"Prostitute, huh?" Peter said. "How much do prostitutes make?"

"It varies, but I make almost six figures a year."

"That much! Holy crap!"

She shrugged it off as if it really wasn't that much money. "And I only have to work three or four hours a week."

"Are you afraid of being arrested?"

"I'm a legal prostitute. I live in Nevada."

"Prostitution is legal in Nevada?"

"Of course it is. Everyone knows that."

"Well, I didn't. When did this happen?"

"It's always been legal there."

"Wow..." Peter thought about it for a minute. "Does that take a lot of the fun out of it?"

"What do you mean?"

"I always figured legalizing something takes a lot of the fun out of it. Kind of like how drinking alcohol was a lot more fun when we were underage."

The prostitute laughed. "Maybe for the customer. For me, legalization takes away the dangerous element. I wish it were legal everywhere in the country. It's bullshit that it's not."

Peter just nodded. "I guess so."

"Have you ever been with a prostitute?" she asked him.

"No interest," he said.

"Why not?"

"Too expensive," he said. "I'd rather spend my money on other things. Besides, I don't think sex is all that fun anyway."

"You're a guy and you don't think sex is fun?"

"Meh," he said. "It's kind of a lot of work for little reward."

She laughed again. "I think you're the first person I've ever met who wasn't either horribly disgusted or creepily intrigued after learning what I do for a living."

"Well, there's always going to be good things and bad things ahead of you, no matter which path in life you choose," Peter said, raising his eyepatch to look at her with both eyes. "Becoming a prostitute might mean you'll be judged unfairly by most people, but you make a lot of money and enjoy what you do." He pointed out at the stars. "And you can afford to travel to another planet, something that very few people will ever get to do."

The prostitute nodded.

"That's what I always tell myself," she said. "If I didn't do what I do, I probably wouldn't have made it out here so many times. And coming out here to space is worth all of it, no matter the cost."

Peter nodded but quit listening when the shuttlecraft entered the planet's orbit. As the ship turned to the side, the planet of Barack could be seen through the window. It was a bright pink mass with white swirls of cloud. Half the size of Earth, but ten times as captivating. A sight that humans were able to see a thousand years sooner than anyone imagined.

Peter and his six-year-old brother, Louie, lay in the back of his pickup truck, admiring the setting of the two suns.

"The new sun is bigger today," Louie said, using the brim of his pirate hat to block the brightness as he looked at the distant star.

Peter smiled at his brother. These moments they spent together were rare, so Peter cherished them. Ever since their mother died, Louie had to move to California to live with his douchebag stepfather. So they hardly ever got to see each other.

"That's because it's coming closer," Peter said, switching his eyepatch from one eye to the next. "It will keep getting bigger as it passes through our solar system. Then it will get smaller as it moves away."

"Will our old sun ever go away?" The thought made Lou hug his pirate teddy bear close to his chest.

"Not a chance," Peter said. "The new sun only moves because it is a rogue star. It isn't stuck in place by gravity like our normal sun."

"Oh," Lou said, as if he understood everything his older brother was talking about. "Sam says there could be aliens living on the new sun's worlds."

"Well, Sam's right," Peter said, pointing at a small dot in the sky. "Barack, the pink one that was named after our president, has alien life."

"Are the aliens bad? Are they going to attack the Earth?"

"It would be as likely as our earthworms attacking their planet," Peter said. "The aliens that live on Barack are just small, unintelligent life forms. Bugs and plants, mostly."

"Bugs aren't aliens."

"Sure they are," Peter said, tipping Louie's hat over his eyes. "They're just little tiny aliens."

"How do you know?" Lou removed his hat and rubbed sweat from his lumpy bald head. "Has anyone been there?"

"Just probes," Peter said. "But people will be going there once it gets close enough."

"Can we go there?" Lou said.

"Only astronauts will get to go," Peter said.

"If we become astronauts can we go?"

"Hmmm..." Peter said. "I don't know if NASA would accept a couple of pirates like us. They'd be afraid we'd steal their spaceships."

A sad look entered Lou's eyes. It was a look Peter had been seeing a lot lately.

"Hey, actually, maybe we should steal their spaceships," Peter said, trying to cheer up Louie before he cried again. "That's what real pirates would do."

"Yeah," Lou said, his face brightening. "We can be space pirates!"

"Space pirates are awesome!"

"Space pirates have robot arms and lasers!"

"Lasers!" Peter grabbed his brother and tickled him, yelling "Lasers! Lasers!"

Louie laughed so hard he went into a coughing fit. His face turned red.

Peter stopped tickling him and hugged him close. "It's okay, Louie."

His little brother continued coughing until blood covered both their pirate shirts.

When he was breathing regularly, Peter asked, "Do you need to go to the hospital?"

Lou shook his head. "I'm sick of going to the hospital."

"My name's Nkosazana," the prostitute said to Peter, offering her hand. "But people usually just call me Zana."

Peter shook her hand with his plastic hook and said, "What kind of name is that?"

"African," she said. "I was born in South Africa, though my family moved to the states when I was two."

"You're mulatto then?"

Zana paused. She was taken aback by his forwardness.

"You look mulatto," Peter said. "You have light brown skin and green eyes."

"Uh, yeah," she said. "My father was of English descent and my mother was native. She had some Khoisan blood in her, which is why my eyes are shaped this way."

Zana pointed at the epicanthic folds in her eyes, which made her look part Asian. It was a common trait among natives of southern Africa.

Peter stared into her eyes for an uncomfortable length of time. He made a box with his hands, as if framing her face in a camera angle.

"I wish I could paint what I'm seeing right now," he said.

14

"The pink planet against your creamy mulatto skin looks so beautiful at this angle."

Zana just laughed at him.

"That might be the sweetest racist thing anyone has ever said to me," she said.

"Huh? That was racist?"

"Well, if it wasn't racist it was at least creepy."

"Yeah," Peter said, nodding his head. "It might have been a little creepy."

"It's okay," Zana said. "Creepy doesn't faze me anymore."

Peter nodded at her as if trying to express an understanding for what it was like to be surrounded by creepy guys all the time. He didn't realize he was petting the pirate teddy bear with his plastic hook hand as he nodded his head.

Peter sat next to his little brother in the hospital bed and presented him with the pirate teddy bear.

"What did you do to Bear?"

"He's not just Bear anymore," Peter said. "Now he's Captain Bearbeard."

Peter's little brother, Louie, was terminal. When the kid was diagnosed, it was just after their mother had died. And it was the anniversary of their father's passing. Peter couldn't handle the thought of losing his little brother as well.

It seemed like his world was collapsing around him. Not only was his family dying off, but it was also around the same time the rogue star, Nimoy, had first entered the solar system. Everyone was predicting the end of the world. The experts all said they would be safe, but nobody believed them. Those same experts also said it would take a hundred years before the star would reach their solar system, but Nimoy only took five.

Whether it was really the end of the world or not, it sure felt that way to Peter. It was bad enough seeing his mother die of breast cancer. Now he had to see his baby brother ravaged by an even more horrible disease.

When Louie's hair fell out, Peter shaved his own head so his brother wouldn't feel so bad. When Louie's left eye became rotten and had to be removed, Peter bought an eyepatch to match his brother's. He never took it off from that day forward.

"We get to be pirates!" Peter said, giving his brother the rest of his pirate costume. "You, me, and Captain Bearbeard here. We're the pirate trio."

"I don't want to be a pirate," Louie said.

"What?" Peter said. "How can you not want to be a pirate? Everyone wants to be a pirate."

"I don't."

"Don't you like swashbuckling and sailing the Seven Seas in search for buried treasure?"

"I don't know," Louie said.

"We'll get Uncle Allen to take us out on his boat and then we'll sail into the sea, drinking rum and singing sea shanties."

In his new pirate costume, Peter got to his feet and sang a sea shanty to his brother. He acted like a jolly drunken pirate, doing a little pirate jig. He wouldn't stop until he saw his little brother smiling. Then his brother's smiles turned to laughter.

"So what do you say, me matey?" Peter said in his best pirate impersonation. "Are ye a pirate or a barnacle-bitten land lubber?"

"Pirate!" Lou said, his face bright with excitement.

"Then a pirate ye shall be," Peter said, putting a pirate hat over the boy's hairless head.

Whenever Louie was feeling okay enough to leave the hospital, Peter would take his brother out on their uncle's boat. Allen wasn't really their uncle, but he had been a friend of their mother's since long before Louie was born.

Peter and Allen would go out to a small island off the coast of San Diego the day before and bury a small chest filled with gold dollar coins. Then Peter would draw a treasure map on an old cloth, burning the edges to make it seem withered and aged.

They would spend the afternoon sailing around the coast, acting like pirates. Even Uncle Allen got into the spirit of things.

Once they reached the X on the map, Peter would take his brother and Captain Bearbeard toward the island in a small boat. They would follow the rest of the directions on the map and then dig up the buried treasure.

The look of excitement on Louie's face when he opened the chest made all the work worthwhile. Peter smiled so hard he cried every time he watched his brother counting each of the little gold coins, listing off all of the great things he would buy with his newfound riches. Being pirates brought so much joy to them both, so Peter tried to take him out as often as he could.

But as time went by, Louie spent more time in the hospital than he spent out. His douchebag stepfather discouraged Peter from taking Louie too far away from the doctors. Then Uncle Allen went into debt and had to put his boat up for sale. Eventually, Peter and Louie could only be pirates at home or in the hospital. They couldn't go on any adventures anymore.

Peter promised he would take Louie on one big adventure someday soon, bigger than any of the adventures they had ever been on before. But what they could do, Peter didn't know. The last great adventure seemed like it was never going to happen.

That was when Peter heard about the trips to the planet Barack. For a period of four months, the distance between Barack and Earth would be close enough for humans to travel. Not only that, but there were hundreds of commercial flights scheduled specifically for civilians who wanted to tour this new planet.

"A once in a lifetime opportunity," they called it.

"More like once in a million lifetimes," Peter would respond.

The company made billions off ticket sales. Although they said the tickets were so affordable that even an average middle-class family could afford them, just one ticket was a year's salary for most people.

But Peter didn't care.

"No matter what," he said. "I'm getting two tickets. No matter what it takes, Louie and I will be space pirates before that pink planet leaves the sky."

The same flight attendant returned to Peter and said, "Is your little brother still in the bathroom? Is he sick or something?"

"Calling him merely sick would be an understatement," Peter said. "But don't let that concern you..." He looked at the flight attendant's nametag. "Suzy."

"Keep him in his seat," she said. "We're about to make our descent."

"Aye aye, Suzy," Peter said, saluting the blond woman in the white suit.

Zana leaned over Captain Bearbeard and whispered into Peter's ear. "What's that bitch's problem?"

"Don't ask me," Peter said.

Peter worked two jobs and started up an online business on the side, trying to save up money to buy tickets to Barack. He hadn't a fifth of the money by the time flights went on sale to the general public. By the end of the first month of tours, all tickets for all shuttles were sold out.

It wasn't until they announced a new series of flights, including cheaper bargain tours, that Peter thought he had a chance. He started taking donations online, after explaining his situation on social media sites. It would be one of the last tours to Barack, but Peter managed to get two tickets. One for each of them.

"We're going to be space pirates!" Peter said to his brother, as he waved the tickets around in the hospital room.

Louie's crusty, scabbed lips curled into a smile.

"Really?" Lou said. "I get to go to the pink planet?"

"Two tickets right here." Peter handed them over. "And those aren't even the cheap fly-by tickets. We actually get to land and tour the biosphere."

"I'll be able to walk on an alien world? Like a real astronaut?"

"Like a real space pirate. Arrgh!" Peter held up the teddy bear. "And Captain Bearbeard gets to come, too."

"When do we go?"

"Two weeks," Peter said. "We get to blast off into space, orbit the planet, and land on the big island where NASA has their research center. We get to eat space food and drive around in moonbuggies. It will be the biggest pirate adventure ever!"

Louie was so excited he could barely speak. For a brief moment, Peter saw his old healthy little brother again. He didn't look like he was sick or suffering or depressed or dying. He looked the way he was supposed to look, like a regular kid.

But Louie's stepfather wasn't too happy when he learned about the flight. He took Peter out of the hospital room into the hallway, a fuming look in his eyes.

"Why didn't you talk to me before buying the tickets?" said the stepfather. "I'm his legal guardian."

"I'm his brother and I wanted to do something nice for him."

"But he's too sick to go to the grocery store, let alone go into outer space," the stepfather said. "Don't you realize what condition he's in?"

"Don't take this away from me," Peter said. "Do you realize all I've gone through to get these tickets? He doesn't have much time left. You have to let him go."

"Absolutely not," said the stepfather. "It's not worth the risk."

"What's the worst that could happen?" Peter said. "He could die? He's going to die soon no matter what he does. Maybe he'd be better off dying in space than in a cold lonely hospital bed."

"He's not going and that's final," said the stepfather.

"Final my ass," Peter said. "Are you going to tell him the one thing he has left in his life to look forward to besides dying is an impossibility?"

The stepfather looked away.

"There's no negotiating this," he said and then walked on.

As Peter watched Louie's stepfather exit the hallway, he vowed to himself he wouldn't let the old son of a bitch get in his way. His little brother was going to see the pink planet and there wasn't anything anyone could do to stop him.

The shuttlecraft's outer shields came down, blocking their view of the planet.

"Why'd they shut the windows?" Peter asked.

"We're about to enter the planet's atmosphere," Zana said. "This is the bumpiest part of the ride."

Peter nodded and faced forward in his seat. As he closed his eyes to get comfortable for the rough ride, a hand tapped him on the shoulder. He looked up. It was Suzy, the flight attendant.

"Where's your little brother?" she asked. "He absolutely must be in his seat now."

Peter looked up with a smile on his face. He picked up the pirate teddy bear next to him and waved at her with the teddy bear arm.

"I'm serious," Suzy said. "Do you want me to get him from the bathroom and bring him back to his seat?"

Peter went into full-on pirate mode, "That be mighty kind of ye, me lassy. But it won't be necessary. Arrgh."

She shook her head at Peter.

"I'll get him," she said, flustered. "This isn't a game."

Then she stormed off down the aisle toward the lavatories. Peter watched her as she walked.

"Why does she keep asking you about that?" Zana said.

"About what?"

"Your brother," Zana said. "She keeps asking you where your brother is, as if he's supposed to be sitting in the seat between us. But the only thing that's been in this seat since takeoff is your weird little teddy bear."

Peter nodded at her.

"Aye," is all he said in response as he stared off into space. The ship rattling its way into Barack's atmosphere was like a jackhammer going through concrete.

Peter tried to hold back his tears as he stood over his brother's hospital bed.

"I can't go, Petey," Louie said to his older brother, his voice scratchy and rough. "I can't be a space pirate."

Peter rubbed his brother's cheek, as if to wipe away a tear. But after his second eye rotted out, Louie didn't have working tear ducts anymore. Just two empty sockets wrapped in a bandage.

"The doctors say I couldn't make the journey," Louie said, "even if I could still see."

His lungs tightened inside his chest as Peter tried to stay strong for his brother.

"Just because you don't get to go into space doesn't mean you can't still be a space pirate," Peter said. "We can be space pirates here on Earth, too. Space pirates rule the whole galaxy!"

Because Louie couldn't see him, Peter had a much harder time raising his brother's spirits. Lou just lay there, his face pointed straight ahead as if staring at the ceiling. Then he held his teddy bear into the air.

"I want you to take Captain Bearbeard instead of me," Louie said.

Peter took the bear out of his hands and looked down at its smiling pirate face.

"I know you spent a lot of money on the tickets," Louie said. "This way they won't go to waste."

"Just me and Bearbeard?" Peter asked.

Louie nodded without lifting his head from the pillow.

"The two of you can still be space pirates without me," Louie said. "Then when you get back, Bear can tell me everything that happened. It'll be almost as good as going myself."

"Are you sure?" Peter asked him. "I could stay here with you and we could play pirates in the hospital."

"No," Louie said. "You two have to go. It's the biggest adventure of all time. You said so yourself."

Peter sniffled and rubbed his nose. Then he put Captain Bearbeard under his arm, stood at attention, and saluted his brother.

"Okay, then, me matey!" Peter said in his best pirate voice. "I accept this mission! I will escort Captain Bearbeard to the pink planet where we will rob it of all its riches! Then we'll bring the booty back to you! If I fail this mission, I agree to walk the space plank!"

When Peter looked at his brother's face, he saw him smiling. It was the last time Peter would ever see a smile on his brother's face.

The funeral was a few days later. It was small and quiet, mostly consisting of distant relatives who lived in the area and his stepfather's douchebag work friends. When Peter and Captain Bearbeard showed up in full pirate outfits, many of the people at the funeral were offended by Peter's choice of attire. But he didn't care. He did it for Louie.

When he saw his little brother lying in his coffin, Peter told him the mission was still on.

"The captain and I still plan to rob the pink planet of all its riches and bring them back to you," Peter told his brother. "I promised I would and a space pirate never breaks a promise."

Then he saluted the coffin, turned around, and marched out of the funeral parlor. He looked back only once to tell his brother how much he loved him.

When he made it out to the parking lot, he looked up at the two suns in the sky. The pink planet was now as visible to the naked eye as the moon at night. Peter stretched his arms and smiled at the sight of it all. He had to raise his eyepatch to wipe away the tears pooling inside.

When the ship made it below the planet's stratosphere, the shields were raised and a bright pink sky filled the windows. Peter looked out at the new world with sparkles in his eyes.

"Look at that, Captain Bearbeard," Peter said, holding the

teddy bear up so it could see out the window. "Have you ever seen anything so magnificent? It's a space pirate's paradise."

White clouds swirled across the shuttle as Peter looked down at the great pink ocean below. Small horseshoe-shaped landmasses speckled the seascape—tiny islands covered in blue vegetation.

"There must be mountains of treasure here," Peter told the teddy bear. "All the space pirates in the galaxy must have used this planet to hide their loot over the centuries. It's going to be our job to find it and bring it back home."

Then Peter hugged Captain Bearbeard to his chest as tightly as he could. He imagined Louie could somehow see out of the eyes of the pirate teddy bear. He wondered what was going through Louie's fuzzy head as he gazed out at the bright pink sky of the alien world.

"Is it everything you hoped it would be?" Peter asked Louie.

It might have just been in his mind, but Peter swore he heard the bear respond, "Even better."

CHAPTER TWO

THE PROSTITUTE AND THE PUPPY FLOWERS

"Zana, stop scratching them," Siphewe told her daughter in a thick South African accent, walking her to elementary school. "How many times do I have to tell you that?"

She had to pull the girl's hand out the top of her dress to get her to stop.

"But they keep growing, Momma," Zana said. "They're itchy."

"They wouldn't itch so much if you stopped scratching them."

Little Zana tried to resist the urge to scratch herself again, but after walking only a block she couldn't take it any longer. She lifted her dress up over her head, revealing dozens of small tumors growing all over her naked body like moles, and scratched herself wildly.

"Zana!" Siphewe cried.

Before the mother could lower her dress, many other kids and parents had caught a look at the strange things growing on Zana's body. They were unlike anything any of them had ever seen. The tumors started as little lumps that swelled to the size of golf balls and then opened up like sunflowers, revealing colorful tendrils similar to those of sea anemones.

Some of the kids giggled at the sight of them, others groaned in disgust. But Zana was used to being constantly teased by the other kids and didn't let their mocking bother her.

Siphewe, on the other hand, could never get used to being mocked. She pushed her daughter along, around the corner to take a different route to the school.

"I keep telling you not to show them in public," she told her daughter. "It's embarrassing. People are going to think we're weird."

"I think my puppy flowers are pretty," Zana said, looking

at one of them in her armpit through the sleeve of her dress.

Zana called her tumors *puppy flowers*, because they reminded her of puppy heads when they started to grow out of her skin, then they looked like flowers once they opened up. They were always a different color. Sometimes they were blue, sometimes purple, sometimes green. Zana was always excited to see what color a new tumor would be as it opened up. It was a surprise every time.

"I wish they just wouldn't itch so much," Zana said.

Siphewe didn't think the tumors were very pretty at all. Ever since they started growing on her daughter's body, Siphewe had been terrified of them. No human ever had anything like them before. The closest comparison the doctors could make was the disease of the Tree Man of Indonesia, who grew giant warts all over his body that resembled the bark and roots of trees.

Not only was she worried about her daughter's health, Siphewe also worried about the attention the disease would bring her family. She didn't want Zana to be known as the "Flower Girl" of California, who grew giant tumor-like warts all over her body that resembled flowers. She didn't want them to be outcasts in their community. That was why she moved away from her home country when her daughter was two years old.

In order to combat the disease, Siphewe cut off her daughter's tumors on a weekly basis. But like warts, the puppy flowers would just grow right back. The things sprouted quickly, faster than hair. If she let them grow, the tumors would probably cover every inch of her body within a year's time.

As she sat in the shuttlecraft, staring through the window at the pink ocean below, Zana tried to be discreet as she reached between her legs and scratched at a puppy flower growing in her pubic region. Although she had grown accustomed to the itchy sensation of freshly forming tumors, there were some areas of her body that were still irritated by them. Her pubic region was the worst of them.

Peter was the only person who noticed whenever she put her hands between her legs to scratch, but he didn't seem to mind. He was much more interested in the alien planet outside.

"So what's the biosphere like?" Peter asked Zana.

She was in the middle of a scratch when the man in the pirate costume tried to engage her in conversation. As he spoke, she just let her hand rest casually between her legs.

"It's just incredible," she said, a peaceful expression forming on her face. "It's the reason I've come here so many times. The Citysphere is a large glass structure that's as big as an airport. It's basically a small domed city. Everywhere you go you feel like you're surrounded by the planet."

"It sounds like it's going to be the awesomest thing ever!"

As Peter's eyes went wild with thoughts of the sphere, Zana quickly scratched at her forming puppy flower and then placed her hand on top of her knee.

"Believe me, it is," she said. "I wish I was rich enough to spend a weekend there."

"They let people stay overnight at the sphere?"

Zana nodded rapidly. "Oh yeah. It's not something they advertise to the general public, but a section of the dome was transformed into a luxury hotel less than a month after it was built. It costs probably a hundred grand per night but for those who can afford it I bet it's worth every penny. If I had the money I'd stay a whole month."

"That would be amazing! But you know what would be even better? Imagine being one of the scientists living in the sphere. Those guys get to travel all over the planet, researching the plants and all the strange alien life forms. I bet they're having the time of their lives!"

"Not all of them," Zana said. "I met one in the cafeteria at the dome. He said he worked his ass off to get there only to become a glorified secretary. His superiors had him working long hours doing incredibly mind-numbing work, while they did all of the fun stuff. He said he wasn't even allowed to leave the sphere, ride on the moonbuggies, or do any sightseeing with the tourists. It didn't sound like much fun."

"How can it not be fun? He's getting paid to work on an alien world. How amazing is that?"

"It seems like it would be amazing to us," Zana said. "But being cooped up in one building for four months would probably get pretty old after a while. If the planet's atmosphere was breathable and you could go outside any time you wanted, then it would be a different story."

"The atmosphere *is* breathable, though," Peter said. "They said so on the Discovery Channel."

"It's only temporarily breathable," Zana said.

"Yeah, still long enough to go outside every once in a while."

"The air is toxic," Zana said. "You can breathe it for a while if you have to, but eventually you'd die."

"Well, I'm going to do it," Peter said.

"What do you mean you're going to do it?"

Peter raised his eyepatch to show he was serious.

"Once we land, I'm going to breathe the air."

"But why?" Zana said, completely amused by the wacky pirate.

"Because it won't feel like I'm really on an alien planet if I don't breathe the air."

"It's probably going to hurt."

"I'm doing it. My mind's made up." Peter raised his chin in the air with determination.

"Okay," she said, raising an eyebrow. "I'll do it, too."

"Really?"

"Once we go out in the moonbuggies," she said. "We can take off our oxygen suits then. Just don't let the guides see us."

"It's a deal."

Then they smiled at each other with conspiratorial winks. Zana felt like a naughty teenager again, like back when she used to ditch class to make out with guys behind the Tech Lab.

By the time Zana became a teenager, she didn't allow her mother to cut off her tumors anymore. It was her way of rebelling. She was sick and tired of having to hide her puppy flowers, which she believed weren't freakish at all. She thought they made her beautiful.

Another reason she didn't want her mother cutting them off was because they had become incredibly sensitive ever since she went through puberty. The stems of the wart-like tumors had very little feeling, but the flowers were incredibly delicate. Caressing the sea anemone-like tendrils was as sensitive as the skin of her nipples or labia. They even grew moist when stimulated. It didn't feel right when her mom touched them.

Not just her tumors, but all of her skin had a heightened sensitivity after she went through puberty. She became easily aroused. She masturbated several times a day. Touching any part of her body was pleasurable to her. It was almost maddening how horny she became. Soon she found herself craving to be touched by other people. She would rub against other students when waiting in lines at lunchtime. She joined the women's basketball team, for intense body contact. Her standard greeting would be an uncomfortably long hug.

Zana didn't start having sex until later in high school, even though sex was all she could think about since she turned thirteen. Because her mother beat the idea into her head that everyone in the world would think her tumors were weird and disgusting, Zana never thought having a boyfriend would be possible. She was right about that. Dating the tumor girl would be far too embarrassing for any guy in her school. But then she learned that pretty much any guy was willing to have sex with her if nobody found out about it.

"Let's go behind the Tech Lab," Zana said to Jake from the wrestling team.

"Uhh…" He looked around to see if anyone was watching. "Right now?"

"Come on," she said, grabbing him by the arm.

He pulled his hand away. "I've got to go to chemistry."

"Fuck chemistry," she said. "Let's go."

She flashed him some cleavage. Despite the puppy flower between her breasts, which reminded him of a blue tarantula, he couldn't prevent himself from getting turned on.

"Sarah will never know," she told him.

In the back of the building, Zana jumped the boy, groping him, forcing his hands to explore her body. Sex wasn't as important to her as being touched, but she knew sex was what the guys wanted.

"You know the deal, right?" Zana asked him.

"The deal?"

She explained the deal she made with all the guys. If he sucked on one of her puppy flowers, she would give him a blow job.

"I'm not doing that," Jake said.

"It's a fair trade."

Jake shook his head. "You can give me a blow job if you want, but I'm not sucking those things."

"They're not contagious."

"I don't care."

"Don't be such a fucking pussy."

Sometimes it would take a while, but Zana would usually get her way. Guys her age were too damned sexually frustrated and their girlfriends weren't putting out. By the end of high school, she had guys begging to suck on her puppy flowers. Sometimes she would have them suck on every single one of them as she masturbated and then give them nothing in return. Just a promise that maybe they would get a little something at some point in the future.

It wasn't long before she started charging money for sex. She didn't really care who she did it with. She just wanted as much physical attention as she could get and thought doing it for money was an added bonus.

"To the left, spanning as far as your eyes can see, is the Ocean of Taco Bell," said a man in a white suit standing in the center aisle of the shuttlecraft. "And the line of tiny blue dots are the Hewlett-Packard Islands."

Zana shook her head when she heard the tour guide list the names of all the landmarks they passed. She couldn't believe they allowed corporations to name different parts of the planet in exchange for sponsorship. She guessed it didn't matter to the scientists in the grand scheme of things, since this planet would leave the solar system by the end of the year and never be seen in human history ever again. Taco Bell Ocean, McDonald's Mountains, Lake Pepsi, and Hot Topic Falls would all be forgotten eventually, but the research collected from their financial support would remain forever.

"Barack's oceans cover 93% of the planet's surface," said the tour guide. "Its land masses include hundreds of thousands of small islands spread across the surface. The largest is Wal-Mart Island, where we will be landing. About the size of Tasmania, it is the home of the Sony-NASA Citysphere and the largest rainforest on the planet—the Amazon.com Jungle."

Zana tried to tune out the tour guide as she did in previous flights. The guide's name was Bill. He introduced himself as a planetologist, but he rarely gave any interesting scientific facts about Barack. It seemed he was mainly there to promote the sponsors of the Citysphere.

"Hey," Zana said to Peter, leaning over the teddy bear to whisper in his ear. "Wanna go with me to the bathroom?"

Peter wasn't really paying attention to her. He was enraptured by the planetologist's speech, not even slightly fazed by the tacky product placement.

"We can join the interplanetary mile-high club," she said.

When Peter looked over at her, she winked.

"Don't worry," she said. "It'll be a freebie."

Since becoming an adult, Zana had gotten used to the sensation of being sexually aroused everywhere she went. She wasn't constantly seeking physical attention anymore, satisfied with what she got from the clients she took in each week. But at that moment, she thought sex in the bathroom of a spaceship flying over an alien world would be a lot more fun than listening to the annoying tour guide's speech for the third time.

"During the presentation?" Peter whispered back.

"You won't miss much," she said.

Peter shook his head. "I don't want to miss any of it."

"Don't be a pussy," she said.

Peter shrugged and then tuned her out.

He was watching a little boy in the front row who was about Louie's age. The kid was exhilarated and hanging on the planetologist's every word. Peter imagined that if Louie were there with him, he would have been reacting the same way.

The little boy kept raising his hand to bombard the planetologist with questions. Whenever he raised his hand, he said "Bill! Bill! Bill!" until the tour guide allowed him to speak.

"When we land, can we swim in the ocean?" asked the boy. "I want to swim in the pink water!"

Bill shook his head.

"No, that would be extremely hazardous," Bill replied. "The Taco Bell Ocean is much different than the oceans of Earth. The liquid is incredibly corrosive, like acid. Imagine what would happen to our oceans if the water were combined with hydrogen chloride rather than sodium chloride. Instead of seas of salt water, you'd get seas of hydrochloric acid. We believe something similar to this is what happened to the seas of Barack, but there has yet to be any conclusive evidence. All we know is that no organic life can survive in Taco Bell for very long."

Many of the passengers on the shuttle suddenly wore uncomfortable expressions on their faces. They didn't like being reminded they were flying over a massive ocean of acid. But this information didn't startle the little boy. Like Peter, he thought it was the coolest thing he'd ever heard.

Zana watched Peter smiling at the presentation. She was annoyed that he was more interested in the planetologist than her.

She raised her hand and said, "Then what happens to us if we crash in the sea?"

Everyone on the shuttle glared at her with evil eyes. She smiled back at them. She only said it to piss everyone off, especially the planetologist. But Bill looked back at her with confidence, fully prepared to ease the passengers' concerns.

"I assure you we are in no danger," Bill said. "The shuttle is equipped to land on the ocean. The seals are water-tight and an emergency signal would be sent out immediately. Within half an hour, rescuers from the Sony-NASA Citysphere would pick us up. It would be but a mere inconvenience. Nothing you should worry yourself about."

The planetologist moved his gaze away from Zana, but she wasn't done with him yet.

"And if the seal breaks open on impact?" Zana asked. "What happens then?"

She was beginning to get under Bill's skin. He gave her a slight sneer, but quickly brushed it off.

"It would be incredibly unlikely with a vessel this sophisticated," Bill said. "But in the one in a million chance we would have to leave the shuttlecraft, we are equipped with life rafts resistant to the corrosive effects of the ocean water and anti-toxic medication that will allow us to safely breathe the planet's atmosphere until help arrives. You're safer aboard this ship than any commercial airliner we've got back on Earth."

Zana gave up. She shook her head and turned to the window. Her questions weren't scaring the other passengers, only making them feel more secure. It wasn't any fun.

"Bill! Bill!" the boy cried, raising his hand again. "Will we get to see aliens? I want to play with the aliens!"

Everyone on the shuttle, except for Zana, thought the kid was just the cutest thing ever.

"Yes, the Sony-NASA Citysphere does have an alien zoo you can visit for a reasonable fee," he said. "However, the largest alien specimen is only the size of a caterpillar, so I don't think they'll be big enough for you to play with."

Then everyone laughed. Zana didn't realize a joke had been told.

"Bill! Bill!" the child said, raising his hand again. "What is that red cloud outside?"

Bill kept smiling at the cute little boy.

"Red cloud?" a flight attendant asked.

The boy was pointing at the window.

"Right there," he said. "A red cloud is coming toward us."

Bill didn't know what he was talking about. He leaned over the boy to look out the window. After he saw it, he froze in place for a few minutes.

Now Zana was interested. Whatever the planetologist was looking at, it was on the other side of the craft where she couldn't see. She stood up in her seat, trying to get a view, but the passengers on that side of the craft all had their heads in the way.

A concerned look came across the planetologist's face. Zana could tell he had no idea what he was looking at. After a few minutes, Bill gave up and shook his head.

"It's just a rain cloud," he said. "Rain clouds on Barack are dark red. It sure looks interesting though."

Zana yelled out, "I thought they were gray, just like on Earth."

Bill just ignored her.

She liked seeing him caught off guard. "Have you ever seen a red storm cloud on Barack before?"

Bill shrugged.

"Black mixed with pink makes red," Bill said. "It's just an ordinary storm cloud. Don't worry about it."

He went back to his presentation.

"Bill! Bill!" the little boy cried. "Look, it's getting closer. It's gigantic!"

Zana smiled with satisfaction as she saw a look of unease crawl across the planetologist's face.

When Zana applied to work at one of the legalized brothels in Northern Nevada, they didn't know what to make of her.

"I've got two conditions or else I won't work here," she told the brothel owner.

They were sitting in an office. The brothel owner, a middle-aged balding cowboy, sat at his desk with a phony smile on his face. Standing by the door, there was an older woman with a hideous fake tan, rock-hard breast implants, and so much cosmetic surgery done to her face that her eyebrows were permanently raised to the top of her forehead. She was the owner's wife and most likely an ex-prostitute herself.

"What do you mean two conditions?" the owner asked. "You're the one looking for work. We're the ones who will be dictating the terms."

Zana found it funny how applying to be a legal prostitute was not much different from applying for any other job. She was never very good at job interviews because it was impossible for her to be anyone else but her genuine self.

"First condition," Zana said, completely dismissing what the owner had said. "I don't do condoms."

Both of the owners freaked out on her.

"What do you mean you don't *do* condoms?" asked the wife. "No sex worker is against condoms."

"They don't interest me," Zana said.

"What about STDs?" asked the wife.

"I don't get STDs," Zana said.

The owner shook his head as if he were speaking to the dumbest of all the dumb girls who had ever come into his office.

"That's impossible," he said.

"I'm immune," she said.

"Nobody's immune."

"I am," Zana said. "I've had unprotected sex with plenty of guys with STDs. HIV, herpes, genital warts. But I've never contracted any of them."

The two owners just laughed. They couldn't believe she actually thought she was immune to all STDs.

"I also can't get pregnant," Zana said. "I don't get a period. So there's really no reason to use condoms."

"It's the law," the owner said. "There's your reason."

"What do you mean?"

"Prostitutes have to use condoms in brothels," he said. "It's state law."

"But if the customer and I agree to do it without condoms, why's it the state's business what goes on his dick?"

"It's just the law," the owner said. "End of discussion."

She was getting on the old cowboy's nerves. She decided not to push it.

"By the way, why don't you have a period?" the wife asked. "Cancer? Birth defect?"

"Sex change operation," Zana said, smiling widely.

Their mouths dropped open in shock.

She burst into laughter.

"I'm just kidding," she said. "You should have seen your faces!"

The owner shook his head at her, twice as annoyed as before.

"Actually," Zana continued, "I don't know why I don't have a period. It just never came. Something went wrong when I was going through puberty. My breasts swelled, sorta, but not much else happened. I never started menstruating and my pubic hair never grew in."

"You have no pubic hair?" asked the wife.

Zana raised an arm, exposing her armpit. The area was completely smooth.

"See," she said. "Not a single hair ever grew. It's like that down below as well." She pointed at her crotch. "And even my arms and legs."

"Interesting..." the owner said, a smile growing on his face as he watched her caressing her arms and legs.

"I wish all the girls had your problem," said the wife. "Myself included. It's a bitch having to wax all the time."

Zana was pleased they were starting to take an interest in her.

"And my second condition..." she said.

The smiles fell from their faces.

"You can't make me cut off my puppy flowers if I don't want to."

Zana pulled off her shirt, revealing a dozen small sprouting tumors on her torso.

"What the heck are those?" the owner said.

"Tumors," she replied. "I've had them most of my life."

"That's disgusting," said the wife.

"Why are they so colorful?" asked the owner.

"Aren't they pretty?" Zana asked with a smile. "They look like tropical flowers growing on my body. I think your customers are going to like them."

"No they will not," the wife said. "You're a freak."

The word *freak* took the smile from Zana's face.

"I'm not a freak," she said.

"Well, nobody else in this world has such freakish things growing on their bodies."

"Well, I'm different. They make me unique."

The cowboy just stared at her, examining her naked flesh. Outside of the tumors, he liked the way she looked.

"You said you could cut them off?" he asked. "If you wanted to?"

"Yeah," she said. "They grow back like hair. But my condition is that I don't want to be forced to cut them off. They make sex a lot more fun for me. That's the only reason I want to work here."

The owner kept staring at her, looking her up and down.

"I think we should give her a shot," he told his wife.

"Are you kidding?" yelled the wife. "Not unless she removes every trace of those things."

"Come on," said the cowboy. "They're not that bad. We'll just tell the guys they're flowers, for decoration. A lot of the girls have piercings and tattoos. How are these any different?"

"She's hideous," said the wife.

The owner shook his head.

"Let's just give her a month," he said. "What harm would it do?"

Then he turned to Zana.

"You can keep them as long as the guys don't complain," he said. "If the flower-things become a problem, then you've got to get them removed. We got a deal?"

He stood from his desk and offered a handshake.

"Sure!" Zana said.

Zana jumped out of the chair and wrapped her arms around him.

"Don't worry," she said. "All the men will grow to love them. You'll see."

The wife watched Zana hug her husband for an uncomfortable length of time, rocking him slowly back and forth. She cringed in disgust as she watched the tendrils of Zana's puppy flowers squirm over the collar of her husband's shirt, as if they were open-mouth kissing his neck.

Zana leaned over the seat in front of her and whispered into the ear of the guy sitting there. He was about college-aged, with curly blond hair. He looked like he had adopted the 1980's surfer-dude style in an ironic kind of way. Zana offered him the same proposition she had given to Peter.

"Hell yeah," said the surfer guy.

When he exited his row, all of his friends gave him high fives on the way.

As Zana exited her row, she said to Peter, "You snooze you lose."

Peter just shrugged and tried to look around her wide butt as it passed in front of him.

When she was in the aisle, Peter said, "We're about to head into the red cloud. You're going to miss it."

"I'll live," she said.

"But it's a red cloud!" Peter said. "It's going to be amazing."

"I won't be long."

With everyone still focused on the red mass outside the windows, Zana and the blond guy didn't bother with discretion at all. It was quite obvious what they were about to do as they squeezed into the shuttle lavatory together, but nobody seemed to notice or care.

"What the hell are those?" asked the surfer kid inside the lavatory, as Zana removed her shirt.

"My puppy flowers," she said, caressing the fleshy petals between her fingers. "Aren't they hot?"

He didn't know what the heck she was talking about.

"Are those really attached to you?" he asked. "Are you fucking with me or something?"

"I want you to suck on them," she said.

"No way, dude."

"Just do it!"

She grabbed his face and rubbed it against the purple tumor growing from her left breast. He tried to push her away, but once she stuffed her hand into his shorts and grabbed hold of his cock, he stopped resisting. Although he didn't suck on the tumors, he didn't stop her from brushing them all over his face and chest as they fucked.

This was how Zana handled her clients during her first month working in the brothel. If her puppy flowers disgusted the men, she would just force herself on them, seducing and pleasuring them until they gave in. There were many horrified by the experience, but lucky for her, they were too embarrassed to ever complain to the management.

Despite the owner's fears, the puppy flowers didn't cause

much of a problem. Some men were too drunk or stupid to even realize they weren't fake flowers taped to her body. Some men didn't care one way or the other, as long as the sex was good. And some men actually said they thought the puppy flowers were pretty. Of course, the customers who said this usually only did so because Zana bribed them with extra sexual favors. But, either way, Zana's boss wasn't hearing any complaints about them.

So Zana got exactly what she wanted—she was able to have sex for a living without having to shave off her tumors. She felt as though she were living her dream, doing exactly what she wanted with her life. Most women might have thought of prostitution as the worst possible job in the world, but Zana saw it as the opposite. She saw it as getting paid to do what she loved. And if anyone ever told her what she was doing with her own body was wrong, she would just tell them to fuck right off.

CHAPTER THREE
THE RED CLOUDS

As the shuttle entered the red cloud, the windows darkened. Moisture appeared on the glass. Then the ship bounced wildly as it went through the turbulence of the storm. The seatbelt signs lit up. The flight attendants rushed everyone to their seats.

Peter looked back, wondering if Zana was okay as the shuttle rattled them around in there.

"I don't like this at all," said a voice next to Peter.

Across the aisle sat a large black man wearing cowboy boots and a cowboy hat. He was staring right at Peter and shaking his head. Peter smiled when he saw him. He'd never seen a real live cowboy before.

"The turbulence?" Peter asked, excitedly.

"It's bad enough back on Earth," said the cowboy. "But turbulence on an alien planet? If I knew I'd have to deal with this, I might have thought twice about spending so much money on my ticket."

Peter loved listening to the black man's deep, manly cowboy-accent. He reminded Peter of Forrest Whitaker if he had been a Texas cattle rancher instead of an actor.

"Isn't it great?" Peter asked.

The cowboy shook his head.

"It doesn't feel right," he said. "Not one bit."

"But look at how red it is out there," Peter said, pointing out the window at the blood-red murk.

The cowboy looked for a second and then turned away.

"It's like we've been swallowed alive by the devil," he said.

Peter nodded cheerfully. "Yeah, it kind of is!"

When Zana and the surfer kid exited the bathroom, she laughed out loud at her inability to walk straight. The turbulence knocked them around like bumper cars. They had to go from seat to seat, balancing themselves the whole way back.

"Have fun?" Peter asked, as she rubbed her way past him.

"Of course," Zana said.

By the look on the face of the surfer kid, he did not seem to have had the same amount of fun. He looked ashamed of the experience, as if he had just been used and abused. His friends high-fived him anyway.

"Look at the sky out there," Peter said to Captain Bearbeard sitting over his shoulders.

"It's red," Zana said.

She buckled herself in and pressed her face to the glass. "I've never seen anything like it." She put her hands up to her face, trying to block out the interior lighting to get a better look.

There was a flash of light coming from inside the clouds.

"Was that lightning?" Peter asked.

Zana squinted her eyes.

Several small sparkles of light erupted from the dark red.

"What does alien lightning look like?" Peter asked. "Is it weird?"

She looked more carefully.

"I don't think it's lightning," Zana said. "Too small."

Peter took off his seatbelt and squeezed in next to Zana, pressing his face against the window next to hers. Then he saw it. Dozens of small, quick bursts of electricity.

"They're like sparklers kids get on 4th of July," Peter said.

Zana smiled. She felt as if they were discovering a brand new phenomena none of the other researchers on the planet had seen before.

"I wonder what the planetologist thinks about this," Zana said.

Peter pressed his finger against the glass.

"What's that!" he said.

"What?"

"There's something out there," he said.

"What's out there?"

"Something," he said. "Lots of somethings!"

Zana looked more carefully. Then she noticed it, too. The sparks were coming from dozens of small dark objects floating in the clouds. The shuttle was going too fast for Zana to get a good look at them.

"What are they?" she asked.

"Alien cloud things!" Peter said.

She snickered.

"They look like they're getting closer," she said. "As if they're floating toward the ship."

Peter put the teddy bear's face up to the glass.

"See that, Captain Bearbeard?" Peter said. "We've made a new discovery. What should we call them?"

"We didn't make a discovery," Zana said. "We can't even tell what they are yet. It could just be a trick of the light."

"It's not a trick of the light," Peter said, lifting his eyepatch. "There's definitely something out there, even if they're just weird condensed sections of cloud."

Zana curled her lips.

"Hmmm..." she said. "I don't know."

Peter looked back to see Suzy the flight attendant shaking down the aisle toward him.

"Sir, you need to stay in your seat and buckle your safety belt," she told Peter.

"But we've made a new discovery!" Peter said.

"What discovery?"

"There are these weird black balls out there that sparkle sometimes," Peter said.

"Very nice," Suzy said. "Now get in your seat."

Peter groaned and did as he was told. But the second he moved out of the way, the flight attendant saw what he was talking about.

"What are those lights?" she asked.

"See!" he said.

"There's a lot more of them now," Zana said.

As the flight attendant leaned in to get a better look, something smacked into the window. All three of them jumped back.

"What is it?" said the black cowboy, looking over the flight attendant's shoulder.

Peter didn't realize he had been watching. The surfer kid and his friends were also looking over their seats at the window.

"What the fuck, dude?" said a friend of the surfer dude.

It was a small reddish-black blob stuck to the outside of the glass.

"It's one of those things," Peter said, holding Captain Bearbeard up so he could see, too.

It looked like a lime-sized ball of mud at first, sludgy and wet, but then it started moving. Long tentacle-like limbs squirmed against the glass. Without blinking or even putting the lens to his face, the cowboy pulled his camera phone out of his pocket and snapped a picture.

"It's alive," Zana said.

The tentacles of the red blob made it look like a squid or jellyfish, but this was no aquatic animal. It was something floating in the air.

"It can't be," said the flight attendant. "It just looks alive because the wind is blowing against it."

Suzy called over Bill, the planetologist, who staggered down the aisle to them.

"We've discovered new alien life!" Peter told him, as the planetologist examined the thing slithering against the glass. "It's like a flying jellyfish."

"And it's much bigger than anything your researcher friends

have at the biosphere zoo," Zana said.

Bill stared closely. He didn't know what to make of the creature. It didn't seem to belong. Not on the window of a shuttle, not on this alien planet.

Then there were gasps and awes coming from all over the cabin. This wasn't the only creature attached to the ship. Dozens of them were stuck to windows on all sides of the shuttle. The craft pitched and reeled as the turbulence worsened.

"Those things are everywhere," said the surfer dude. "Where are they coming from?"

Zana pointed out the window.

"The cloud," she said. "The things live in the cloud."

"That must be why the cloud is red," Peter said, looking up at Bill. "Because it's full of flying jellyfish."

Then electric sparks glimmered through the creature's flesh. All of them jumped back.

"Wow," Peter said, nodding his head with excitement. "It's like an electric eel."

Bill didn't seem as excited about it as Peter. He looked over at the flight attendant with concern.

"Tell the pilots to change course," he whispered into Suzy's ear. "Now. We need to get out of here fast."

"What's wrong?" she asked.

"These things could be dangerous," he said. "We don't know anything about them."

Suzy nodded in agreement, but she didn't move an inch. Her eyes were locked on the creature. Bill glanced at what she was seeing and his eyes also widened.

"What's it doing?" Zana said, scooching away from it.

The blobby jellyfish creature squeezed through the glass as if it were swimming through water and entered the cabin. It floated slowly past Zana's face. Her eyes brightened with amazement. Her mouth dangled open.

"Are you seeing this, Bearbeard?" Peter said to his teddy bear, as the creature passed them. "It can move through walls like a ghost."

Bill was unable to move as the creature floated toward him. It glimmered in his eyes, pulsing up and down in the air. He removed his white coat and held it out like a net.

"What are you going to do?" Suzy asked.

"Catch it," he said, his eyes locked on target.

Peter held up Captain Bearbeard so the teddy bear could get a closer look.

"You can't catch a ghost," Peter said.

But Bill wasn't listening to him. He scooped the jellyfish up in his coat, wrapped it up, and held it in his hands.

"It's soft and spongy," Bill said, as he felt it through the fabric. "Like cotton candy."

Everyone cheered the planetologist. The flight attendant patted him on the shoulder. The cowboy had a chubby-cheeked smile on his face. The surfer dude and his two friends leaned over the seats, clapping their hands.

But it wasn't the only one that entered the ship. All over the shuttle, the creatures were seeping through the windows, floating into the cabin.

The surfer dude was too busy laughing and high-fiving his friends to notice one of the red blobs coming up behind him.

"Don't move," Zana said to the surfer dude.

He looked at her, his laughter fading to a soft chuckle.

"There's one right behind you," she said.

The surfer dude froze. His friends backed away from him. Without moving his head, he tried looking at it through the corners of his eyes. It shimmered and swayed along his shoulder.

Then panic took over. The kid tried to jump out of the way, although he didn't have enough room. He rammed his neck right into the floating creature. An electric charge exploded from the jellyfish and rippled through the kid's skin. In an instant, his body went limp and fell to the floor.

Zana and Peter jerked in their seats at the sight of the electric flash. Then they looked over at the planetologist. Their eyes locked on the thing wrapped in his white coat.

Bill looked down at the creature in his hands. It was seeping through his coat as easily as it passed through the glass. Before he had the chance to throw it away, it wrapped itself around his wrist and filled him with an electric current. His eyes went blank. He dropped to Peter's feet.

"Don't let them touch you," Peter yelled to everyone on the shuttle.

The passengers looked back at Peter and noticed their tour guide's body lying in the aisle. Panic flashed across their faces as they returned their attention to the red blobs floating above them. They were surrounded.

Screams erupted throughout the cabin as other people were electrocuted by the floating creatures. Despite the violent turbulence, people jumped out of their seat to get away only to be tossed into the sparkling jellyfish hovering in the aisle.

"Is he dead?" Suzy asked Peter, staring down at the planetologist's body.

Peter placed his hand on the man's neck. There was a bit of a vibration in his skin, but no pulse. He looked up at the flight attendant and confirmed her suspicion.

The creatures seemed to be getting agitated by the screaming people running through the aisle. They became violent, whipping chaotically in the air to attack the passengers. The flight attendant curled up into a ball next to the cowboy for safety.

"Get down!" Zana yelled, as one buzzed over Peter's head.

Peter lowered his eyepatch and used Captain Bearbeard as a bat, smacking the red blob toward the ceiling of the ship. But just as that one went flying, another seeped through the window next to Zana. Peter pointed it out to her before doing anything.

"Keep calm," he said, without raising his voice.

Zana curled in terror as Peter used the teddy bear to shovel the creature over the seat in front of them.

"No problem," Peter said.

She couldn't tell he was winking behind the eyepatch.

The lights flickered on and off.

"What's happening?" Zana said, as she looked around the cabin.

Peter's mouth widened at the strobing lights.

"Those things must have gotten into the wiring," he said. "They're shorting out the electronics."

The lights went out. All they could see were the electric sparks coming off the creatures in the dark as they attacked the screaming passengers.

"Buckle your seatbelt," Peter said.

His voice was finally serious.

"What?" Zana cried.

"The creatures have gotten into the cockpit," Peter said, as he strapped in himself and Captain Bearbeard.

He turned to Zana, barely able to make out her silhouette in the dark red light of the window. Even in the lighting, she could clearly see the severe look in his eyes.

"If the pilots are stung..." he began.

He couldn't get himself to finish the statement, but he didn't need to. Zana understood. She buckled herself in with shaking hands, as Peter yelled out to the other passengers.

"Get back to your seats and buckle yourself in," he yelled. "Quickly."

But he wasn't loud enough to be heard over their screams. They were too busy panicking, desperately trying to get away from the electric creatures they couldn't see anymore. The only person who listened to him was the cowboy across the aisle. He buckled up and braced himself.

"Forget about the creatures," Peter yelled.

But it was too late. The ship was already falling out of the sky. It took a nose dive, plummeting toward the ocean. Thundering booms sounded all around them as the metal shook violently through the atmosphere. Bodies, living and dead, were tossed out of their seats and tumbled through the cabin.

Peter and the cowboy tried to grab the flight attendant in the aisle between them, but she slipped away before they could get a solid grip. Once they fell out of the red clouds and pink light reentered the cabin, Peter saw that Suzy had caught herself on the legs of the seats three rows ahead of them, holding on with all her strength. She stared at Peter with a terrified look in her eyes, screaming so hard that no sound escaped her lungs. There was nothing he could do to help her.

The floating creatures were thrown to the back of the ship, splatting against the ceiling and walls. One of them landed on Zana's chest. As she screamed, it passed through her body, seeping into her lungs and out her back. It didn't electrocute her. It was just trying to escape.

Outside the window, the pink ocean was rapidly approaching. Zana's breaths quickened, hyperventilating, as she saw her death approaching.

She felt something grab her hand. It was Peter. He smiled at her with a warm, peaceful expression. Holding his hand was comforting to her, calming.

It was as if he were telling her *everything will be fine*.

She smiled back at him, as if to say *thanks for dying with me*.

When they made contact with the ocean surface, the front end of the ship crumpled like paper on impact. Half the seats were ripped from the floor. Water exploded into the cabin. Suzy the flight attendant was thrown down the aisle, her neck snapping against every seat on the way down.

As the wind was knocked from Peter's lungs, all he could think to do was hold his teddy bear's paw tight. He wasn't ready to let it go just yet. But then he realized it wasn't the teddy bear he was holding. It was the hand of the scared woman sitting next to him.

The ship was twisted up, ripped apart, and sinking fast. Although the tour guide had said the shuttle would stay afloat if it were to land on the ocean, there was no sign of that capability. The front of the cabin was filling with water. The few who were still alive up there didn't even have the time to unbuckle themselves before the alien fluid engulfed them.

A hand grabbed Peter's shoulder.

"Come on," said the cowboy, shaking him back to life. "We need to get out of here."

Peter snapped himself out of it. He was in shock and wasn't immediately thinking straight. By the empty look in Zana's eyes, he could tell she was in similar shape. She just sat there, casually holding his hand in a deathgrip.

Half of the seats around them had been torn away, thrown to the front of the craft. The other half was filled with dead bodies—people who were either electrocuted or died on impact. Those still alive were in a state of panic, screaming and thrashing in their seats.

One shrieking woman held the hands of her husband and child. The rest of their bodies were nowhere to be seen. She was just holding their hands.

"The pilots and flight attendants are dead," said the cowboy, unbuckling his seat belt. "We've got to save ourselves."

Peter tried to undo his safety belt, but Zana wouldn't let go of his hand. He had to pry open her fingers one at a time. It wasn't until he was free that she realized where she was and what was going on.

"What do we do?" Zana asked, her eyes darting around the cabin.

The water level was rising fast. Those who were already in the acid pool couldn't climb out. The ship was at too steep an angle and the walkway was too slippery.

"Help me," cried a hairless elderly woman, pulling herself over a seat to get out of the liquid.

The flesh was already melting from her face and arms. Her bones could be seen poking out of the soggy mess that was once her chest. The planetologist had compared the ocean water to hydrochloric acid, but this acid was a hundred times stronger than that.

Not only the woman, but all of the passengers submerged in the liquid were dissolving faster than they could move— their clothes and skin slipping off of them like caramel sauce. But they didn't give up for a second. Even after they were reduced to screaming skeletons, they still struggled to escape and survive.

The sight of those in the acid caused a riot among the other passengers. They pushed and shoved each other to get away from it, knocking the weaker passengers to the ground. A young boy was trampled to death inches from his father's arms.

"Make for the exits," the cowboy yelled.

Peter tucked Captain Bearbeard into the front of his pants like a baby kangaroo in its mother's pouch. Before he could get up, Zana climbed over him, knocking him back into place. He got up and joined the frenzied mob of passengers trying to escape. A woman grabbed him by the shoulder and tossed him back so she could get ahead. A fat kid pushed hard against his kidneys. Peter took it one step at a time, focusing on keeping his balance and not losing his teddy bear.

"Get the door open," somebody yelled, as a crowd piled against one of the emergency exits.

But the guy at the front couldn't open the door with everyone shoving up against him.

"Quit pushing me," he yelled.

Nobody heard him over the thundering sounds of bending metal as the shuttle went deeper into the sea. Another guy had to use all his strength to push everyone back so the lever could be pulled.

Once the door opened, a violent gust of wind poured inside. Alien air filled their lungs. Peter inhaled deeply. It was cold and ticklish to his throat. The odor was metallic. Many people held their breath, terrified of what might happen if they ingested the toxic air.

The life raft exploded into view, inflating instantly as the door opened. Everyone kicked and punched their way out of the exit. The man who opened the door was pushed forward so far he fell off the other end of the raft into the rolling pink waves. He wasn't the only one. So many people tried to force their way onto the raft that those who were already on were knocked backward into the water.

"It's full," yelled the cowboy, grabbing onto the lady who was trying to force herself through the exit. "Go to the next one."

The mob rushed for the next exit. But as this emergency door was opened, the life raft didn't engage. The mechanism to inflate it had been damaged on impact. But those in the back of the crowd didn't know this. They pushed and shoved until those at the front of the line fell into the sea, with no life raft and no way of getting back up.

Zana was the first to make it to the next emergency door, but wasn't strong enough to get it open before the rest of the crowd barreled into her back. She was slammed headfirst into the handle and knocked out cold. Nobody helped her. They just tossed her body over the back of a seat on their way out of the exit, leaving her there to die.

When Peter reached Zana, he shook her shoulders and lifted her head.

"Are you okay?" he asked.

She didn't respond.

Peter held Zana's arms tightly around his shoulders, her head dangled limply against his neck. He could feel her breath on his ear, telling him she was still alive. When he went for the closest exit, the people on board waved him away.

"No more room," they cried. "We've got too many already." Even though a third of the raft was still available.

As Peter turned away, a violent wave hit their raft, slamming them into the side of the ship and covering them with acid. Their eyes filled with panic as droplets of the fluid ate holes through their clothes and skin.

"This way," the cowboy shouted at Peter. He was waving him over from another emergency exit.

Peter pulled Zana up the aisle, her feet dragging behind him. The cowboy helped them onto the raft, giving them the last spot in the center. He almost fell over the side as the raft thrashed up and down.

"She hit her head," Peter announced, brushing her hair out of her wound. Nobody seemed to care.

When the cowboy cut them loose, the waves tossed the life raft into the wilds of the pink sea. Everyone looked back at the shuttlecraft as they were pulled into the distance. Dozens of screams echoed from inside the ship. There weren't any more life rafts, but there were still plenty of people left on board.

Just before the shuttlecraft went under, three passengers jumped out and tried to swim for the raft.

"We have to do something," a teenage girl cried, a horrified look on her face as she watched the desperate survivors swimming toward them.

The cowboy shook his head.

"Nothing we can do," he said.

The swimmers only made it halfway before they were completely dissolved by the sea.

Small islands poked out of the pink water in every direction, but the waves were pushing them toward the largest one: a cocaine-white beach with blue jungles and cliffs so jagged they looked like a demon's face leering over them. The closer they got to the island, the bigger the waves became.

"Brace yourselves," the cowboy yelled, pointing at a massive wave coming at them.

Peter covered Zana with his body as he braced for impact. They bounced against the water when the wave hit, but everyone held tight. A group of survivors on another raft were not as lucky. They were on the wrong side of the wave as it crashed, getting flipped over and tossed into the sea. A couple of people were able to hang on, but most of them were left behind, treading acid water as their life raft was sucked toward the demon's mouth.

The next wave hit harder, knocking a woman over the side. Her husband reached out for her hand only to be pulled in after. Another wave splashed over them, hitting a young man directly in the eyes. He turned back, screaming in Peter's face with nothing but soggy white balls in his sockets.

Peter looked away. Then he moved his eyepatch to the other side of his face, covering his eye closest to the water.

Until they made it to the beach, everything was a blur. Only half of the people they started with were still inside the raft. Peter had no idea how or when most of them had fallen out. Two people lay dead in the raft—one with her throat melted out, another whose left side was nothing but bones and stringy organs.

Not a single person was left unscathed by the acid, but Peter and Zana seemed to be in the best condition due to their position in the center of the raft.

"Help me with them," the cowboy said to Peter.

The right side of the cowboy's face was horribly burned by the acid spray, giving his flesh the consistency of raw hamburger. But he didn't let it slow him down.

"We got to get them out of the water," he continued.

They jumped out of the raft, ankle-deep in the acid, and pulled the others to shore. Once everyone in their group was safe, they removed their acid-covered boots and wiped their toes in the white sand. The alien beach felt more like snow than sand, but wasn't at all cold.

A scrawny frat boy with a brohawk was already on the shore, jumping up and down at them and yelling at the top of his lungs.

"What the fuck, bro," he screamed at Peter. "What the fuck just happened!"

The college kid was in too much shock to realize that most

of his left arm was melting away.

"We fucking crashed!" He waved his arms around, spraying liquefied skin across the beach. "What the fuck! We're on an alien planet. What do we do? Why are you dressed like a pirate? Everyone's fucking dead. We're so fucking dead!"

With the kid following him, Peter tried to revive Zana. She still wouldn't wake.

"How's anyone going to find us?" cried the frat kid, as Peter pulled Zana into a safe area higher up the beach. "We're not even on the same planet anymore. The air is poison. What's with the fucking teddy bear? We're breathing poison!"

Peter pushed past the scrawny kid and went toward the cowboy.

"We need to rinse the acid away," Peter said, pointing at three wounded people lying in the sand. They writhed on the beach as the acid slowly ate its way deeper into their flesh.

"With what?" the cowboy asked.

"Water," Peter said.

"I don't know if we have any water," said the cowboy. "And even if we did we'd never have enough. We need to use sand."

"Will that work?"

"I have no idea."

Rubbing the wounded with sand only caused their skin to peel off quicker. Even when Peter wiped away the liquid as gently as he could, it still removed the skin like oatmeal.

"Not like that," said the cowboy. "This way."

He packed the sand on one man's face. It was the young guy who was sprayed in the eyes.

"The sand seems to absorb the acid," said the cowboy.

When he brushed away the sand, the young man's eyes were dryer than they had been. The acidic foam was gone.

"Think of it like a sponge."

As Peter assisted the wounded, the other life rafts started to come ashore.

"Help them," the cowboy told Peter, as the first raft hit the beach.

The frat kid tried to follow Peter, but the cowboy grabbed him by the shoulder and pulled him back.

"Stay here," said the cowboy.

"What the fuck," the frat boy whispered, tears forming in his eyes. "This is so fucked."

"Calm down," said the cowboy. "Let me help you with your arm."

Once the kid realized the condition he was in, he became very quiet and let the cowboy pack sand on his arm.

Peter went for the other raft as it arrived on the shore. It was the same group who refused to allow Peter on board. All of them were dead, except for one. He was a large man in a leather trench coat. He had gotten through completely unscathed, because he had used the bodies of his dead companions as shields from the acid.

"I need help with the wounded," Peter said to him.

He leapt out of the raft onto the beach and shoved past Peter without saying a word. Then he walked up the beach as if he had something more important to do.

The next life raft that arrived was filled with acid. Two dead bodies lay soaking in it. Both had almost completely dissolved to skeletons.

The final raft arrived completely deflated, with no sign of passengers living or dead. Peter assumed it had been ripped apart against the rocks as it came ashore. Anyone else still out there was surely dead by now.

As Peter went back toward the others, he came across two new survivors who must have come ashore on the raft with the frat kid. It was a middle-aged woman and her teenaged daughter.

"Help me," the woman cried out for Peter. "Help!"

She was hunched over and choking. Her daughter rubbed her back, hugging her close. Judging by their tacky yet expensive clothing, Peter could tell they were upper middle-class suburbanites. The kind of people who thought they were much richer than they really were.

"What's wrong?" Peter asked.

Her words coughed out of her. "The air. I can't breathe."

Peter tried to see if she had any acid on her throat or chest, but there was nothing. She was choking on the toxic atmosphere.

"But it should take hours before the poisons in the air have any effect," Peter said, looking at the daughter. "I don't understand why she's reacting to it like this."

"Don't worry," said the teenage daughter, holding her mother tightly as she went through her coughing fit. "She's a hypochondriac. It's just psychological."

The mother shook her head, trying to choke out the words, "No, it's not!"

Peter understood. "Try to calm her down. Help should be on the way soon."

The daughter nodded.

"The pills," the mother said, grabbing at Peter's pirate shirt. "The tour guide mentioned anti-toxin pills. I need them."

Peter looked at the daughter. The pills most likely went down with the ship. He felt his pocket for some loose aspirin. He always carried around loose painkillers for the sake of his brother, who was always getting headaches and stomach cramps.

"I have some right here," Peter said, holding out his hand.

The aspirin pills were covered with lint and dirt.

"Take one of these and you'll be fine for the rest of the day," Peter said. He gave one to each of the women.

The daughter played along. She took the pills from Peter.

"Take it, Mom," said the girl, putting a pill between her lips. "It will neutralize the poison."

The mom put it in her mouth and swallowed. The second it went down she breathed easier, as if instantly cured.

"Thanks," she said to Peter, breathing heavily.

Peter smiled and saluted her. "No problem."

Then he led them down the beach toward the others.

"How are they doing?" Peter asked the cowboy, leaning over the wounded.

The black man shook his head. "There's not much I can do to help them. They're slipping fast."

One of the wounded, a young Hispanic woman with curly black hair, lay dead in the sand. It wasn't the acid that killed her. She had bled to death from a wound in her stomach she must have received in the crash. There was a gentle smile on her face, as if the cowboy had been joking around with her just seconds before she died.

"Name's Jim, by the way," said the cowboy, holding out his hand to Peter.

As they shook hands, Peter told him his name and said, "Good to meet you."

The frat kid interrupted them in a panic. "Where's the rescue ships? We need to get out of here, bro!"

He was sitting next to the Hispanic girl's corpse, his half-melted arm strung up in a sling.

The middle-aged mother removed her yellow sunglasses and looked up at the sky. There weren't signs of any rescue crafts in the area.

"The tour guide said the rescue ships would come get us in half an hour," the mother said. "Why aren't they here yet?"

"The electronics shorted out," Peter said. "It happened too quickly for the pilots to have sent out the emergency signal."

Panic crossed the mother's face. "Then nobody knows we're out here?"

"They know we're out here," Peter said. "And they surely know our flight path. But who knows how long it will take them to come get us."

Jim shook his head.

"It could be a long time," he said. "I'm not sure what kind of resources the Citysphere has at its disposal. They might not be equipped for this level of search and rescue."

"So we're fucked?" asked the frat boy.

"Not necessarily," Jim said.

"But we can't even breathe the air on this planet," said the mother. "If they don't come soon, we'll all be dead."

"We'll just have to hold out until they make it," Jim said.

"And how long will that be?" asked the mother.

Before Jim had a chance to respond, they were interrupted by a gurgling moan coming from the water. They looked back to see a man stepping out of the ocean onto the beach.

"Heeeellp mee," the man groaned.

Much of his flesh had melted away. His clothes, his skin, his face. He was a bloody bag of meat on bones, reaching out for them like a walking corpse.

Then there were other half-melted people coming out of the sea, moaning and gurgling. Some of them didn't even have voice boxes in their throats anymore. The only sounds they made were the sizzling noises coming off their dissolving flesh. They were the people who had fallen out of the life rafts before they made it to the beach.

The teenaged girl screamed.

"What the fuck," cried the frat boy. "They're still alive. How are they still alive?"

The second they stepped onto the beach, some of them fell apart into soggy pieces and died right there. But others lingered, hopelessly grasping for life. They crawled across the sand toward Peter, screeching in agony, leaving a trail of their liquefied flesh behind them.

"What do we do?" asked the mother, hiding behind her own daughter.

"There's nothing we can do," Jim said. "They're already dead."

He took off his cowboy hat and said a prayer to the dying sacks of flesh writhing before him. It was all he could think of doing. He knew they would be better off being put out of their misery, by either smashing their skulls open with rocks or tossing them back into the sea. But he decided that would be too horrifying for the other survivors to witness. For their sake, it was better to allow these poor melting souls to die on their own, in excruciating agony.

CHAPTER FOUR
THE COCAINE-WHITE BEACH

Zana awoke to a pink sky with a purple moon peeking out behind the clouds. It took her a few moments to realize the moon staring down at her was actually Earth. It looked like an alien world from this view. She sat up, rubbing a soft bump on her head and wondering why her clothes had so many tiny holes in them. Things didn't really connect with her until she saw the life rafts and the pink waves crashing against the shore.

Dead bodies lined the beach. She couldn't believe they were real when she saw them. Most were skinless. Some were just empty bags of meat. A couple were still moving and attempting to scream. Two men were tending to the bodies. She recognized the cowboy who had been seated in her row on the ship. But there was also an Asian man in a yellow blood-stained turtleneck sweater who was assisting him.

"What happened?" she asked the cowboy, who was kneeling over one of the bodies with his back to her.

Jim didn't respond. She heard the Asian man praying for the dead man below them. The corpse was a young man with a melted face and empty eye sockets. Acid from the ocean had sprayed the kid in the eyes, eaten through the sockets to his sinus cavity, and finally killed him when it dissolved his brain. There was nothing anyone could have done to save him.

When the Asian man was finished praying, Jim looked back to Zana.

"So you've come back from the dead?" he said to her.

She pulled herself to her feet, balancing on the deep crunchy sand.

"What happened?" she asked. "The last thing I remember was the ship going down."

Jim shook his head.

"Some people made it." He dropped a ragged coat over the face of the dead kid in the sand. "The majority of the passengers did not."

"How did I make it?" she asked.

Jim went to the life rafts and pulled them up the beach, dumping the acid back into the sea. "You were knocked out, but we pulled you to safety. You were lucky."

"You saved me?"

"It wasn't me," Jim said. He pointed across the beach to Peter. "He's the one. If it weren't for him, you'd never have made it out alive."

She looked at Peter.

"The weird guy saved me?"

Peter was across the beach, sitting with his knees spread and red toes wiggling in the white sand, gazing out at the ocean with a big smile on his face. She looked back at the cowboy and the dead bodies. Then she shook her head in disbelief. If it weren't for him, she would be just another skinless corpse on the beach.

"Why did he save me?" she asked.

The cowboy shrugged.

"You'll have to ask him that question," he said.

Zana looked around the beach. Besides Peter, the cowboy, and the Asian man, there were only a handful of people who weren't skinless bodies dying in the sand. There was the frat boy with a brohawk cradling his half-melted arm. There was the teenaged girl and her mother. And in the distance she saw a man in a black trench coat following the shoreline and smoking a cigarette.

"Is this everyone who made it?" Zana asked.

The cowboy looked up and scanned the beach.

"Yeah," he said. "Just the eight of us."

"What about the wounded?" Zana said, pointing at the line of bodies in the sand. A couple of them were still breathing.

The cowboy didn't want to say it out loud, so he just looked up at her and shook his head.

"So what do we do now?" Zana asked.

"Well, everyone else thinks we're going to be rescued at any minute." The cowboy looked up at the empty sky. There was no sign of passing ships. "So they're just waiting around."

"You don't think we're going to be rescued any time soon?"

The cowboy didn't want to respond so close to the others. He picked up a couple purses and a backpack and carried them up the beach. Zana followed.

"I think it's possible we could get picked up at any second," he said. "But I'm not going to depend on it."

He dropped the purses and backpack in a pile of bags and assorted junk. It was all of the belongings of the dead, as well as four orange packs that came with the life rafts.

"So what are you going to do?"

The cowboy opened one of the orange packs. It was a survival kit. He poured its contents out into the sand.

"I'm going to inventory our supplies," he said.

Zana nodded. "Need help?"

"Yeah," Jim said, as he scanned through the kit's contents. Once he found the bag of pills he was searching for, he handed them to Zana. "Here. Give the others one pill each."

"What are they?" Zana asked, as she held them up to the dim sunlight.

"Anti-toxins," he said. "So we don't get sick breathing this air."

Zana pulled one of them out and swallowed it.

"Just don't give any to the dying," he said.

The prostitute nodded and looked back at a skinless person writhing in the sand among the dead. Even now, the acid was still eating away at his flesh. She was amazed he was still alive.

"It would just be wasted on them."

Zana handed out pills to the people she passed on the beach. Nobody spoke to her. They were all still in shock. She walked along the line of corpses toward Peter. Close up, the bodies didn't look real. They didn't even look human anymore. The jungle on her other side was more pleasing to look at. The trees were similar to palm trees from Earth, but they were covered in what looked like a blue moss. The leaves were a dark indigo and appeared almost soft and fluffy.

When she made it to Peter, she sat down in the sand next to him. He smiled at her and then looked back at the ocean. Unlike the others, he didn't seem like he had just been through a horrific experience at all. He seemed more like someone on a relaxing vacation.

"Isn't it beautiful?" he said.

She didn't respond, but stared out at the ocean. The sight of the crashing acid waves made her skin curl. They sat in silence for a few moments, just watching the alien scenery.

Then Zana said, "That cowboy guy said you rescued me."

Peter nodded.

"Why?" she asked.

Peter shrugged.

"Out of all the people you could have saved," she said, "why me? I'm a prostitute. You could have saved a kid or somebody important."

Peter shrugged again.

"You deserved to be rescued just as much as anyone else," he said.

She leaned her elbow on his shoulder and said. "Personally, I think I deserve to be rescued *more* than anyone else. But that's just my perspective. Most people wouldn't bother saving the whore."

"We were friends on the flight," he said. "Friends have to look out for each other."

"So we're friends?" Zana asked.

"Yes." He nodded confidently.

Then he shook her hand as if an agreement had just been made.

"Okay," she said. "We're friends."

She handed him one of the pills. He didn't swallow it. Instead, he put it in a pocket on the teddy bear in his lap. Then he stood up and brushed sand from his pants.

"Let's go," he said, holding his hand out.

"Go where?"

"To explore the island of course," he said with a smile. "We can't crash land on an alien planet and just wait on the beach until we're rescued. We have to check this place out."

Zana smiled back at him.

"I guess it is pretty exciting," she said, taking his hand and getting to her feet. "I bet not even the Citysphere researchers have been to this particular island before."

"We're explorers," Peter said, raising his plastic hook hand into the air. "We'll be legendary by the time we get home."

They started up the beach toward the blue jungle.

"We'll be legendary alright," Zana said. "We're already the first humans to get shipwrecked on an alien planet."

As they stepped into an opening in the trees, they passed the man wearing the black trench coat. He pushed past them to get out of the jungle, going back toward the beach.

"Hold up," Zana said to the guy.

He looked back at her. She noticed he wasn't actually wearing the trench coat. It was just draped over his shoulders like a cloak.

"Here," she said, handing him one of the pills. "So you can breathe the air."

The guy took the pill.

"What's it like in there?" Peter asked him, nodding toward the jungle.

"Blue," said the man in the trench coat.

Then he spit out the pill.

"What did you do that for?" Zana asked, trying to retrieve his pill from the sand.

"It's just a sugar pill," he said.

"What?" she asked, looking down at the wet pill in her hand.

"It's a placebo," he said.

"It can't be." Zana licked the wet pill and could taste the sweetness. "Why would they bother putting placebos in the survival kit?"

The man rubbed spit from the stubble on his chin and shrugged.

"To make the passengers feel safer," he said.

Then he walked on.

Zana put the wet pill back into the bag and watched the man as he walked down the beach.

"Just because the pills are sweet doesn't mean they're sugar pills, right?" she asked Peter.

A gust of wind blew the man's trench coat from his shoulders. He grabbed it before it could tumble into the acid waves, and then wrapped it back around himself. Zana wasn't sure exactly what it was, but she saw something unusual attached to the man's body before he covered himself up with the coat. It was an extra appendage.

"Did you just see that?" Zana asked Peter.

"What?"

Peter was already stepping into the jungle to examine the blue trees.

"I might just be seeing things," she said. "But I swear it looked like that guy had three arms."

"Three arms?"

"I'm serious," she said. "Three arms."

But Peter was no longer paying attention to her. His eyes were bedazzled by the sight of tiny alien snails sliding up the blue trunk of the tree. They were about the size of ladybugs, and shiny black with long red spikes on their shells. He put his hand on the tree next to one of the snails, but once Zana saw what he was doing, she pulled him away.

"Are you nuts?" she said.

"What?" Peter asked. "I just wanted to pick one up."

"They're called black widow snails," she said. "I've seen them at the Citysphere. Their spikes are supposed to be incredibly poisonous."

"They're cute," Peter said.

She pulled him away from the tree.

"I don't care if they're cute," she said. "Don't touch them. In fact, don't touch anything out here."

"You're no fun," he said.

She groaned and pushed him deeper inland.

The jungle was alive. Every inch of it slithered and breathed. They felt as though they were walking through the insides of a living creature, the trees and vegetation pulsing around them like a human heart.

"Why are the trees blue?" Peter asked.

He rubbed the bark of a smooth tree. It looked like a blood vessel growing out of the white fleshy soil.

"They're not." Zana pulled his hand away and showed him that his fingers had turned blue. "The blue comes from a type of algae that grows on everything."

Peter rubbed his fingers together. "It's slimy."

"I told you not to touch anything," she said, rubbing his fingers against her shirt. "Don't get any of that in your mouth. It'll probably make you sick."

He put his fingers to his nose and smelled the residue, wondering what would happen if he tasted just a little.

"Come on," she said, pointing up a rocky slope. "Let's get up as high as we can. I want to check this place out."

Peter followed her up the slippery algae-covered rocks to the top of the craggy hill. It wasn't the tallest peak on the island, but it was high enough to get a good view.

"It's a bit bigger than I was expecting," Zana said, as she looked off in the distance. "Maybe five or six square miles, I would guess." She pointed out to the sea. "The other islands in the area are probably a tenth the size."

"How far away do you think the Citysphere is from here?" Peter asked.

"Not that far, but too far to see from here," Zana said. "The island it's on is probably thirty minutes away by shuttlecraft."

Peter nodded.

Then they stopped talking and just breathed in the view.

The pink sky, the rolling alien waves, the Earth hovering behind the clouds above them, the blanket of blue trees pulsing below— it was one of the most beautiful sights either of them had ever seen. Both of them suddenly had stupid smiles on their faces they couldn't wipe away. They looked at each other. Their smiles grew even bigger.

Zana leaned in to kiss Peter. He pulled away.

"What?" he asked, still smiling.

"I'm trying to kiss you," she replied, also still smiling.

"Why?"

"Don't you think it's beautiful?" she asked. "I always get the urge to kiss someone when I see something beautiful."

Peter continued to smile and nodded his head.

"You said we were friends, right?" she said. "Just give me a friendly kiss."

She leaned in to kiss him, widening her lips to give him a lot more than just a friendly kiss. As their mouths connected, Peter jumped back and cried. "Wow!"

"What?"

"Déjà vu!" he said.

"Huh?"

He stepped away from her.

"I just had déjà vu all of a sudden," he said. "Isn't that weird?"

"Uh… not really… People get déjà vu all the time."

"But on an alien world?"

"Sure, why not?"

"But I've never been on an alien planet before, so how could I have remembered doing this before?" He rubbed his chin. "I always wondered if time was circular. You know, where we live our lives over and over again, repeating the same things. My theory is that déjà vu happens when we remember something from our past lives."

Zana laughed at him.

"What's so funny?" Peter asked.

She said, "Déjà vu is basically just a brain fart where your short term memory gets mixed up with your long term memory. It's usually caused by dehydration."

"Well, that's not as fun," Peter said.

"Why does it have to be fun?" she said. "It is what it is."

"I guess so…" he said.

She shook her head and went to the other side of the summit.

"Did you still want to kiss?" Peter asked.

Zana snickered. "The moment's passed, pirate boy. You might want to refrain yourself from getting déjà vu the next time a girl wants to kiss you."

Peter shrugged, more interested in something peeking out of the jungle.

"What's that?" he asked.

He pointed at a spot toward the center of the jungle, about half a mile inland. Zana followed his finger.

"I don't see anything."

"There's something shiny over there," he said.

Zana squinted. There was something reflecting sunlight at them, twinkling like a star.

"Do you think it's a piece of the ship?" Peter asked.

Zana shook her head. "It could be anything."

"Want to go check it out?"

"Later," Zana said. "We shouldn't go too far from the beach."

"Where's your sense of adventure?"

"Nobody knows where we are," she said. "And I'd hate to be on the other side of the island when rescue arrives."

"Let's at least hang out here for a while," he said. "We'll have a better view if the rescue ship shows up."

"Sure," she said.

They sat on the edge of the cliff and dangled their legs off the side, looking down at the pink lagoon. The smiles on their faces quickly returned, as did Zana's urge to kiss someone. The second their lips touched, Peter got déjà vu again, but this time he decided to refrain from mentioning it.

When they returned to the beach, Jim had finished the inventory. The equipment was separated into five groups: food and water, first aid, signaling devices, fire and shelter equipment, and multi-purpose items. Every single thing he found in the dead passengers' bags had a use.

"Where have you two been?" Jim asked.

"Exploring," Peter said, raising his plastic hook hand.

Zana said, "We climbed up the peak to get a better view of the place."

"Any sign of a rescue ship?"

She shook her head. "Nothing but empty sky as far as the eye can see."

"We'll use rocks to build an SOS in the sand," said the cowboy. "Then wait a couple of hours. If rescue doesn't show up, we're going to have to prepare ourselves to stay the night. Create a shelter. Build a fire."

"Can we do that here?" Zana asked.

The cowboy pointed at the pile of supplies.

"Let's hope we can," he said. "Or else it's going to be a very long, hard night."

"Has anyone gotten sick yet?" Zana asked.

Jim shook his head. "Not yet."

"Somebody said the pills are just sugar pills. They don't actually do anything."

"Who said that?"

"The guy in the trench coat."

"Adam?"

"I guess."

"Well, don't go telling anyone else that," Jim said. "You'll start a panic."

"You think he's right?"

"Who knows. We should still take them though. Better to be on the safe side. It's not like they'll harm us if they turn out to be fake."

"I feel fine so far," Zana said.

"I'm sure you'll feel fine for quite a while," said the cowboy. "If it's anything like radiation sickness you won't notice the damage that's being done until it's too late. You'll be fine for days and then all of a sudden you'll get horrible headaches, then begin vomiting, then lose your hair and teeth, then your skin falls off."

Zana stared at him blankly. "Uh, thanks..."

"Just be prepared for the worst."

Then the cowboy went back toward the others to check on the wounded.

A couple hours passed, but rescue didn't come.

"Why aren't there any ships in the sky?" cried the middle-aged mother. "Shouldn't we at least see the other flights coming to and from the Citysphere?"

"Our ship might have gone way off course," Zana said.

"Or all ships could be grounded until they figure out what happened to us," said the cowboy.

"Or both," Peter said.

It was the first time all of the survivors had gathered together into one spot. Jim used the opportunity to get them organized.

"There's a good chance we're going to be stuck here for a while, at least overnight," Jim said. "We're going to need to build shelters and get a fire going. I want us to gather as much wood as we can."

"Are you in charge now?" asked the middle-aged mother.

"I don't need to be in charge if you'd prefer somebody else," said the cowboy. "But my father taught me basic wilderness survival skills when I was young. I plan to put those to use whether I get your help or not."

"We'll help you, Captain," Peter said, as if he just volunteered everyone in the group instead of just himself.

They split up and entered the jungle. Zana planned to go

alone, but the two women and the wounded frat kid all followed her. All of them were useless.

"Be careful of the insects," Zana said. "Most of them are poisonous. I also wouldn't touch anything covered in the blue algae."

After hearing this, the middle-aged mother started wiping at her hair and arms as if she suddenly felt bugs crawling all over her. Embarrassed of her mother, the teenaged girl sped up toward Zana.

"What's your name?" the girl asked.

Zana introduced herself.

"I'm Jill," she said. "My mom's name is Tori."

The frat boy stepped forward. "I'm Shane." He squeezed between them. "But people call me Long Shane, if you know what I mean." Then he raised his eyebrows.

Even with one arm, the frat kid was trying to pick up girls. It was like he had forgotten he was in pain again. The women ignored him.

"Look for dry sticks," Zana said.

They searched the area, but most of the wood was slimy with algae. Zana told them to take what they could anyway.

"But what about the blue stuff?" asked the mother. "Isn't it dangerous?"

"I'm not sure," Zana said. "It might be okay. If it's toxic or prevents the wood from burning, we'll have to figure a way to scrape it off later."

"What about getting it on our skin?" asked the mother. "I don't want to touch it if it's poisonous."

"Then take off your shirt and wrap it around your hands."

"Then I'll be topless!"

"Just carry the fucking wood," Zana said.

They picked up as much wood as they could carry. The mother was having itching attacks as she held the wood. The frat boy only held one stick in his good arm.

"So what do you do for a living?" Jill asked Zana, as they went back toward the beach. "My mom's a caterer."

"I'm a prostitute."

The women went silent.

"Whoa, awesome," said the frat boy.

"How could you admit something so horrible?" asked the mother.

"I don't think it's horrible," Zana said, eyes forward.

"Of course it's horrible," said the mother.

"I'm not ashamed to be a sex worker," Zana said. "It's a lot less degrading than most jobs, if you ask me."

"Hell yeah," said the frat boy, checking his wallet to see how much money he had on him.

"But it's illegal," said the mother. "How do you know I won't tell the police about you once we get home?"

"Go ahead." Zana laughed. "I work at a brothel in Nevada. Prostitution is legal there."

"Well it shouldn't be."

"Why not?" Zana said. "Prostitution has been legal all over the world for most of history. It was legal in this country up until Prohibition when it was outlawed by the same Christian conservatives who got alcohol banned. If sex wasn't so taboo in our culture then prostitution wouldn't be such a big deal."

"I'd hardly call sex taboo these days," said the mother.

"The day I see a naked couple having sex in public or on prime time television without causing an uproar is the day I'll call sex *hardly taboo*."

"I can't believe you're defending prostitution," said the mother. "Do you know how many women's lives are ruined because of prostitution? All the abuse they endure?"

"Yeah, I know exactly how bad it can be. But the reason it's so bad is because of narrow-minded people like you who shun and criminalize it."

The mother dropped the wood she was carrying. "I can't believe you'd say all of this in front of my daughter."

Then she grabbed the teenaged girl and pulled her away from Zana, out of the jungle.

Zana shook her head and turned to see the frat kid staring at her. He was curling a fifty dollar bill around his fingers and raising his eyebrows.

"I totally agree with you," Shane said.

She groaned and gave him a *shut the hell up* face. Then she went for the beach.

Peter and the Asian guy were building a fire on the beach.

"Does the wood burn?" Zana asked as she came out of the jungle with a bundle of blue sticks.

"No," Peter said, holding a match to a slimy log.

"The algae is probably making the wood too wet," Zana said. "You should probably scrape some of it off."

"With what?"

"Use a rock or something."

Peter found a rock in the sand and rubbed it against one of the sticks in the fire pit.

"This is going to take forever," Peter said.

Zana turned to the frat kid who was following her around like a puppy.

"Help him out," she said.

The frat kid obeyed and tried to scrape blue slime from the sticks with his one remaining arm.

"So why are you dressed like a pirate, bro?" the frat kid asked Peter.

"Me and Captain Bearbeard here are space pirates," Peter said, not in a silly pirate voice but in a matter-of-fact tone. "We came to loot this planet of buried treasure."

"You look more like an ass pirate if you ask me," he said. Then he looked at the Asian guy as if to give him a high five.

"You were sitting in front of me, weren't you?" Peter asked the kid.

The kid shrugged. "I don't know."

"Your friend," Peter said. "The one with the surfer hairdo. I'm sorry about what happened to him."

"You saw him get electrocuted by one of those floating

73

creatures?" the kid said.

Peter nodded.

"My other friend was killed in the crash," he said. "He didn't get to his seatbelt in time. I'm the only one of us left."

"At least one of you made it," Peter said. "Over two hundred people died today. It's a miracle any of us made it at all."

The frat kid nodded. "I don't know what I'm going to tell their families..."

"I'm sure you'll think of something."

"Did you lose anyone in the crash?" he asked Peter.

Peter shook his head and held his teddy bear tightly.

"What about you, Chinese Guy?" the frat kid asked the Asian man. "Did you lose anyone on the flight?"

The Asian guy was annoyed by the way the frat kid asked the question.

"I'm not Chinese," he said.

"Fine," said the frat kid. "Japanese. Korean. Whatever."

"I'm Kazakh."

"Huh?"

"Kazakhs are the native race of Kazakhstan."

"Kazakhstan? Like the country Borat comes from? How come you're Asian then?"

The Asian man groaned.

"Kazakhs are Asian," he said. "The guy who created the character of Borat knew nothing about Kazakhstan. The majority of people in Kazakhstan are Asian. We're also mostly Muslim."

"There are Asian Muslims?"

"Of course there are. It's the second largest religion in the world."

"Huh," Shane said. "What do you do for a living?"

"I work with computers."

"They have computers in Kazakhstan?"

The Kazakh man stood up and walked away.

"I think you offended him," Peter said.

The frat kid shrugged. "It's not my fault he's from a stupid country."

The cowboy passed out energy bars to everyone.

"Take only a couple bites at a time," he said. "Make it last until tomorrow night. We have only a couple days' worth of food."

"Is that going to be enough?" asked the mother.

"I'm not worried about the food," he said. "What I'm worried about is the water. The average human can go only two days without water, but can go two weeks without food."

"That's not true," said the teenage girl, scarfing down her entire power bar in two bites. "I have a friend who went on a fast for six weeks and she was fine."

The cowboy shook his head. "In high-stress survival situations, you don't want to go more than two weeks without food."

"So how much water do we have?" Zana asked.

"Not enough," said the cowboy. "Only a couple of quarts per person."

"How long will that last?"

"We should be drinking at least a quart a day."

"So two days with water and two days without?" Peter asked. "Four days to live?"

"Hopefully, we'll be rescued by then," Jim said. "But if not we'll need to figure out another way to get water."

"There's supposed to be fresh water on this planet," Zana said. "The bugs and plants wouldn't survive if there was only the acid ocean water to drink."

"Yeah," the cowboy said. "But I really doubt it will be safe for human consumption. Let's not try it until we have absolutely no other choice."

Everyone agreed. Then they went back to removing algae from the wood so they could start a fire.

"What the hell did you just do?" said the mother as the daughter came out of the jungle alone.

"Nothing," said the daughter, rubbing her mouth of tan goop.

"Did you just puke?" cried the mother.

The girl shook her head.

"I know when you're lying, young lady."

"What's going on?" Zana asked the mother.

"Jill's bulimic," she said.

"You mean she just threw up the food she was given?" Zana cried. "On purpose?"

"I'm sorry," the girl said, lowering her head.

"It's not her fault," said the mother. "It's a disease. She can't control herself."

"But somebody else could have used that food," Zana said. "She wasted it."

Adam, the guy in the trench coat, stood up and glared at the women.

"She's not allowed to eat anymore of the food," he said.

"But she has to," said the mother.

"If she can't control herself, then food will be wasted on her," he said. "She's cut off."

"No she's not," said the mother. "I'll make sure she doesn't do it again."

Adam looked the girl directly in the eyes. "If you waste one more bite of food, I'll toss your ass into the sea."

The mother shivered and her teeth chattered. "It's so cold. When are you going to get the fire lit?"

"Soon," the cowboy said.

It was not yet night, but one of the two suns had set, dimming the sea and sky to a darker shade of pink-purple.

"It's not cold at all," Zana said.

"I'm freezing!" said the mother.

By the time they got the fire lit, the mother pushed everyone else out of the way, even her daughter, to absorb all of the warmth herself.

"Hey guys?" Peter asked.

Everyone looked at him.

"Whatever happened to all the bodies?" he said.

Zana didn't know what he was talking about until she looked at the shore. All of the skinless people who had been lying there were missing.

"Did somebody move them?" Zana said.

They all got up and went toward the shore. Only the mother remained at the fire, shivering and holding her hands inches from the flames.

The cowboy led them down to the place he had left them.

"They were right here," he said.

"Are you sure?" Peter asked.

Adam took a puff on a cigarette.

The cowboy took off his hat and rubbed the mangled side of his face. "Yeah. There's still blood in the sand."

"Do you think the tide came in and melted them?" Peter asked.

"I don't even know if this planet has a tide," said the cowboy.

"It's got a beach," Peter said. "It probably has a tide."

"Nobody touched them?" Jim asked the group, staring directly at Adam.

Adam shook his head and blew smoke into the air.

"This is fucked up, bro," said the frat kid. "What if the aliens got them?"

"What aliens?" Zana said.

"You know," he said, rubbing sand from his brohawk, "what if there are some kind of flesh-eating creatures living on this planet that nobody's seen before?"

"First of all," Zana said, "*we're* the aliens on this planet. Any life form we come across would be called a *native*, not an alien. Second of all, the scientists have been dying to find alien life larger than insects since they've landed and they haven't found shit."

"But the scientists didn't know about the creatures that

attacked our ship," Peter said.

"Yeah," said the frat kid. "There could be all kinds of creatures that they don't know about."

Zana shook her head. "The only reason they didn't find those creatures was probably because they didn't think to search the clouds for life forms."

"Whatever happened," said the cowboy, "let's assume the worst and keep on our toes. It could have been anything."

"You think it really was some kind of creature?" Zana asked him.

"Or creature*s*!" Shane added.

"In all honesty," said the cowboy, staring directly at Adam, "I think one of you were sick of looking at them and tossed their corpses into the sea while everyone else was out collecting wood."

Adam puffed on the cigarette.

"Weren't a couple of them still alive?" Peter asked.

The cowboy nodded.

"Well," Adam said, "at least they were finally put out of their misery."

"It's still murder," Zana said. "If somebody actually did it…"

Everyone looked at each other.

Shane broke the silence by saying, "I still think the aliens got them."

Zana was about to say something when she saw Jill's mother writhing in the sand up the beach.

"What's going on with her?" Zana asked.

The woman was coughing and holding her throat, thrashing in the dirt. When the cowboy saw what was happening, he ran toward her.

"It's probably nothing," Jill told Zana, not moving from her spot. "My mom's a hypochondriac. She has fits like that all the time."

Zana left the girl by the shore, following the others toward the writhing woman.

"Are you okay?" the cowboy said to Tori, holding her by the shoulder.

"She's a hypochondriac," Zana told the cowboy.

Then the cowboy started coughing. He looked at the fire and then brushed the smoke out of his face.

"Get away from the fire," Jim yelled.

He pulled the woman away from the smoke. Everyone stepped back. Then he quickly dumped sand onto the flames, covering his face with his shirt, trying to put the fire out. Peter and Zana helped him.

"Get back," Jim said, pushing Peter and Zana away as the fire went out. "Get far away from it."

There was more smoke in the air now that the fire had been smothered. The cowboy led everyone back.

"The wood is toxic," he said. "We can't burn it."

"How is it toxic?" Peter asked.

"I don't know," Jim said. "The sap could be poisonous. Or maybe the bark was saturated with sea water. You know what happens when you burn acid?"

Peter shook his head.

"You get poisonous gas," Jim said. "And with the strength of the acid from this ocean…"

Jim looked at Zana who was standing over Jill's mother. The woman wasn't coughing anymore.

"How is she?" Jim asked.

Zana looked up at the cowboy and shook her head. The woman's heart had stopped. They all looked back to the woman's daughter standing by the shore. The girl shook her head, tears hitting her cheeks.

"No," Jill yelled. "She's just a hypochondriac. She does this all the time."

Jill went to her mother.

"Even car exhaust makes her go into a seizure," Jill said.

She shook her mother.

"Come on, Mom," she cried. "Get up. It's all in your head."

Zana pulled the girl away and hugged her as tightly as she could.

"She's fine," Jill kept repeating. "It's all in her head…"

As the second sun went down over the horizon, everyone kept quiet. Even though they had all seen so many people die that day, for some reason Tori's death hit them the hardest. It might have been because they had gotten to know her a little. Or it might have been because it happened in front of her daughter's eyes. They all had sat in silence, having a moment of peace. Then they buried Jill's mother in the crunchy white sand.

After the burial, Zana and Peter lay on the beach, staring up at the stars.

"It doesn't seem like we're on another planet at all anymore," Peter said, his teddy bear on his chest. "Almost like we're back home."

"Without the sunlight, the pink sky becomes black," Zana said. "So does the ocean. Even the stars are pretty much the same ones we'd see from Earth."

Peter said, "If I didn't know any better, I'd say we've been teleported back home. Just lying on a normal beach, somewhere in Northern California."

"Except the air doesn't smell like salt water," Zana said.

"No." Peter smelled at the air. "It smells more like pennies and Dimetapp."

"Dimetapp?"

"That purple cough syrup," Peter said. "I can't stand the stuff."

Zana laughed and then looked over at Peter.

"Hey," she said at him until he looked her in the eyes.

He turned his head to face her, then lifted his eyepatch.

"Do you think we're going to die here?" Zana asked.

Peter thought about it for a minute. Then he said, "No."

"No?" Zana asked. "You sound so confident about your answer."

"That's because it's not going to happen."

"Why?"

Peter put his eyepatch back on and turned back to the stars. Then he said, "Because I've just decided it won't."

Zana smiled at him and shook her head. Then she looked up at the stars, rubbing a puppy flower with one of her hands and holding Peter's plastic hook with the other.

CHAPTER FIVE
THE COWBOY AND THE BEACH BABIES

Using a glow stick to light his way, Jim climbed up the highest peak on the island. He was all by himself. Nobody knew where he was going. He dropped the glow stick onto the ground and built a second fire. He felt guilty for the woman's death. Even though he didn't know the smoke would kill her, he should have been more cautious burning unknown vegetation. If he hadn't left the fire, she might not have died. Of course, he knew deep down that if the missing bodies hadn't distracted the group, it was very possible all of them would have died right there. Not a single survivor left. And it would have been all because of him.

That's why he was willing to risk his own life to build this second fire. They needed a signal fire, one that could be seen from miles away in any direction. It didn't matter if the smoke was poisonous way up here. It was only a danger to the person who had to keep it burning.

Jim had a bandana wrapped around his mouth and handmade goggles covering his eyes, but he still held his breath and ran away the second the wood caught flame.

"You call that a fire?" Jim said to his dad as he walked down the hill toward their camp, carrying a bundle of dried sticks from the nearby desert trees.

His dad curled up his gray mustache and said, "It's comin' along, boy. Hold your horses."

Jim laughed at the old man as he tossed kindling over the miniature flames.

Ever since he was a kid, Jim's father took him out on week-long camping trips into the Texas wilderness. The point was to bring as little equipment as possible and live off the land. His father wanted to teach him how to be a real man. A real cowboy.

Even though he grew up a black man in an era where black men had few opportunities, Jim's father had been a cattle rancher his whole life. And he wasn't just a ranch hand either. He owned his own ranch by the time he was twenty-six. That was in the 1930's. There weren't many black men in Texas who were successful young business owners during that time.

It was 1973. Jim was sixteen years old. And he couldn't have been more proud of his father. When he was younger, Jim hated the camping trips his father forced him to go on. They were hard and not fun at all to a young boy. Building their own shelters, killing their own food, finding water in 103 degree weather—that wasn't young Jim's idea of a good time.

But as a teenager, Jim grew to appreciate what his father was teaching him on these camping trips. He grew tough and self-reliant. He grew into a man. A cowboy.

"Now that's what a fire looks like," Jim said, patting his father on the back.

"Well, look at you," his father said in his old cowboy accent. "Aren't you Mr. Special, making a fire better than your old man. So what you get us for supper, Mr. Special? Better be something besides those grubs you had us eat last time."

"Just wait," Jim said, opening his satchel.

He dropped a long fat lizard onto the rock by his father.

"A chuckawalla?" his father said. "Where'd the heck you find a chuckawalla?"

"It was just lounging in the sunlight over on those rocks up the hill."

"Well, that's what chuckawallas do," his father said, picking the lizard up by its tail. "That's how they get so fat. They just bask in the sun all day long like your beached whale of a mother."

Jim laughed and took the lizard from his father. He whipped open his pocket knife and began to gut the reptile.

"Why're you always picking on Mom?" Jim asked.

"Because the woman deserves picking on, boy," his father

said. "If she got a little work done every once in a while I wouldn't pick on her so much."

"Nobody deserves to be picked on," Jim said.

"You'll see," his father said. "One day you'll have a woman in your life and you'll see the way it is."

"I don't know about that, Pop. I don't think I'm the marrying type."

"Don't you have yourself a girlfriend yet?"

"Nope," Jim said, emptying the lizard's guts into a cup.

"Lone wolf then, huh? When you're older, you'll see. Trust me. You'll see."

Jim just chuckled at his father and shoved a stick up the lizard's ass to roast it over the fire.

After the signal fire was burning bright, Jim went down to the others and set up a quick shelter. He just propped up the life rafts between the trees to break the wind.

"I'll make a real shelter in the morning," he told the others. "But this one will be good enough for us tonight."

"No thanks," Zana said.

"We're good," Peter said.

Nobody was willing to sleep there except for Jim. They were afraid of sleeping near the trees after what happened to Tori. They also worried about the rafts that had been covered in acid.

"I dried them out," Jim said. "They're perfectly safe."

"Not going to risk it," Zana said, completely fine with sleeping out in the open.

Zana, Peter, and Jill were bundled together, using raggedy coats for blankets and body heat to keep warm. Shane tried to join the girls and the pirate under their covers, but Zana shooed him away. She found the boy's half-melted arm creepy and didn't want him anywhere near her.

"Suit yourself," Jim said.

The cowboy figured they'd be fine as they were. He'd have a better shelter for them the next night.

Jim decided not to bother Adam or the Kazakh man. They were separated down the beach. Each of them seemed like they wanted to be alone for their own reasons. Neither of them seemed like they were planning on getting any sleep. The Kazakh was sitting near the supplies, as if keeping watch. All Jim could see of the man in the trench coat was the red light of his cigarette on the other side of the beach.

"If you see a rescue ship coming, light this," Jim told the frat boy, as he dropped a flare next to him in the sand. "Before you go to sleep, hand it off to whoever is still awake."

Shane just nodded up at him.

Because nobody wanted to sleep in Jim's makeshift shelter, he decided to build a better one. It was easier building a shelter for just one person. He dug a ditch in the sand using a flat rock. Once it was deep enough to fit his whole body, he dropped one of the life rafts over the top, making sure it was completely dry of sea water. Then he crawled in and buried the opening behind him. He lit a candle from one of the survival kits, stuck it in the sand, and then curled around it. In a properly made shelter, just one candle could keep him warm all through the night.

"The key to a good shelter is insulation," Jim's father told him, as he demonstrated how to construct a burrow. "If your shelter is insulated good enough, all you need is your own body heat to keep yourself warm."

The old man had a long branch just about a foot taller than he was leaned against a tree stump. Then he placed smaller branches against both sides of the long branch, as if creating a tent made of wood. After that, he covered the exterior of the shelter with leaves.

"Go inside of there," the father said.

85

Jim peeked through the opening next to the tree stump. There was just enough room for one man to barely fit inside of there. It didn't look comfortable at all.

"See any sunlight getting through?" his father said.

"A bit," Jim said.

He stood up and pointed at the places where the light was coming through. The father tossed leaves over the areas his son pointed.

"You don't want to see even a speck of sunlight coming through," the father said. "If there's no sunlight then that means the shelter is well insulated."

Once the father was done, the thing looked like a giant pile of dead desert leaves.

"It looks like something a beaver would sleep in," Jim said.

"Yeah, that's how critters keep warm in the wild," his father said. "They build burrows like this one."

"You're actually going to sleep in that thing?" Jim asked.

"That's the plan," his father said. "Now it's your turn. I want to see you build one."

"I'll build one," Jim said. "But I'm not sleeping in it."

"Oh, you're not, huh?"

"By morning, that thing's going to be full of scorpions and wolf spiders," Jim said.

"Well, in a survival situation you just have to put up with wolf spiders and scorpions."

"Or what happens when a rattler comes in and curls up next to you for warmth?"

"Then I'm having rattlesnake for breakfast," the father said, patting his belly.

"That is if it doesn't bite you first."

"I'll bite *it* first."

"Good luck with that," Jim said.

"So where are you going to sleep, Mr. Scared-of-Snakes?"

Jim pulled a bundle of netting out of his pack and unrolled it.

"I've got a hammock," he said. "I'm sleeping off of the ground and away from the bugs."

"That's contraband, boy," his father said. "When'd you sneak a hammock into the supplies?"

"When I learned you were planning to make us sleep like hedgehogs."

Jim chuckled as he strung his hammock up in a palo verde tree.

"Besides," Jim said. "It's not even cold enough to need a shelter at this time of year."

"I know it's going to be a warm night but that's not the point, boy."

When the hammock was set up, Jim jumped into it and lay back, covering his eyes with his cowboy hat.

"Have fun with the rattlesnakes," Jim said.

"If I do catch me a rattlesnake for breakfast don't come around begging me for some," his father said. "Cause you're not getting any."

"Fine by me," Jim said.

"Fine."

"Fine."

Then his father pushed the hammock with his boot until his son rolled off into the dirt.

"Whoops," his father said. "Better watch out. Those things can be tipsy."

His son glared up at him for a moment. Then they both laughed. They kept laughing as they threw punches at each other, play-fighting, kicking dirt into the air and barking like coyotes.

Jim awoke to a burning sensation on his hands and face. At first, he thought it was the candle, but the candle had gone out hours ago. He realized it was acid.

The first sun was rising in the sky as Jim burst out of his shelter. He wiped his face with the white sand until it stopped burning. Then he investigated his shelter. Using one finger, he felt around in the area where he had slept. The sand there was moist. He decided he must have dug too deep in the sand the night before. Like most beaches, there was water under the sand. The only thing he didn't get was why he didn't realize it sooner. He wondered if he had dug deeper in his sleep as he dreamed. Whatever happened, he learned the hard way that digging a shelter wasn't safe.

"Awake?" Peter said, standing behind Jim's shoulder.

Jim looked at him, rubbing grains of sand away from the raw hamburger side of his face. "Yeah."

"Want to explore?"

"Huh?" asked the cowboy.

"Everyone else is either asleep or in a bad mood," Peter said.

The cowboy noticed only Zana was still asleep.

"I want to check out the island with someone," Peter said.

"That's probably a good idea," Jim said. "We should see if we can find a source of fresh water, just in case it comes down to that."

"If water's here, we'll find it," Peter said, tapping his forehead with his hook hand.

Before they went off on their hike, they told Adam where they were going. Then they each took one of the anti-toxin pills. The two suns hovered over them in the pink sky like glowing devil eyes.

"Three miles long, maybe seven miles wide," Peter said. "We've got a bit of ground to cover."

"Then we better shove off," Jim said, tipping his hat.

They walked into the jungle, aiming for its heart.

"Is that a cat?" Peter asked, pointing at a tree about a mile into the wilderness.

"I don't see anything," Jim said.

"I swear I just saw a cat," Peter said.

"On this planet? Was it an alien cat?"

"No, it was a fluffy gray cat. Like the one my neighbor had when I was a kid."

They went toward the tree where Peter thought he saw the cat.

"Are you sure you saw something?"

"Yeah. It had a collar and everything. It must have gotten scared and ran off."

"There's no cats here, boy," Jim said. "It was probably just a shadow of a leaf rustling in the wind or something like that."

Peter went to investigate. There was no sign of a cat, nor paw prints in the sand. He began to doubt what he had seen.

"We're breathing in a lot of alien pollen," Jim said, looking up at the tall blue blood vessel-shaped trees. "It could be toxic like the wood. Maybe it's got a hallucinogenic effect that's making you see cats."

"Maybe it does," Peter said, pointing into the jungle, "because I also see a giant snake over there."

Jim laughed at the pirate, but then realized Peter was serious. He looked where the kid was pointing and saw movement in the trees. It wasn't a hallucination. Jim saw it too.

They moved forward, cautiously. If it was a snake, it would have been the largest one either of them had ever seen. It was the width of a tractor tire and so long they couldn't tell where it ended and where it began.

"Maybe we're having a shared hallucination?" Peter asked.

The cowboy put his finger to his scabby acid-burned lips and shushed him.

Upon closer inspection, about fifteen feet away, they could tell it was definitely some kind of living creature. Its flesh was rubbery, soft, and translucent like gelatin. They would have been able to see right through it if it weren't coated in white sand. As it passed, the tail end was more like that of a slug than a snake. They went to where the creature had been and watched it as it slithered through the jungle. It moved more like a worm than a snake, but a heck of a lot faster than either.

Jim looked over at Peter and saw the pirate was holding a

rock in his hand. He held it as if he were a baseball pitcher.

"You're not planning on throwing a stone at that thing, are you?" Jim asked.

Peter froze in his pitching stance, trying to make a casual I'm-not-doing-anything-wrong face.

"You know that thing could be extremely dangerous, right?" Jim asked. "You don't want to piss it off, do you?"

Peter dropped the rock behind his head.

"I thought so," Jim said. Then he turned to go in the opposite direction of the creature.

As Jim had his back turned, he heard a loud *thud*. When he turned back to Peter, he saw the boy's arm outstretched as if he'd just thrown a football.

"You didn't just throw a stone at it anyway, did you?" Jim asked.

He looked at the creature. It was no longer moving. A rock was lying on its back as if stuck to its gelatin flesh. When he saw it, the cowboy froze in place.

"Don't move a muscle," he said to the pirate.

The pirate did not move, the cowboy did not move, the giant worm did not move. All three of them were frozen in place, as if waiting to see what the other was going to do next.

"Now what?" Peter whispered to Jim.

"Just keep still," Jim whispered back.

"Okay."

A minute passed.

"Why'd you throw the rock when I told you not to?" Jim whispered to Peter.

"I couldn't resist," Peter whispered back.

A few minutes later, the creature moved on, sliding through the trees toward the hills. Once it was out of sight, the cowboy and the pirate relaxed. Jim took off his cowboy hat and smacked Peter over the head with it.

"Don't you do anything stupid like that ever again," Jim said.

"Whoa!" Peter said. "When you hit me with that hat, it gave me déjà vu!" He rubbed his head. "I guess my short term memory was mixed up with my long term memory due to dehydration."

The cowboy shook his head. "No, you're probably just remembering an episode of Gilligan's Island."

Peter thought about it for a minute. A deserted island... A fat, serious Skipper... A skinny, goofy Gilligan... Skipper hitting Gilligan with his hat for doing something stupid...

"You're like the Skipper and I'm Gilligan!" Peter said, excitedly.

"Let's keep moving," Jim said, heading deeper into the jungle.

"Zana would be Ginger," Peter continued, but the cowboy was no longer listening. "Only she's a prostitute instead of a movie star. Jill would be Mary Ann. Shane couldn't be The Professor. He only has one arm..."

Peter yelled at the cowboy. "Hey Jim, who would be The Professor?"

Jim thought about it. "The planetologist who died in the crash."

Peter looked down, feeling kind of bad their Professor was dead.

"I guess the Howells died on the ship, too..." Peter said, his voice a solemn murmur.

"A jelly worm," Peter told the cowboy a couple hours later.

"Huh?"

"What do you think?"

"About what?"

"My name for the creature back there," Peter said. "I saw it first, so I get to name it. I'm calling it a jelly worm."

Jim wiped the sweat from his brow. "I guess it's as good a name as any," he said.

"It's perfect!" Peter said.

Jim took a leaf from one of the nearby trees.

"We've been all over this island," Jim said. "But I don't see any sign of fresh water."

He rubbed the leaf against his arm.

"What are you doing?" Peter asked.

"I'm seeing how my body reacts to the vegetation," Jim said. "We can get water from these plants if they're not poisonous."

"How do you know if they're not poisonous?"

"Touch them to your skin, then wait and see what happens," Jim said. "If your skin itches or burns it's no good. You'll want to stay away from it. Then try touching it to your lips and wait. Then your tongue."

Peter was about to rub a leaf against his arm, but Jim pushed it away. They didn't need two people testing the vegetation.

"You do the same thing for food you find in the wild," Jim continued. "Only the next step would be to take small bites and wait at least half an hour before eating anymore. You'll know if you're eating something you shouldn't be."

The cowboy's arm was already growing red and itchy. He tossed the leaf onto the ground.

"Well, that's obviously no good," Jim said, as his skin went from itching to burning.

He went to the next species of tree and picked some small round leaves to sample. The second his fingers touched them, they started to burn.

"This one is especially poisonous," Jim said, rubbing his fingers in the dirt. "Remember what it looks like. Stay far away from this kind of tree."

Next he went for a patch of purple grass they could see up ahead.

"How do you get water from leaves?" Peter asked.

"All you need is a plastic bag," Jim said.

He pulled a plastic bag out of his pocket and handed it to the pirate. Peter looked through the plastic, as if expecting something magical to be hidden inside.

Jim's father checked on the plastic bags that had been lying in the sun for a few hours. Each bag was full of leaves with straws sticking out the top like juice boxes.

"Thirsty?" he asked his son.

Jim took one of the bags and saw it was a quarter of the way full of water. The sun caused the moisture to evaporate out of plants and condense in the bag. Not as good as finding a river or lake, but it worked in an emergency.

They sat down in the dirt together and looked out across the desert landscape. There was no sign of life for miles.

"So how long have we been coming out here?" his father asked.

"Since I was nine," Jim said.

"And how old are you now?" his dad said. "Twenty? Is that so... Twenty." He leaned back and folded his hands over his large metal belt buckle. "Eleven years. Seems like just yesterday you were whining to stay home and play dollies with your sisters. Look at you now. You've grown into a fine man."

"Like you, Pop?"

"Well, maybe not quite as fine a man as me," said his father with a jokingly smug expression hiding behind his bushy gray mustache. "You've got quite a long way to go before you're of an equal caliber to your old man. Maybe ten or twenty years from now you might come pretty close."

"More like five years," Jim said, chuckling. "At most."

"So now that you're a man," his father said, "I guess I can't force you to go on these little excursions with me anymore. I think I've taught you everything I know."

"That's all you know, old man?" Jim said. "I guess you're not exactly an encyclopedia of information."

"Well, look at Mr. College Man thinking he's better than his old pop," his father said. "If you decided to work on my ranch instead of going to that fancy school of yours, I'd show you just how much information an old cowboy can have. I've got a whole library of knowledge you're missing out on."

"I don't need to read books on how to shovel horse crap," Jim said.

"There Mr. College goes again," his father said, looking up at the clouds. "Thinking he's just too good for his old man…"

Jim drank from his bag of water through the straw. It tasted of grass and dirt.

"So…" his father began. "How long are you going to keep humoring your old man by going out on these annual camping trips? I'm sure you've got better ways of spending your summer vacations than roughing it in the middle of nowhere with this gray-haired old timer."

"I'll keep coming as long as you keep inviting me," Jim said.

"I'm serious," his father said. "I'm giving you an out here. If you don't want to come any more, you don't have to."

"No, really," Jim said. "I want to come. I couldn't imagine a summer without roasting prairie dogs or drinking cactus water, stranded in the middle of the desert with you."

"Don't make fun of your old man," he said. "I know you're just joking around."

"Serious, Dad," Jim said. "I look forward to these trips all semester. There's no way I'd stop coming. Not for as long as I'm alive."

His father grew quiet. It was one of the first times he could tell his son was being genuine with him. Jim could see the beginning of tears growing in his father's eyes.

"Thanks, boy," his father said. He choked out his words, trying to stop himself from crying because cowboys don't ever cry. "I was really hoping you'd say that. I have to admit that I look forward to these trips all year myself." He squeezed his son's knee through his jeans. "If you keep coming, I'll keep bringing you. For as long as I'm alive."

Jim smiled. "For as long as you're alive, huh?" he said. "At your age, I guess that means you've only got about two or three more trips left in you." He chuckled. "I don't think it'll be a problem committing to that."

"Oh, you're asking for it now," his father said, getting to his feet and holding up his fists. "I'll show you how many years I have left."

"Sit back down, old timer," Jim said. "You're going to give yourself a heart attack. I don't want to have to carry all the supplies back by myself."

"Show me what you're made of, Mr. College." His father kicked at his boots.

When Jim got to his feet, they just laughed and smacked each other on the shoulders. They didn't notice or care they had just stomped the water out of their plastic bags.

Jim and Peter tried every species of plant they could find, but all of them caused Jim's skin to itch and burn. His arms were covered in red splotches.

"None of these are going to work," Jim said. "We're not going to be able to get water this way."

"Maybe it will rain soon and we can get water that way," Peter said.

"Maybe," said Jim. "Though I hope the rain water is safe. If it rains acid on this planet, we might all be in a whole lot of trouble."

"Best not to think about it then," Peter said.

"No, it's best to think about it and prepare for the worst."

By the time they got back to the beach, both Peter and Jim were nauseous and had intense headaches. They weren't sure if it was because they had been breathing in toxic pollen all day or if it was the poisonous atmosphere finally taking effect.

"Where have you two been?" Zana said, approaching Peter and the cowboy as they sat down in the sand to relax.

"Looking for water," Peter said.

"What did you find?"

"No water," Peter said. "But we did find a jelly worm!"

"Anyway," Zana said, not too concerned about what a jelly worm might be. "I've been looking all over for you. Is Shane still out there?"

"Shane?" Jim asked.

"The kid with the dumb stubby mohawk," Zana said. "Didn't he go with you?"

Jim and Peter looked at each other.

"No, it was just the two of us," Jim said.

Zana paused. "Are you serious? Nobody's seen him all day. We thought he went with you."

Jim got to his feet and pushed the sand from his pants. "When's the last time anyone's seen him?"

"Not a single person here has seen him since last night," Zana said.

"We need to find him, quickly," Jim said.

"Why?" Zana said. "He probably just went exploring like you two did. I'm sure he'll find his way back."

"Not necessarily," Jim said. "Not if he went into the jungle alone."

"What's in the jungle?" Zana asked.

"We found a rather large creature," Jim said.

"A jelly worm!" Peter said.

"What kind of creature? Is it dangerous?"

"I have no idea if it's dangerous, but it's very large. It was some kind of giant snake-like creature."

"You know those tube slides at water parks?" Peter raised his eyebrows to the top of his head. "It was as big as one of those."

"It can't be a predator," Zana said. "Something that big wouldn't have anything to eat on this island."

"It was a bit slug-like," Peter said. "Maybe it's a giant slug that eats the blue algae on the trees."

"We can't be sure what it is," Jim said. "We've got to play it safe. Nobody goes inland alone. Now let's split up into pairs and search for him."

They gathered everyone else together and let them know the situation. Then they split into three groups. The Earth was setting in the east and one of the suns was setting in the west. They only had a few hours before it would be dark. After what happened to Jill's mother the night before, Jim refused to lose another survivor.

Sitting in front of the campfire with his father, listening to the coyotes howling at the moon, roasting barrel cactus fruit like marshmallows, Jim felt at peace with the world. Sometimes he wished his life could always be this way. It was easy to forget all of his problems when he was under the stars with his dad. He didn't have to worry about exams or bullies. All he had to worry about was food, water, and finding a place to sleep.

"I think I need to learn myself the harmonica," Jim's father said, as he lounged in the dirt. "I think that's what's been missing by the campfire all these years—some kind of dusty trail music." His father pretended he was holding a harmonica to his lips. "Yep. Some good old-fashion cowboy music."

"How the heck are you going to learn an instrument, Pop?" Jim said. Then he took a bite of his barbecued cactus fruit. "You're the most tone-deaf man I know."

"Don't you worry about me learning the harmonica. Trail music is in my blood."

"If you get to bring a harmonica, then I'm bringing my guitar," Jim said.

"You can't bring no electric guitar to the campfire, boy," said his father. "Is Mr. Jimi Hendrix too good for dusty trail music?"

"I'll bring an acoustic guitar then," Jim said.

"Now you're talking," his father said. "Harmonica and acoustic guitar. That'll be some good desert music."

"If you can learn how to play in key, that is."

"I'll learn. I'm good at learning."

"Sure you are, Pop."

This was the kind of night Jim loved best when out on these trips with his father. It was the kind of night where it was warm enough to sleep out under the stars, so they didn't need to build a shelter. They already found a good source of food and water, so all they had to do was relax and talk. Get to know each other, father and son.

"So," his father began, "you seeing anyone at that fancy college of yours? Have your first young romance yet?"

Jim blushed. "Actually..." he began, then shook his head and laughed.

His father raised up his hat. "Well?"

"I'm seeing somebody," Jim said.

"It's about time, Mr. Lone Wolf. Are you in love?"

Jim nodded. "Yeah. I really think I am."

"Of course you *think* you are," his father said, laughing. "When you're young you fall in love at the drop of a hat. But you really don't even know what love is yet. You'll see."

"Are you trying to ruin it for me or something?"

"No, no," his father said. "Forgive me. Go on. What's the girl's name?"

Jim paused for a second, building up courage.

"Actually, it's not a girl," Jim said.

"A *woman* then?" his father asked, chuckling. "Exactly how old is this lady? I'm beginning to get a little worried over here."

"His name is Shawn," Jim said.

His father went quiet.

"We've been seeing each other since last semester," Jim said. "He was on the same floor as me in the dorms."

His father just stared blankly at his son.

"I think he's the one, Pop," Jim said. "I really love him."

His father kept staring. Then he burst into laughter.

"You had me going there for a minute!" his father cried. "Mr. In-Love-With-A-Guy-Named-Shawn trying to put one over on his old man!" He laughed until he wheezed. "Really, now. What's the girl's name?"

"I wasn't joking, Pop," Jim said. "I'm in love with a man."

"You can't be in love with no man. People are going to think you're a fairy."

"A fairy?"

"A gay boy."

"I *am* a gay boy."

"No you're not. I didn't raise you to be no ass-poker."

"I like men," Jim said. "I've always liked men. I thought you knew this by now. Mom knows."

"She does?"

"Yeah. It's not like I've been keeping it a secret all these years."

"But you're a man's man. A cowboy. You're no fruit."

"Haven't you noticed I've never been interested in girls?"

"I thought you were just shy," his father said. "I was shy around women when I was your age, too."

"I'm sorry it was such a shock to you," Jim said. "But it's the truth. Shawn and I are in love. We plan to move in with each other in the fall."

His father couldn't speak for a few minutes. The old man's eyes were squinting shut, his lips rolled out, as if he was about to say something but the words just wouldn't come.

Then, in a deep venomous tone that Jim had never heard before, his father said, "You're going to *hell*, boy."

Jim couldn't respond.

His father turned his head away. "It's a vile, disgusting, immoral sin."

Then his father turned his back and lay in the other direction. He didn't speak another word for the rest of the night. The next morning when Jim woke up, his father was gone. He waited around for a while, thinking he might have gone for water or to use the bathroom or just gone on a long walk. But his father didn't return. He had gone home and left his son behind.

Jim didn't need his father's help to make it out of the desert alive. The old cowboy had trained him well. In a couple of days, he made his way to the nearest highway and hitchhiked his way into town.

When he got back to the ranch, his father was there but he didn't speak to Jim. In fact, Jim and his father would never really speak to each other ever again. Jim would try to talk to him from time to time, but his father would just brush him off. He wouldn't even look his son in the eyes anymore. All the love and pride his father once had in his son had vanished in an instant. The old man resented him, as if he had been betrayed somehow.

And no matter how much Jim loved his pop, no matter how much he tried to reconnect with him and get him to understand, the old man didn't want to have anything to do with him.

Just before dusk, they called off the search. There wasn't any sign of the kid.

"No luck?" Zana asked Jim and Peter, as they gathered on the beach.

Peter shook his head.

"What could have happened to him?" Zana asked. "He was just sitting here on the beach all night."

As she said that, Jim decided to investigate the beach for clues. He walked along the shoreline, searching for his Nike shoe prints. Peter and Zana followed him. Once the cowboy came across the prints that he clearly identified as Shane's, he followed them down the beach.

"Can you see where he was headed?" Zana asked.

Jim stayed focused. The kid's tracks went all the way toward the water and then stopped.

"He went in the ocean?" Peter asked.

"Was it suicide?" Zana asked. "Did he get confused which planet he was on and try to go for a swim?"

The cowboy picked up a flare from the dirt. It was the one Jim had given the kid before he went to sleep the night before. The end was black with charcoal. It had been used.

"What's that?" Zana said.

"A flare," Jim said. "The kid lit it for some reason."

"Do you think he saw a rescue ship?" Zana asked.

"I don't know," Jim said. "That's what I told him to do with it."

"Maybe he got so excited about the rescue ship that he didn't realize he was running into the ocean?" Peter said.

"But why didn't he yell out to us?" Zana said. "If he saw a rescue ship, I'm sure he would have let us all know first thing."

"Not necessarily," Jim said. "These waves create a lot of white noise. If he was standing right here, we wouldn't have been able to hear him from down the beach where we were sleeping."

"What are those?" Peter said, pointing at a couple of lines in the sand.

Jim took a closer look. He hadn't realized exactly what they were before.

"It looks like somebody was dragged into the water," Peter said.

Jim bit his lower lip and then backed away.

"That's exactly what it looks like," Jim said.

Zana shifted in the sand. "What do you mean? Are you saying something pulled the kid into the ocean?"

"I think there's a good possibility that's what happened to him," Jim said.

"So now there's some kind of creature living in the acid?" Zana said. "And another in the jungle? Is nowhere safe?"

"Let's just keep a good distance from the water," Jim said. "And nobody should ever wander alone. Not even on the beach."

"What about the rescue ship?" Zana asked.

"What do you mean?" Jim asked.

"If the kid ran to the shore with a flare because he saw a rescue ship," Zana said, "but was pulled into the ocean by some kind of creature, what happened to the rescue ship? Did they see him? Is it coming back? Or was that our one chance and we blew it?"

"We have no idea what the kid saw," Jim said. "He might have tried to use the flare to defend himself. We'll never know."

"Best to just hope rescue is still coming, right?" Peter said.

"Right," Jim said, staring down at the tracks in the sand.

Jim didn't take his boyfriend to his father's funeral the next year. He didn't think it would be appropriate. Instead, he took his acoustic guitar and played the old man a dusty trail cowboy song with harmonica accompaniment. He was sure nobody in the room knew the significance of the song, but there wasn't a dry eye in the house by the time he was finished. His uncles told him the song captured his father's character down to the last note. He was a good old-fashioned American cowboy through and through.

Back at the ranch, after the wake, Jim sat with his mother and drank bourbon-spiked coffee.

"Your father left you the ranch," his mother said, her belly hanging out of her widow dress. "You can sell it if you want."

"Where are you going to live then?"

"I can't stay here anymore," she said. "It'll remind me too much of him. I plan to move back home to live by my sisters in Georgia."

Jim stared into his coffee, watching the ripples across his reflection.

"What if I don't want to sell it?" Jim said.

"What would you do with this big old ranch?"

"Maybe I want to run it," Jim said. "Follow in the old man's footsteps."

"You? A rancher?" His mother laughed. "If he heard those words three years ago, he'd have caught fire he'd be glowing so bright."

"I think I would make a pretty good ranch man."

"Oh, hush," his mother said. "You don't have to try to make your father proud just because he went and died. You should live your own life the way you want to live your life."

"But I think this might be what I want to do with my life," Jim said. "College doesn't suit me. And I'm having my doubts about the business world. I think I might want to give this a try."

His mother laughed. Then she sighed. Then she shook her head.

"My grown-up little boy," she said.

She stood up and kissed him on the forehead. As she held her lips there, Jim could feel her cry against him—her tears trickling into his hair, her mouth trembling against his eyebrows.

"He loved you so much," his mother said. Then she sniffed

back her tears. "No matter what you think he thought of you in the end, know that he never stopped loving you."

She looked him in the eyes, brushing his hair from his face. "And up until the day he died I know with all my heart he couldn't have been more proud to have you as his son."

His mother stepped back and dried her eyes.

"He was just afraid," his mother said. "That's all it was. They don't teach cowboys how to have that kind of courage."

Jim had to break eye contact with his mother so he wouldn't start crying himself. He just sat there quietly, holding in the tears, waiting for her to leave the room.

Cowboys never cry. And no matter what his sexual orientation, Jim was a cowboy. Just like his father.

Jim didn't go back to the others for a while. He sat alone, in the sand, staring into the ocean waves. He was thinking about his father. He often thought about his father when he sat alone in the outdoors.

The ranching business didn't end up working out for Jim in the end, but he never sold his father's ranch. Instead, he turned the place into a wind farm. He used the land to harvest wind power that he sold to electric companies. It turned out to be a pretty lucrative business. He was able to retire at the age of fifty, with enough extra income to pay for vacations like this trip to an alien planet.

Jim never married, due to Texas laws, but he had his share of memorable relationships. The only thing Jim felt he missed out on due to his sexual orientation was that he never had any children of his own. He would have loved to have had a son to take on camping trips like the ones his father took him on. He would have loved to have had a little cowboy of his own.

As Jim thought about this, he saw something crawling out of the ocean toward him. He inched back in the sand, but then realized it was too small to be dangerous. It was the size of a puppy or maybe a...

"A baby?" Jim said.

Just as Jim had been imagining, a naked human baby boy crawled out of the ocean across the beach. One that looked like it could have been Jim's son.

"What in the world?" Jim said, as he kneeled down to the child as it crawled across the sand.

It was as if his dream had come true...

But then two more babies crawled out of the sea. White babies. Then ten babies crawled out. The acid seemed to have no effect on them. Jim backed away and went toward the others.

"What the hell is going on?" Zana said.

Peter lifted his eyepatch.

Then dozens, maybe hundreds, of naked human infants appeared on the beach, crawling and gurgling toward them.

CHAPTER SIX
THE THREE-ARMED MAN

Adam and the Kazakh man came out of the jungle, giving up their search for the missing frat kid.

"Fuck it, we're not going to find him," Adam said. "If he's not dead already, he'll find his own way back."

They went toward the supplies. After hiking through the jungle, Adam was dying for something to eat. He knew there wasn't much food to spare, but he just wanted a small bite of something. Anything. His stomach was burning with so many acids it was as if he had been drinking the ocean water all day.

Sweat had become a thick brown sludge in his crotch and armpits. It itched as he bent down into the sand, searching through the equipment. He took a swig of water—just the tiniest sip to moisten his crusty dried-up lips, even though he wanted to chug it all right there. He dug through the first aid, wiping away the white sand crystals that covered everything. Then he rummaged through the backpacks and purses. He couldn't find what he was looking for.

"Hey, where's the rest of the food at?" Adam asked.

The Kazakh man shrugged.

Adam went over every inch of the supplies. Twice. All the food was gone.

"Somebody swiped it," Adam said.

The Kazakh rubbed his temples, as if an intense migraine was swelling inside his skull.

"Maybe the missing kid took it with him," replied the Kazakh, his eyes closed tight as the headache spread across his brain.

Adam punched the dirt. "He better not have."

Stomping down the beach toward the others, his trench coat flapped in the pink wind. Adam was aiming to kill somebody.

"Who took the rest of the food?" he yelled across the beach.

He wasn't even sure if they could hear him at that distance.

But the prostitute had good ears. She looked at him, shrugged, and moved on. Adam felt like strangling the woman as she turned his back to him, even though he was sure she had nothing to do with the missing food. He was just in a strangling mood.

Coming from the jungle, there was coughing and puking sounds. It was the teenaged girl, puking up her lunch.

Adam clenched a fist, glaring into the blue trees. He saw her. He saw what she was doing.

"You better run," he said, too quiet for anybody to hear.

He stormed into the trees and found Jill bent over a mound of vomit. Judging by the contents of her puke, Adam could tell this girl had binged herself on all the food they had left and was now throwing it up. The last of their rations... Ruined by a selfish little brat...

"What did I tell you?" Adam said.

When the girl looked back and saw him, she froze mid-puke.

"I told you if you did this one more time, I was going to toss your ass into the sea."

She just stared up at Adam. His face was very serious. The whiskers on his chin were so rigid they could peel the skin off anyone who tried to kiss him.

"I'm sorry," she said, beginning to cry. "I can't stop eating when I'm upset."

He grabbed her by the hair.

"Get ready to burn," he yelled, dragging her out of the jungle onto the beach.

Jill shrieked and grabbed at his wrist as she felt her scalp tearing. He pulled her up to the acid foam and looked her in the eyes.

"You thought I was joking?" Adam yelled. "Do you know what it's like to die of starvation?"

"I'm sorry!" Jill shrieked.

Zana, Peter, and Jim had gone to the other side of the beach, investigating the shoreline. They didn't see what Adam was doing. Only the Kazakh man came to help.

"You starve to death when your body begins to digest itself," Adam said, pulling her closer to the acid. "After it dissolves all the fat in your body, it goes after the muscle. Your body starts eating your organs, your lungs, your heart. You are basically digested alive until your organs fail."

He held her over the acid waves.

"Let me show you what it feels like," Adam said.

The Kazakh grabbed the screaming girl's arm and pulled her from the water. Adam kept his grip on her hair, refusing to let go.

"What are you doing?" yelled the Kazakh.

"She wasted the last of our food," Adam said. "The bitch deserves to burn."

They pulled on her like she was a human tug of war. Her blond hair was getting speckled with blood near the roots.

"She just lost her mother," yelled the Kazakh. "She's upset."

"I don't care if she lost her whole damned family," Adam said. "This is about survival."

"You're not judge, jury, and executioner." The Kazakh loosened his grip on the girl the second he heard her scalp rip.

"Like hell I'm not," Adam yelled.

Jill grabbed Adam in the crotch and squeezed with all of her strength until he let go of her hair. Then she threw sand in his eyes and crawled away.

As Adam bent over in pain, the black trench coat fell from his shoulders. The Kazakh and the teenaged girl froze in place as they saw it: a third arm.

It wasn't an arm that grew out of his body. It was somebody else's arm—a bloody limb that had been cut off of another person's torso and sewn onto his, connected at the elbow.

The Kazakh and the teenager stepped away from the three-armed man. They had no idea what the severed arm was all about, but suddenly he seemed even more dangerous and deranged than before.

"What the hell are you looking at?" Adam asked them.

He retrieved his trench coat and wrapped it around his shoulders. With the extra arm sewn to his elbow, he couldn't use the coat's sleeves.

"I said what the hell are you looking at?" Adam repeated.

But the Kazakh and the teenager were no longer staring at him. They stared at something behind him. Adam turned around to see dozens of human babies crawling out of the sea.

Like baby turtles, they squirmed through the sand across the beach, wiggling past Adam's legs toward the jungle.

"What the fuck is going on?" Adam said. "What the hell are these things?"

"They're babies," Jill said.

"I mean besides that," Adam said. "What are they doing here?"

They forgot all about their conflict and just watched the scurrying infants for a while. Besides the fact they just came out of the acid, there was something else inhuman about the babies. They didn't open their eyes as they crawled. And they didn't make baby noises, only weird fizzling sounds similar to those made by shellfish when water levels are low.

"Where'd they come from?" Jill asked.

They watched the babies entering the jungle.

"And where are they going?" Adam asked.

They followed the infants up the beach into the jungle.

"Wait..." Adam said, his eyes focused on one infant in particular. "Is that what I think it is?"

"What?" asked the Kazakh man.

"It's impossible..." he said, shaking his head.

Adam went toward a baby girl and lifted it out of the sand. The thing's limbs squirmed in the air, like those of a crab. It wasn't the baby that was familiar, but there was something about the infant...

"What do you recognize?" the Kazakh asked.

On the baby's cheek, just below its left eye, there was a large birthmark shaped like a horseshoe. Adam would have recognized that birthmark anywhere.

"I know it sounds crazy," Adam said, staring at the wiggling infant. "But I think this is my wife."

The three of them looked down at the baby in his arms as

its eyelids slowly opened to reveal two translucent gelatin orbs where its eyes should have been.

The bitch was back. She had been coming into the pizza shop on a weekly basis for over a year, always with the worst damned attitude, always giving everyone around her a hard time. She locked eyes with Adam as she entered. A pissy look on her face. She always had a pissy look on her face. Adam couldn't stand the woman.

"Fucking assholes smoking in front of the store," she said to Adam in her thick accent. He didn't know where she was from but was sure it was some small Eastern European country he'd never even heard of before. "Why do you let them get away with it?"

"They're standing over twenty feet away from the entrance," Adam said. "It's no big deal."

"You should tell them to go away," she said.

"Why would I do that?"

"It's bad for business," she said, dropping her giant purse onto the counter. "Nobody wants to come here for lunch with that smell outside. I absolutely loathe inconsiderate people."

Adam changed the subject. "So what can I get for you, Moonlight?"

Adam called her Moonlight, but he didn't know her real name. She told him her real name a few times in the past, but it was such a strange foreign name he couldn't even pronounce it, let alone remember it. But she said the name meant *moonlight* in her native language. So Adam just called her Moonlight out of laziness. He would have just called her *that bitch* if he could get away with it.

Moonlight looked at the menu, squinting her eyes, thinking out loud as she went down every item on the menu.

"I don't want anything greasy," she said, tapping her long melon-colored fingernails on the counter. "I just washed my hands."

Adam wondered why she came to a pizza shop if she didn't want anything greasy.

"I'll have an order of garlic knots but hold the garlic. And give me a garden salad. Large."

"What kind of dressing?" Adam asked.

"No dressing," she said. "I brought my own."

As Adam got her food together, Moonlight just stood there watching him with the bitchy expression on her face, complaining about how he prepared her food. She paid with a fifty and wanted her change in fives. She left everything that wasn't a five-dollar bill in the tip jar.

"Here you go," Adam said, handing her the food.

She pulled away with her hands raised, refusing to touch the bag.

"Can you carry it to my car for me?" she asked. "My wrists are sore."

"It's not that heavy," Adam said.

"Just carry it for me," Moonlight said. "You have to go the extra mile for regulars. It's good for business."

Adam looked in the back at the manager, sitting on his ass and reading a newspaper like he always did in the afternoons after the rush. The manager overheard the conversation and waved Adam away. The jackass loved tormenting him with the overly demanding customers.

"Fine," Adam said, stepping out from behind the counter.

"I'm parked only a few blocks away."

Moonlight led Adam like a puppy dog down the street. She was parked a lot farther than a few blocks away.

Every time Adam asked, "Are we almost there?"

Moonlight would say, "Yeah. Just another block."

As she passed smokers on the street, she coughed at them and then looked at Adam as if she was expecting him to do something about it. He shrugged her off, wondering why it would be his responsibility to stop smokers several blocks from the pizza shop.

When they entered a parking garage, she pointed out a

sports car in the corner of the lot.

"That one," she said.

"The red one?" Adam asked, his mouth dropping open.

"Yeah."

It was a Ferrari Enzo, one of the most expensive cars on the market. It would take 40 years' worth of Adam's pizza shop wages to afford such a vehicle.

"You have an Enzo?" Adam asked, a wide smile on his face. "How the hell can you afford an Enzo?"

Adam knew the bitch had money, but he had no idea she was that loaded.

"Oh, the car?" Moonlight said. "Is that a good model?"

"An Enzo? Are you kidding?"

"I don't know anything about cars," she said. "My family has an extensive car collection. I just picked it out because the color matched my dress."

She opened the door so Adam could put the food in the back. He used the moment to get a good look at the interior. It was so new it seemed as if that day was the first time it had ever been driven.

"Do you like it?" she asked him.

"It's beautiful," Adam said, not taking his eyes off the car.

Two arms wrapped around Adam's chest from behind. It took a few minutes to realize it was Moonlight. She groped him, rubbing her hands down his shirt, kissing his neck. When he turned around, she kissed him gently, staring into his eyes. Adam didn't know what to do. He just kissed her back.

"I want you to be my boyfriend," she said to him.

Before Adam could answer, she kissed him again. Her thin lips pressed mechanically against his. Adam had no idea the woman was attracted to him until that moment. She had probably been attracted to him the whole time. He wondered if that was why she came in to the pizza shop every week yet rarely ever ordered pizza.

She had always been such a horrible bitch to him. Until that moment, he never thought of her as attractive. Her personality was just so ugly he always thought of her as an unattractive person. But at that moment he saw her as beautiful. She wasn't his usual type. Too bony, small breasts, conservative clothing style, but she did have a very pretty face. And a very nice car.

"Uh, sure I'll be your boyfriend," Adam said, assuming she wasn't as serious as she really was.

She smiled at him and kissed him again, just a peck on the nose. "But you must convert to Phyleaism," she said. "I'm not allowed to date outside of my religion."

She was serious. She didn't want him for just a casual fling; she was ready to get serious. He didn't even know the woman yet she was already asking him to change religions for her. That should have been his first warning sign. He should have just kindly turned her down and walked away, but he couldn't stop staring at the Ferrari Enzo in the corner of his eye. He couldn't refuse a woman with that kind of money.

"No problem," he told her. "I was planning on converting to that anyway."

He had never actually heard of Phyleaism.

Moonlight smiled at him. It was somewhere between a happy smile and a smug I-got-you smile.

"I also have to make sure you have the right blood type. I am only allowed to date men of a certain blood type."

Adam shrugged. "I'm O positive."

He wondered why blood type mattered. The only logical reason he could imagine would be that she always wanted to have a blood donor on hand.

"Perfect," she said.

As she wrote down her phone number on the back of Adam's hand, he noticed a weird shape on her face. On Moonlight's cheek, just below her left eye, there was a red horseshoe-shaped birthmark. It almost looked like a tattoo.

"How is that possible?" the Kazakh man asked, staring at the baby in Adam's hands.

"The birthmark," Adam said. "My wife had the exact same birthmark in the exact same spot on her face. It can't be a coincidence."

The others came toward them, dodging through the swarm of babies that crawled up the beach like fiddler crabs.

"Don't touch them," Jim yelled at Adam, pointing at the baby in his hands. "We don't know what they are."

"Are they dangerous?" Jill asked, looking down at the infants crawling past her ankles.

"They could be for all we know," Jim said.

Adam shook his head. "I think I know what they are."

The others stared at him.

"I think these are the shuttle crash victims," Adam said. He held up the baby in his hands. "I know it sounds crazy, but this infant is my wife. I'd recognize her anywhere, even as a baby." He pointed at the birthmark. "The number of infants on the beach seems to be about equal to the number of passengers on the shuttlecraft. They also seem to be the same variety of races and genders."

"So what are you saying?" Zana asked. "None of them died in the crash? They were all turned into babies?"

"Something like that," Adam said. "What if the ocean isn't really made of acid? Maybe it's some kind of giant fountain of youth?"

Jim pointed at the acid burns on his face. "You call this youthful?"

"I don't know how it works," Adam said. "But I swear this is, or *was*, my wife."

Jim pointed at the baby's face. "Look at its eyes, man. That thing ain't human. I don't care if it looks like your wife. It's not. Get rid of it."

The last of the infant horde entered the jungle, leaving the beach empty of everything but their tracks in the sand. Peter and Zana followed after them.

"Where are you two going?" Jim yelled, watching the two entering the trees.

"We want to see where they're going," Peter yelled back. "Aren't you curious?"

Jim turned to Adam. "Your wife is dead," he said. "I know you want her back, but this isn't her. Let it go."

Jim helped Adam lower the wiggly baby-creature to the sand. As his grip loosened, the infant flopped quickly up the beach to catch up with the others.

"Let's go," Jim told him, patting him on the third arm through his coat. "Maybe they'll lead us to water."

Jim, Jill, and the Kazakh went into the trees, leaving Adam by himself for a moment.

Adam stared down at the wiggling baby as it struggled up the sand. He hoped the cowboy was right about the infant. He hoped it really wasn't his wife.

"We have to do *what?*" Adam yelled at his fiancée.

Moonlight looked at him with her usual pissy face. "Why do you have to be so difficult all the time?"

A waiter gave Adam another cactus blossom martini and removed his half-eaten dinner plate of duck eggs and smoked fish. He had suddenly lost his taste for overpriced yuppie food.

"I'm not being difficult," Adam said. "You're completely insane."

"It's an important part of being a Phyleaist," she said. "We can't get married unless we go through with it."

"Is it even legal?" Adam said. "How are we supposed to live the rest of our lives like that?"

"My family has been doing it for generations," Moonlight said.

Adam slammed his drink.

"Listen," he said. "I've put up with all of your religion's other psychotic rituals. I go to your backward church every Monday and Thursday. I pray to your gods during breakfast. I save all of my cut hair and toenail trimmings in little jars. I bathe with the lights off. I even killed that fruit bat with a ball-peen hammer before we started having sex. But I'm not going to become your Siamese twin."

They were having dinner that night to discuss their wedding plans. Adam didn't know just how insane his fiancée's religion was until she explained what a traditional Phyleaist ceremony entailed. Couples were not just betrothed by a priest, but by a surgeon. They were literally sewn together in a bond of matrimony.

In attending Moonlight's church regularly, Adam had met several Phyleaist couples. He always wondered why they constantly held hands when they walked or sat together. He assumed they were just deeply in love. He had no idea they were physically attached to each other.

This was the reason Moonlight had asked for his blood type before they became romantically involved. Phyleaist couples become conjoined in a similar way to conjoined twins. They share the same circulatory system.

"Why can't you just see this as a beautiful thing?" she said. "We will become one being. My heart will pump blood into your body and your heart will pump into mine. Don't you want to be a part of me for the rest of your life?"

Adam decided to tread carefully. He was about to marry into a family worth billions and didn't want to mess it up. But he wondered if all that money would be worth it.

"Of course…" Adam heard himself saying. "But… it just seems impractical. We would always have to be in the same place at the same time. I'd never be able to ride a motorcycle again. I can't even imagine what going to the bathroom will be like."

He also wondered how he was going to have all of those affairs he planned to have after marriage.

"We'll have toilets designed for two," said Moonlight. "And you can ride motorcycles with side cars. With my family's money, we can have everything custom-built around us. The only thing you'll have to give up is your individuality. We will

115

become one being."

Adam shook his head, not sure what to say.

"I don't want to force you to do this," she said. "You have to truly want to do it. The man I marry must love the idea of becoming a part of me. I couldn't be with anyone who didn't feel strongly about it."

"It's that important?"

She nodded. "Otherwise, the wedding's off."

Adam let out a long breath.

"I'm not saying I don't love the idea," he said, attempting to sound convincing. "I really do. It's just a very serious thing. It would change my life forever…"

At that moment, Adam realized he was willing to go through with it. To have that much money, to never have to work another day in his life, to have an army of personal servants—it was worth sewing himself to the crazy bitch. He couldn't imagine anyone arguing against that.

"Marriage is supposed to change your life forever," Moonlight said, raising a glass of wine to her lips.

As she drank, Adam envisioned the red fluid flowing down her throat was not wine but his own freshly drained blood.

The horde of infants disappeared in the blue jungle. As Adam followed them, their numbers fell from hundreds to dozens to just a few crawling slowly over roots and vines.

"Where did they all go?" Zana asked, coming back toward the others.

"We lost sight of them," Peter said behind her, dangling his teddy bear sadly across his knees. "They spread out and found good hiding spots."

"Hiding spots?" asked the cowboy.

Peter pointed. "I followed one into some bushes. It went in but didn't come back out. I didn't see it in there. Must have dug a hole."

"Babies can't dig holes," Zana said, and punched Peter on the arm.

"I keep telling all of you." The cowboy scratched his nose. "These can't be real babies. We have no idea what they're capable of."

Then there was only one infant left: the one Adam believed was his wife. The six of them followed the remaining baby, watching carefully as it crawled across the ground. It went for the bushes, but Jim blocked its way with his boots.

"Keep it out in the open," he said. "Don't let it hide."

The baby tried crawling around Jim's feet, but he just walked with it, continuing to block its path so it would be forced to move on. Squishy fizzing noises rose from its mouth as if it were growling with frustration. It crawled forward until it got to a tree and then wrapped its limbs around the tree's trunk as if hugging onto a mother's leg.

"What's it doing?" Zana asked.

It hugged the tree tighter.

"Is it trying to climb?" Peter asked.

They watched as the infant creature snuggled against the tree, rubbing its naked flesh against the smooth blue bark.

"Moonlight?" Adam asked. He got down on his hands and knees. "Is that you?"

Jim put his hand on Adam's shoulder.

"It's not your wife, pal," Jim said. "Trust me."

"Can you understand me?" Adam asked.

The infant tilted its head and looked up at the large man hovering overhead. Adam looked into its gelatin eyes. There seemed to be no life within.

"You're not real, are you?" Adam asked. "You're dead. There's no coming back from the dead."

The baby opened its mouth to speak, but words did not emerge. Its lips opened wider. Then its face stretched, twisting into a deformed expression.

"What's happening?" Jill cried.

The infant became like putty. Its body transformed into

a shapeless blob.

"It's melting," Peter said.

"Why is it melting?" Jill cried.

The blob oozed toward the ground, sliding down the trunk of the tree. Its flesh became a creamy slime.

Adam stared down at the pile of meat soup. He raised his voice to it.

"Don't you dare haunt me," he said. "I've finally gotten rid of you. Don't you dare haunt me."

But there was nothing left of the infant to hear him. It was just a puddle of goop dissolving into the soil.

"Quit scratching," Moonlight said.

Adam kept scratching.

"I can't help it," he said. "It keeps itching."

His nails dug into the skin between their conjoined arms.

"It hurts when you do that," Moonlight said. "Stop."

"It feels good to me," Adam said, continuing to scratch their shared patch of flesh.

The itching was supposed to stop a few months after the wedding surgery, but it never did. Two years went by and Adam still couldn't get used to the feeling of being connected to another person. It was especially awkward in the area of their skin where their nerves mingled together. For a few inches of flesh, they couldn't tell whose skin was whose.

"One at a time," said the guard at the security gate, pointing at the wealthy couple.

"We can't exactly do that," Adam said, lifting his arm to show they were attached at the arm. "We're conjoined."

The guard didn't know what to do. He'd never had to deal with conjoined twins. He looked at his supervisor who shrugged in response.

"Come in sideways, maybe?" the guard asked.

They went through the metal detector sideways. When

118

their arms passed through, the alarm went off.

"We have metal wires in our arms," said Moonlight. "They are in place so we can't easily separate."

"You attached yourselves together on purpose?" asked the guard.

"It's part of our religion," she said.

He waved them through, shaking his head in disbelief.

They normally didn't have to deal with airports. They only traveled on their family's private jet. But this time they were going to another planet and didn't own their own spaceship to get there.

"I can't believe we're taking a budget flight," Adam said, leading them to a patio outside the terminal. "This is going to be hell."

"It's your fault," Moonlight said. "You waited until the last minute to order the tickets. You're lucky we're going at all."

"We should have just gone to Jamaica again."

"Jamaica's gross."

Adam lit up a cigarette and inhaled.

"What do you think you're doing?" Moonlight said as her husband blew a cloud of smoke over their heads.

He inhaled again. She gave him a pissy look.

"I'm having a smoke," he said.

After they were married, Adam picked up smoking. Not because he liked to smoke, but because he knew how much she hated it and he wanted to piss her off. There was a lot of crap she did that he had to put up with on a daily basis, so smoking was his way of getting back at her. Because they were conjoined, she had no choice but to tolerate it.

"At least we don't share the same lungs," Adam said.

Moonlight faux-coughed a few times and waved the smoke away. "That's the last pack you're getting," Moonlight said.

Then she pulled her scarf over her nose and mouth and leaned as far away from him as possible. A smile cracked Adam's lips. Smoking had become one of his most satisfying activities as of late.

Living with his wife attached to him was even more difficult than he thought it would be. Scheduling was particularly annoying. He was forced to sleep at the same hours as Moonlight, but she was an insomniac who could never get comfortable in bed. They only slept a maximum of five hours a night, almost always awake by sunrise. And going to the bathroom was an absolute nightmare. Moonlight constantly complained about the smell when they used the bathroom together, as if he should have had some kind of control over the odor of his feces. And sometimes she wouldn't even let him go if she didn't have to, especially if she was in the middle of doing something. Walking and jogging lost all of its enjoyment. They didn't share the same taste in television or film. There really weren't many interests they shared, outside of spending lots of money.

On the shuttle, Moonlight complained about how he still smelled like cigarette smoke. She even covered her nose until the ship was ready for blast off. Adam just ignored her and read an old issue of *Unknown Soldier*. He was really into military comics. Because Moonlight never let him watch the war movies he liked, he picked up comic book reading as a supplement. It took him a while to get used to the medium, but eventually he found comics addicting to read.

When they blasted off into space, Adam was so involved in the storyline of his comic that he didn't even care what was happening to him in the real world. With Moonlight's bankroll, they had gone on many excursions. They went on a safari in Kenya, danced through the streets of Brazil, visited the pyramids in Egypt, swam with turtles on the Galapagos Islands, toured the Australian Outback, and even fed penguins in Antarctica. They had done and seen so much that little impressed them anymore. Adam was more interested in his comic book than space travel.

"I can't see anything," Moonlight complained once they got through the atmosphere.

Adam looked over her shoulder and saw the window was pure blackness.

"It's a black void," Adam said. "What did you expect?"

"Stars," she said. "I at least want to see stars."

"You can't see stars in space," Adam said. "Not until the Earth blocks out the sun."

Everyone was staring out the windows on the other side of the shuttle. They were able to see the Earth. By their expressions and tears flowing down their cheeks, Adam could tell that it was probably a wonderful sight. But he couldn't see anything. Neither could Moonlight.

"Tell him to move," his wife said.

A morbidly obese giant of a man was seated across the aisle, blocking Moonlight's view of the shuttle window, blocking the supposedly breathtaking view of Earth from space. She nudged at Adam, but he didn't care. He'd seen pictures of Earth from space. It wasn't anything new. He'd rather just read his comic until they got to the new planet.

But Moonlight was not going to let it go.

"Hey, fat head, get out of the way," she told the man.

The fat guy looked at her with an annoyed face.

"I can't see," she said. "Can you please move?"

She shouldn't have insulted him. The large man decided to block her view even more.

"Can't you hear me?" Moonlight asked.

She turned to Adam. "He's so rude. Make him move out of the way."

Adam just snickered. She was always trying to make him fight anyone who pissed her off. But how could he fight anyone anymore with the woman attached to his left arm? She turned her attack dog into a lap dog, and he wasn't about to start shit with anyone if he wasn't physically capable of following through with it. He just sat there, tuning her out, reading his comic book.

Moonlight was so annoyed she jerked their conjoined arm, knocking the book out of her husband's hands. She married him because of his size. He was tall and strong. A real man. A tough guy. But there was nothing more unattractive to her than

121

a man who was afraid of a fight.

The Kazahk man pushed Adam into the dirt when he wasn't looking.

Not accustomed to using his left arm much anymore, Adam didn't catch himself and went straight into the ground, landing on his third arm. He heard a wire in his elbow tear a bit of his flesh.

"What did you push him for?" Jim asked.

The Kazakh had his fists up, standing between him and Jill.

"He tried to kill the girl," said the Kazahk. "He would have thrown her into the ocean if I hadn't stopped him."

"And I still plan to," Adam said.

He got to his feet and punched the Kazahk twice. Once in the face and once in the arm protecting his face. But the Kazahk took the punches, not moving from his spot. Jim separated them.

"Now, what's this all about?" Jim yelled.

Adam yelled over Jim's shoulder. "That bitch ate the rest of our food, then puked it up."

"Is that true?" Jim asked the girl.

Tears flowed down the girl's cheeks. She nodded.

"Did you drink all the water as well?" Jim asked.

She shook her head.

"Then it's fine," Jim said.

"What do you mean *it's fine?*" Adam yelled, getting in the old cowboy's face. "Because of her we're going to starve to death."

"The food isn't important," said the Cowboy. "It takes a very long time to starve to death. Water is the main thing we have to worry about. We won't last long without water."

In the background, though nobody was listening, Zana said, "Am I the only one who's weirded out by the fact a baby just melted by our feet?"

Adam wouldn't stand down. "You're just going to let her get away with that? This isn't a game. Our lives are at stake."

"Her mother just died," Jim said. "She was upset. I think we can forgive her this one time."

"We already forgave her the last time she did it," Adam said. "If we have to resort to cannibalism because of her she's going to be the first eaten."

"We're not resorting to cannibalism," Jim said. "We'll either be rescued or we'll die of thirst long before it will come to that."

"Maybe I'll eat the bitch out of spite then," he said.

Then Adam's eyes glared red. It looked as if he were ready to strangle every single person standing there. Everyone stepped away. Even Jim felt the need to step back a little. But, instead of backing up, one person came forward.

It was Peter. He raised his hand, waiting to be called upon. The others looked at him, wondering why he had such a big smile on his face.

"I've got a solution," Peter said, his hand still raised.

"What?" Adam said.

"We can eat the puke," Peter said.

Then he smiled wider and lowered his hand. Everyone cringed at him.

"Shut the fuck up," Adam said. "I'm not eating no puke."

"Why not?" Peter said. "The puke has just as much nutrition as the food did in its original form. It just doesn't taste as good anymore."

Adam glared at Peter. He wanted to punch that stupid pirate hat right off of his head.

"He's right," said the cowboy. "We should gather it up and use it for emergency rations."

"You're sick," Adam said.

The cowboy smiled. "You're the one who's so concerned about starving to death. Is eating a little vomit where you draw the line? Trust me, I've eaten a lot worse in survival situations."

Adam shook his head. "I'd rather resort to cannibalism…"

The cowboy laughed out loud.

"That reminds me," Jim said, between laughs. "I've been meaning to ask you something…"

Then the smile dropped from Jim's face and in a serious voice he asked, "What's with the severed arm you've been hiding under your coat?"

Everyone went silent. The question had come out of nowhere.

Adam broke eye contact with the cowboy. He let the coat fall from his shoulders. The extra limb was much smaller than his own muscled arm. It was stiff and mangled. The upper half of the arm where it had been severed was shredded, as if it had gone through a lawnmower. The limb was already beginning to stink.

"It was my wife's," Adam said. He held her cold dead wrist with his other hand. "We were sewn together when we were married, like conjoined twins."

The others were confused by what he was saying, but it didn't faze the cowboy one bit. As if it was something he'd seen or read about before.

"She was killed in the crash, wasn't she?" Jim asked. "You were combined together as one person, but then the shuttle ripped you apart."

Adam folded his fingers into his wife's fingers, but didn't respond.

"I'm sorry," the cowboy said, placing his hand on Adam's shoulder.

The three-armed man jerked him away, turned around, and stormed back toward the beach. He was trying to block out his memory of the crash. That experience was over and done with. He didn't need to think about it ever again. He survived and she didn't, that's all he needed to remember. It was all he wanted to remember.

Adam didn't realize the shuttle was crashing until they hit the water and all of the seats crumbled together in a pile at the front of the cabin. It took him a few moments to realize he had been buried inside a ball of twisted metal and dead bodies.

He pushed a seat off his head and scanned his surroundings. People were screaming all around him. Acid was pouring into the cabin. Not many people were left alive in his section of the ship.

He tried to stand up, but he was pinned down. Moonlight was deeper inside of the junk pile. Adam couldn't tell her apart from the other corpses curled below. All he could see of her was her face staring up at him, blood leaking down her lips, emptiness in her wide-open eyes.

Adam saw the acid was coming in faster, getting closer to him. He tried pulling Moonlight's body out of the wreckage, but she was completely stuck.

The other survivors were already exiting the ship onto escape rafts. He knew he had only a small amount of time left to get out of there, but he was trapped in place.

"Help me," Moonlight said.

Adam looked down at her face. She blinked. His wife was still alive.

"I can't move," she said. Her voice was distant and dazed, perhaps from shock. "Why can't I move?"

"I thought you were dead," Adam said. Then Adam began to dig his wife out of the wreckage. "I'll get you out," he said. "Hold on."

Moonlight blinked at him.

The pool of acid continued to rise.

Then Moonlight shook herself into a more conscious state, sobering up, beginning to realize what was actually happening around her.

"I don't want to die," Moonlight said, panic filling her face as reality began to sink in. "Don't let me die."

Once Adam had dug far enough down to find Moonlight's body, he realized her condition was a lot worse than he expected. Her legs were coiled like snakes behind her back and around the legs of seats. Her other arm seemed to disappear through the floor of the cabin and reappear out the back of her neck. She was practically fused to the metal, like taffy that had melted around a cluster of nails.

"Get me out of here," she cried.

Adam just stared at her. He had no idea where to begin.

"Hurry!" she yelled.

Adam shook off her words and focused on untwisting her legs from the seats.

"We're going to die if you don't get me out of here," she said.

He pulled with all of his strength, but some parts of the wreckage were unmovable. She touched his knee with her conjoined arm. Tears filled her eyes.

"Please..." she cried. "You have to save us."

Adam kicked and thrashed at the metal, but it wouldn't budge. The acid was rising.

"It's no use," he said.

She tried to smile. "Don't give up. I know you can do it."

"I can't," he said, snapping at her. His face turned red. "Not with only one fucking arm."

"Don't give up," she whispered.

But there was nothing he could do. He couldn't free her. She was dead. She was probably dead even if he got her out of there. He knew he had to focus on freeing himself or they would both die.

"I'm sorry," he said. "There's no way to get you out."

Tears flooded Moonlight's eyes as she accepted the hopelessness of the situation. She looked up Adam. He looked down at her.

Adam yanked on Moonlight's arm with all his strength, trying to separate them, trying to pry them apart.

"It's not going to work," Moonlight said.

She didn't seem shocked at all that he would try to separate them and save himself.

"We can never be separated," she said. "The metal wires are woven into our bones. You're wasting your time."

But he kept trying. He screamed out as he attempted to dig his fingers through the skin between their connected limbs.

She hushed him, touching his knee with her dangling fingers.

"Let it go," she said. "It doesn't matter anymore."

Adam wouldn't give up. "I'm not going to die here."

"We don't have a choice," she said. "We're one being. If you can't free me then we will die."

As Adam tuned her out, focusing on getting himself free, she just looked up at him with a smile.

"I know I can be a horrible bitch to you sometimes," Moonlight said. Her voice was soft now, less frantic. Her deep black eyes peered up at her husband, absorbing him. "I know you probably wouldn't have married me if it weren't for the money."

She paused for a moment to sniffle. Blood filled her nasal cavity.

"But I want you to know," she continued. "The day we were combined together into one person... The day I felt your blood rushing inside of mine... That was the happiest day of my life."

He could tell she wanted him to hold her, accept their fate, and die gently together...

"We are one being," she said. "We lived as one and must now die as one."

But Adam wasn't going to do that...

He pulled a jagged piece of metal out of the pile. It was sharp. Sharp enough to cut through flesh.

"You can't," she said, staring at the metal. "You'll never cut through the wires."

"I'm not going to cut the wires," he said, raising the piece of metal like a machete.

"The only way to separate us is to cut off your arm," she said. "But it won't work. You'll only bleed to death. Just give up and be with me for our final moments together."

She smiled up at him. He looked down at their conjoined arms.

"I wasn't planning to cut off *my* arm," he said.

The smile fell from her face. She feared the serious look in her husband's eyes. She tried to pull her conjoined arm back inside of the wreckage, but his strength overpowered hers. He stretched her arm across the back of a seat, then he brought the blade of metal down into her shoulder.

As blood sprayed across the seats and his wife's screams filled the cabin, Adam realized he was smiling. Something was exciting him. It took a moment before it dawned on him, but he was happy because he was about to be free. If he were to get out of there alive, he wouldn't have to worry about Moonlight ever again. He would inherit her fortune and could continue his life as a rich man without having to be conjoined to the horrible bitch. All he had to do was survive.

The acid was beneath them, melting the lower half of Moonlight's body as he finally ripped her arm from her torso. He stood up, backing away from the acid.

They stared at each other.

"It was the opposite for me," he said to her. "The day I felt your filthy blood pumping into my body… That was the most disturbing and horrible day of my life."

Then he turned and ran, leaving her behind with the rising acid.

The ship was sinking fast, but he was determined to make it. He had to survive. Only one life raft hadn't left yet. When he got to the exit, he looked down at the cowering people trying to cut their raft free. They saw him and waved him away.

"No more room," they cried. "We've got too many already." Even though a third of the raft was still available.

Adam calmly stepped down into the raft. Picked up the closest person and tossed him into the acid sea.

"Is there enough room now?" he asked the others.

They slowly nodded and inched away from him, scared of the severed human arm he seemed to be holding like a club.

As the raft rolled through the waves toward the island, Adam did everything he could in order to survive. He stole a leather trench coat from one of the other passengers to give himself extra protection from the acid spraying against them. The passenger didn't dare object. He sat in the middle of the raft, where less acid would hit him. Those who tried to get too close were kicked back to the outside of the raft.

Many passengers fell overboard from sitting too close to the edge. Those who didn't fall overboard were sprayed with the burning seawater. They shrieked and writhed as the fluid ate away their flesh. Adam broke their necks to put them out of their misery, then used their bodies as cover, protecting him from the corrosive fluids.

The only surviving passenger was an old woman who was so frightened of Adam she curled up on the far side of the raft.

"Come here," he said, reaching out his hand. "It's safer in the middle."

But she didn't hear his words. She just saw him reaching for her. And she was so frightened of what he would do to her that she jumped overboard into the acid sea to get away from him.

Adam watched the woman dissolve into bones as she swam away. It made him laugh. Everyone else could die for all he cared. All that mattered was his survival. He was about to become an incredibly rich, unmarried man. All he had to do was survive.

And he was determined to do so, no matter what measures he had to take.

That night, Adam stayed away from the others. He kept the signal fire going on top of the mountain and sat far enough away so he wouldn't breathe any of the toxic smoke.

He wondered if the baby he'd seen that day was actually Moonlight. It wasn't missing an arm, so he doubted it was really her. The way the thing melted into the tree, it was as if feeding itself to the soil in order to help the tree grow. He wondered if that's what it was really doing. Maybe something in the sea dissolved animal matter into proteins, then reformed them into baby-sized packages of nutrients that crawl themselves up the beach to the trees. There had to be a logical reason for it, but not one Adam was expecting to ever learn.

Staring at the billowing smoke, some of the flames were green and pink in color, as if slow-burning fireworks had been thrown into the fire. It seemed magical the way the unnatural colors curled together in the night air.

For a moment, Adam saw his wife's face in the fire. She was glaring at him. The same expression she gave him right after he had cut her arm off. The same expression she died with.

"Don't you dare haunt me," Adam told the fire.

In the Phyleaist religion, couples are supposed to die together. When they are married and share the same blood, they become one being, one soul. In the afterlife, their thoughts, memories, and feelings mix together, become inseparable from each other. If the wife dies without the husband, she cannot go to the afterlife without him. She would be incomplete.

"Go away," Adam said to the smoke hovering overhead. It looked as if it were his wife reaching out for him.

The smoke seemed to tell him, "But I have nowhere else to go..."

As a Phyleaist wife, it was Moonlight's job to haunt him, drive him insane, and force him to end his own life so they could go to the afterlife together. Adam didn't believe in any of that nonsense, but even if he did, he wasn't going to let her beat him. He was finally free of her.

"Go head and try to haunt me," Adam said. "You'll never make me give in."

Moonlight's face faded from the smoke. Only her bleeding lips remained, hovering over the fire.

Just as Adam's eyelids were falling shut, he heard something in the distance. Carried on the wind, through the hills, it was the sound of a baby crying. At first there was just one, but then a dozen cries could be heard. Then the whole jungle was screaming with the sound of a hundred howling infants. They were lost souls trapped forever within the roots of the blue trees surrounding him.

"Be quiet," Adam growled.

The screams grew louder.

"I said be quiet."

He stood up and tossed a stone into the trees, but the cries wouldn't stop. They continued through the night like drills burrowing through Adam's auditory canals.

CHAPTER SEVEN
JELLY WORMS

"Why aren't they coming?" Zana said to Peter.

They were sitting on the beach, staring up at the sky. It was the morning of the third day and there was still no sign of a rescue ship.

"It's a big planet," Peter said. "It's probably not easy to search every little island."

The pink ocean rolled and whirled in the distance. The sight was as beautiful as it was frightening. It did not seem like easy terrain to search.

"They probably gave up on us already," Zana said. "I mean, if I were in charge of the Citysphere I wouldn't send a rescue party out here for longer than a few hours. The ship didn't stay afloat. I'm sure they think we're all dead by now."

Peter lay back and raised the teddy bear into the air, staring up at it like an airplane.

"But they should know we might have made it to an island," Peter said. "I'm sure they're just going island to island in the area. It's going to take a while. There's a lot of islands."

Zana brushed sand out of her underwear.

"Do you know how expensive that would be for them?" Zana said, scratching at her sandy areas. "They don't have that many resources. The staff at the Citysphere has more important things to do than rescue a bunch of middle-class idiots from a budget flight who are more than likely dead already."

Peter dropped the teddy bear from the air, as if it were a ship falling from the sky to crash-land on his chest.

"We'll either be rescued or we won't," Peter said. "I'm not going to waste my time worrying about it too much. I'd rather enjoy the experience while I still can."

Peter stuck his tongue out at the sky. He wasn't going to let bad thoughts ruin his mood.

"You still think being on this island is fun?" Zana asked him.

"Yes," he said, without a second thought.

Zana smirked. She looked at him and then looked back at the waves.

"Yeah," she said. "Me too."

"This is the last of the water," Jim said, handing Zana and Peter a plastic bottle of water. "You have to share it."

"It's barely twelve ounces," Zana said, shaking the bottle.

"It's all that's left."

"You said we had two quarts per person," Zana said. "I haven't even drunk a full quart yet. I've been conserving it."

Jim shook his head. "Some of the water's been contaminated."

"What do you mean contaminated?"

Jim said, "Acid crystals formed on the insides of some of the bottles, the ones that didn't have lids. The water has become acidic. Not as strong as the ocean water, but it's not safe to drink."

"How the hell did acid crystals form on the insides of the bottles?"

"The sand is probably full of acid crystals," Jim said. "And the sand gets into everything."

Peter and Zana hadn't thought about that before. They knew that beach sand on Earth is salty from the ocean water. It made sense the sand on this island would be full of dried acid particles.

"You might not want to sit directly in the sand," Jim said. "Although the acid is safe to touch in crystal form, it's dangerous when mixed with liquid, including your sweat."

Zana stood up and wiped all the sand off her skin. She wasn't sure if it was just her imagination, but the sand in her moist underwear was beginning to burn.

"How long can we last on this much water?" Peter asked the cowboy.

"Not long," Jim said. "We need to find another source of water. Today."

"What do you want us to do, Captain?" Peter asked.

"We're going to comb this island, every square foot of it," Jim said. "I want the two of you to start on the south side. I'm going to take a volunteer to the north. The others will stay on the beach in case rescue shows up."

"What should we do if we find water?" Peter asked. "Do we need to bring containers?"

"Just leave it and meet me back on the beach," Jim said. "Whatever you do, don't drink any of it."

Before Peter and Zana prepared themselves for a long hike through the jungle, Jim told them, "And one more thing… Keep an eye out for any sign of Shane. I know it's unlikely that he's still out there at this point… but you never know."

Peter and Zana strolled down the beach toward the south side of the island, listening to the pink waves. Zana continuously itched herself.

"That damn cowboy's got me paranoid," Zana said, her hands under her shirt. "I keep thinking I'm covered in acid particles that are burning my skin."

Peter laughed. "Yeah, it's like when you find an ant on your arm and then go the rest of the day thinking ants are crawling all over you."

Mentioning ants only made Zana itchier. She lifted her shirt up into her teeth and scratched every inch of her torso with both hands.

Peter's eyes widened when he saw Zana's body was covered in brightly covered tumors.

"Whoa…" Peter said, barely able to speak. "What are those?"

Zana realized she was exposing herself and removed her shirt from her mouth.

"They've been growing on me since I was a kid," she said.

134

"They're like giant moles."

At first she hesitated. She didn't want to scare Peter the way they usually scared people. But Peter's face wasn't scared or disturbed. He had the expression of excitement.

"Wow!" Peter said, leaning in closer.

She turned her body so he could get a better look, holding up her shirt as if showing off a new tattoo.

"I call them *puppy flowers*," Zana said.

Peter kneeled down, his eyes dazzling as if he'd just seen the most amazing thing in his life, more amazing than being on this alien planet.

"They're so pretty," he said.

Zana's mouth dropped open when he said the words.

"You really think so?" she asked.

Peter nodded. "It's like you grow flowers from your body! And they're so colorful!"

She could tell he was sincere and that put her into a state of shock. Nobody had ever told her they were pretty before and actually meant it.

"They're absolutely beautiful," he said.

Zana wanted to cry right there. She had been searching her whole life for somebody who actually saw her tumors as beautiful, in the same way she thought they were beautiful. Her eyes started to tear up.

She said, "I think so, too."

"Can I touch them?" Peter asked.

She smiled and nodded rapidly, biting her lower lip.

He touched her tumors in the way that someone might feel a bouquet of roses or pet a sea anemone at an aquarium. With each of his strokes, Zana's breaths grew heavy. She licked her lips and closed her eyes. He didn't know he was touching something similar to genitalia. He thought he was just examining something strange and interesting. But to Zana it was as if they were making love in the most intimate way possible.

135

"I think I might be falling in love with you," Zana said to Peter, as they continued down the beach.

Peter scratched his neck. "Really? That's weird. We just met each other."

Zana shook off his words. "You probably don't realize it yet, but I'm sure you're falling in love with me, too."

"Why do you say that?"

"It's nature," Zana said. "Haven't you seen all of those deserted island romance movies? When a man and a woman get stranded on a deserted island together, they always fall in love by the end."

"But those are just movies."

"They're based on real life, though. When two people are stranded together, your instincts start telling you to mate with each other. It's so you can increase your numbers. Even if you start out hating each other, you'll eventually find yourself deeply attracted to one another. Instincts just take over. You don't have a choice."

"But we won't be here long enough for that," Peter said.

"You never know. It could just take a few days of feeling isolated from civilization."

"But there are other people on the island besides the two of us," Peter said. "Maybe you'll end up falling in love with one of them."

"When there are multiple people on an island, a woman will instinctually be more attracted to the one who's most beneficial to her survival."

"Like Jim?" Peter asked.

"More like you," Zana said. "You saved my life. I'd say someone who's willing to risk their life for mine is the most beneficial to my survival."

"But anyone could have done that…"

"It's not just that, though," Zana said. "Even more important is your attitude. You're confident and optimistic. When I'm around you, I feel like everything's going to be all right. In a situation like this, there's nothing more attractive than somebody who makes you feel safe."

She took his hand and held it against one of her puppy flowers as they strolled down the beach.

"You think too much," Peter said. "It's only been a few days. It's not time to start choosing who you'll be mating with."

Zana laughed. "I know, I know. I'm just saying... if this was an island on Earth that we could actually survive on for the rest of our lives, there's no doubt about it—you'd definitely become my mate."

Peter didn't know what else to say. He just shrugged and said, "If you say so..."

"You act as though you don't want to fall in love with me," Zana said.

Peter was about to open his mouth to respond, but she cut him off.

"Be careful how you respond to that," she said, smiling. "I'm easily offended."

"I'm sorry," Peter said. "I don't see myself falling in love with you."

"Is it because I'm a prostitute?" she asked.

"Not at all," Peter said. "I just don't fall in love very easily."

"Sounds like a challenge," Zana said.

They continued walking for a few moments in silence, trudging through the thick white sand.

Then Zana said, "Have you ever been in love before?"

Peter looked over at her, then down to his teddy bear.

Peter only had one girlfriend in his life. It was when he was in college. He was an art major and she had a thing for artists. Tracy was her name.

She used to hang out on Peter's floor of his dorm, scoring weed and beer from some of the guys who lived there. Her skirts were always too short to hide her ass. Her breasts were always spilling out of her shirts. All of the guys on the floor wanted her, but she didn't put out for just anyone.

Tracy was playing drinking games with some guys across the hall, while Peter was building a house of cards the size of a washing machine. Sitting at his desk, he heard them laughing and talking. Though Peter wasn't all that social with the people on his floor, he liked leaving his door open. It made him feel a part of the conversation.

"So what's your type?" he heard some guy ask Tracy.

Peter could tell the guys were all trying to hook up with her. Every question they asked had something to with sex or her body. The guys also constantly insulted each other in order to prove which one was the most worthy. She didn't seem impressed by any of them.

"Artists," she said. "I only date artists."

"Yo, I'm an artist," one of them said.

"Bullshit." She giggled.

Peter shoved his tongue into the side of his cheek as he placed two more cards onto the top of the stack.

"You've not seen my tags?" the guy said. "I'm a tagger. Street art."

There was a pause, as if they were watching the guy draw some bubbly graffiti letters on a napkin.

"Nah, that's not the kind of artist I like," she said. "You're not good enough."

"I'm all about art," said another guy. He sounded like somebody from the cast of Jersey Shore. "I'm not a painter, but my life is a work of art."

"Shut up," she said. She was clearly drunk. "Just shut it."

"I'm all about performance art," the guy continued. "I'm a poet and a dancer. My moves are pure art."

Peter chuckled and almost knocked over his cards.

"You're not what I'm looking for," she said.

"What kind of artist then?" the guys asked.

"I want like... a crazy brilliant artist boyfriend," she said.

"You know, like a real eccentric. Somebody who's just weird and awkward, but deep down he's a misunderstood genius."

"Fuck that," a guy said. "Those guys are all fake. They just pretend they're deep but they're really just losers."

"I don't want a fake artist," she said. "I want a genuine weirdo. Someone who's so wrapped up in their work they forget to put their pants on half the time."

"You don't really want someone like that," a guy said.

"I really do," she said, laughing. "Seriously."

"Bullshit."

"I do."

"No, you don't," one of them said. "And I'll prove it to you."

"How?"

"I know the weirdest, most eccentric art major on campus," he said. "The guy's from another planet."

"Oh yeah?"

"Yeah, and he's got mad talent. But one look at him and you'll change your mind."

"Is he ugly?"

"He's short and scrawny," he said. "Looks kind of like that kid from Star Trek."

"Wil Wheaton?"

"Yeah, Wil Wheaton!"

They all laughed and bantered about Wil Wheaton.

"So who is he? Where's he live?"

"Across the hall," one of them said. They all laughed.

Peter looked over and saw them peeking out of their room at him. When they locked eyes, the four heads hid back inside and giggled.

"He's not that bad," she said.

They laughed harder.

"His name's Peter," one guy said. "If you want a weird artist, go get him."

"I'm going to," she said.

"Then go do it," one said.

"Yeah, have fun," another said.

"Suck on his tiny cock," the last of them said.

Peter could tell there was bile behind their words. They were jealous, angry at the girl. They told her about Peter just so she would get turned off by the idea of an eccentric artist and go for one of them instead. But their plan backfired. She fell for Peter within seconds.

"You're Peter?" she said, stepping into his room.

When Peter turned to her, she could tell he was exactly what she was looking for. He was building a house of cards as casually as one would stack books on a shelf. A grape vine was dangling out of his mouth like a cigarette. His shoes were mismatched and held together with duct tape. His jacket had a hole in it the size of his whole back. And yes indeed he was not wearing any pants. He was wearing shoes, a shirt, a jacket, and boxers, but no pants.

"They say you're a talented artist," she said, closing the door behind her.

"Meh," Peter said, pointing at the other side of the room.

His walls were covered in his art.

"Whoa, crap," she said. She nearly fell over when she saw his work. "This is really yours? Holy shit."

Peter shrugged and continued building his house of cards.

"I don't really have any talent," Peter said. "I just majored in art because it sounded like fun."

Peter wasn't trying to be humble. He really didn't care for his work. Despite his own opinion, everyone in the art department thought he was one of the most stylistically complex and brilliant artists in the school.

"Shut up," she said. "This is genius. Are you kidding me? You're like M. C. Escher, but sexy as hell."

Peter's style was mostly nudes with intricate patterns in the flesh. All were black and white, using pen and ink. The effect was very surreal.

"My name's Tracy," she said.

She sat up on the desk next to his house of cards, careful not to knock it over.

"Hello," Peter said.

140

"I'm sure you heard everything I said across the hall," she said. "But artists turn me on."

Peter didn't know what to say in response to that. The next thing he knew she had thrown off her clothes and jumped on his desk in front of him, smashing the house of cards with her big naked ass.

As she fucked him, Tracy moaned loudly so the three guys across the hall could hear. Peter could sense their jealousy. In childish attempts to get them to quit having sex, the three guys banged on his door, put shaving cream in his keyhole, and even pulled the fire alarm. The same things they did when anyone was trying to get laid on their floor. But nothing they did could keep her hands off of Peter. He was exactly the guy she had been looking for all semester. She wasn't going to let them ruin it.

She came to see him every day after that. Sometimes they had sex. Sometimes they just talked. Sometimes she watched him draw. Sometimes she posed naked for him. Peter had no idea what the heck was going on until Tracy started to refer to him as her boyfriend. That's when it clicked with him that he was in a relationship.

But he never really had any feelings for her. She just invited herself into his life and he went with the flow. He didn't really know how to connect to the girl. They had nothing in common. And even though everyone on his floor thought she was the hottest girl on campus, he really wasn't attracted to her at all.

"Grab my tits," Tracy said, as she was naked on top of him. "Why aren't you grabbing my tits?"

Peter was busy reading a manga called *Cage of Eden* as she tried to fuck him.

"Wait!" he said. "This is the best part!"

"Aren't you done with that yet?" Tracy asked.

"Oh, wow!" Peter cried. "This kid is getting eaten by a hyaenodon!"

"What the hell's a hyaenodon?"

"Hold on," Peter said, holding up his finger. "I'm on the last page."

Tracy huffed at him and tossed the book across the room. Peter's eyes followed it, trying to read the last page as it flew through the air.

"Pay attention to me," Tracy said.

Peter stared at the book on the floor, as if able to read through the cover to the last page.

"I am paying attention to you," Peter said, a wide smile on his face as the manga story replayed in his head.

"Make me feel sexy," she said. "Don't you think my breasts are sexy?"

"Sure."

"Sure! That's all you've got to say? Sure? Most guys would kill for a girl with tits like these."

"I don't know," Peter said. "Your nipples are too dark."

"What!"

"I think it's prettier when nipples are lighter in color than the breasts, and glossy like scar tissue."

"Are you fucking with me?"

"And they're also too round," Peter said. "I like when nipples are kind of shapeless. If they're shaped too perfectly round, they seem artificial for some reason. I also think it's neat when nipples are inverted."

"Stop being an asshole!"

Peter then realized he was insulting her.

"Oh, don't feel bad," he said. "I just think your breasts aren't your best physical attribute."

"Then what is my best attribute?"

Peter pointed at a large coffee-colored splotch on her stomach.

"That's my favorite part," he said.

"My birthmark?" she asked. "You like that ugly thing?"

He rubbed his finger along her birthmark.

"It's beautiful," he said, his eyes following the patterns inside of the mark. "It's like a snail shell with so many textures inside."

"But it's so big and splotchy. I wish I could get it removed."

"I love it," Peter said. "I could just stare at it for hours."

She looked down at it with new eyes.

142

"I guess it does kind of look like a snail tattoo," she said.

"It's a work of art," Peter said.

Tracy smiled at him.

"That's why I only date artists," she said. "You can find beauty in anything."

She pulled off his pants.

"But you better find the beauty in my too-perfectly-round nipples or I'm going to kick your ass," she said.

As they made love, Peter thought about the exciting manga he had been reading. He just couldn't get it out of his head. He wanted to know what was going to happen next.

After Tracy had her orgasm, Peter jumped out of bed and began scribbling in his sketchbook.

"What are you doing?" she said. "Did you come?"

But he just ignored her and focused on his work.

"What are you doing?" she asked. "Did my body inspire you?"

After he finished the first panel, he held it up to show her.

"The Cage of Eden manga!" he said. "The next volume doesn't come out for a few months, so I'm going to continue the story on my own."

Tracy just lay there in his bed, staring at him with bewilderment. Peter's excited eyebrows rose to the top of his forehead as he sat naked at his desk furiously sketching manga characters being attacked by prehistoric beasts.

"Nah, I've never been in love," Peter said.

Zana stepped in front of him, walking backward, "You should try it sometime. You might like it."

"I don't know…" Peter said.

"Why are you so resistant to it?"

"I'm just not attracted to women," he said.

"You're gay?" Zana sounded disappointed.

"No," he said. "I'm not attracted to men either."

She asked. "If you're not heterosexual or homosexual, then

what are you?"

"I'm asexual, I guess," he said. "I've never been sexually attracted to another person before."

"What do you mean you're not sexually attracted to me?" Tracy yelled at Peter in front of a dance club where everyone could hear them. "How the hell could you not be attracted to me?"

"I don't know," Peter said, tugging on an inside-out pants pocket.

She said, "So every time you called me pretty was a lie?"

"I wasn't lying," he said. "I totally think you're pretty, but in the way that a sunset is pretty."

"I have no idea why we were even together in the first place," she said. "If you didn't like me this whole time, why didn't you tell me sooner?"

Peter shrugged. "You seemed to be having fun being in a relationship with me. I didn't want to ruin it for you."

"Whatever," she said. "I'm through wasting my time. You're such a loser. I can't believe I slept with you."

All the drunk college guys smoking outside of the dance club were laughing their asses off at every word she said. Tracy hoped to humiliate Peter by speaking as loud as she could, but he seemed completely unaffected by the experience.

"Sorry about that," Peter said. "We can break up if that'll make you feel better."

"Of course we're breaking up, you moron!"

The college guys nearly fell over with laughter, pointing at Peter and hollering something about his dick size. Tracy just rolled her eyes, turned her back, and walked away from him.

"Goodnight," Peter said with a smile, waving at her as she went down a side street behind the club.

"Fuck off," Tracy said.

She gave him the middle finger but didn't bother looking back.

"I don't know if I buy it," Zana said. "There's got to be at least one person in the world you've found sexually appealing."

"Nope," Peter said. "Nobody."

"Then what the hell do you fantasize about when you masturbate?"

Peter blushed and looked away.

"You do masturbate, don't you?" she asked.

"Yeah, I do masturbate from time to time. But I don't fantasize about having sex when I do it."

"What else is there?"

"I fantasize about airplanes."

"Airplanes?"

"I always wanted to learn how to fly an airplane," he said. "Whenever I think about it, I get really excited."

Zana's face was a blank stare at him.

He continued, "Sometimes I imagine I'm parachuting or riding on roller coasters or going down water slides. I also sometimes fantasize about being really good at basketball."

Zana laughed at him.

"Those aren't sexual fantasies," she said. "They're daydreams."

"Well, sometimes I get aroused when I think about that stuff."

"You're so weird!" she said.

She laughed and pointed.

"What the hell is wrong with you?" she said.

Then she stopped laughing and curled her fingers into fists.

"You're such an asshole," she said.

Then she sped up, walking far ahead of him, ignoring him.

Peter wondered what the heck that was all about. She seemed to have suddenly gotten offended when she realized Peter didn't find her attractive. It reminded him of the time Tracy had broken up with him.

"Wait up," Peter said.

But when he sped to catch up, she only increased her pace to avoid him. He didn't understand what was wrong with her. He was hoping he could figure out a way to make her feel better.

"Are you okay?" Peter asked.

Zana turned around to look at him. There were tears in her eyes. Peter wondered why the heck she would have tears in her eyes.

Then something exploded out of the sea and Zana disappeared into its gaping cavernous mouth.

It was a giant worm. The same kind as Peter and Jim had seen in the jungle, only this one was much larger. It slurped Zana's body inside of its mouth so fast she didn't even have enough time to scream.

Peter just froze. He couldn't tell if any of this was real or not. As the worm slid slowly back toward the water, he could see through its translucent skin. He saw Zana inside of there, struggling and fighting to climb back out. Farther down the massive tunnel of jelly-flesh, Peter could see the other contents of its stomach, all the other things it had eaten. There was another human inside of the worm, only this one was almost completely digested. Though very little flesh remained on its body, Peter recognized the corpse.

It was Shane.

That's what had happened to him. The first night on the island, Shane must have been attacked by this creature while he was sitting on the beach watching for rescue ships. It sucked him up and pulled him into the acid sea.

As the giant creature inched its way across the beach, Peter watched Zana struggling inside of it. He couldn't let what happened to Shane happen to her. He had to get her out of there somehow.

Although the creature was almost the size of a subway car, he couldn't let fear get in his way. He made up his mind. He was going to save Zana at all cost. He just had to be brave.

Peter knew how to be brave. Even when the odds were against him, he was the kind of guy who would stand up to anything or anyone.

It was the same night Tracy had broken up with him. Peter was on his way home, excited to draw a new chapter of his manga, when he heard someone screaming. A woman. He followed her cries into the graveyard, which separated the dorms. It was common for people to hop the fence as a shortcut home late at night. It was the route Tracy usually took.

He wasn't sure it was her until he saw her lying in the grass. Tracy was being held down by four guys as a fifth was trying to remove her pants. She kicked and screamed, but they only laughed at her efforts.

They outnumbered him five to one, each of them twice Peter's size, but he couldn't let that frighten him. He had to do something. He had to stop them.

"Does anyone have a cigarette?" Peter said, as he stepped out of the shadows toward the five men. "I could really use a cigarette right now."

All of them froze when they saw him. Even Tracy, with her pants down to her knees, was surprised.

"Who the fuck is this guy?" one of the guys said.

Peter didn't recognize any of them. They were around his age, but they didn't appear to be students at the college.

"Peter!" Tracy yelled. "Call the police!"

One of them put his hand over her mouth. As she struggled in their grasp, the guy who was trying to pull off her pants stood up and approached Peter. Two of his friends followed.

"You two know each other?" the guy asked.

Peter nodded. "Yeah. She used to be my girlfriend, but we broke up a little while ago."

"So what are you trying to do? Save her or something? Think you can win her back by playing the hero?"

"Nah," he said, shaking his head. "As I said, I was just

wondering if any of you had a cigarette I could bum."

Tracy pulled her face away from the guy restraining her and said, "What the fuck are you doing, Peter? Run! Call the Police!"

The guys all laughed at her.

"Yeah, Peter," said the leader, cocking his head. "Run. Call the police."

Peter looked at Tracy then up at the guy standing in his face. He smiled.

"Can't," Peter said. "I don't have a cell phone."

They laughed at him.

"Then what good are you?" he said.

The guy pulled a cigarette out of his pack and handed it to Peter.

"Here's your cigarette," the guy said. "Now get lost."

Peter took the cigarette then gave it back.

"Can you light it?" Peter asked. "I don't have a lighter."

It made the guy smirk. He lit Peter's cigarette for him and handed it back to him.

"You'd be dead right now, if I didn't find all of this so amusing," the leader said.

Peter held the cigarette in his hands and just stood there, staring at the men with a smile on his face.

"Aren't you going to smoke it?" the leader asked.

"Nah," Peter said. "I don't smoke."

"Then why the hell did you have me light it for you?"

"To do this," Peter said.

He lunged forward and stabbed the cigarette into the guy's face. The leader tumbled back, shrieking. It only burned the outside of an eyelid, but he yelled as if his retina had been scorched away.

Being small and quick, Peter was able to slip by the leader's two friends before they could grab him. Then he jumped headfirst into one of the guys holding Tracy. With all his weight, he slammed his skull into the guy's chest, nearly breaking his neck in the process. It knocked the wind out of the guy and caused him to let go of Tracy.

"You fucking asshole!" Tracy yelled.

Peter couldn't tell who she was referring to.

She was able to jerk herself out of the other guy's hands and once she was completely free, she ran. Peter ran with her. They took off into the woods of the cemetery, trying not to trip over headstones.

It was a stupid plan, but it worked. Tracy was free. He knew he would think of some way to save her. He knew all he needed was the courage to try.

"It's all your fault," Tracy yelled at Peter. She seemed delirious, an emotional wreck. "This wouldn't have happened if it weren't for you!"

As they ran through the cemetery, the five guys followed close behind yelling and threatening to kill them both.

"Just get to the gate and we'll be fine," Peter said, cutting through a row of tombstones. "They won't do anything once we're back on campus."

"I hate you," she said through her tears. "I fucking hate you."

Once the gate came into view, Tracy turned and slapped Peter.

"How could you do this to me!" she yelled.

Then Tracy kicked him in the testicles. Peter cried out and crumbled to the ground in pain. She spit on him. Then she continued running, leaving him in the dirt.

When the five guys caught up to Peter, they kicked and stomped him as he lay writhing on the ground.

"Grab the bitch," the leader said to one of his friends.

But before his friend could run after Tracy, Peter grabbed him by the ankle. The guy tripped and fell to the ground. Another guy tried to go after Tracy, but Peter wrapped both of his arms around his legs. The guy didn't fall, so he dragged Peter with him.

"I won't let you get her," Peter yelled, his bare stomach ripped open against the corner of a grave marker as he was pulled.

The other guys continued kicking and stomping him, but Peter wouldn't let any of them go after his ex-girlfriend.

"Why the fuck are you protecting her?" the leader said to

Peter. "That bitch just kicked you in the balls so we'd get you instead of her."

"I don't care," Peter said, blood dribbling into his eyes.

"You still in love with her or something?" He leaned down and punched Peter in the face. "That bitch doesn't give a fuck about you." Another punch, breaking open Peter's lip. "She screwed you to save herself."

"I don't love her at all," Peter said, a copper flavor flooding his mouth. "Not at all."

As they pummeled him, Peter watched Tracy hopping the fence in the distance. She looked back for just a second, then ran off toward campus. She didn't call for help. She didn't try to get the police. She just went home.

Peter said, "But what kind of person would I be if I let her get hurt?"

As blood leaked down his cheeks, a broken smile grew on his face. It didn't matter what happened to him. He was just happy Tracy had gotten away. He was relieved knowing that she would be safe.

Peter's bravery had paid off once before and he was hoping it would pay off again. His mind was made up. He was going to rescue Zana no matter the cost. He tightened Captain Bearbeard into his belt, switched his eyepatch to the other eye, and grunted with commitment.

Then, without knowing what the heck he was going to do to save Zana, Peter charged the monster.

"Hang on," he yelled at Zana, but he couldn't tell if she could hear through the worm's flesh.

He leapt onto the creature's head and straddled it. Zana's hands stretched out the back of its throat and clung onto the rubbery flaps of the worm's mouth. Peter grabbed her hands and pulled.

"Come on!" Peter yelled.

The creature's flesh was incredibly slimy and he had difficulty keeping his grip. The worm roared and rose into the air. When it slammed down into the sand, Peter tumbled over the side and landed in front of its lips.

"Let go of her," he told the worm. "She's my friend!"

He put his feet on each side of the worm's eyeless slug-like head and pushed, pulling Zana with all of his strength. When her face pierced through the worm's mouth-flaps, she gasped for air. Her hair was wet with slime. Her clothes soaked.

"Get me out of here," she shrieked.

When she was halfway out of its mouth, the worm opened its lips. The mouth-flaps stretched out three times the width of its body, like a snake unhinging its jaw. Inside of its gaping maw, Peter saw dozens of fish-like eyeballs staring at him. The worm did have eyes, but they were inside of its mouth.

As Zana's legs were freed, she crawled over Peter to get away. It was only an accident, but as she desperately scurried over the pirate's body her knee connected with his face. It slammed right into his forehead, nearly knocking him out.

"Run," Zana yelled.

But Peter was dazed from the knee to the face. She crawled to safety, but for Peter it was too late. The monster's mouth had stretched so wide it could have swallowed a house. The creature's head blocked out the pink sky as it descended upon him.

"Come on," Zana cried, even though she knew escape for him was impossible.

Peter just stared into the monster's gaping maw. He didn't move a muscle.

Zana cried out as the worm's mouth closed around Peter's body. She gasped and stepped back. A tear fell down her cheek as she watched the creature return to the acid water with new prey in its belly.

The five men left Peter broken and bloody in the cemetery.

Before they left, the leader asked Peter, "Was it worth it?"

Peter coughed up blood.

The leader lifted Peter's head out of the dirt by his hair. "Was it worth getting your ass busted up for the sake of that bitch?"

Peter's fist was shaking as he took it off the ground and moved it toward the man's face. Then, slowly, he raised his thumb.

"Fucking idiot," the leader said.

He dropped Peter back into the dirt.

"Word of advice," the leader continued. "Don't risk your life to save some stupid bitch who doesn't give a shit about you. Next time, you're going to get yourself killed."

Then the five men turned to walk away. But Peter told them to wait. He pulled himself to his feet and staggered forward.

They looked over at him, watching him sway back and forth. With the blood and dirt covering his body, the weird college kid looked like a deranged ghoul.

"Next time, I won't get killed," Peter said. He spit blood. "This only happened to me because I was too weak to fight you. But I'm not going to be weak forever. I'm going to become strong. I'll be strong enough to beat ten or twenty guys like you all at the same time."

He raised his fist into the air.

"Next time, I'm not going to get myself killed," Peter yelled. "Because next time, I'll save the girl and defeat all the attackers without getting a scratch on me!"

Then Peter fell over face-first into the dirt and the five men burst into laughter.

"Let's get out of here," the leader said. He chuckled and patted his friends on the back as they walked on.

But Peter wasn't joking around. He had made up his mind. Once his injuries had healed, he began training. And he didn't stop training until he was the most powerful fighter his city had ever known.

Before it made it back into the ocean, something happened to the jelly worm. Zana couldn't figure out what was going on, but the worm began thrashing and shaking its head. Then its gelatin flesh burst open.

An explosion of worm guts and mucus burst across the sand. When the rain of goop ended, Zana saw him. Standing there, where the worm's head used to be, Peter was in a fighting pose. His arms were out to his sides, as if he had destroyed the creature's head just by punching in both directions at once. His pirate teddy bear still strapped into his belt like a baby in a sling.

Zana didn't recognize Peter at first. He seemed like a completely different person. His eyes were calm and distant. He seemed serious, focused. He was no longer a goofy kid dressed up like a pirate. He was deadly.

The headless worm fled back into the sea. Peter changed his fighting stance. He didn't take his eyes off the water. Another giant worm exploded out of the sea. It shrieked at Peter so loudly it shook the island. The noise made Zana fall back, covering her ears. But Peter just stood there, unfazed.

The jelly worm went for him. It took Zana a minute to realize it wasn't a new worm. It was the other end of the same worm.

Peter didn't run. Instead, he charged the worm as it came toward him. He leapt into the air as the worm widened its mouth, and kicked it in the largest of its internal eyes. The worm squealed as Peter held tightly to one of its mouth-flaps and repeatedly punched at its fish-like eyeballs. Although the creature had incredibly strong cartilage eyelids designed to protect its eyes from its prey, Peter's fists were well-trained. He could punch through a brick wall if he needed to.

The thing whipped its head around. Although Peter had the strength to hold on, the slime covering its mouth-flaps was too slippery. He lost his grip and was tossed across the beach.

When he landed, Zana ran to him and tried to stand him up. The worm didn't attack them. It continued thrashing its head, shrieking and whining.

"What the hell is that thing?" Zana cried. "What the hell are *you?*"

Then Peter noticed the jelly worm wasn't shrieking because of its injury. It was shrieking to call for help.

"We need to get out of here," Peter said, getting to his feet.

Before Peter and Zana had run ten meters, three more giant worms emerged from the ocean and squirmed up the beach.

"Into the jungle," Peter said.

The other jelly worms were smaller than the first one, but they moved faster. They slithered through the blue trees like snakes, tearing violently after their prey.

"What do we do?" Zana said. "We can't outrun them."

Two more jelly worms were up ahead, coming at them from deep in the jungle. They would soon be surrounded.

"Up a tree," Peter said.

They targeted the tallest, sturdiest tree they could find. Zana went first. Once they were high enough that none of the worms could get them, they relaxed. They took deep breaths and looked down. The five jelly worms coiled around the trees below them, slithering slowly, following their scent.

"They can't climb?" Zana asked.

Peter shrugged.

"Maybe they don't see us," he said.

They watched the worms.

The creatures didn't try to come after them, but they also didn't leave.

"Now what?" Zana asked.

Peter pulled his teddy bear out of his belt, examining it to make sure it was all right.

"We wait," Peter said.

They waited there patiently for an hour, but the worms didn't leave. The creatures stayed on the ground below them as if they knew Peter and Zana would have to come down eventually.

Zana scratched her arms and whined in agony. While climbing the tree, they had gotten the alien blue algae all over them. Their skin was itching and burning like crazy now. It was impossible to get all of it off.

"I'm sick of it," Zana said. "Why won't they leave?"

Peter curled his lower lip and blew air into his nostrils.

"They must be hungry," Peter said.

"What do you think they eat?" Zana said. "They're obviously predators, but there's no prey big enough for them to eat on this planet."

"There's us," Peter said.

"But what did they eat before us?"

"Maybe they ate each other."

A moment of silence as Peter thought about it.

Then his eyes lit up and he said, "Or maybe there are tons of other animals on this planet we don't know about yet."

"But where are they?" Zana asked.

"They could be hiding," Peter said. "Those jelly worms are huge and we didn't notice them right away."

"Do you think there are more creatures in the ocean?"

Peter thought about it. "I don't know. The ocean is made of a powerful acid. I'm still amazed those worms can survive in it."

"I'm not," Zana said. "Haven't you heard of tapeworms?"

"The parasite?"

"They can live in a mammal's stomach and intestines without getting digested," she said. "They generate a mucus that protects them. Those giant worms probably have something similar."

Zana pointed at her arm.

"Look," she said.

The skin on her arm was red from the reaction to the blue algae in the tree, but there was a spot on her arm that was her natural skin tone.

"This area was covered in slime when we climbed the tree," she said. "It was like a layer of protection."

"Whoa," Peter said. "Jelly worms are awesome."

Zana shook her head at him.

"You really didn't know about the mucus?" she asked.

He shrugged.

"You know if the worm didn't have this stuff covering its body you would have been killed by jumping on top of it," she said. "The thing came from the acid ocean. It would have burned your skin off."

"Really?"

"I can't believe you just jumped on top of it without realizing that."

Peter shrugged.

"It seemed like the right thing to do at the time," he said.

She pulled his hand into her lap. She didn't care he was using that hand for balance and nearly fell out of the tree.

"You were amazing back there," she said, folding his fingers between hers. "I think I'm going to fall for you whether you like it or not."

Peter didn't know what to say. He just sat there in the tree with her, staring down at the worms below. Then he felt a puppy flower beneath her shirt, its tendrils becoming erect as it brushed against his wrist.

"What's that?" Peter said.

At first, Zana thought he was talking about her aroused tumor poking into his arm, but then she noticed he was looking at something in the distance.

"Where?" Zana asked.

Peter removed his hand from her lap and pointed at a tree deeper in the jungle. There was something inside of it.

"Is that what I think it is?" Zana said.

Peter squinted his eyes.

"Yeah," he said.

"It can't be," she said. "It's got to be some kind of an illusion."

"No, I'm pretty sure it's real," he said. "There's a football player in that tree over there..."

The jelly worms eventually left, but it took a few hours. They made sure the things were gone for good before making their descent. Then Peter and Zana climbed down as quickly as they could and went straight for the tree they had seen—the one with the football player.

They called up to him.

"Is somebody there?" Zana yelled.

No response.

"Maybe it was an illusion after all," Peter said.

They climbed the tree. The closer they came, the more they were sure it was a football player. However, the guy wasn't moving. When they got to him, the smell was unbearable. They saw the belt tied around his neck like a noose. He was dead.

Jim whipped his cowboy hat in front of his face to get rid of the corpse's decaying odor.

"How long do you think he was up there?" Zana asked.

"I'd say it's been a month or two," Jim replied.

After getting down from the tree, Peter and Zana met up with the others back on the beach and brought them to see the football player's body. Nobody believed it until they saw it. They searched the body and found no belongings, no suicide note, no ID, nothing.

"Was he on the ship with us?" Jill asked. "I don't remember seeing a guy in a football uniform."

"He wasn't on our ship," Jim said. "He's been here for a lot longer than we have."

"Then how the hell did he get here?" Zana asked.

"Some other way," Jim said. "Either there was another shuttle crash in the area a couple months back that wasn't mentioned on the news or he came from the Citysphere. I'm guessing he was part of some tour group that got washed out to sea or maybe the son of one of the researchers who got lost on an expedition. Something like that."

"It's creepy," Jill said. "The babies coming out of the sea and now this…"

"I'm sure everything has a rational explanation," Jim said. "But I'm not really worried about why he's here. What I want to know is what he's been up to since he's been here."

"What do you mean?" Zana asked.

"I want to know if he made a camp on this island," Jim said. "I want to know if he had left behind food and water. I want to know if there's a wrecked vessel on the island he couldn't repair himself. I want to know if he was alone or if there are still others here somewhere."

"So we need to keep searching the island?" Peter asked.

Jim nodded. "Yeah, we need to check out every inch of this place. If he did come in some kind of exploration vessel, we need to find it."

He looked at Zana and Peter. "We also need to find a safer place to camp. If those worms are as dangerous as you say they are, we can't stay on the beach anymore."

Adam was standing behind the group, trying to chisel off his third arm with a sharp stone.

"We're not going to find anything," Adam said. "We searched this island all day. There's nothing here but poisonous plants and dirt. There's no way a ship is out there we didn't find."

"We don't have a choice," Jim said. "We have to keep looking. If we don't find water or a way out of here, we're going to die."

Peter nodded. "Then we'll keep searching this island nonstop until we're dead."

The others were silent for a moment, but they all agreed. They didn't have any choice but to keep searching.

The cowboy looked up into the tree. He removed his hat.

"But first we should cut this poor boy down," he said. "We should give him a proper burial, whoever he is."

They searched the island all day, but there was no sign of where the hanged man had come from. There was no campsite, no ship to be found.

"Where the hell could he have come from?" Zana asked.

Nobody knew the answer to that question.

"It's like he was stranded here with only the clothes on his back."

There also wasn't any water in sight. There were puddles of slime that seemed to help plants grow. There was moisture forming over the blue algae that covered the trees. But there were no ponds or streams.

Apart from a few areas they decided to avoid due to the presence of roaming jelly worms, they had looked everywhere. They didn't know what else to do.

When night was beginning to fall, they decided to give up the search until morning. They gathered on the beach. Not a single one of them went anywhere near the water. Those who had seen the jelly worms constantly eyed their surroundings for any sign of movement.

"We're exerting ourselves too much," Adam said. "It's only going to make us dehydrate faster."

"We have to keep looking," Jim said. "We just haven't been searching thoroughly enough. Water can be anywhere. It's in the ground. It's inside of fruits."

"But everything's toxic," Zana said. "Any water we find in fruits or in the soil will probably kill us."

"Not necessarily," Jim said. "We don't know anything about this world. Scientists said it would be impossible for humans to survive on this planet, but they also said the largest living creature here was only the size of a human thumb. Those giant worms are proof they have no idea what they are talking about."

Peter raised his hand lightning-fast.

"Oh!" he cried.

They all looked at him as he jumped up and down with his hand raised like a hyperactive 2nd grader.

"What's with you?" Zana asked.

"I forgot!" He turned to Zana. "Remember that shiny thing we saw the first day we were here?"

"What shiny thing?"

"The first day on the island we climbed the peak to get a good look around. We saw something shiny in the distance. It looked like metal."

"Is this true?" Jim asked.

Zana said, "We saw something that reflected light. It wasn't necessarily metal. It could have been anything."

"Still," Jim said. "We should check it out. It might be something we missed in our search. How far away was it?"

"Not too far," Peter said. "Maybe half a mile away. A mile at most."

Jim looked up at the sky.

"I think we might be able to get there and check it out before it gets too dark," he said. "Show me."

Only Jim and Peter climbed the hill to get a look at the thing that was reflecting the light.

"A lot of things besides metal can reflect light," Jim said. "For instance, water. That's what I'm hoping it is."

"I doubt it was water," Peter said. "It was really shiny."

"We'll see," Jim said.

When they made it to the top of the hill, Jim and Peter scanned the terrain.

"Over there," Peter said, pointing at the spot between the trees that was reflecting the pink sky.

Jim squinted his eyes.

"Is it water?" Peter asked.

He shook his head. "I can't tell from here."

They went down the hill and hiked into the jungle.

"Maybe it's a helicopter," Peter said. "Does the Citysphere use helicopters to get to the different islands? Do you know how to fly a helicopter if it is one?"

"They didn't bring helicopters to this planet," Jim said. "They explore the islands using vehicles built especially for this place. They're kind of like hovercraft that can move over both land and sea."

Peter pointed up ahead.

"Do they look like that?" he said, pointing at a ship behind the trees in front of them.

Jim hadn't realized they already arrived at their destination. Up ahead, there was definitely a ship just lying in the dirt as if waiting for them. Once the entire thing was in view, Jim stopped in his tracks. He couldn't believe what he was seeing.

"That thing didn't come from the Citysphere," Jim said.

Peter looked at the cowboy and then more carefully at the spaceship behind the trees.

"In fact..." Jim continued. "That thing didn't come from Earth at all."

That's when Peter realized the strange design of the ship. It was conical and about the size of a city bus, made of some kind of metal that glimmered like nothing Peter had ever seen before.

CHAPTER EIGHT
THE ALIENS

"It's from another world?" Peter asked. "Which world?"

They hid behind webby bushes, examining the ship from a distance.

"Who knows," Jim said. "This planet and the sun it orbits have been tumbling through the galaxy for millions of years. It's likely passed several worlds along the way. This must have been some kind of alien exploration vessel that crashed here a long time ago."

"How long has it been here?" Peter asked.

"Centuries maybe," Jim said.

"That long? But it's so clean and shiny, like it's brand new."

Jim pushed his way through the bushes.

"I'm going to take a closer look," he said.

Peter followed.

They entered the crash site. The area was wide open, as if the ship had leveled a large section of the jungle during its emergency landing, scorching it in such a way that nothing was able to grow there ever again.

"Do you think they died in the crash?" Peter asked, looking up at the shiny cone-shaped vessel. "Or were they stranded here on the island like us?"

"We'll be in luck if they died in the crash," Jim said. "There might be supplies still on board. If we're in luck, maybe there's even preserved food and drinkable water."

"Even if it crashed here centuries ago?"

Jim tipped his hat at him. "You never know. They could have storage technology far superior to ours."

They examined the ship, looking for a way in.

"So where's the door?" Peter asked.

There were small slit-like windows along the outside of the

craft, but no entrance was in sight.

"Got to be one here somewhere," Jim said. "Maybe it's on the roof like a submarine."

Jim stepped forward to see if he could climb up to the roof. As he touched the outside of the vessel lights brightened inside of the ship, emanating through the window slits. The engine whirred as though powering up.

"They're alive," Peter cried, excitedly. "The aliens are still alive in there."

Jim stepped away from it.

"Get back," he told Peter. "I think they're taking off."

"We should ask them to take us with them," Peter said.

"Get back!"

A flash of light burst from the ship. Then a silver beam hit Jim square in the chest. The cowboy stopped moving.

"Jim?" Peter yelled, from the bushes.

Jim kept standing there for a moment. Then he fell back. When he hit the ground, Peter saw a shiny silver spear in his chest. He had been shot by some kind of weapon.

If the passengers of the crashed vessel were still alive in there, they were far from friendly.

The ship fired again, aiming for Peter. The silver beam sliced through the bushes, grazed his ear and pierced into the rock behind him. Peter ducked behind a tree trunk as two more beams were fired.

It appeared as though the ship were firing some kind of liquid metal that hardened into razor-sharp blades as it traveled through the air. But that didn't make much sense to Peter because the ship's armaments looked more like camera lenses than gun barrels. Peter wondered if the aliens had the technology to turn energy into matter.

Jim moaned. He was still alive. Peter watched as the cowboy tried to pull the blade from his chest, but he didn't have the strength. He had been completely impaled, nailed to the ground.

"You alright?" Peter yelled at him from behind the tree.

The cowboy couldn't speak. His lungs were filling with blood. Peter had to save him. Like he rescued Zana from the jelly worms, he had to save Jim from the angry alien beings. But this time he wasn't going to use his fighting skills to save him.

Peter stood up and stepped out into the open. He raised his arms in surrender. He kept his distance and made no sign of aggressive behavior.

"I just want to help my friend," Peter told the spaceship. He pointed at Jim. "Then we'll leave you alone."

The ship reacted to Peter's hand gesture and fired at him twice. The pirate turned sideways and the two blades sliced past him, grazing both his back and chest.

Peter glared back at the ship. His expression began to change. It grew darker and more serious.

"Not nice," he said.

Another beam fired directly at Peter's face, but he caught it in midair with one hand. The liquid metal was still solidifying as he gripped it, stretching forward into a needle-like point only centimeters from his eyepatch.

Then Peter charged the ship. He used the silver blade like a bat, swatting away the other metal beams as they were fired at him. He stabbed one of the lenses on the side of the ship, smashing it open. Then spun around and drove the blade into the other lens. The whirring sound faded after the ship was disarmed.

Peter caught his breath against the side of the vessel for a moment. Then he went to Jim.

"Are you okay?" he asked the cowboy.

Jim pulled the metal rod from his chest and tossed it aside.

"Never better," Jim said.

His voice was a wheezy croak that could barely be heard.

He sounded as if he had doused his voice box with gasoline and set it on fire.

As Peter got Jim to his feet, the ship whirred back to life. This time the sound was several times louder than before. Several flaps slid open on the upper half of the ship, revealing more of the lens weapons. But this time there weren't only two. There were hundreds. Peter wouldn't be able to dodge them this time.

Just as the weapons lit up to fire, something ran out of the bushes toward them. It looked like some kind of yellow creature. It flew past Peter and Jim to the side of the ship, slid open a panel, and began to press buttons as fast as lightning.

Before Peter or Jim knew what was going on, the engines on the ship faded out. Lids closed on the lens weapons. Everything went quiet. Then Peter recognized who had saved them. It wasn't a creature.

The Kazakh man in the yellow turtleneck sweater closed the panel and turned to his comrades.

"You saved us," Peter said. "How the heck did you know how to turn it off?"

The Kazakh looked at him with a blank expression.

"I'm good with computers," he said.

The others showed up at the crash site soon after. They had heard the sounds of the alien ship through the jungle and had to see what was going on.

"There's no one living inside," the Kazakh told Peter, pointing at the vessel. "You set off the ship's automated defense system."

"How do you know that?" Peter asked.

"As I said, I'm good with computers."

Everyone gathered around Jim. They set him down and tried to treat him. He instructed them on what to do, but his medical knowledge was limited to first aid. Also, the twilit sky was quickly becoming night, making it difficult to see. They were able to stop his external bleeding, but they had no idea whether he was still bleeding internally or not. He continued to cough up blood, but he no longer seemed in danger of drowning in it.

"You'll be fine, right?" Zana asked him. "You're too tough to let a little wound like that do you in."

Jim just nodded and half-smiled up at her. He wasn't in good enough shape to pretend he was going to be all right.

Peter and Adam examined the spacecraft as the girls watched over the wounded cowboy. They were praying to find a stock of food and water inside, as unlikely as that seemed. The Kazakh found another panel on the side of the ship. He tapped some buttons and a hidden door revealed itself. It opened up like an elevator door.

"Who the heck are you anyway?" Peter asked the Kazakh.

"I don't think I introduced myself to you yet," he said, holding out his hand to shake. "My name's Morgan."

"And you know how to operate alien spaceships?" Adam asked.

"No," he said. "I'm just figuring it out as I go."

He slid open another panel and clicked buttons as if he knew exactly what he was doing. The keyboard was more like a metal jigsaw puzzle with strange markings around the exterior. Peter's brain went numb just trying to understand the shapes of the keys.

"I have a reputation for being able to hack anything," Morgan said. "It now appears I'm even able to hack alien technology."

When he finished what he was doing, the power went on inside of the ship. The interior was illuminated by a pale green light. Ancient dust rose into a cloud and drifted from the entrance of the ship, into the night air.

There was nothing inside. The main room was filled with metal storage compartments, just boxes on shelves and covering the floor. Perhaps they contained cargo once, but they were empty now. The cockpit was big enough to seat three passengers, but their bodies were not there.

"Looks like whoever crashed here got rescued," Peter said.

"And they took everything with them."

Morgan agreed. He added, "Then they must have armed the security system, as if they planned to return for the ship at some point."

"But they never ended up coming back..." Peter said.

The three-armed man suddenly kicked a box across the glossy metal floor.

"So there's no fucking food or water here?" Adam said. "Nothing we can use?"

Peter and Morgan looked at each other.

"At least we have a good shelter," Peter said. Then he pointed at the ceiling. "And light."

"Can't we fly this thing out of here?" Adam said to Morgan. "Can't you fix it and get us home?"

Morgan shook his head. "I'm sure I could figure out its computer systems. But fly it? No. Fix its engine? No. I understand programming, not engineering."

"Bullshit!" Adam yelled.

He kicked the wall of the ship and stormed outside. Everyone watched the hot-tempered man as he nearly trampled over Jim's wounded body on his way into the jungle, to go back to the beach. The alien spacecraft might have been good shelter, but if it wasn't going to get him home it was worthless. Adam would rather stay out in the cold and keep the signal fire going.

In the morning, they went out to continue the search for water. But without Jim accompanying them, they didn't really know where to look. The excursion was long, tiring, and absolutely fruitless.

The day after that, everyone was really beginning to feel the effects of hunger and dehydration. In addition to the thirst, many of them were beginning to feel sick. Zana described it as a hangover that wouldn't go away. They wondered if the poisonous atmosphere they had been breathing was finally catching up to them.

That night, they ate Jill's puke, hoping to ease their starvation a little. The food was sour and full of sand. It only made the group feel worse.

On the third day without water, everyone just sat there, too thirsty and exhausted to do anything. Jim's condition was not improving. He wasn't bleeding internally, but the pain was unbearable. They were worried about infection.

Peter and Zana sat on the beach, praying the rescue ships would come that day. But the sky was dark and thick with clouds. It didn't seem like a good time for a search and rescue mission.

Zana was topless, allowing her puppy flowers to curl in the breeze. The tumors had grown larger and fluffier since she had been on the island.

She had a fat puppy flower in the palm of her hand, squeezing juice out of it. Peter's teeth clicked as he watched her lick the juice from her fingers.

"Is that as gross as it looks?" Peter asked.

She squeezed more of them, popping the tendrils like zits and licking frantically like a ravenous dog.

"It's kind of good," she said, and sucked every droplet of moisture from her hands.

"What's it taste like?" Peter asked.

She pointed a large purple one at him.

"Want to try?" she asked.

Peter cringed and backed away. He knew the growths were basically big colorful warts. No matter how thirsty he was, he couldn't imagine being desperate enough to drink wart juice. Zana squeezed another one and sucked on her fingers.

"It's thick like saliva," she said, "but tastes tangy and a bit sweet."

"It looks like you're eating pus," Peter said.

Zana looked at the milk on her fingers. Then she shrugged

and put it in her mouth.

"It tastes kind of like pus, too," she said.

As they were walking like zombies back toward the shelter, they heard a loud rumbling sound.

"What is that?" Peter asked.

"It sounded like a tree collapsed," Zana said. "Maybe there's a jelly worm in the area."

They listened. Another rumbling noise.

"No, that's not what it is," Peter said.

Then Peter recognized the sound. He didn't notice it at first, because he'd never heard it on this planet before.

"It's thunder," Peter said. "It's a higher pitch than on Earth, but it's definitely thunder."

Then something hit Peter on the forehead. It was cold. He wiped it away and examined his fingers. Water.

"It's raining," Peter said.

He smiled up at the sky. More droplets were continuing to fall. "Water!"

They jumped into each other's arms and laughed, shaking each other with excitement.

"We're saved," Zana said, trying to cup her hands to catch the droplets.

"Come on," Peter yelled.

He grabbed her by the hand and rushed her through the jungle back to the ship. When they got there, everyone was pulling boxes and plastic bags out into the rain.

"Hurry," Jill told them. "We need to catch as much as we can."

Peter and Zana helped bring everything that could possibly hold water outside. Then they took off their clothes and danced naked in the wet.

Zana leaned her head back and opened her mouth to catch water on her tongue.

"Don't drink it now," Peter said to her. "We don't know if it's safe yet."

The rain was showering harder. His voice was barely audible over it.

"If it's not safe we'll die anyway," she said.

Peter thought about it for a minute and then said, "What the hell."

But as he opened his mouth to the air, he felt a burning sensation. Zana coughed and grabbed her throat, then looked at Peter. They felt it at the same time. Their entire bodies were beginning to feel like fire. They were soaked from head to toe in acid rain.

Inside the ship, everyone was desperate to wipe the rain water from their skin. They stripped down and rubbed themselves against the sides of the ship, shook their hair violently to splash all the droplets out. Jim let them use his dry clothes to wipe it off, but soon his clothing was just as wet.

When there was nothing else they could do, they just sat there and suffered through the itching and burning. Their flesh was rubbed so raw they didn't want to let it touch anything anymore. They could feel their hair beginning to fall from their scalps. They curled into little balls and watched the rain through the door, cursing it with all of their venom.

Jill asked Zana what the heck those flowery things were covering her naked body. Zana told her to go fuck herself. Her voice was rough and weak from the acid that burned the inside of her throat.

"It's not necessarily hopeless," Jim said to them in his scratchy tone. "There might be a way to separate the acid from the water."

They all looked at him.

"Are you serious?" she asked.

"As a last resort, I was going to try this method with the ocean water but feared it would be too dangerous due to the strength of the acid. But the acid content in the rain is a lot less than in the ocean water. It's worth a try."

With that, everyone felt a little better about the rain. It might have been a godsend after all. They stared out at the falling water, imagining what it would taste like without the acid burning through their flesh.

Something moved through the jungle, heading toward the ship. When it got closer, they realized it was Adam. He stomped slowly through the trees, carrying one of the life rafts over his head like an umbrella.

When he got to the ship he tossed the raft aside, stepped through the threshold and sat down in the back of the ship. He said nothing. There was a look of rage in his eyes and his face was blood red. At first they thought the discoloration was due to an intense level of anger, but on second glance they realized he was red because all the skin on his face had been peeled away by the rain.

"It's a way you can get the salt out of salt water," Jim said, lying against the doorway of the ship as the others followed his directions. "Maybe it will also get the acid from the acid rain."

The sky was clear and the ground was mostly dry when they put Jim's plan into action. They dug a hole and put a metal box filled with rainwater inside. Placed an empty water bottle in the center and covered the hole in plastic. A pebble was placed on top of the plastic, above the water bottle.

"The plastic will collect condensation," Jim said. "Then it will slide to the center toward the pebble and drip into the bottle."

"And then we'll be able to drink it?" Zana asked.

"We'll try," Jim said. "But if even the rain water is toxic, I'm not sure how much better condensation will be."

"How long will it take?" Peter asked.

"It takes a long time to make just a little water," Jim said. "Set up as many of these as you can. Make sure they're all in direct sunlight."

Hours later, when the first bottle was half filled, Peter decided to be the one to test it.

"Just rub a little of it on your skin first," Jim told him. "Choose a spot that's not already burned."

Peter wet his hands and rubbed the moisture on his inner arm.

"Now wait a while and see if it burns at all," Jim said.

They waited. It didn't burn him.

"Now try putting some in your mouth, just a tiny sip."

Peter did so. Then he waited. It seemed fine in his mouth as well. He swallowed and waited. His stomach didn't react.

They all got to drink a little from the bottle. Then they sat around, watching the condensation, waiting to get their water one drop at a time.

"Why don't you cut that fucking thing off?" Zana yelled at Adam, pointing at his third arm. "It's beginning to reek."

Adam just glared at her as if he was going to kill her. His wife's arm was rotting while still attached to his body.

"If I could remove it I would have already," he said. "Just leave me alone, you fucking freak."

Zana looked back at him like she was going to rake her fingernails across his skinless face.

"Nobody calls me a freak," she said.

"Those growths on your body make you a freak," he said.

"My puppy flowers make me beautiful," she said. "You're the freak."

They were all incredibly irritable. After a couple of days drinking the water, everyone began to feel sick. Some of them believed it was from the atmosphere, others thought it was from drinking the water. Jim told them it was possibly both. Whatever it was, the sickness was only getting worse with each passing day.

Zana vomited into the corner. It was the third time that day. The nausea was unbearable. Of what water they drank, they could only keep about half of it down.

"Only drink a little each day," Jim said about the water. "Just enough to keep you alive. If it's what's making us sick then large quantities will only make us sicker."

"If it's the cause of the sickness, aren't we better off drinking nothing at all?" Zana asked.

"Dehydration will definitely kill us," Peter answered for Jim. "But all we know about the water so far is that it might be making us sick. It's the safer gamble of the two."

Peter looked over at Jim and the cowboy nodded in agreement.

Peter and Zana were on the beach. Their clothes had been completely ruined by the acid rain, but Peter continued to wear his pirate outfit despite the multitude of holes. He thought it only made him look more like a genuine pirate. Luckily, Captain Bearbeard was safe inside the cargo hold of the alien vessel when it rained, leaving his pirate outfit completely intact.

Zana, on the other hand, decided to go trash her ruined clothes and take on a more primitive style. She wore a single green leaf to cover her pubic region. Other than that and the puppy flowers growing all over her body, she went naked.

"It's my Garden of Eden look," Zana said, pointing at her leaf crotch.

Although Jim had a severe reaction to the same leaf when it made contact with his skin, Zana seemed fine wearing it as clothing. Not much of it was actually touching the sensitive areas of her skin. She also used her ration of the water to wash the toxic blue algae from the leaf.

"I don't care what you guys think," Zana said. "I can't handle the sickness from drinking that water. I'm not doing it anymore."

"But you'll die," Peter said.

"No I won't," she said.

Then she ripped a puppy flower off her shoulder like an old bandage and sucked the pus-like fluids out of it.

"Why'd you rip it off?" Peter said.

She swallowed the tangy juice and said, "I need to trim them from time to time. They've been growing like crazy since I've arrived on the island."

Peter noticed her tumors were getting insanely large and shaggy. It was like she was covered in a rainbow of clown wigs.

"It's almost as if these things thrive in this environment," she said. She paused to rip off another one and cringed at the pain. "They're growing faster than weeds. I love having them grow from my body but when they get too big they become annoying."

She removed all the ones that were too large and tossed them in a pile. The stumps left behind on her body trickled with blood.

"Maybe you should eat them," Peter said, laughing. "Then they wouldn't go to waste!"

As Peter laughed, Zana looked at him with a serious face. Then she said, "That's what I *have* been doing."

Peter stopped laughing.

"Huh?" he asked.

"I haven't told anyone," she said. "I wanted to keep it a secret, just in case things got desperate."

"You've been eating them?" Peter asked. "Isn't that like feeding on yourself?"

"Not exactly," Zana said. "These things are separate organisms that grow on my body, but they're not really a part of me. Think of my flesh more like soil. They grow like flowers out of me."

"So you can't feel them?" Peter said, rubbing his finger along a tendril of one of the puppy flowers.

A chill ran through Zana's spine. It felt as if he were caressing her nipples.

"No, I can feel it," she said. "For some reason my nerves are connected to them. They're actually incredibly sensitive to the touch."

Peter pulled his hand away.

"It's okay," Zana said. "You can touch them."

Peter touched another of them, but just for a second. When

he saw her smiling as he fingered her, he hid his hand under his thighs, worried he did something weird.

"I'll let you have one," Zana said, motioning toward her severed puppy flowers. "You must be starving."

"You want me to eat a part of you?"

"I just said they're not really parts of me," she said.

"Still, I'd feel like a cannibal."

"It's okay." She picked up a bright blue one and showed it to him. "Just try it."

She put it in his hands. "Take a bite."

Peter brought the fluffy thing to his lips and pressed it against his tongue. The outer skin tasted like Zana, the way she smelled. It was covered in her sweat.

At that moment, he really felt as though he were about to eat a piece of her. But he found his mouth salivating. His stomach awoke from hibernation and growled as if it were letting out a long yawn. He looked over at Zana. She was smiling at him. He could tell she would be disappointed if he didn't go through with it.

As he bit into it, juices splashed down his throat. The texture was like that of a jellyfish. The fluid was like milky syrup. He chewed the first bite quickly and swallowed. Her breaths were rapid as she watched him eat.

"What do you think?" she asked.

He didn't want to offend her.

"Yummy," he said, hoping his acting didn't come off as too fake. "It's pretty good."

"You liar!" she said. Then she laughed. "It tastes like pig snot, doesn't it?"

Peter had no idea what pig snot tasted like.

"A little like pig snot," he said, taking another bite and savoring it like a sip of wine. "But I also detect a hint of tamarind with an oaky finish."

She punched him in the arm. "Stop teasing me and eat it already."

Peter choked the rest of it down, trying as hard as he could not to cringe. He instantly regretted eating it. Something about consuming a tumor-like growth from the body of a woman who hadn't bathed in many days didn't sit well with him.

"We'll share them," Zana said, holding up the other puppy flowers. "My body will be like a garden, growing fruit for us to eat."

She smiled at him, pressing her tumors to her nose as if smelling a bouquet of roses.

"Just don't tell anybody," she said. "It'll be our secret."

Peter didn't smile back at her. He was beginning to feel queasy. The squid-like tumor felt as if it were trying to escape his stomach and crawl back up his esophagus.

For several days after that, Peter kept Zana's secret. They ate her tumors when nobody else was around. The fluids they contained were juicy enough they didn't need to drink the toxic water anymore. The puppy flowers were all they needed. Soon the sickness that had been afflicting them went away. Their health returned.

"I think we should tell the others," Peter said, as they shared a tumor in secret.

"No," she said. "Don't you dare tell anyone. You promised."

"But everyone else is so sick," Peter said. "And they're so hungry. They could die."

"I don't care," she said. "There's not enough for everyone."

"I'll share my portion with them," Peter said. "Even a morsel of nutrients is better than nothing."

"You have to swear you won't tell anyone," Zana said. Her eyes were beginning to tear. "It's important. They can't eat my puppy flowers."

"But why?"

"You won't understand." She held both of his wrists tightly, staring into him with watery eyes. "Just don't tell them. Promise me. Please?"

"Okay," he said. "I won't tell them no matter what. But if things get really bad, where it's the difference between life and death…" He hugged her closely and whispered into her ear, "I want you to share them with others."

Zana didn't respond. She buried her head in Peter's chest and wiped her tears against his collar bone.

Jim's condition only worsened over time. He continued coughing up blood for a while, but toward the end, he started coughing up thick, yellow phlegm that smelled of rancid fish. His wound had become infected. He was going to die. Everyone knew it, but nobody talked about it.

On his last day, he asked to speak to Peter alone. The others complied and left them together in the ship's cargo hold.

"It's up to you now," Jim said to him. "You've got to take care of everyone after I'm gone." He blinked slowly. He spoke as if he were half asleep. "I know you can do it. I know, more than anyone, you've got it in you."

"Thanks," Peter said. "It's okay. I think we'll be fine."

The cowboy shook his head. "No, you won't."

He paused for a moment before explaining himself.

"It's not going to be easy," Jim said.

"Everything's worked out so far."

Jim grabbed his hand. "No, that's not what I mean. You have to forget about getting rescued and focus on rescuing yourselves."

He pointed out the door at Earth in the pink sky. At first, Peter didn't recognize it. The Earth looked so small.

"This planet is moving farther and farther away from Earth every day," Jim said. "Soon it will be too far away for human beings to reach this planet. The people at the Citysphere aren't looking for us anymore. They are getting ready to pack the place up and fly back home."

Peter hadn't realized how much time had passed. They all

knew they only had a limited amount of time to be rescued, but he didn't know the time was already running out.

"You've got to figure out a way to get to the Citysphere on your own," Jim said. "Build a boat or use a life raft. It'll be incredibly dangerous and I'll admit the odds you'll make it are incredibly slim. But you really have no other choice. Human beings weren't meant to live on this planet indefinitely. If you die in the sea, at least you gave it a shot. If you stay here, you'll die no matter what."

Peter took a deep breath. He didn't say a word. He just nodded.

"I wouldn't have had the guts to go back out into that acid sea," Jim said. "That's why I didn't bring it up even though I've known for a while it's the only hope of ever getting out of here. I'm only able to suggest it now because I don't have to go with your goofy pirate ass." Jim laughed. "It's your problem now."

He continued to laugh until he coughed up black fishy-smelling blood. After he wiped the goop from his mouth, he said, "I hope you're a braver man than I am."

They buried him that evening, out on the beach next to where they buried Jill's mother. Peter placed Jim's cowboy hat over his grave marker. Zana left flowers that would have been too poisonous for him to touch had he still been alive.

As the sun set over the horizon, Morgan said a Muslim prayer for the great man who selflessly did everything he could to keep the group going from the first moment they became stranded on that island.

Peter turned from Jim's grave and looked at the others. They were all gathered around him.

"So," he said, straightening his back and switching his eyepatch from one eye to the other. "Are we ready to do this?"

They all nodded at him in unison.

"Good," he said. "Now let's get the hell off this island."

Zana applauded his words, clapping and hooting.

Nobody knew how they were going to traverse the acid ocean, but they were all determined to try. As they walked down the beach carrying a newfound confidence on their shoulders, Peter realized he had just been promoted from pirate to pirate captain.

CHAPTER NINE
ESCAPE

Everyone pulled together the following day. They all gathered supplies, brainstormed ideas, and did everything Peter asked them to do. Even Adam joined them. In fact, he worked harder than anyone.

The life rafts that brought them to the island were too deflated to use, but the acid-proof rubber was going to come in handy. They had to build their sailing vessel out of wood, even though it was poisonous to the touch. The jungle vegetation seemed unfazed by the acid rain, so they assumed it must have had some kind of resistance. They tested it by dipping a tree branch in the ocean water. It fizzed quite a bit, but the wood was fine. It was resistant enough to use in their ship.

"We can't remove the blue algae," Zana said. "That's what stops the wood from dissolving."

"Then we're going to have to use one of the deflated rafts as a protective covering," Peter said. "We can't have our skin covered in that stuff the whole trip."

Adam and Morgan carried large pillars of wood onto the beach as Jill collected vines to be used for rope. Peter and Zana focused on planning.

"I need you to be the navigator," Peter said to Zana. "You're the only one who's ever been to the Citysphere. You're the only one who has any chance of getting us there."

"I'm not sure I can get us there," she said. "I know which direction to head. I know it's about half an hour away if we were flying. But I've never been out at sea before. It's got to be easy to lose our way."

"Study the stars every night until we take off," Peter said. "You might have to use them to guide us."

"One good thing is the Citysphere generates a lot of light,"

Zana said. "We'll be able to see it from miles away."

"Good," Peter said, nodding proudly at the naked girl. "Now let's see if we can't make a sail. Without that we're not going anywhere."

Jill discovered a few dead jelly worms had washed up on the beach. They were enormous, even larger than the one that attacked Zana. Large sections of their bodies had been burned, scorched to a crisp.

"What happened to them?" Jill said. "Why are they all burned like that?"

"I'm no expert," Peter said, "but they look like lava burns if you ask me."

"There's an active volcano on this island?" Jill said.

"No," Peter said, "but there could be one anywhere under the ocean."

"The smell is horrible," Jill said.

"I would have suggested eating meat from these things but they've gone rancid," Peter said. "But there's something else we can use them for…" He looked at Morgan. "Hand me a lance."

Lance was the name Peter gave to those silver spears that shot from the alien spacecraft. The strange blades had become very useful tools for building their raft. There were enough of them for everyone.

Morgan pulled a lance from his belt loop and handed it to Peter. The pirate boy scooped some of the fluids oozing out of the worm.

"This mucus protects the worms from the acid," Peter said. "We should collect it. The stuff will come in handy."

"But it's rotten," Jill said.

"Get used to the smell," Peter said. "We'll be covering our bodies with this stuff while we're out at sea."

"You're joking, right?" Jill said. "You have to be."

Peter looked at Morgan. "Get another lance. We're also

going to use the skin. We'll use it for extra protection. Also, we might just be able to make a sail out of it."

Morgan nodded and they got to work.

Adam was having difficulty cutting the wood into the right shape. He tossed his lance into the ocean and roared with frustration.

"This isn't going to work," he said. "We need to think of some other plan."

"What kind of other plan?" Jill said, wrapping vines around logs.

"I still think the flying saucer is our best bet," Adam said.

"It's not a saucer," Jill said. "It's a flying cone. The ship is cone-shaped."

"Whatever," Adam said. He looked at Morgan. "You can fix it. I know you can."

"I can't," Morgan said.

"You should at least try."

"Just because I understand its programming doesn't mean I can fix its engines. I understand that ship as much as you understand airplanes on Earth. Could you fix the engine of a commercial airliner? Could you fly it across the globe and land it safely? You'd have a better chance of pulling that off than I would flying that thing."

"We also don't know how the thing crashed," Zana said. "It could have run out of fuel. I don't think we have any alien fuel handy."

"What about its communications equipment?" Adam said. "Can we reach the Citysphere using that thing?"

"That was the first thing I tried when we found the ship," Morgan said. "I couldn't find anything resembling a communications device. For all we know, they don't communicate using verbal language."

"Or maybe they used some kind of alien cell phones," Zana

said, "and didn't leave them in their vehicle."

Adam lay back and kicked his feet up on the partially constructed raft. "There's got to be a way that ship can help us. Maybe we should see if it floats."

But the others had stopped paying attention to him.

The group's high spirits didn't last long. The stench of dead jelly worms was thick in the air. Nobody could stomach sewing the worm skin into a sail, so Peter had to do that task himself.

Without having any food and with the water making them sick, the group's energy levels had bottomed out. Jim told them they could only survive in the wild for two weeks without food. The two week mark had come and gone. Only Adam was still working, but the work he was doing was all wrong and had to be redone. When Peter tried to explain this to him, the three-armed man looked like he was going to rip his throat out.

Peter took Zana for a walk to share an emerald-green puppy flower.

"We can't do this anymore," Peter said to Zana. "Everyone else is starving."

"I'm not giving them any of my fruit," she said. "It's just for us."

"If they don't eat anything they'll never be able to finish work on the raft," Peter said. "They're going to die."

"Fuck them then," Zana said. "We don't need them. We can build our own raft. It wouldn't have to be very big if it were just the two of us."

"And just leave everyone else behind?"

"The only other person worth saving would have been Jim," she said. "Adam's an asshole, Jill's useless, and that Asian guy doesn't even talk."

Peter stopped walking and looked into her eyes with his serious face.

"I can't believe what you're saying," he said. "I know you're a better person than this."

"I'm not a better person," Zana said. "I'm petty. I only care about myself."

"Stop saying that," Peter said. "I've seen you help a lot of people since you've been here."

"That's when I thought we'd only be here a couple of days," Zana said.

"You've been nice to me the whole time," he said.

"Only because my stupid animal instincts have chosen you as a mate," she said. "You don't like women and I can't even have children, but my body keeps reacting that way whenever I'm around you. It's driving me fucking crazy."

"Everyone else is able to control themselves."

"It's not the same," she cried. "I'm sick of this island." She turned and walked away from him. "I'm sick of being me."

As she stepped farther away from him, Peter looked down at the teddy bear in his belt loop.

"Did you hear that, Captain Bearbeard?" Peter said. "It wasn't in her words, but you could clearly hear it in her voice..." He smiled up at her as she walked in the distance. "She really does care an awful lot about everyone."

He petted the teddy bear's sandy fur.

"She's just trying to save them from herself."

They had to rebuild the raft several times. Not just because Adam kept messing it up, but because their design was all wrong. They needed something that would not only sail but completely protect them from every drop of ocean water. And it had to stay together for the entire journey.

Jim probably would have been able to design a perfect vessel, but he was gone and nobody else knew what they were doing. They could hardly tie knots that stayed together longer than three minutes. If they went out to sea in any of their earlier efforts they would have all been killed before they got past the breakers.

"We'll get it right next time," Peter said. "We have to."

Because everyone was so weak, Peter did three times as much work as everyone else. Zana did a little more than her share as well, but wouldn't touch anything having to do with the jelly worms. She was still rattled over having been eaten by one.

A little after they started a new raft, Adam puked blood into the sand. He had been puking a lot that day and had ripped up the insides of his throat. He didn't look good. His eyes were yellow and he was getting horribly sunburned on his already skinless face. He was a walking corpse. The stench of his wife's arm completed the illusion.

Peter looked at them. It wasn't just Adam. They all looked like death. Only Zana resembled a human being. The difference between those who were eating the puppy flowers and those who were starving was very clear. The only way they were going to escape the island was if everyone was able to eat.

Peter looked over at her. Their eyes met. He just stared at her, but she knew what he was thinking. She shook her head at him.

He frowned and then opened his mouth to speak.

"Don't you dare," she said.

Peter paused.

"I'm sorry," he told her.

Then he looked at the others and told them all about Zana's puppy flowers.

Nobody wanted to eat them at first. When Zana threw a temper tantrum about sharing her food, they were fine with it. The idea of eating tumors from her body disturbed the lot of them. Their bodies had grown accustomed to not having food in their bellies. Starvation didn't give them hunger pangs; it just made them weak. They were fine with her saving them all for herself.

But it only took a few hours before they all changed their

mind. They wanted to get home. If they had to eat tumors in order to survive, then they were all willing to do it.

They gathered around Zana, just staring at her like starving wolves around a wounded gazelle. She contemplated fighting them off with the lance by her feet. She contemplated running away. In the end, she decided to give in.

"Fine," she said. "I'll give you one each. But that's it."

When she handed out the puppy flowers, cutting them off with the edge of a lance, she didn't give one to Peter. She just ignored him. Her hands and lips were quivering. She didn't look him in the eyes.

The three starving people sat in a circle, holding the brightly colored tumors as if they were living things. Then they sucked the tendrils into their mouths and bit into them like slices of rubbery watermelon.

Zana watched them carefully as they ate. Gooseflesh appeared on her arms and legs. The puppy flowers on her body were growing erect like angry porcupines.

Peter sat away from the group with the teddy bear sitting next to him. He viewed them as a spectator, from a distance.

"That's what I meant when I told you Zana wanted to save them from herself," Peter said to Captain Bearbeard. "Look at what she's doing."

Zana was licking her lips and stroking a green tumor between her fingers.

"The puppy flowers are like sex organs to her," he continued. "It arouses her when people eat them. They're getting her off and they don't even know it."

Zana's mouth widened as the teenaged girl tongued her pink, quivering fruit.

"It's like she's molesting them," Peter said. "She's tricking them into doing something sexual for her. But as I said, she's really a good person deep down inside. She doesn't want to be this way. I noticed it when I ate one of them with her. After the experience was over, she felt ashamed of herself. She felt as though she did something wrong, something she didn't want to do to me."

Zana's puppy flowers squirmed all over her body, shimmering, dancing, as if they were approaching orgasm. She could still feel what the tumors felt as they were being licked and chewed, even after they had been disconnected.

"That's the reason she didn't want to share with anyone else," he told the teddy bear. "It was for their sake. She knew she wouldn't be able to control herself. She knew it would be sexual. And she didn't want to molest anyone else in the way she had with me."

Zana was sweating, feeling herself inside of their mouths.

"She has a dark side," Peter continued. "I knew I was letting it out. But what choice did I have? There's no other food on the island."

Zana knew Peter was watching her as she had orgasm after orgasm, but she didn't care anymore. She blamed him for doing this to her.

Eating the strange flesh helped the group's energy levels a little, but it also made them queasy. Jill puked up most of hers. They weren't sure if it was due to disgust, bulimia, or the sickness from the toxic atmosphere. Zana nearly killed her for wasting it.

Still, they were able to continue work on the raft. Everything was back on track. That is, until they were hungry again.

"The first one was free," Zana told them. "But from now on you have to pay for them."

"Buy them?" Adam asked. "Are you fucking kidding me?"

"These growths are my pride and joy," she said. "They are my babies. I can't let you eat my babies for nothing."

"Fine," Adam said. "I'll pay you whatever you want for

them once we get back home."

"No," Zana said. "I don't want money."

"What do you want then?"

"I want you to do favors for me," Zana said.

"What kind of favors?" Adam asked. "Rub your feet? Bring you martinis?"

Zana laughed. "Something like that. But for now, I want you to work twice as hard on the raft. No slacking. No whining."

"Fine," Adam said.

"And tomorrow you can rub my feet," she said.

They went back to work. Peter smiled up at Zana. He saw what she was doing. She was trying to get them to work harder, using the puppy flowers as an incentive. At least, that's what Peter originally thought she was doing. After she continued speaking, he began to get a little worried.

"Your survival depends completely on me," she said, leaning on a lance like a cane. "Remember that. If you don't do as I say, you won't get anything to eat. If you piss me off, you won't get anything to eat. I want to be treated like a goddess until we get back to the Citysphere."

Everyone looked up at her. She was completely serious. Something dark inside her was coming to the surface.

"I want to make this perfectly clear," she said. "I'm the one in charge now."

She pointed her lance at them.

"And you are all my bitches."

In exchange for the tumor fruit, Zana had people do all sorts of things for her. Sometimes she had them do important tasks nobody wanted to do, such as collect boxes of mucus from the dead jelly worms. Other times, she had them waste time doing something to make her happy, such as build her a canopy on the beach so she could get some shade.

Adam was getting increasingly angrier with every task she

had him do. He threatened to kill her on more than one occasion, but she just laughed off his threats.

"Zana, you have to stop," Peter said. His voice was serious, dropping the pirate act.

It was the first time they had been alone together in days. They were on the alien vessel while everyone else was on the beach. Zana sat on a metal crate like a throne. Stripes of white mud were on her face and arms, as if she were a primitive islander wearing war paint.

"We don't have time for you to be distracting people with useless tasks," he said. "If you keep it up they're going to turn on you. They might even get violent."

Zana smiled and cat-walked toward him. Peter could tell something weird was going on with her.

"I'm not in any danger," she said. "I've got you to protect me."

She went to him and slid her finger down his firm muscled arm.

"You could save me from anything," she said.

"I'm serious," Peter said. "We only have two days left to get to the Citysphere. If we don't finish the raft by the end of the day tomorrow we're not ever going home."

"Then I'll make sure everyone works hard," she said.

Peter nodded, and then turned to leave.

"Is that all you came here for?" she asked.

Peter stopped.

"You haven't eaten in days," she said. "Aren't you hungry?"

Peter looked back at her.

"You don't have to pay like the others," she said. "I told you before. I'm growing them for us."

Peter nodded. "It's been difficult to concentrate."

"Here," she said, taking his hand. "Have one. I have plenty."

She guided him to his knees.

"It seems the more I cut them the faster they grow," she said.

He looked up at her. A large blue puppy flower tickled his face.

"But I want you to eat it off of my body," she said, wetting her lips as she looked down on him.

Peter was hungry but he didn't have time to play her game.

"Can't this wait?" he asked. "There's not much daylight left."

She hushed him and placed the tumor in his mouth.

"Don't talk," she said. "Just taste."

Her tumor filled his mouth. Like touching a sea anemone with a finger, the blue tendrils of the puppy flower curled around his tongue. It was getting warmer inside of him, as if Zana's body temperature was rising.

"Now suck on it," she said, removing his pirate hat and stroking his hair.

She wasn't just playing a game with him. She was trying to get Peter to do her a sexual favor in exchange for food. He knew he couldn't go through with it. If he let her take advantage of the situation once, she would only do it again, perhaps with other people.

He tried to pull away, but realized he was stuck. The tumor petals wrapped tighter around him, sucking his tongue out of his mouth. Zana moaned and relaxed her muscles toward his face. She grabbed his neck and held him in place.

"Let me go," he said, but his words were mumbled nonsense to her.

As she became more heated, Peter decided the best course of action would be to just bite the tumor off and leave. But by the time he built up the courage to do so and chomped his teeth down into the tumor stalk, Zana squealed out in climax and a pool of warm fluid gushed down Peter's throat.

He stood up with a cheek-full of milky fluid. He wasn't sure if his bite had squeezed juice out of the puppy flower or if Zana had somehow ejaculated inside of his mouth. Either way, he didn't know what to do with it.

A satisfied smile grew on Zana's face as she watched Peter swallow. He glared back at her.

"What's wrong with you, Zana?" Peter asked. "When did

you become so weak?"

She looked away from him and rubbed the saliva from her lips.

"I'm sorry," she said.

She pulled the tumor from her stomach and handed it to Peter.

"Please," she said. "Don't tell anyone. Pretend it never happened."

He touched her on the shoulder.

"We have just one more day here," Peter said. "Keep it together until then."

Zana slapped his hand away.

"Get the fuck away from me," she said.

Peter turned and left the ship. As he entered the jungle, he could hear her screaming at the top of her lungs and throwing boxes of acid rain across the floor.

Only one day left to fix the raft, but they had no idea how they were going to do it.

"We'd need at least five more days to make this safe enough," Morgan said.

"We don't have five days," Peter said. "By tomorrow night, there's not going to be a single human being left on this planet besides the five of us. If we don't get it done today we're not going home."

Adam pointed at their incomplete vessel. "We still have to figure out the sail, build the barrier, test the canopy, create a safe compartment for drinking water, and reinforce the damn thing a billion times."

"Forget about the drinking water," Peter said. "We need space for the jelly worm mucus. We'll be applying it to our bodies the entire way there."

Everyone cringed in disgust just at the thought of that smell all over them. They didn't realize Peter was actually going to have them go through with that plan.

"How can we leave without water?" Jill asked.

Peter said, "We can survive without water for one day. And if we don't make it in time, we're dead anyway."

"We should at least bring some water bottles," she said.

"We need them to make goggles," Peter said. "Our eyes are going to be the most vulnerable out there. Seeing will be more useful to us than drinking."

He also knew the tumor fruit had enough moisture to keep them going, but he didn't want to bring that up. The night before, Zana had refused to share her puppy flowers. They were all seconds away from strangling her to death.

"We've got to give it our all today," Peter said. "Work harder than you've ever worked before. Our lives depend on it."

Everyone went straight to it, determined to succeed. Everyone but Zana. She spent most of the day alone, strolling down the beach or wandering through the jungle. Peter asked her to do some minor tasks, but she just ignored him. A couple of her puppy flowers had grown so large they were about to pop like water balloons, and they were so overwhelmingly sensitive that even the wind sent orgasmic ripples through her body.

The raft came together quicker than Peter expected. He and Morgan worked in unison to build the barrier, which was a wall tall enough to keep the waves from splashing inside. Then they put several layers of jelly worm skin inside and outside of the raft. After the mast was raised, they used the rubbery skin to create a canopy. The raft was beginning to look more like a grotesque camping tent made of flesh than a sailing vessel.

Despite the repulsive smell that made her nearly puke every two minutes, Jill forced herself to sew together sheets of the worm skin into sleeping bags. If the waves were too fierce out there and the raft began filling with water, they would be able to seal themselves up into individual protective bags. Once the sea calmed they would be able to scoop the ocean water out with metal boxes and continue on their journey.

They labored all day. Adam, Peter, and Morgan didn't rest

for a second until its structure was complete. Anything that could be constructed back at the spaceship, like the goggles and backup sail, they held off on until dark. By the end of the day, it was finished. They weren't sure if it was going to be good enough, but they knew they did the best they could have done. If they failed to make it to the Citysphere, they knew it wouldn't have been for lack of trying.

"We go at the crack of dawn," Peter told them. They were passing out from exhaustion, lying on the floor of the spaceship like a pile of corpses. "By this time tomorrow, we'll either be on a flight back to Earth or we'll be at the bottom of the sea."

He looked over at the others. They were already out cold, trembling in their dreams.

"Either way," Peter continued, speaking to Captain Bearbeard, who wore his own pair of tiny plastic goggles. "Tonight's the last night on the island."

Not quite able to sleep, Peter went outside and took a deep breath of the night air. He had gotten used to the tangy metallic flavor of the atmosphere, but just now remembered how sharp it was on his lungs. It woke him up, gave him a shot of adrenalin.

"It's not going to be easy, Captain Bearbeard," Peter said to his teddy bear. "But we'll make it there. The two of us just need to be strong for everyone."

He saluted the teddy bear's paw and hugged him to his chest. Then he looked away from the bear, into the blue jungle.

"Real pirates are always brave, no matter what," he said. "That's what you taught me. You're the bravest pirate of them all. You never cower in the face of danger, you never cry when times are tough, you never give up when the odds are against you, and you always have a smile on your face even when you know tomorrow could just be the last day you'll ever draw breath."

Then his eyes turned red. Tears would have formed if the

ducts weren't dried to a crust.

"I'm so happy you didn't come with me, Louie," Peter said to the teddy bear. "I don't know what I would have done if you were here."

Peter lowered his face into the belly of the stuffed animal and inhaled deeply, trying to find his brother's scent. All he could smell was dirt and rotten jelly worm mucus.

"You talking to yourself again?" said a voice from behind.

He looked back to see Zana sitting on the roof of the spaceship. She had been watching him the whole time.

"Where have you been?" Peter asked.

She didn't answer the question. She paused for a long moment of silence.

"I did what you asked," Zana said, looking up at the sky. "I've been studying the stars every night. I think I can get us to the Citysphere."

"You think?"

She paused. "No, I *know* I can get us there."

Peter nodded at her.

"I'm sorry for how I've been acting," Zana said. "I get like that sometimes, especially when I'm stressed out."

"It's okay," Peter said.

"I think I was just sexually frustrated," she said. Then she snickered. "I'll be better once we get out of this place."

"We'll need you at your best tomorrow," Peter said. "You should get some sleep."

She nodded.

Just as Peter headed back into the ship, Zana stopped him with her foot as she dangled above the doorway.

"I'm happy I met you, Peter," she said, smiling down at him. "You've made me a better person."

Peter smiled back in response. On his way inside, he wrapped his arms around her dangling feet and hugged her toes to his chest. Her toenails poked into his skin like the claws of kittens as she curled her toes around the fabric of his raggedy pirate shirt.

The raft was on fire the next morning. They could smell the smoke as they walked through the jungle and then rushed as fast as they could to figure out what was going on.

The blaze had already consumed the entire vessel. Zana was standing at a safe distance, staring at the flames. There was nothing left of the ship to save.

Peter ran down to Zana and pulled her away from the deadly smoke. Tears were pouring down her cheeks.

"I can't go back there," she cried. "Don't make me go back there."

The others rushed toward her. Their expressions were exploding with rage.

"What the hell happened?" Adam yelled. "What the fuck did you do?"

"It doesn't matter." Her words were hysterical. "We never would have made it anyway."

Peter had to get between them so Adam didn't snap her neck right there.

"You crazy bitch!" Adam swiped his hands over Peter's head at her, his rotten third arm smacking off his pirate hat.

"It would have been suicide," she said. "I just saved all your lives."

"Saved us?" he said. "You fucking killed us. That was the only chance we had."

When Peter pushed Adam away from her, the three-armed man went toward the bonfire, picked a lance out of the sand and came at Zana.

"You're fucking dead, bitch," Adam said.

Peter raised his hands and blocked his path.

He pointed the lance at Peter, "Get the fuck out of my way or you're dead too, faggot."

"Kick his ass, Peter," Zana shrieked. "Kill him. He's gone crazy."

Peter wasn't going to fight him, but had to disarm him

quickly. As long as they didn't fall apart, there was still hope. He just had to reach them.

"You don't want to do this," Peter said. "Let's think of another way."

"Fuck that," Adam said. "She killed us."

He raised the lance like a javelin.

"Now I'm going to kill her," he said.

Peter got into a fighting stance, ready to take the three-armed man down if he had to. But Adam did not attack. Something seized his attention.

They all looked out at the sea. The shoreline was quickly receding. Within minutes, it had completely vanished into the horizon.

"Where the hell did the ocean go?" Jill asked.

The sea had become a barren desert, leaving behind only small puddles here and there. Hundreds of jelly worms squirmed through the white hills of mud, some of them ten times the size of any they had previously seen. It was as if Moses had parted the sea for them, so they could go by foot all the way to the Citysphere.

"Get to higher ground," Peter said. "It's a tidal wave."

They all looked at each other. For a moment, none of them could move or speak. Their thoughts were racing. Their heads were trying to fathom what a tsunami from this ocean would do to an island.

Then they ran. Adam went first, into the jungle.

"We need to get to the ship," Jill cried, running after Adam.

Morgan followed after her.

"No," Peter yelled to them. "It's not high enough. Get as high as you can."

But they were already gone.

Peter turned to Zana.

"Come on," he said.

She was catatonic, staring out at the horizon.

"Come on!"

He grabbed her shoulder and tugged her away from the beach. They went straight for the peak where they had built the signal fires. It was the highest they could get to in so short a time. Peter had to pull Zana all the way up to the summit or she never would have budged.

Looking out at the sea as the massive wave appeared on the horizon, Zana grabbed Peter's hand and held it tightly. Peter hugged his teddy bear like a baby against his chest.

"I'm sorry I burned the raft," Zana said to Peter.

He hushed her.

"Don't worry," he said. "It doesn't matter anymore."

She let go of his hand and wrapped herself around him, embracing him with all her strength. Even the tendrils on her puppy flowers squeezed firmly around the curves of Peter's body.

"Wait a minute," Peter said.

He pulled away.

"What the heck is that?" he asked, pointing at the shore.

Zana looked. Something was moving below them.

"Is that a truck?" Zana asked.

Peter just nodded at her, dumbfounded.

A sports utility vehicle drove casually down the beach toward the bonfire. It was neon green with a portrait of Jerry Garcia painted on the roof. When it stopped, two middle-aged men stepped out.

"Where the hell did they come from?" Zana said.

"Are they from the Citysphere?" Peter said. "Did they come to rescue us?"

The two men wore tie-dyed polo t-shirts and pink surfer hats. They strolled along the beach, scanning the area around the bonfire. They seemed to have no idea a tsunami was headed their way.

"We have to warn them," Peter said.

He went to the edge of the peak and yelled down at the

men, waving his hands in the air.

"Run," Peter yelled. "Get out of there!"

It took a few yells, but Peter eventually got their attention. They walked toward the bottom of the hill.

"Get to high ground!" Peter said.

When they got close enough to hear, one of the men shouted up to Peter.

"What the hell is going on?" said the man.

"A tidal wave is coming," Peter shouted. "Get off the beach."

"Who are you?" he asked.

"Look behind you," Peter yelled.

"Where are we?"

They didn't look until they saw Peter pointing in the direction of the ocean. When the two men saw the wall of water heading for them, they ran back to their SUV.

"Not that way," Peter yelled. "Up here."

But it was too late. The SUV only drove a few yards before the tsunami hit the island.

The acid wave was so high it blocked out both the suns. Jelly worms swam in and out of the pink water. It towered over their heads, far larger than they ever could have expected.

"We're not high enough," Peter said.

The neon green SUV disappeared into the rolling mass of acid.

"Nowhere on this island is high enough."

As her last act, Zana closed her eyes and grabbed onto Peter, kissing him deeply with all of the life inside of her. Then the roaring tsunami swallowed them whole.

Jill, Morgan, and Adam heard the thundering wall of water crashing behind them as they raced through the jungle. Morgan separated from them and went for the mountains. He was far behind them and knew he wouldn't make it to the spaceship in time.

Adam made it into the alien vessel first and tried desperately to close the door.

"Wait for me," Jill yelled up ahead.

But he wasn't going to wait for her. He could already hear trees being ripped from the ground by the impact of the tsunami. He had only seconds to figure out how to close the doors.

Jill made it inside as he continued hitting tiny metal buttons on the control panel.

"Close it," Jill yelled.

"I'm trying."

"Hurry!"

When the wave hit, they were thrown back. The vessel barrel-rolled through the jungle. It smashed over trees and slammed into rock. Jill fell into the cockpit and her head was driven into the jagged control board. Blood gushed out of her face and she went limp against the pilot seat.

Adam tried to hold on as the vessel tumbled with the wave. Acid poured inside and splashed across his chest. He didn't have time to feel the pain.

He pulled himself to the control panel and punched at it, trying to get the door shut. But the electronics short-circuited and sparks flew out of the panel into his face. The door closed on its own as the ship crashed against the side of a cliff face, bending them back into place like an aluminum sardine lid.

When he got to the highest hill he could find, Morgan climbed up a tree. He knew it wasn't enough, but he kept climbing anyway.

The water hit and ripped the tree out by its roots. As it tumbled over, Morgan fell to the next tree over. He held tightly to the branches for a split second before he fell to the next one.

Like dominoes, the forest tumbled over onto itself, and Morgan rode like a surfer on top of it. He thought the trees were going to roll him to safety, until they all came together on the back end of the mountain.

The massive pillars of lumber landed in a pile against the thickest, sturdiest tree in the forest. And Morgan was crushed in the middle of it. His blood drooled out into the violent river of acid flowing beneath him.

When it was all over, the tidal wave had washed completely over the land, wiping it away like writing erased from a chalkboard. In that moment, the island was gone. It had been completely swallowed up by the sea. And then, in the belly of the sea, it began to digest.

CHAPTER TEN
APOCALYPSE

Adam kicked open the door of the spaceship and stepped outside. He was covered in rotten jelly worm skin and mucus. The scraps they had left behind in the cargo hold had saved his life. But he wasn't unscathed by the acid. The right side of his face had burned completely away. His right eye was blinded, now just a white marble in a mangled eye socket. The meat of his right leg had been eaten away to the bone. His ribs were visible through his chest.

He stepped out onto a craggy piece of rock the size of a king bed and looked out across the landscape. The island was no longer recognizable. The trees had been ripped to shreds. Dead jelly worms floated by like wrecked submarines after a sea battle. Most of the island was still under water.

It was a wasteland and Adam was like an undead zombie crawling out of the wreckage into the sunlight. The only land he could reach from his position was a small hill. He had to jump from the roof of the ship to a boulder in order to get to it. When his face slammed into the side of the rock, Adam realized he didn't have any sensation left in his skin. The blow caused no pain.

He staggered up to the top of the hill and looked around. There was nothing left. The wave had completely decimated the island.

At that moment, he felt like the only person left on the planet. The Citysphere had probably been evacuated. Everyone else was killed in the tsunami. It was just him, floating through space, far away from home, on a planet he had no hope of ever surviving upon.

But then he heard a cough.

He looked around, trying to find its source. Then there was a moan. He followed the sound to the other side of the hill.

Then he saw it. Across a pool of acid, on top of a pile of swampy blue trees sticking straight up out of the sizzling pink fluid, he saw Morgan's body. He was banged up, dangling from a tree limb, blood leaking from every orifice. But he was still alive.

Morgan's eyes opened to a bloody skull glaring down at him. He thought it was a dead body hanging in front of his face until the skull blinked.

"You finally awake?" the corpse asked.

"Adam?" Morgan said.

He was lying on a rocky surface beneath the pink sky. He tried to get up but the mangled man pushed him back down.

"Don't get up," Adam said. "Both of your legs are broken. You might have some broken ribs as well."

Morgan lay back down against the rock.

"You look horrible," he said.

Adam laughed. "You don't look much better yourself."

"Where is everyone?" Morgan asked.

Adam shook his head.

"The tidal wave destroyed everything," Adam said. "There's nobody else."

Morgan closed his eyes and took a deep breath.

Adam pulled some supplies out of a bag, setting them up against the rock.

"What are you doing?" Morgan asked.

"I'm trying to make drinking water," Adam said.

"Out of the ocean water?"

"I'm not sure if it will be as drinkable as the stuff we got from the acid rain, but we've got to try."

"Maybe if you dilute it several times," Morgan said. "You might eventually be able to get something drinkable."

"I'll try that," Adam said.

The sound of vegetation being digested in the acid water

sizzled all around them. They heard more trees collapsing in the distance.

Morgan's head rolled to the side. In the moat of acid at the bottom of the hill, several small jelly worms fed on the corpse of a larger worm. They were only about twenty yards away. It was like watching an alligator feeding at the zoo, without a safety barrier between them.

"So what's next?" Morgan asked.

Adam looked up at the sky. The pink clouds reflected in his melted white marble eye.

"First, we're going to wait for the water level to go down," Adam said. "Then you're going to fix the spaceship so we can get out of here."

"Are you serious?" Morgan said, lifting himself upright. "I told you it's impossible."

Adam slammed Morgan back into the rock with all of his strength, popping one of his ribs out of place.

"I told you, don't get up," Adam said, as Morgan coughed and wheezed beneath his hand. "You have to save your strength."

Before Morgan could object again, Adam looked at him with demon eyes.

"You'll fix the ship," Adam said. "Your life depends on it."

Then he grabbed a metal box and walked away, toward the shore to collect some ocean water.

Morgan held his chest and coughed a thick wad of blood and phlegm into his lap. That's when he realized how broken his legs were. They had been pulverized. One looked broken in five places with his foot twisted backward. The other was crushed beyond recognition. He didn't feel any pain. He was paralyzed from the waist down.

He crawled across the surface of the rock until he made it to the edge and looked down at the spaceship sticking halfway out of the water.

The vessel was twisted around a boulder. Large cracks divided the frame into several pieces and the cockpit was impaled by a tree. Even if Morgan knew everything there was to know about alien spaceship technology, there was no way he ever had a prayer of fixing it.

"Morgan Douglas?" said the man waiting at the gate.

Morgan nodded and shook his hand.

"That's a shit name they gave you," said the man, a prematurely balding white guy in a navy blue suit.

"They didn't want anyone to suspect me for being Muslim," Morgan said. "A background check would have been tricky."

The white man introduced himself. "Call me Chase. Another shit name. Nice to meet you."

Chase picked up Morgan's bag for him.

"So, welcome to Barack," Chase said, gesturing to the pink sky and rolling blue hills outside of the glass dome. "The tackiest tourist trap in the solar system."

Morgan followed him through the Sony-NASA Citysphere, traversing a maze of gift shops and astronaut-themed cafes. The place was thick with wide-eyed tourists, staring out the glass walls at the alien planet, taking pictures of men in oxygen suits driving little moonbuggies through fields of purple grass.

"It's your first time on Barack, isn't it?" Chase asked. "You want to take a look at the observation tower before we go downstairs?"

"No," Morgan said. "I'd rather get straight to work."

Chase nodded.

"My thoughts exactly," he said. Then he shrugged. "You see one alien planet with an ocean made of acid, you've seen them all."

Chase pointed to the right and they took a side passage into the private sector of the dome. The wild clatter of tourists disappeared as the security guard closed the gate behind them.

Leading him down the long quiet hall, Chase whistled the theme to Doctor Who and snapped his tiny bald head to the beat as they went. His whistling reverberated against the glass walls.

"So they say you started out as a hacker?" Chase said, as they entered an elevator at the end of the hall. "Like that movie *Hackers* with Angelina Jolie? Back when she was actually hot?" The elevator door closed. "That movie was stupid."

"I did freelance work," Morgan said, as they rode the elevator to the underground levels. "My specialty was erasing histories for people."

"What do you mean erasing histories?" Chase asked. "Like making people disappear?"

"I erased internet histories," Morgan said. "You know how stupid teenagers get bored sometimes and go online to post sexist and racist comments all over message boards and social network sites just to piss people off?"

"You mean trolls?" Chase said.

Morgan nodded. "Well, sometimes those trolls grow up to become governors or congressmen. And a lot of those distasteful comments they posted as teenagers still exist out there, just waiting to be found by their political opponents. People hired me to track down all of their embarrassing online content, hack into the sites containing them, and wipe them out."

"With all of your talent, that's what you used it for?" Chase said, laughing as he led them off the elevator into another long echoing hallway. "Do you realize because of you we now have trolls out there in important government positions?" He mockingly shook his head. "You did your country a horrible disservice, good sir."

"It's not my country," Morgan said.

"Of course it is," Chase said. "As long as you're calling yourself Morgan Douglas, you sir are a proud God-fearing American."

"Can we get on with this?" Morgan said.

"Relax," Chase said. "You have a full week's access to it. There's no rush."

"How many others were found?" Morgan asked.

"Three on this continent," Chase said. "We've only brought the one down here. It'll take at least a month to bring over the big one."

"I'll be fine with just examining the small one during this trip," Morgan said.

"You're lucky your predecessor died last week or you wouldn't be examining anything at all."

"How did he die anyway? They didn't fill me in on the details."

Chase stopped them at two large bay doors at the end of the hallway.

"When they first came in contact with it," he said, pushing open the door to reveal a glossy cone-shaped spacecraft. "They set off its security defense system. The whole team was impaled to death by metal spears that seemed to just appear in midair."

Morgan's eyes lit up when he saw it. A few researchers were already there, documenting every inch of the alien vessel. In the past five years, Morgan had become one of the country's leading experts in extraterrestrial technology, but he had never seen anything quite like this before.

"But don't worry," Chase said. "We'll show you how to disarm it just in case the damn thing goes off again."

Adam carried Morgan into the alien vessel's control room. Most of the acid had dried inside but the muddy soil outside the ship was still dangerous.

"I set up my camp at the top of the hill," Adam said. "But you'll get the run of the ship. I figured you could use the space."

The second Adam set him down, Morgan rolled over and puked into a corner. The water they had been drinking was making them incredibly ill. Even after using Jim's process of distilling water from acid five times over, it still wasn't good enough. Although the water wasn't burning holes in their throats and stomachs—as far as they knew—it was incredibly toxic. They felt even worse drinking this than they did drinking the acid rain.

Morgan leaned back against the tree trunk that now

centered the cockpit. Everything around him had been obliterated on impact. The seats were shredded, the floor and ceiling torn apart, the control board shattered. Morgan had no idea what Adam expected him to do with this mess.

"Let me know if you need a hand," Adam said.

"Yeah, you can help," Morgan said, adjusting his back against the itchy blue algae. "For starters, you can cut this tree out of here. I can't even reach the ship's computer with it in the way."

Adam shook his head. "You'll have to figure a way around it for now. I'm busy with the water." He picked up a lance from the floor of the ship. "I'm also thinking about trying to hunt down one of those smaller worm creatures. If we're lucky, they might be edible."

Morgan gave him a faux-smile.

"Whenever you have the time," he said.

As the three-armed zombie left the ship, Morgan put his face into his hand. The task Adam gave him was so hopeless it almost made him laugh.

But he didn't laugh, because he knew there was another way.

"If anybody can do it, you can," Morgan told himself.

He had no intention of actually making an effort to rebuild the ship. There was something more conceivable he wanted to try. If he could get the computer system working again and use it to network himself into one of the other alien vessels left behind on the planet, he might just be able to figure something out.

In secret, he had already attempted this several times since finding the ship. But all attempts failed. Though the alien ships on the planet were all linked together via their computer systems, he could not access them. He gave up his efforts once he realized escaping via raft was the more prudent option.

Now he didn't have any other option. He had to figure out a way to make the previous plan work. But this time he would also have to repair the control board.

As Morgan looked across the shattered computer panel wrapped around the tree trunk, he wondered if even that were possible.

"What do you mean you can't get it working?" said Mr. Mike, a thick-necked dwarf with a white comb-over. He was the leader of the excavation team. Morgan's superior. "They said you were the man to go to if I needed to make the impossible possible. Why aren't you making the impossible possible?"

"Miracles take time," Morgan told him, adjusting metal coils beneath the control panel. "I'm still figuring out what is what."

"This planet's not going to stop its journey through our solar system just so you can finish your job," said Mr. Mike. "Time is of the essence."

The dwarf's enormous muscles flexed beneath his white button-up shirt. Then he bent a metal rod in his hands and stormed out of the cockpit.

"The guy's a tough little bastard," Chase said, as he entered from behind. "Did you see him bend that thing? It was like he was trying to be intimidating or something."

"He's right though," Morgan said. "I'm taking too long with this. A computer system is like a language. Once you learn how to speak the language, then a whole world of information opens up to you. I thought I was a master at deciphering these languages, no matter how foreign they might seem. But this one has me stumped. It's not reacting at all."

"Try taking the hardware apart and putting it back together again," Chase said. "It's what we're doing with the engine."

"I just need to approach it from different angles," Morgan said. "If I listen closely enough, I just know it's going to speak to me."

"Just take it apart," Chase said. "You can get intimate with it later."

Morgan's tongue between his teeth for concentration, his face covered in ancient dust, as he twisted angler coils inside of a control panel. Then the lights in the ship lit up into a bright lime-green color and Morgan shouted in triumph.

"Got you!" he yelled at the light. He slid down the wall and laughed with relief. Just accomplishing the first, tiniest step gave him hope.

When he opened his eyes, he saw Adam's skinless face staring back at him. The man was sitting in the corner of the ship, where the shadows used to be. He had been there watching him the whole time.

"Is it ready now?" Adam said, his dead eye oozing from its socket.

The large man was looking worse than ever. The area where his elbow connected to his wife's dead arm was turning yellow and the blood vessels were dark purple in color.

"I just got the lights working," Morgan said, and then he cringed as a creamy fish-stenched pus oozed from Adam's wound. "Is your arm okay?"

The arm was infected. The bacteria from the dead flesh spread into Adam's body. His wife's rancid rotting blood flowed through his veins.

Adam ignored the question.

"But is it ready to fly?" Adam asked. His tone became angry. "I want to leave now."

Morgan shook his head.

"I've just barely gotten started," Morgan said. "It's going to take time."

Adam jumped to his feet and slammed his hand into the side of the ship.

"We don't have time," Adam yelled.

Morgan pointed at the surroundings. "Look around you," Morgan said. "How quickly do you think any of this can be fixed?"

"I don't care," Adam said. "Figure out a way."

He was even worse than Mr. Mike.

"Why don't you help?" Morgan said. "You still haven't cut away any of that tree in the cockpit."

"I don't have time," Adam said, rubbing his fist into his good eye. "No time."

"Still hunting those worms?" Morgan said.

"There are some smaller ones I've been watching," Adam said. "If I could get one alone I think I can kill it."

"If you keep trying, I'll keep trying," Morgan said.

Then Adam mumbled some words and exited the ship. He left Morgan alone for the next few days.

"What the heck was that?" Chase said, staring at the golf ball flying off into the pink sky. "I thought you knew how to play?"

Morgan lowered the sun visor on his oxygen suit to see where his ball had gone, leaning his golf club over his shoulder. He had hit it a hundred feet over the hole. It landed in the thick purple grass on the edge of the course.

"I'm just not used to this gravity," Morgan said.

"Lame excuse." Chase patted him on the back. "It's not *that* much different than Earth."

Then Chase hit his ball straight down the line, landing it only a few feet from the hole.

"That's how you do it," Chase said. "Right on the lavender!"

"The lavender?" Morgan asked.

"Yeah, well, we felt kind of stupid calling it *the green* when all the grass is light purple," Chase said. "At least the tourists get a kick out of it."

Morgan hadn't used any of his break time in days and Chase finally convinced him to take a few hours off. Getting outside of the dome to play a nine-hole game on the Alan Shepard Golf Course was something Morgan was actually willing to try.

"So nobody's given me a straight answer yet," Morgan said as they searched the purple grass for his ball. "The aliens—where exactly did they come from?"

"That's the five trillion dollar question," Chase said and pointed at the ball, which had been hiding near a slithering black widow snail. "But I don't expect either of us will ever know the answer to it."

Morgan swiped at his ball and missed, accidently hitting the tiny snail, which went flying through the air across the golf course.

Chase snickered at the poor snail and then he continued, "The more interesting question at the moment isn't where they're from, but how the heck they got here."

"Oh?" Morgan said, concentrating on his next swing.

"They say the ships weren't designed to land in a place like this," Chase said. "They would have burned up in the planet's atmosphere upon entry. And their landing gears weren't designed for the high gravity. Every single one of them, even the big one, crash landed."

"So they weren't research vessels coming to explore this planet?" Morgan asked.

Morgan hit his ball onto the lavender. It knocked Chase's ball farther away from the hole.

Chase shook his head at his opponent's lucky shot, "They aren't even deep space vessels. They seem like they were designed to transport cargo between a planet's moons."

"That's all?" Morgan asked.

"We've started calling them *The Truckers* now," Chase said. "Because that's basically what they were—space truckers."

"With weapons systems?" Morgan asked. "They seem a little too deadly to be cargo ships."

Chase lowered his club behind his golf ball.

"Who knows," he said. "Maybe they needed to defend themselves from space pirates."

Then he took his shot and sunk it into the hole. He raised his fist in triumph.

"So what are a bunch of space truckers doing on this

planet?" Morgan asked.

"Exactly," Chase said. "The ships obviously weren't manu-factured on this planet, they were only designed for short range moon travel, and they would have burned up in this planet's atmosphere if they tried to land. So how the hell did they get here?"

Morgan was lined up on the lavender, ready to take his shot. He shrugged at Chase.

"I don't know," Morgan said. "Maybe something brought them here."

When Morgan took his swing, he hit way too hard again. The ball flew past the hole, off the lavender, and deep into the dark purple thicket.

"Stop haunting me, you bitch!"

Morgan heard Adam yelling at someone on the hillside. He pulled himself along the floor to the exit of the ship. It was dark out there. His eyes were too accustomed to the green lighting within the ship to see in the dark outside.

"Get away," Adam continued. "I'm not giving up. You'll never make me give up."

Morgan couldn't tell what was going on. There was nobody else out there. The three-armed man seemed to be getting crazier by the day.

"You're dead," Adam yelled. "Stay dead. Don't fucking haunt me."

Morgan rolled over and tried to go back to sleep. Just as he began to slip out of consciousness, he heard a woman's voice. He sat up, wondering if he had just imagined it. Then he heard it again. It wasn't a voice, more like a moan.

"Fucking, fucking, fucking bitch!" Adam screamed.

Morgan continued to listen, but didn't hear the woman's voice again. He just heard Adam yelling at the top of his lungs like a banshee in the wind.

It was a couple of nights later when Morgan heard the woman's voice again. This time, it sounded more like the wind blowing through a crack in the ship, so he paid it no mind.

He had just finished assembling the section of computer board he needed for his plan, but it still wasn't working. The power wouldn't come on. All the pieces were in the right place, exactly as they were when he assembled it back on the Citysphere. It was just dead.

He was about to raise it over his head and smash the thing to pieces when he heard a whimpering. Then he heard a moaning sound. It wasn't the wind.

Setting the panel down carefully, he continued to listen. Another moan. It wasn't just his imagination. He had to check out where it was coming from.

Morgan pulled himself to the exit of the ship, dragging his dead legs through the rubble, dumping over the box he was using as a toilet.

With urine and feces covering his lower body, saturating his festering wounds, he grabbed a crack on the side of the ship and began to climb. There were plenty of dents and cracks in the frame of the ship to get good handholds, but he was so weak he could hardly pull his body up.

When he got to the top of the vessel, he looked up the hill and saw Adam's camp. There was a shelter built of fallen timber. Morgan could make out the bust of a female figure lying inside. He recognized the blond hair. It was Jill.

She moaned and writhed on the ground, her head rolling back and forth. She wasn't wearing any clothes.

The shambling corpse that was once Adam staggered through the blue grass toward the shelter. He leaned down to Jill and smacked her across the face.

"Shut up," he said.

The girl continued jerking her head, but didn't react to his slap.

Adam pulled off his pants and lowered himself on top of

her. Then he slapped her again and spread her legs. Using jelly worm mucus as lubricant, he entered her.

Morgan shouted across the hill at them as Adam slammed into the teenaged girl. The grunting and crying drowned him out. He could do nothing but watch as the grotesque zombie foamed at the mouth, ravaging her innocent flesh.

"You're raping her?" Morgan yelled at Adam as he delivered the next day's ration of water.

Adam's face grew annoyed.

"It's none of your business," Adam said.

Morgan could see Adam's teeth grinding together through the side of his face where his cheek was missing.

"You said nobody else was alive," Morgan said.

"She's brain dead," Adam said. "Been unconscious since the wave. What she doesn't know won't hurt her."

"She's just a kid."

"I don't fucking care," Adam said. "She owes me. I'm keeping her alive. I'm cleaning the shit off her."

"How does that justify rape?"

"She's only alive because she serves a purpose."

"She needs help, you fucking asshole," Morgan shouted.

"Back off," Adam said, stepping forward as if ready to bash Morgan's head in with a rock.

Morgan hesitated to say anything else. With his legs crippled, he wouldn't be able to defend himself.

"You, too, are only alive because you serve a purpose," Adam said. "Remember that."

And he left.

From that moment on, Morgan could not un-hear what was being done to the teenaged girl on the hill above him. He stewed with disgust, covered in his own shit. He wanted to murder Adam, stick a lance in his stomach the next time he came close enough. But he needed Adam for his survival.

Jill, despite what he was doing to her, also needed him for her survival. Morgan couldn't take care of her on his own.

He had no choice but to work harder. It would take a miracle for him to succeed at his plan to save them, but it was their only hope.

"We found them," Chase said, charging inside of the cockpit.

Morgan didn't look at him, busy trying to reassemble the flight system of the control board.

"Found who?" Morgan said.

"The Truckers," Chase said.

Morgan slowly looked up from his work. He noticed Chase had a look of overwhelming amazement on his face. He couldn't tell if the white guy was saying exactly what he thought he was saying.

Then Chase confirmed it.

"They're still alive."

The team took a Sony-NASA hovercraft across the continent, twenty miles away from where the largest spaceship had been found. There were people all over the site, many of them carrying weapons. Morgan, Chase, Mr. Mike and three other researchers stepped out of the hovercraft in yellow oxygen suits. The Citysphere's chief biologist, Dr. Richards, met their team at the entrance to the cavern.

"What's with all the guns?" Mr. Mike asked Richards, hobbling over the blue algae-covered rocks like a white-haired tank.

"There have been a few incidents," said Dr. Richards, who was wearing a pearl-colored coat beneath his translucent oxygen suit. "Two men were killed. Five severely injured."

"They're dangerous?" asked Mr. Mike.

Dr. Richards just gave them a stern expression.

215

"Come with me," he said.

The team followed Dr. Richards into the cave. The smell was unbearable, like rotting frog bellies. The deeper they descended, the stronger the stench became.

"They have been stranded on this planet for nearly eighty years," said Dr. Richards. "We don't know the lifespan of the species, but we're assuming these are the children or grandchildren of those who originally crashed on the planet."

"How could they have possibly survived for so long?" asked Mr. Mike.

"This cave system has an underground water source," said Dr. Richards. "It's highly toxic, but a resilient life form could survive on it. That's why they moved down here. Also, the species would have had difficulty living on the surface. They appear to be from a low-oxygen planet."

"How has communication been going?" asked Mr. Mike.

"It's not," said Dr. Richards.

"What do you mean?" asked Mr. Mike.

"You'll see."

Morgan was tossing and shaking in his sleep when he woke to Adam staring down on him.

"What do you want?" Morgan asked.

Adam handed him a chunk of meat the size of a fist.

"Here," Adam said. "Have some."

Morgan picked it up. The meat was bloody and still warm, flabby to the touch.

"It's all we have to eat," Adam said.

Red goop dripped down a lance in Adam's hand. His palms were wet with blood.

"What is this?" Morgan asked. "It doesn't look like worm meat."

Adam shook his head.

"I gave up on the worms," he said.

He cleaned the lance with his shirt.

"Then where'd you get it?"

Adam stared at him for a moment. Then he stood up, lifting a slab of meat over his shoulder. A trail of blood dribbled behind him as he walked out of the ship.

Morgan looked down at his legs. The pants were cut open and large pieces of flesh had been removed. The entire front of one thigh was missing, both calves were severed. He could see the white of his kneecap shining through the blood.

The limbs were paralyzed, so he felt nothing. He didn't even wake when Adam had carved him up like a Christmas ham.

"You sick motherfucker," Morgan yelled, loud enough so his voice could be heard outside. "What the fuck is wrong with you!"

He picked up a bent lance and held it up like a tire-iron.

"Think I'll let you get away with this?" he yelled. "Get back here!"

A warm puddle formed around his hips. The wounds were still bleeding. He dropped the lance and used his ripped pants as a tourniquet.

"You come near me again and I'll kill you," Morgan said. "Cannibal rapist motherfucker!"

He wrapped his arms around his legs and leaned forward, crying out words that no longer made sense.

Richards led them to a heavily guarded containment area deep in the cave. When Morgan saw the creatures, he almost fell to his knees. There were seven of them: four-armed insect-like humanoids with locust-textured skin, brightly-colored caterpillar fuzz for hair, and red mammalian eyes. One of them locked eyes with Morgan and snarled at him like a vicious dog.

"Barack's atmosphere causes severe neurological damage," said Dr. Richards. "If humans were to attempt to live on this planet and breathe its atmosphere, we would die in a matter of months.

217

But during that time we would become increasingly psychotic."

Dr. Richards tapped on the glass and all seven of the creatures turned their hungry eyes to him.

"These creatures, on the other hand, were strong enough to endure," he said. "The toxicity level this deep underground isn't as strong as on the surface. Not enough to kill them. However, it was enough to alter their minds. It turned them into wild animals."

As the creature eyeing Morgan continued to growl, another one crept up behind it. This one appeared to be female with a swollen pregnant belly. The female grabbed one of the male's arms and ripped it off, then ran away with it. The male shrieked and gripped its shoulder.

"What was that?" asked Mr. Mike.

The other creatures gathered around the female, drooling and begging for bites of the arm.

"Their food source," said Richards. "Their species has the ability to regenerate limbs. So for the past eight decades, that's all these beings have had to eat."

"They've been eating each other?" asked Mr. Mike.

Dr. Richards nodded.

"There's absolutely no edible food on this planet," he said. "The only way to survive is to resort to cannibalism."

The next time Adam came for meat, Morgan wasn't going to give it up without a fight.

"Get the fuck away from me," Morgan yelled, aiming the lance at him.

Adam stood there and wouldn't back off.

"We need to eat," Adam said.

"Eat your own fucking legs," Morgan said.

"Your legs are useless now," Adam said. "You don't need them."

He stepped closer and Morgan raised the lance as if to

throw it at him.

"Would you rather I eat the girl's legs?" Adam said.

Morgan froze.

"You wouldn't dare," Morgan said.

"As I told you, you're only alive as long as you serve a purpose," Adam said. "It's your choice. We can eat your dead, crippled legs or I can start cutting pieces off coma girl."

"Touch her and I'll rip out your throat," Morgan said.

Adam leaned down and glared at Morgan with his skeletal face, tapping his lance against the cripple's mangled legs.

"I'll cut you a deal," Adam said. "Every day I'll slice one piece of meat off your legs. If you can finish repairing the ship before the meat runs out, I won't have to carve up the girl."

Morgan shook his head, fuming at him.

"You son of a bitch," Morgan said.

"So what's your answer?" Adam asked. "Your legs or the girl?"

Morgan said nothing. He tossed his lance aside.

"That's what I thought," Adam said.

As he sawed a strip of flesh away from Morgan's ankle, Adam said, "It's what needs to be done."

He paused to lick the blood from his fingers.

"In order to survive…"

On his way out, Adam took Morgan's lance with him just in case he tried to defend himself again.

Baby cries came from the jungle. More of the infants had crawled out of the ocean, looking for trees to fertilize, as they had the second night on the island. But all the trees had been uprooted by the tidal wave, so the infant creatures had nowhere to go. They just wandered through the darkness, wailing, lost.

Morgan looked outside but couldn't see any of them. He could only hear their cries. He could also hear Adam's voice, hollering from the top of the hill at them.

"Shut up!" Adam cried.

He was tossing rocks at everything that moved.

"Stop haunting me! Get away!"

The baby cries continued into the morning. After the cries were gone, Adam could be heard yelling at the babies as if they were still all around him. He continued throwing rocks at bushes, screaming at them to leave him alone. He spent hours at a time running through the hills, yelling at the top of his lungs at somebody he was trying to kill. Somebody who wasn't really there. If Adam hadn't already gone completely insane, he had now.

"You have one more day," said Mr. Mike. "Then you're out of here."

"I'm on it," Morgan said.

"Don't make me have to tell your people you were a waste of money," he said, then left him alone.

Morgan still had no clue how to decipher the operating system. Even with his experience and reputation, he might as well have been a two-year-old trying to reprogram an AI processor.

"No luck?" Chase asked, poking his head in for his hourly check-up.

"Nope," Morgan said. "I just can't wrap my brain around this one."

"Weren't you the guy who deciphered the coding on that alien probe they found a couple years back?"

"Yeah, that was me."

"I heard you figured that out in one day."

"It took five hours," Morgan said.

"Five freakin' hours!" Chase said. "Where's the guy who pulled that one off?"

"I don't know," Morgan said. "Maybe I can manifest him five hours before they send me back to California."

"Need any help?" Chase said. "I'm a good target for bouncing ideas off of."

Morgan shook his head.

"I can focus better when I'm alone," Morgan said. "Thanks anyway."

As Chase walked back to his station, he joked, "Too bad you can't just ask the Truckers how to run the damn thing."

Morgan chuckled and went back to work, but then he paused and thought about that for a moment. Though deranged and incapable of language, he wondered if there wasn't a way the aliens could help him figure this out.

He went to the caverns with the next group, a team of botanists who said they found a new species of mushroom growing in the cavern that wasn't native to this planet. They thought it might have been brought over by the Truckers.

For hours, Morgan watched the aliens. He studied the way they moved, the sounds they made. He believed if he could get an understanding of the way they thought, the way they behaved—even as deranged lunatics—he might gain some kind of insight into how they would go about programming an operating system.

So he sat there in the dark foul caves with them. Fourteen hungry red eyes glued to his exotic flesh.

Adam was yelling in the night again, running through the labyrinth of fallen timber on the hillside.

When Adam first screamed, it surprised Morgan so much that he hit his head against the control board. The scream had a shrieking tone to it that reminded him of the deranged alien creatures he had studied in that dark putrid cavern. The looks on the monsters' faces haunted his dreams for many restless nights after Morgan returned to California.

When he looked back at the control board, the thing was lit up. It was working. Something must have jiggled into place when he hit his head against it.

"Son of a bitch," Morgan said, staring at the now-functioning console.

He was finally able to get to work.

Adam's head peeked inside the ship.

"How much longer?" Adam asked, exhausted from running wild in the night. "This place is driving me insane."

"It's going good," Morgan said. "I have the operating system up and running. If all goes according to plan I'll be able to—"

Adam cut him off by staggering across the room and biting into one of his legs. Even though he felt no pain, Morgan screamed at the sight of someone tearing flesh from his inner thigh.

"What the fuck are you doing?" Morgan cried.

Adam looked at him with a bloody piece of meat dangling from his mouth. He didn't say anything. He just chewed.

"Mr. Mike?" Morgan said, entering the small man's office.

Mr. Mike rubbed his callused fingers through his white comb-over and said, "What do you want now? An extension? Not going to happen."

"I need to see the big ship."

Mr. Mike cackled loudly, jerking his whole chest up and down.

"Right," he said. "Like I have the clearance for that."

"I think I figured it out," Morgan said.

"Figured what out?"

Morgan pointed back at the cone-shaped ship.

"The operating system."

The entire team gathered in the hangar. Mr. Mike said he probably couldn't clear bringing Morgan to the big ship, but he'd try to pull some strings if his findings were worthwhile.

"I was studying the behavioral patterns of the Truckers," Morgan said.

Chase interrupted, raising his hand, "They're not called Truckers anymore. Richards's team renamed them *Acriditoids* due to their locust-like features."

Morgan waved him off. "Acriditoids then. The point is, while studying them, they clearly showed signs of pack mentality, like wolves. Richards was the first to agree with me. It seems there's a female, an alpha female, in control of the group. None of the gammas will eat, drink, sit, or even urinate without the alpha's permission. Just like pack animals."

"What's your point?" said Mr. Mike. "They've reverted to primitive beings. Of course they'd act like animals. What's this have to do with the operating system?"

"It has everything to do with it," Morgan said. "At first, I also thought their pack behavior was the psychosis bringing out their primal instincts. But then I thought about it. What if they always had that pack mentality? What if their ships were designed with pack dynamics in mind?"

"Go on," said Mr. Mike.

"The operating system hasn't been responding at all," said Morgan. "I should have been able to make at least some progress by now. It feels as if I'm locked out of it, like trying to access an adult website on a computer with parental control. After seeing how the alpha female controlled her underlings, I believe that is exactly what's happening here. My theory is the big ship is like the alpha. It has complete control of the smaller ships. It can fly them, land them, crash them into a pink planet. The little ships can't fly themselves unless they get permission from the big ship."

Morgan stepped toward the team leader.

"Give me permission to check out the alpha ship," he said to Mr. Mike. "Once I get this system unlocked, I'll be able to wrap my brain around it in no time. Five hours. That's all I'll need."

Mr. Mike sneered at him.

"That's it?" said Mr. Mike. "That's all you've got? It's wild speculation at best. I can't get you clearance with just that."

"But I can prove it if given the chance," Morgan said.

"It doesn't matter," said Mr. Mike. "They'll never allow it. If that's all you've got then we're done here."

Then the little man stomped off, back to his office. Morgan fell back, leaning against the ship.

"Don't worry," Chase told him, patting him on the shoulder. "If you're right they'll find out soon enough. You just won't be there to tell the short bastard *I told you so.*"

Morgan just sighed and closed his eyes as tightly as he could.

One night, while Adam was away from his camp, Morgan decided to check up on Jill. It took a lot of effort, climbing out of the ship and up the mountain using only his hands. But his legs were light now that they had been mostly eaten.

The girl looked okay from what he could see of her in the moonlight. She had severe swelling and bruising on her head and the side of her face. Her naked body was also covered in dried blood, but it didn't appear to be hers.

"It's okay," Morgan said to the girl, brushing her hair out of her eyes. "Everything's going to be fine."

She moaned as he touched her. Then she opened her eyes and looked at him.

"Morgan?" she said, a drunken smile appeared on her face. "You're alive?" Her voice was slow and rough. "He told me everyone else was dead."

"Jill..." Morgan said. "He told me you were in a coma. Are you alright?"

"I'm fine," Jill said, smiling. "Just fine."

She was conscious but her mind wasn't all there. Either she had a severe concussion, was delirious from lack of food and water, or had gone crazy from being raped every night by the horrifying zombie man.

"Don't worry," Morgan said. "I'm going to get you out of this.

I've found a way. You just have to hang on."

"We're going home?" Her eyes blinked a long blink. "Please take me home."

"I will," Morgan said.

He kissed her on the hand. His tears touched her sandy knuckles.

"But first, can you do me a favor?" Jill asked.

"Anything."

"Can you take it out?" Jill said.

"Take what out?"

Morgan looked around, wondering what she was talking about. Then he noticed, when his eyes adjusted a little better to the moonlight, what she was referring to. She had a lance between her legs, shoved deep inside of her.

"He was mad," Jill said. "Because he can't get it up anymore."

The sight of it made his eyes shiver and his heart peel open like a grapefruit. He turned his head away. He wanted to shove twenty lances up Adam's asshole for this. He wanted the bastard dead.

"And he said I was dry," Jill said. "Too dry."

Morgan pulled himself farther into the shelter, down toward her legs. When he tried to remove the lance, it didn't come out, pulling her whole body with it. That's when he realized the lance was the one Adam had taken from him, the one that was bent like a tire-iron. But with its sharpened end inside of her, the lance seemed less like a tire-iron now. It was more like a meat hook.

As Morgan was leaving the Sony-NASA Citysphere to go back home, Chase walked with him to the gate.

"It's bullshit they won't be bringing you back here next month," Chase said. "I bet you would have been more useful than any of those other idiots they got back in California."

"I'd have to agree with you there," Morgan said. "But I'll

still be able to continue my work on it once they transport the ship back to California."

"Yeah, but they don't have the resources to bring the big one back," Chase said. "Your alpha ship will be left on this planet, floating through the cosmos without you."

"It's fine," Morgan said, as they arrived at the gate.

"Well, look on the bright side," Chase said. "If you came back, you'd have to take one of those new *budget* flights that they're using to save money from now on. I hear they're about as safe as Apollo 1."

Over the intercom, a gate attendant announced the shuttle-craft was ready to board.

"That's me," Morgan said. "I better get going."

He held out his hand.

"Nice working with you," Chase said, shaking his hand goodbye. "For a slanty-eyed Muslim commie, you're not such a bad guy."

"Who said I was a commie?" Morgan said. "At the moment, I'm Morgan Douglas. All-American asshole."

On his way into the shuttle, Chase yelled at him, "Hey Morgan, next time a planet comes through our solar system, let's have another game of golf."

Morgan smiled and waved him away.

A few weeks later, even though he had been removed from the project, the team decided they wanted Morgan back. It appeared the people who replaced him discovered his hypothesis about the ship's operating system was completely correct. The operating system was indeed locked by the alpha ship and they wanted Morgan's help unlocking it.

But on his second flight to Barack, his shuttlecraft crashed into the sea and he became stranded on the deserted island. He thought he was never going to get a second chance to look at the Acriditoid vessels, until they found one on that very island. He thought their prayers of rescue had been answered. Unfortunately, the control system was still locked by the alpha ship.

But Morgan had an idea that he wanted to try to save them

from the island. He thought about beta wolves. When an alpha wolf dies, he is replaced by a beta wolf. Morgan had a theory that maybe the smaller ships were capable of being beta ships. If anything happened to the alpha ship then a beta ship could take over and control the rest of the fleet.

Although the ship Morgan was currently in had been completely destroyed, he hoped he could control another ship from elsewhere on the planet, get it to fly over the sea to their island and pick them up. Then they could fly that ship to the Citysphere and call for help. If they were lucky NASA might just have the resources to come and get them, even given the current distance between Barack and Earth.

When Morgan got the control panel working again, he realized the system was no longer locked. Somebody over at the Citysphere must have finally figured out how to unlock it from the alpha ship. It was actually possible for them to get home. That was if Morgan could decipher the operating system.

"All you need is five hours," Morgan told himself, working nonstop without sleep. "Figure it out in five hours."

It took nine hours, but Morgan succeeded in his task. Luckily, he wouldn't have to fly the ship himself. He wasn't a pilot. It wouldn't have been possible. But he was able to program a flight plan. The ship could fly itself.

After entering commands to the third ship on the planet, the one they didn't take back to California, Morgan held his breath and clicked a metal button with a single finger.

"And we're off," Morgan said, as the commands were sent.

When Adam arrived for his daily feeding, Morgan held up his hands.

"Not today," Morgan said. "I got it working."

"What did you say?" Adam asked, almost angered by Morgan's words.

"I succeeded," Morgan said. "We're going home."

"Bullshit," Adam said. His hands were shaking, his black flesh dripped from his third arm. "You're lying."

"It's true," Morgan said. "I can get us to the Citysphere. We'll try to call for help."

"Don't fuck with me," Adam said. "This ship isn't going anywhere."

"Yeah, this ship is totaled," Morgan said. "We never had a chance getting anywhere in this. But there's another ship on the main continent. I was able to program it to come here."

Adam's good eye was wide with shock.

"Now all I need to do is keep this signal going," Morgan said. A smile grew on his face. "And it will fly right to us."

"I'll believe it when I see it," Adam said.

"It should be here in an hour," Morgan said. "Maybe less."

"You're just buying time," Adam said. "I see through it. You're not going to stop me from taking my meat."

Morgan yelled at the ceiling in frustration. Then he looked at Adam.

"Fine," Morgan said. "But it's the last piece of my leg you'll ever need."

Adam staggered toward him. His left arm looked just as rotten as the dead arm it was connected to.

As the zombie-like man leaned down to take a bite of his leg, Morgan gripped the bloody hook-like lance behind him. He had been able to remove it from Jill and brought it back with him. He contemplated driving it right into Adam's skull.

But he still needed Adam. Neither he nor Jill could walk. They likely would need the psycho to get them onto the ship once it arrived.

Adam was about to take a bite of Morgan's leg, but then paused. He sniffed at the air around his lap.

"It's rank," Adam said. "The meat on your legs must be spoiled."

"It's your arm," Morgan said. "You're just smelling your own gangrenous flesh."

Adam smelled Morgan's legs again.

"No, they're rotten." He stood up and shook his head. "I can't eat that."

He turned toward the door.

"Wait a minute," Morgan said. "What are you going to do?"

"I'm going to cut a steak off of that bitch," Adam said. "I'm bored of fucking her anyway."

"No," Morgan yelled. "Just wait one hour."

Morgan crawled across the ground toward his feet.

"Please," Morgan said. "Just wait an hour. I promise you a ship will arrive."

Adam shook his head. "I'm through with you."

When the zombie went for the door, Morgan uncovered the lance and drove the hook-end into Adam's upper thigh. Adam screamed. Morgan took it out and aimed for his spine, but the enraged zombie blocked it with his rotten arm.

"Are you fucking kidding me?" Adam yelled at him, ripping the lance from Morgan's hand. "After all I did for you?"

Adam swiped it across Morgan's chest. The legless man flew back. Blood sprayed from his collar bone. Adam charged him and stabbed him twice more in the ribs.

"Stop!" Morgan said. "We can get off this island. You don't have to do this."

But Adam wasn't listening. He was crazed, just as the aliens in the underground were crazed. He grabbed Morgan by the head and bashed it against the ship's control panel.

"I am not the meat," Adam cried. "You are the meat."

After the fifth time his head slammed into the control board, Morgan felt it crumble into pieces. The signal died. The ship he had called would no longer be able to reach them.

"You are the meat!"

Adam let go of his head and went for his stomach. He ripped open Morgan's shirt and sank his teeth into his freshly opened wounds.

"But we had it," Morgan said, looking down at the ferocious creature chewing on his guts. "We actually had it…"

Adam wasn't listening. He had found Morgan's intestines and was pulling them out with his teeth, like a dog tugging on a rope of sausage.

CHAPTER ELEVEN
THE LIVING DEAD

"They're dead," Zana said to Peter as they walked through the wasteland of shredded trees. "Give it up already."

Peter jumped on top of a slimy jagged stump.

"I swear I heard somebody yelling out there last night," Peter said.

He used his hand to block the sun from his eyes. The second sun, Earth's sun, was too small to be much of a bother. It just looked like a bright white dot in the pink sky.

"It's just the ocean waves crashing," Zana said. "You're just hearing what you want to hear."

"I'm not giving up until I search every inch of this island."

"It's been days," she said. "You saw how big that wave was. Nothing could have possibly survived. The fact we're still alive is an absolute miracle."

As the wave came crashing down on Peter and Zana, they had accepted the fact they were both going to die. They held each other, allowing the wave to wash over them. But something unexpected happened. One of the jelly worms inside of the wave got to them before the acid could. Its head emerged from the water and swallowed both of them whole, before it crashed on the rocks.

Peter and Zana had no idea what had happened to them. They could only feel themselves being smothered and squeezed by a blanket of blubber, their air supply getting thin. The jelly worm smashed against cliffs and trees, but its gelatinous body was enough cushion to protect its two passengers from the blows.

When it was all over, Peter punched his way out of the

creature's stomach. The jelly worm was lying on a pile of dead jelly worms on the far side of the island. They didn't recognize where they were exactly. Everything had been demolished.

They went searching for the others, but large sections of the island had been blocked off by pools of acid. The alien vessel seemed like the best place to look for them, but the ship had been swept away with the wave.

Days passed, but Peter never gave up hope. He forced them to keep traveling through the collapsed jungle until he found some sign of what happened to them.

"You're just trying to keep busy," Zana said. "Even though you know they're dead, you keep searching because you need something to do. You need to keep your mind off the fact we're stuck here with no hope of ever going home."

"No," Peter said, completely sure of himself. "They definitely are alive. I heard them."

"Just let it go," Zana said. "Let's just enjoy our time left together."

She rubbed her puppy flowers and smiled.

"We have the whole planet to ourselves now," Zana said. "We can be like Adam and Eve on an alien world. I know we'll eventually die, but that's the way I want to spend the rest of my life—on this island, in this world, just the two of us."

"But it's not just the two of us," Peter said. "There's Captain Bearbeard. And the others are here somewhere. I know it."

Zana groaned and sat down on a rock. She didn't care that residual acid moisture was burning her bare butt.

"Are you taking a rest?" Peter asked.

"Fuck you," Zana said. "I'm staying here."

"We shouldn't split up," Peter said.

"I don't want to split up," Zana said. "I want us to stay together. Right here."

Then she stopped talking to him and stared at the rotting

jelly worm corpses in the distance. Peter sat next to her and snuggled Captain Bearbeard to her shoulder. But his effort to comfort her just pissed her off more.

She grabbed Captain Bearbeard.

"What's up with this fucking thing anyway?" she said, holding up the bear.

"Give it back," Peter said.

"Why should I?" she said. "Why is it so important?"

Peter didn't answer. He just reached for it.

"Stay back," Zana said, holding her hand around his head, threatening to harm it.

"Don't," Peter said.

She ripped its neck a little, white cotton fluffed out of the hole.

"Answer me," she said. "Why do you carry this thing around? You care more about it than you care about me."

She tore it a little more.

"You have to be nicer to me," Zana said. "I'm all you've got left."

She squeezed the head with all her strength as if she were about to rip the bear in half.

"Please," Peter said. "It's my little brother's. It's all I've had left of him since he died."

Zana stopped and looked at him.

"Don't," Peter said, as if he were about to cry. "Please don't."

"Fine, you big baby," she said, tossing the half-ripped bear into his lap. "Choose your stupid toy over me."

She stood up and continued down their path.

Zana was getting sick of Peter's lack of interest in her. She wanted him and didn't care that he was asexual. She just didn't take well to being rejected. It was one thing that always pissed her off.

Working at the brothel in Nevada, Zana faced rejection a lot.

Whenever a customer arrived at the ranch, all the girls lined up in the front room and the customer would get to choose whom they wanted to buy. If Zana wasn't chosen, she would always get angry.

"What the fuck!" she yelled, as the tall record producer from Seattle chose a blond woman instead of her.

"Her?" Zana yelled at the guy. "Are you serious? Instead of me?"

Everyone looked at Zana as if she were a psychopath, especially the customer who wanted nothing to do with her. But she was still new and learning the ropes. She didn't realize how disrespectful she was being.

"What the heck do guys see in her anyway?" Zana said, turning to the others as they broke away from the line. "She's so plastic."

Zana sat down by one of the older girls at the bar and ordered a diet Dr. Pepper. She thought it was bullshit she wasn't allowed to drink alcohol on the job.

"I'm a million times hotter than she is," Zana said, twirling her straw in her drink. "These guys are idiots."

The girl sitting next to her was Yamaya, a latina with short curly hair. She shook her head at Zana when she called the customers *idiots*. If the bosses heard, she would have paid a fine for it.

"It's because she's white," said Yamaya. "And you're black."

"I'm both, actually," Zana said. "Besides, what's that have to do with anything?"

"White girls sell better," Yamaya said. "That's also why she costs more than you do."

"She makes more money than me?" Zana yelled. "Just because she's white? That's bullshit. We should sue their asses for discrimination."

Yamaya laughed.

"Good luck," she said. "The law doesn't care about what goes on in here. They're allowed to be as racist as they want to be."

"We should go on strike," Zana said. "Or start a union."

"Girl, I don't think you realize what kind of life you got yourself into," Yamaya said. "They don't call these pussy penitentiaries for nothing. When you signed the contract, you signed your rights away."

Zana shrugged. "So?"

"You try to protest and they're going to kill you," Yamaya said.

"Bullshit. No they wouldn't."

"Maybe not," Yamaya said. "But they'll make you wish you were dead."

That's when Zana learned her dream of becoming a sex worker was not at all what she imagined it would be. Although the brothels were legal, they were not well regulated. The laws were in place to protect brothel owners and customers, not the women who worked in them. The system was easy for brothel owners to manipulate and the women were easy to extort. The brothel owners took half of the women's earnings, yet also charged them rent for their rooms, expenses for items such as condoms and towels, they had to share their tips, pay their customer's cab fares, and even pay for their own mandatory doctor checkups once a week to make sure they were STD free.

Not only that, but the women were driven like slaves. They had to work fourteen hour shifts and were never allowed to leave the property. If they broke any of the rules, they would get fined. It was $100 if they were late to a lineup, $500 for refusing a customer, and sometimes up to $1000 just for taking a drive down to the liquor store for a pack of cigarettes. And there was only one way to pay off those fines—service customers for no pay.

Zana heard there were some brothels that weren't so bad to work at, where the employers treated their employees with respect, but she didn't know which ones they were. Some of the women who had been around for a while said that such a place could only be a myth.

No matter how bad it got, Zana still insisted she loved her

work. Like any career, she knew it all wouldn't have been fun and games. She had to take the bad with the good.

And though she might have been getting taken advantage of by her employers, when it came to her customers, she was the one taking advantage of them. In the bedroom, she was the boss. And that's the way she liked it. No matter how strong or aggressive the customer, she always had a way of turning him into her bitch.

It was time to eat, but Zana wouldn't give Peter any of her puppy flowers.

"Things are going to have to change around here," she told him.

"How do you mean?" Peter asked.

"Back on Earth, I was a prostitute," Zana said. "I'm sick of being the prostitute."

"You don't have to be a prostitute ever again," Peter said. "That lifestyle is behind you now."

"That's not what I'm saying," Zana said. "I don't want the lifestyle I had to end. I just don't want to be the prostitute anymore. I want to be the customer."

"I don't understand what you mean."

"I'm not letting you eat for free anymore," Zana said. "If you want food you'll have to sell yourself to me. I want you to be the prostitute."

"You're really going to threaten me like that?" Peter asked.

Zana nodded. "You either give me what I want or you'll starve to death."

She bit into a puppy flower and swallowed. Then she held it out for him to eat.

"I'll give you this bit," she said, "if you can make me come with your mouth."

Peter pushed it away.

"No, thanks," Peter said. "I don't sell myself like that."

"What do you mean?" she asked. "You'll starve to death otherwise."

"No, I won't," Peter said.

"Why not?"

"Because you won't let me," Peter said.

He walked into the jungle.

"Fuck that," she said. "You're going to give it up or you're going to die."

"Maybe you'll let me starve," Peter said. "But there's no way you'd let me die. You're too nice a person."

"I'm not nice," she said. "Fuck you."

"You *are* nice," Peter said. "And you'll only hate yourself if I let you take advantage of me."

"You don't understand." Zana pointed her puppy flowers at him. "These things growing on my body intensify my sex drive beyond anything you could ever imagine. I've been stuck on this island far too long. I *need* sex. Every inch of me is ready to explode. If I don't get it, I know I'm going to die."

"You'll live," Peter said. He felt like he was trying to fend off a horny frat boy.

She screamed with frustration. "It's driving me insane!"

"Think about something else. I'm not going to do sexual favors for you."

"Fine," she said. "We'll see how long you can hold out. You'll need to eat some time. Good luck finding food anywhere else on the island."

Peter pointed toward a pile of trees.

"Maybe there's food inside of there," he said.

Zana saw him pointing at something behind a rock. When they got closer, she realized it was a refrigerator. Her eyes trembled with confusion.

"Where the hell did this come from?"

The refrigerator was just sitting there, as if it had always been there. It was white and covered in magnets. Most of the magnets were advertisements for pizza companies but some were shaped like butterflies. They held up pictures of a four-

237

person white family and their dog. A grocery list was also posted on the freezer.

Unlike everything else around it, the refrigerator looked completely untouched by the acid.

"Am I imagining things?" she asked. "Are we sharing a delusion?"

Peter opened up the refrigerator. It was filled with food.

"There actually is food in here," Peter said.

He pulled out a can of RC cola and opened it. When he took a drink, a smile stretched across his face.

"How is it?" Zana said.

"It's warm!" he said, as if warm soda was the best thing he'd ever had in his life.

Zana pulled out a tupperware container. It was filled with meat, like somebody's leftovers from dinner.

"Meatloaf?" Zana said.

When she opened it, a rancid smell poured out. The meat was green and fluffy. She tossed it aside.

"It's rotten."

They investigated all the food. Most of it was old and moldy.

"Looks like everything's gone bad," Peter said. "It's probably been here without electricity for a while."

"Why is this thing here at all?" Zana said. "You act like it's no big deal."

"I'm not looking a gift horse in the mouth." Peter found an apple in the crisper. It wasn't bruised or rotten yet. "Maybe God felt sorry for us."

He took a bite of the apple and looked up at Zana with excitement.

"Apple!" Peter said.

She grabbed another apple from the refrigerator and ate it so fast her bites were like a chainsaw, splashing juice all over her chest.

Peter examined the other contents in the fridge. "It looks like some of this stuff is still good. There's jarred food and condiments. We should stay away from all the meat though."

Zana opened a can of cola and guzzled it down.

"I guess I'll be able to hold out for quite a long time," Peter said. "I won't need your tumor fruit while I have all of this."

When Zana realized he was right, the smile fell from her face and was replaced by an expression of rage. She threw her RC can at the ground and pushed the refrigerator over face-first into the mud.

"You should get used to not getting everything you want," Yamaya said to Zana.

The sex Zana was having at her job was getting boring. The guys just couldn't satisfy her. They didn't think that's what they paid her for.

"This job is getting shittier every day," Zana said. "I should have just kept doing it illegally."

"Don't let *him* hear you say that," Yamaya said, pointing at the new customer walking through the entrance.

It was a police officer, still in uniform.

"Don't let him pick you," Yamaya whispered to Zana. "Slouch a little. Look lazy and disinterested."

"Why?" Zana whispered back.

"He's a cop," Yamaya said. "Cops don't have to pay."

"You mean I'd have to service him *for free?*" Zana whispered, clenching her fists.

The cop saw Zana with her fists clenched, standing in an aggressive manner toward Yamaya.

"I see you have some new girls," the cop said, smiling.

He approached Zana. She gave him a dirty look, telling him *don't you dare pick me* with her eyes.

"She looks like she's trying to be a tough chick," said the cop. Then he looked her in the eyes. "Do you think you're a tough chick?"

"She's the least obedient girl we've gotten all year," said

the brothel owner.

The cop looked her up and down, licking his crusty pencil-thin lips.

"So she's a wild horse, is she?" asked the cop, rubbing his sausage-fingers through his salt and pepper hair. "Guess old Officer Croc will have to break her for you."

Zana looked at the brothel owner with a bored expression on her face.

"I'm not going to fuck him," she said.

The owner's eyes lit up as if she had just stomped on his nuts.

"Are you fucking serious?" said the owner.

"Fine me if you want," she said. "But I'm not doing it. If he's not paying, then I'm not servicing him."

"Oh, you'll be fined alright," yelled the owner. "Fined out your asshole!"

Officer Croc held up his hand.

"It's okay," he said. "This time I'll pay. I'll even pay double."

He rubbed a callused finger down Zana's chest.

"But I'll make sure I get every single penny's worth," he said.

Despite her disgust, Zana agreed. For double, she wasn't going to say no. But she didn't know until afterward that the brothel owner would still fine her for her outburst. In the end, she would end up paying two hundred bucks of her own money for the honor of servicing the greasy cop.

"Wake up," Peter said to Zana, as she was curled up in the sand with her elbow over her eyes. "You're not going to believe what I just found!"

She did not care. Her head was killing her.

"It better not be another magical refrigerator," Zana said.

"No, it's not!" Peter was hopping up and down. "You're going to flip out!"

Zana got up and followed him down the shoreline. When she saw what he wanted to show her, she did indeed flip out.

"The tidal wave must have brought it in," Peter said.

She couldn't believe her eyes, but there it was. The shuttle-craft that had crashed into the ocean was now on the beach, dangling out of the jungle on its side.

"That's not what I was expecting at all," Zana said.

Inside, there was not much left of the ship. The acid had eaten away all the fabric from the seats. The paint, the plastic, the human remains—it had all been dissolved under the waves. Just the metal parts remained, but they were also curled and warped.

"Seems like it's been years since the crash," Zana said. "I hardly recognize this ship anymore."

They carefully balanced themselves on the twisted metal parts of the seats and hiked their way to the cockpit.

"Maybe the communications equipment still works," Peter said. "We could see if it reaches Earth."

When they pried open what was left of the cockpit door, he said, "Nevermind."

The entire cockpit had crumpled in on itself, crushed upon impact. Any semblance of a dashboard had been melted into fluids caked on the floor.

"There's nothing here," Zana said. "It's not even safe enough to use as a shelter."

The ship rocked and squealed as the trees supporting it began to collapse. Zana lost her balance and fell, rolling backward toward an exit.

"Look out," Peter yelled, jumping after her.

When Peter landed on his belly, grabbing her by the wrist, there was an explosion. They just heard a loud boom all around them. Then they fell out of the emergency exit and slid down to safety.

"What was that?" Zana said.

It took them a couple seconds to register what had happened. Above them, hanging from the emergency exit they fell from, was a yellow slide. The exploding noise was actually the sound of it inflating.

"It's a life raft," Peter said.

"I thought all the life rafts were used," Zana said.

"No, one of them didn't deploy," Peter said. "Remember? It malfunctioned."

Zana vaguely remembered. Everything had happened so quickly after the crash, it all seemed like a crazy dream.

"Too bad it didn't work at the time," Zana said. "It's kind of useless now."

Peter examined the raft.

"No, it's not," Peter said. "We can use this."

"For what?" Zana said.

"To get to the Citysphere."

"But it's deserted now," Zana said. "Nobody's going to be able to rescue us."

"So?" Peter said. "Wouldn't you rather spend the rest of your life at the Citysphere than on this island?"

Zana thought about it. Her eyes widened with excitement.

"We could sleep in real beds," she said. "And the whole place was wave-powered. We'd have electricity."

"There might even be food and vehicles to explore the continent," Peter said. "Who knows what they left behind."

Zana looked at the raft.

"But it's going to be dangerous," she said. "So many people died just getting from the shuttle to the island using these rafts..."

"We can acid-proof it," Peter said. "And build another sail. I know we can make it if we try."

Zana shook her head.

"I don't know..." she said. "It might not be worth the risk."

She thought about it for a while. The thought of living in the Sony-NASA Citysphere was appealing. There would likely be beds, furniture, and heat. It would be a return to civilization. But she didn't think it would be possible to make it there and she was so close to getting Peter to put out for her.

There was something lying beneath the raft. Peter lifted up the yellow rubber and picked it up. It was some kind of pile of dried meat.

"What is that?" Zana asked.

"Some kind of skin," Peter said.

It looked like the shedded skin of a snake or lizard, or the exoskeleton of a scorpion after molting. But the bag of skin was the size of a human. A reptilian human.

The girls gave him the nickname Officer Crocodile, or Officer Croc, because the skin on his back looked like the reptilian scales of a crocodile. He had been in a fire early in his career as an officer of the law and suffered third-degree burns across large sections of his body. The texture of his skin was rough and seemed diseased. The brothel workers were all disturbed by it.

At first, the nickname was meant to be an insult. But Officer Croc liked it and embraced the handle. The fact they were all scared and disturbed by his appearance only excited the cop.

"Get on the bed," said Officer Croc. "Take off your clothes."

Zana turned her back and pulled off her shirt.

"And take those stupid flowers off of your body," he said. "You look like an idiot."

Zana gave him a dirty look. He didn't like that.

"Did you hear what I said?" he asked, as he removed his shirt.

"They don't come off," she said.

He looked at them and examined one, holding it in his palm. She quivered as his calloused hands scratched against the sensitive surface of her puppy flower.

"So they don't," he said. "You're a freakish little cunt, aren't you?"

She pushed his hand away.

"I don't like them," he said. "Take them off."

"They are a part of me," she said. "They don't come off."

"Cut them off," he said. "They disgust me."

She backed away.

"Fuck you," she said. "Cut your dick off."

He removed the belt from his pants and held it like a whip.

"You're going to have to learn to do what you're told," said Officer Croc. "Now be a good little whore and I won't have to spank you."

"Get out of here," Zana said. "You can keep your money."

The cop laughed.

"It's too late now, my milk chocolate bunny," he said. "The transaction has already been made. Now get on the bed and show me your ass."

Zana realized she was shaking. She couldn't believe the man had the upper hand on her. She had to be stronger. She had to gain control.

"No," she said, raising her voice. "You get on the bed and show me *your* ass."

The smile fell from his face.

"You giving me an order, whore?" the cop said, stepping toward her. "I'm an officer of the law. I *give* the orders around here."

"In the bedroom, I am the highest authority," she said. "You will follow my orders."

"Now you're beginning to piss me off," said the cop. "You think you're a tough chick. Well, I got news for you."

He slapped her across the face with the belt. Zana heard a popping sound and then found herself falling back onto the bed.

"There's no such thing as strong women," he said, unzipping his fly. "Girls who act tough just haven't been fucked hard enough yet. They need a real man to show them their place in society."

He pulled down his pants to reveal a penis the size of a middle finger. Though erect, it was warped and deformed. Its texture was even rougher than the skin on his back. When he was burned in the fire, it was his genitalia that got the worst of it.

"Think I'm going to fuck that, you ugly prick?" she said.
He shook his head.

"Don't worry, sugar pie," he said. "You won't be doing any of the fucking."

Zana kicked him in the testicles and ran for the panic button. She hit it five times. The red light went on.

"Security's coming, asshole," Zana said. "Get the fuck out."

The cop stood up. He seemed perfectly all right. Even though she heeled him with all of her strength, he felt nothing.

"I lost my nuts in the fire ages ago," said Croc, slapping his crotch. "But that still caught me off guard. No whore has ever had the nerve to strike me before."

Zana hit the panic button four more times.

"Think anybody's coming to save you?" he said. "They don't give a shit about what happens to you. When I'm in the room with you, there's no such thing as a panic button."

Zana ran for the door, but he intercepted her like a football player and slammed her against the wall.

"Now I told you," Croc said, rubbing his hand along one of the puppy flowers on her hip, "to take these stupid fucking things off."

Then he ripped the tumor off and a splash of blood squirted onto his penis. Zana shrieked. He grabbed another one and ripped it off.

"Get off me!" she screamed, punching and kicking at him.

He picked her up and body-slammed her onto the bed, ripping her tumors off like picking weeds in a garden. The bed became splattered with blood. When they were all gone, he held her down and spread her legs.

"You fucking rapist," she yelled. "Get away from me, you rapist."

The cop picked her up off the bed and body-slammed her again, this time on the floor. It knocked the wind out of her. She stopped screaming. She could only gasp for air.

"Calling me a rapist?" he said.

The cop laughed and moved her now-docile limbs to where

he wanted them.

"You're a prostitute," he said. "You can't *rape* a prostitute."

Zana closed her eyes as tightly as she could, as she felt his deformed little penis squirming its way inside her.

For the next few days, Zana didn't help Peter build the sail or reinforce the raft. She sat in the sand, hugging her legs, as Peter did all the work. He didn't mind. It gave him something to keep him busy. The job took much less time than the previous rafts. He had enough practice constructing them to know exactly what to do.

Peter still kept telling Zana he heard shouting noises coming from the far side of the island. Zana heard nothing. There was one weird noise she heard the day before, but it didn't sound like a human scream. It sounded closer to the shrieks of a jelly worm. He wanted to make sure the others weren't still alive before they left, but Zana assured him there was no way anyone else could have survived the tsunami.

"It's ready," Peter said on the afternoon of the third day. "We can leave within the hour if you want."

Zana nodded her head and rubbed tears from her eyes. "Sure. If you think it's safe."

"I would like to get some extra jelly worm mucus just in case," Peter said. "Then we can go."

He held out his hand.

"Want to come with me to get some?" he asked.

Zana stood up and wiped the sand from her legs.

"It'll be nice to sleep in a real bed," she told him, as they strolled into the destroyed jungle.

"Tonight you will sleep in the best bed on this planet," Peter said. "I promise you this."

They came across a hole in the ground, just a dozen yards inland. It was more like a well, going deep into the ground. Peter looked inside.

"What is it?" Zana asked.

Peter squinted his eyes.

"A cave," Peter said. "It looks like it goes pretty deep."

He waved away the smell rising up from the darkness.

"You think anything lives down there?" Zana asked.

"Not anymore," he said. "The place is flooded from the wave. If any animal was living down there, it either drowned or fled to the surface."

Zana didn't like the look of the deep, dark pit. It seemed like something was down there, staring up at them, ready to jump out and grab her. The pit was obviously the home of a living creature, like a jelly worm or something even more horrible.

"We should keep moving," Zana said, "before it gets dark."

They continued on. A wind drove chills across Zana's bare flesh. She wrapped herself around Peter for warmth, curling her head into his neck. Her puppy flowers pulsed against him.

"Things haven't been easy for you, have they?" Peter asked.

She kept walking, closing her eyes and allowing Peter to guide her.

"You seem like you've had some hard times," he said.

"I don't want to talk about it," she said.

They walked in silence for a couple of minutes.

Then Zana said, "They piss me off."

"Who does?"

"People," Zana said. "I'm glad to be rid of people."

"What's wrong with people?"

"Not all people," she said, rubbing Peter's shoulder. "Just the assholes."

She suddenly jerked her head away from Peter and stomped on a mound of purple grass.

"Why are assholes so afraid of sex?" she said. "People should be allowed to have sex for any reason they want. The government has no right to tell us why we can and can't do it. If I want to do it for money that's my own business. It doesn't hurt anyone."

Peter didn't say anything. He just followed her and listened. He knew she just needed somebody to rant to.

"If the law actually protected a sex worker's rights in the same way any other human being's rights were protected, there wouldn't be any problems," Zana said. "Even where prostitution is legal, women are abused and taken advantage of. Because people let them. Because deep down they think people like me deserve everything that happens to us."

Zana cried and hugged Peter. He put all his strength into his embrace when he hugged her back.

"It's a new world," Peter said. "You can create your own ideals here."

Zana looked him in the eyes and then kissed him. She knew he wouldn't kiss her back, but she didn't care. She wanted to kiss him anyway.

But then he did kiss her back. He just did it because he knew she wanted him to, but Zana's signals became crossed. She put her tongue in his mouth, squeezed his ass, pressed his body against the puppy flowers in her pelvic area.

"Zana," Peter said, trying to pull away.

But he gave her an inch and Zana was going to take the whole mile. She stuck her hand down his pants and sucked on his neck.

"Stop it," Peter said. "You don't want to do this."

"Shut up and fuck me," Zana said, and then she bit into his lip, drawing blood.

He pushed her away.

"I said stop."

Zana looked at him with an angry face. Then she attacked him. With all her strength, she ripped open his zipper and grabbed for his penis. She tried to make him hard. He wouldn't be able to resist if she could just get him hard.

"I'm going to fuck you whether you like it or not," she said.

Every time Officer Croc came to the brothel, he chose Zana to service him. Whether she fought him or submitted to him or put on a show for him or acted completely apathetic toward him, the cop didn't seem to care. He always wanted her. So Zana started tuning him out, blanking her mind when she was with him and blocking out her memories after it was over.

Zana had only one way to cope with what the cop was doing to her and that was to take it out on the other customers who came to see her.

"Take off your clothes and get on the bed," she told a skinny college kid with a shaved head.

The brothel was a couple of hours away from a college campus and they regularly received visits from groups of college guys. There were four in this group and the kid with the shaved head was the youngest. His friends told him to choose Zana because they thought it would be funny. They knew she was the freak.

"Are you a virgin?" she asked him.

It was a question she was not supposed to ask the college guys, because they found it humiliating. Most of them were. But Zana wanted to humiliate him. She knew he was a virgin. She just wanted to watch him squirm.

"Hell no," he said, not looking her in the eyes.

She took off his clothes and then removed her own. Her body was covered in bloody marks from where Officer Croc had removed her puppy flowers.

"How about an ass virgin?" she said. "Have you ever been fucked in the ass?"

"Fuck no," he said. "What do you think?"

"So you're not an ass virgin?" she said, giggling. He didn't get the joke.

"Then I guess it's time somebody deflowered you," she said.

He didn't understand. She had to spell it out for him.

"I'm going to fuck you in the ass."

The kid freaked out.

"What?" he said. "Are you some kind of tranny? Get the hell away from me."

"I'm all woman," she said. "But I bet my dick's bigger than yours."

Zana opened her legs. There was one puppy flower Officer Croc did not rip away, because it was hidden inside of her vagina. The tumor became erect and emerged from her labia, the tendrils squirming with anticipation.

"Now suck it," she said. "Suck my dick."

The boy jumped from the bed and tried to run for it, but Zana cut him off. He saw the panic button and hit it with his fist.

Zana laughed. "You think anybody's coming to your rescue? They stopped answering my calls for help a long time ago."

He tried to force his way through her, but she shoved him back. She planted her knee in his testicles and he fell to the ground.

Then she began to visualize the kid as Officer Croc.

"You think you can rape me and get away with it?" she said to him. "This is my domain. I eat deformed fuckers like you for breakfast."

She held out her foot to the boy.

"Kiss my feet, cop," she told the kid. "I'll teach you how to show a woman proper respect."

The kid continued to cringe on the ground.

She smothered his face with the bottom of her foot.

"Lick my toes, pig," she said. "Stick your tongue between them like you're eating a girl out."

The kid opened his mouth and just pressed his tongue against her feet, unable to lick due to the pain. A stream of drool trickled between her toes.

"You think women are weak?" she said.

She brought her longest toenail down the center of his face

and cut a line of blood across the tip of his nose.

"I'll show you how strong a woman can be," she said, pressing her foot against his neck and applying half of her weight. "You need a real woman to put you in your place."

When she released her weight from his throat, the kid gasped for air. Then he began to cry. He no longer resisted her attacks. He just cried.

Zana hushed him and stroked his hair.

"There now," she said, whispering in his ear. "Don't worry. It'll all be over soon."

Then she slid her vaginal tumor inside of him and fucked him against the floor. With every thrust, she regained a little more of the inner strength Officer Croc had stolen from her. She could feel herself becoming whole again.

When she was done with him, the college kid sniffled as he put his clothes back on. He was probably the same age as Zana, but at that moment, she felt older and stronger than him. She felt as if she were a superior species, an alpha female bossing around a gamma wolf.

Zana told him, "You might want to tell a lie about what went on in here. If your friends find out you were fucked in the ass by a tranny prostitute, you're going to have one hell of a freshman year."

Every time Officer Croc paid her a visit, she needed to abuse at least three other men until she felt better about herself. She picked on the smaller guys or the sheepish ones who let her get away with it. Sexual abuse became the cycle of Zana's life.

By the time Officer Croc stopped choosing her in the lineups, Zana was too far gone to quit. She still had to make other men pay for what he did to her. The darkness inside of her had swallowed her up alive.

Peter didn't hit Zana as she yanked at his penis. She knew he could fight and would seriously injure her if he wanted to. But

Zana knew him. She knew he would never hurt her no matter what she did to him. A smile grew on her face as she succeeded in making him hard.

"Zana, cut it out," Peter said.

As he pulled her hands away from his penis, Zana went for his pants and pulled them down to his ankles. Then she pushed him back. He tripped on his pants and fell into the purple grass.

She was so wet that all she had to do was drop herself on top of him and he slid right in.

"Zana!"

She grabbed his throat as she bucked on top of him.

"Just lay there and take it," she said.

Within a minute, Zana burst into orgasm. Peter went limp inside of her. Her breaths were heavy against his chest.

Then she began to cry.

"It's okay," Peter said.

He stroked her hair.

When she looked at him, he was smiling at her as if concerned. He hoped she had gotten it out of her system.

"You're smiling?" she said.

She pushed off of him and got to her feet.

"You're such an asshole," she said and charged off back toward the beach.

Then she turned around and yelled back, "How can you be such an idiot!"

Peter didn't know what to say. She was mad he let her do that to him. She knew he could have stopped her, but he didn't. She'll never forgive him for that.

Peter went on to get mucus from dead jelly worms. He took deep breaths, trying to keep the calm smile on his face. He was looking forward to their adventure on the sea.

But Zana did not let the event slide from her mind so easily.

As she walked in the opposite direction, back toward the beach, she hissed and spit at the thoughts racing through her mind. She squeezed her thumb into the tender area in the center of her wrist, causing a shooting pain to rip through her arm.

"What the hell's wrong with him?" Zana said. "He thinks he can comfort me after what he did."

She hit the side of her head, trying to forget what just happened, trying to figure out a way to remember the experience differently. But then her nerves quivered and her mind cleared. She felt as if she were no longer alone.

Up ahead, there was something on the path. Leaning over the hole they had passed on the way into the jungle, a man was standing there. Zana froze in her tracks and looked again. It wasn't exactly a man. It was some kind of creature, an insect-like lizard with four arms and red eyes.

The thing hadn't seen her yet. She ducked into the bushes and observed it more carefully. It looked deranged and angry. Its mandibles clicked back and forth, as it peered into the pit at its feet. Zana had no idea where the thing had come from, but she knew it most likely lived underground. It had probably been under their feet the entire time they'd been on the island, only now coming out after the tidal wave destroyed its home.

The thing didn't look very friendly. Zana backed up. She had to get to Peter. They had to get off the island immediately. The thing looked up just as Zana stepped back onto the path. Its red eyes glared at her. Then it shrieked like a howling wolf.

Zana raced down the path toward Peter. The thing came after her. It used its hands to run faster, as if it were some kind of insectoid gorilla charging after Zana on all six limbs.

"Peter!" she screamed, but he was too far ahead to hear.

If she could have gotten over the next hill, she would have been able to see Peter in the valley with the jelly worm corpses. He would have been able to see what was after her and come to her rescue. But she couldn't go over the hill. There were three more creatures stepping out of the jungle, blocking her path.

Zana turned to run into the jungle but there was another creature coming at her from the side, and another from her other side. She was closed in.

"Peter!" she screamed at the top of her lungs, but the echo of her voice ricocheted in the wrong direction.

The creatures circled Zana like wolves, growling and gnashing their insect jaws at her. Their eyes were bloodshot. They were like mad demons.

Zana didn't know what to do. She couldn't outrun them. She wasn't armed and couldn't fight them.

The six creatures howled into the sky. Their voices like the high-pitched screeches of bats.

"Peter, where are you!" she called at the top of her lungs.

Then she began to cry and fell to her knees.

"Motherfucker," she yelled at him. "You asshole!"

She punched the ground. Then she threw sand at the closest creature, trying to blind it. The thing backed away.

The six insect men just circled Zana like sharks, but they did not attack. It was as if they were waiting for something.

"Peter!"

Then she saw what they were waiting for. It was the alpha. It was standard pack animal behavior to allow the alpha to eat first. The creature was twice the size of the others. A female. Zana looked up at the powerful creature as it slowly crept toward her. The muscles of her four arms were like those of a bodybuilder, pulsing beneath her green exoskeleton. Her mandibles were so large they could easily have decapitated any of the males surrounding her.

"Peter!" Zana cried.

Her voice was becoming hoarse from yelling so loud. The next time she tried to yell, hardly anything came out. Her vocal chords were damaged.

The alpha roared. Then it lunged at Zana and collapsed on the ground in front of her.

Zana looked up. Peter was standing in front of her with his elbow pointed upward. Like a Muay Thai kickboxer, he had planted his elbow into the back of the creature's skull and knocked it unconscious.

"Get back," Peter yelled.

Zana crawled into the jungle as all six of the creatures came at him. He used their limbs to toss them into each other, then jabbed their faces so hard their exoskeletons cracked.

As Peter fought the creatures, Zana ran away, abandoning him to take care of them. She couldn't help him anyway. She had to find someplace safe, just in case he lost. She wouldn't stand a chance against them on her own.

So she ran aimlessly through the swamp of blue algae and didn't look back. There was nothing else she could do.

Zana charged through the hills of the island, her bare feet breaking open against the rocks she trampled. The acid in the soil burned skin away from the inner arches of her feet.

Thirty minutes of running and still no place felt safe to hide. There was movement in the trees behind her. She looked back to see one of the creatures coming after her. It was a smaller one, perhaps an omega who had been cast out of the main pack. It was missing three of its arms, but the one remaining had claws sharp enough to tear her throat open if it got within reach.

Down in the valley, Zana saw something glitter in the sunlight. She didn't know what it was. She just went for it. Behind her, the creature was no longer in sight, but she could still hear its hungry shrieks.

When she got to the bottom of the hill, she saw what had been reflecting the light. It was the cone-shaped spaceship, the one that had washed away with the tidal wave. It was in ruins, twisted around the rock face of a small mountain. She ducked inside. The green light was still shining within. The thing still had power.

Her eyes darted across the vessel, looking for a way to close the door of the ship. The door was bent open. There was no way to block it.

The creature shrieked as it came into the clearing near the ship. It was too late for her to get out of there. She was trapped inside. Her only chance was to find a good hiding spot.

In the cockpit, Zana tripped over Morgan's half-eaten corpse. When she looked back at him, she had to cover her mouth to stop herself from screaming. Then she had to keep covering her mouth so she didn't vomit at the sight of his body.

The meat on his legs was missing, as if he'd been gnawed on all the way to the bone. His stomach was sliced open and his intestines were hanging out. His face and arms were also heavily chewed upon. He obviously didn't die in the tsunami.

The creature stalked the area outside of the ship, snarling and sniffing out Zana's trail. She saw a lance on the ground near Morgan's body. It was bent like a meat hook, but could still be used as a weapon.

As she bent down to get it, Morgan grabbed her wrist and squeezed it tightly. Zana stepped back, nearly screaming. She looked Morgan in the eyes. He was staring up at her. He was still alive.

Morgan continued holding her wrist and listened to the creature as it snarled and wheezed.

"They're called Acriditoids," Morgan whispered. His nose and lower lip were missing, which made it difficult for Zana to look at him as he spoke. "They're the descendants of the aliens who came here on this ship. The chemicals in the atmosphere made them go insane, turned them into animals."

He released Zana's hand. She held the bent lance and ducked, getting closer to him as if the half-dead man was some kind of protection.

"What happened to you?" Zana asked.

"Those things out there have been feeding on me for the past couple of days," Morgan said. "They must have smelled my open wounds."

She looked around the ship.

"What about the others?" she asked. "Is Adam still alive?"

Morgan chuckled quietly.

"He's been feeding on me too," Morgan said.

The Acriditoid outside shrieked. Then there were three more shrieks in the hills around them, as if answering its call. More of them were coming.

"We're surrounded," Zana said, holding the lance tightly.

Morgan lifted his finger and pointed at a control panel. The finger was mostly just bone poking out of dead flesh.

"There's a way," he said. "Activate the automated defense system. It'll kill anything that comes near the ship."

"How?" Zana asked.

"I'll instruct you," he said.

Zana looked over at the control panel and back at Morgan. She heard the area outside the ship crawling with those shrieking abominations. She wondered if she'd be able to get it working in time.

After Zana got the defenses up and running, she heard the creatures outside screaming as beams of gray light fired across the landscape like a volley of liquid metal arrows. She looked out the doorway to see two of the creatures impaled by lances. One of them was fleeing into the trees. But the omega was still standing there, staring at Zana. It was not moving. The ship could not detect it.

The omega ran for the entrance and Zana backed away. All the lances fired at it, but missed as it charged full speed into the ship.

The creature crashed into the wall of the inner cargo hold, then turned back to Zana. It snarled and gnashed its mandibles as it crept forward. Upon closer examination, what scared Zana the most was the creature's eyes. Although they were tinted red, they looked so human. She felt as if there was a man hiding behind that insect exoskeleton.

As the omega attacked, Zana tripped backward. Its one remaining arm swiped at the air, missing her. She buried the hook-shaped lance in its belly. Then she pried open its shell like cracking the meat out of a lobster. It fell to the ground, convulsing in a seizure as its stringy meat dangled from its abdomen. Zana watched as it died slowly at her feet.

When she went back to Morgan, she noticed he was having trouble keeping his eyes from rolling to the back of his head.

"You have to save her," Morgan said.

He still whispered even though the Acriditoids were gone. "Who?"

"The girl, Jill," Morgan said, trying to hold on. "Adam's gone completely insane. He isn't human anymore."

He paused as air fell from his lungs.

"You have to save her from him," he said. "He's been raping her. He said he would cut her up for meat if he had to."

"Peter built another raft and we plan to get off this island today," Zana said. "I'll make sure the two of you come with us."

Morgan shook his head.

"Not me," Morgan said. "Just Jill."

He took the lance from Zana.

"I'm already dead," he said.

Then he cut his own throat and bled out before Zana could say another word.

Zana turned off the defense system and stepped outside. She grabbed two lances that were sticking out of the dead Acriditoids and went up the hill in search of Jill and Adam.

There was another alien corpse on the hillside, but it wasn't killed by the ship's defenses. It looked like it had been impaled several times. Then its head was bashed in with a rock. Some of its flesh had been eaten away. A few feet from the body, the meat was in a pile where it had been puked up.

She heard shouting at the top of the hill. Adam was yelling at the top of his lungs. He held a lance in his hands, fighting off two Acriditoids who were trying to flank him.

"I'm not going with you," he yelled at them. "Send all the demons you want. I'm not giving up!"

Although it sounded like Adam, the man fighting off the aliens did not look like him any longer. He looked more like a living skeleton. Half of his face had been burned away by acid, his clothes were shredded rags. Zana was terrified by the sight of him. Morgan was right. Adam was no longer human.

Zana zoomed her eyes into the shelter and saw Jill lying within. The girl was covered in blood and wasn't moving. Zana knew she had to get her out of there. She had to get her away from that monstrous man.

"Let her out of there, asshole," Zana told the owner of the brothel.

A new girl named Gillian, an 18-year-old from Scottsdale, Arizona, was locked in a room in the attic. Although Zana didn't know the girl very well, she didn't like the way she was being treated.

"First of all, you're getting fined a hundred bucks for calling me an asshole," said the owner. "Second of all, it's none of your fucking business."

"You can't just lock her up in a room like a damned prisoner," Zana said.

The owner looked up from his desk. "Officer Croc thinks she's too fat. He wanted us to put her on a diet."

"So?" Zana said.

"She refused," the owner said. "So we locked her up and put her on a fast."

"You're starving her against her will?" Zana said.

"She could lose a few pounds," said the owner. "It's not going to kill her."

Zana left the office and met with a few of the other girls in the hallway. She told them the story.

"We need to get her some food," Zana said.

The girls broke eye contact with her.

"You shouldn't get involved," Yamaya told her.

"I can't just sit back and let it happen," Zana said.

"Next time it's going to be you locked in the room," Yamaya said.

Zana flipped her off and left the hallway.

It had been two weeks and they were still starving the girl. She only received glasses of water through the bars on the door. She also got some vitamins and fiber pills, but she didn't take any of the vitamin C because she said it made her empty stomach burn.

"Here," Zana said, yelling up to the attic window from outside the brothel.

Zana tossed granola bars through the window. The girl looked down at Zana. She threw the food back down.

"You're going to get me into trouble," the girl said.

Then she went back inside.

But Zana wasn't going to give up. She decided she was going to save that girl. She couldn't let their asshole boss do that to her.

Zana crawled up the side of the hill, watching Adam and the two aliens carefully. He stabbed one of them in the stomach, but the other slashed him across the back. Whoever won the fight, Adam or the creatures, would quickly discover Zana and come after her. She had to be fast.

She ran up the hill toward the shelter and ducked inside. The girl was unconscious. Rotten jelly worm skin covered her like a blanket.

"It's okay," Zana said. "I'm going to get you out of here."

The girl's eyes opened and looked up at Zana. She blinked weakly.

"We have a raft on the other side of the island," Zana said. "We're leaving right now."

"Let me die," Jill said.

"I'm not leaving without you," Zana said.

Zana pulled the blanket away and the reason the girl wanted to die became very clear. She looked over to her right, outside of the shelter, and saw the bones lying in a pile. She saw strips of meat hanging from tree branches, being dried in the sun to be preserved like beef jerky.

Then she looked back at Jill's body. Both of her arms and both of her legs had been amputated by the crazed man. He had been feeding on her just as he fed on Morgan.

Jill looked up at Zana and smiled.

"Let me die," she repeated.

Zana looked down at Gillian's body as Officer Croc tightened his belt.

"What the hell did you do?" Zana said.

She had come to the girl's room when she heard the screaming. But when she arrived, it was too late. The cop had killed her.

"I guess I was too much man for her," said Officer Croc, looking back at Zana with a blistered smile. "Her heart gave out on her."

Zana got into his face.

"Her heart gave out because you had my idiot boss starve her for the past five weeks," she said.

"I didn't tell him to do anything," said Officer Croc. "I just told him the bitch was too fat."

"It was baby fat," Zana said. "She was still just a kid."

"She's not anything anymore," said the cop.

"You're not getting away with this, motherfucker," Zana said.

Officer Croc finished buttoning his shirt and then faced her. Then lunged at Zana and grabbed her by the throat.

"I can get away with whatever I want," he said. "Because I'm the law. And you're all just a bunch of whores."

He tossed her to the ground.

"You're just meat," said Officer Croc. "Nothing more."

The cop left Zana with the body. She looked down at the dead girl and held her hand over her mouth. It was her fault the kid was dead. She promised herself she would save the girl but she did nothing. In the end, she was as useless as the other women. The girl's death was dismissed as an accident, and officially, the disgusting cop who killed her didn't even visit the brothel that day.

Zana wanted to get the truth out about what happened, but was worried nobody would listen. She knew nobody would be on her side.

But this time she wasn't going to just let another girl die. Even though Jill was already severely crippled by the three-armed man, Zana was going to save her life.

She rolled Jill onto her back and used the putrid worm skin to tie her into place, the girl's arm stumps hanging over Zana's shoulder.

With the two lances holding the skin tight against her chest, Zana lifted the girl up and carried her out of the shelter. She was hunched over, trying to balance Jill on top of her. Even though the girl had no arms or legs, she was still incredibly heavy.

Zana looked back at Adam and met his eyes. He was stabbing the last of the Acriditoids through the head with his lance when he saw them.

"Where the hell did you come from?" he yelled at Zana

from across the hill.

Zana turned and ran as fast as she could with Jill on her back.

Adam pulled his lance from the dead alien and charged across the hill toward her. Even though he was staggering on skeletal legs, he was still faster than Zana with the girl on her back.

"Get back here," he yelled.

But Zana wouldn't stop. She ran down the hill into valley. The sun was beginning to go down. The jungle was getting dark.

She couldn't let anything happen to the girl. Not this time. She wasn't going to let him hurt her anymore.

"Fucking bitches," Adam yelled. "Get back here, you bitches."

Zana tried to lose him in the jungle, but he was too close and her strength was giving out on her. The adrenalin wasn't enough to keep her going anymore. Malnourishment slowed her down.

She hid Jill under some fallen trees and then raised a lance like a sword. She was going to have to fight him. Hopefully, he was in an even weaker state than she was.

After what Officer Croc did to the young girl, Zana couldn't just let him get away with it. He had been torturing the women in that establishment for too long. He had to be stopped.

She knew she couldn't find a legal way to make the cop pay for his crimes. She was going to have to take him out somehow and make it look like an accident. There was one method she could think of. It would be perfect retribution for what happened to the girl. Zana just didn't know if the method would make the cop suffer enough. The next time Officer Croc came to the lineup, he chose Zana right away. He didn't like the way Zana had stood up to him after the girl had the heart attack.

"It's time to teach you another lesson," the cop said to her. "And this time you better learn it good."

Zana smiled. She took him in her arm and escorted him up to her bedroom.

"This time I'm not playing any games," he told Zana.

He held out a pair of handcuffs.

"Put these on," he said, and then tossed them at her.

"No," Zana said and threw them aside.

He came at her and slapped her across the face.

"Go ahead and struggle," he said. "I get mean when you struggle."

As he leaned down to pick up the handcuffs, Zana slammed something into his neck. He stood up and looked at her. A syringe was sticking out of him.

"Fucking bitch," he said.

His voice was soft from the shock of being stabbed in the neck. He pulled out the syringe and looked at it.

"What the hell was in here?" he said, his voice shivering. "What the hell did you do to me?"

Zana smiled. He was scared. She couldn't believe she actually got to see him scared.

"Nothing," she said. "Nothing at all."

Officer Croc sniffed at the syringe. There was no trace of any chemical.

"Just air," Zana said.

The cop didn't know what to do. He sat down, sweat pouring down his neck.

"The air bubble is traveling farther through your veins every second," Zana said. "The moment it reaches your heart, you will lose a beat. You will have a heart attack and you will die. Just like the girl you murdered."

He searched his body, as if looking for the air bubble.

"And nobody will know what happened," Zana said. "They'll just believe you had an ordinary heart attack. It's an open and shut case. A guy your age found dead with a prostitute.

Obviously, your poor elderly heart just couldn't take it."

When Adam staggered toward Zana, she was swinging her lance in the air like a samurai. She didn't know the first thing about fighting with a sword, but she was good at baton-twirling and thought she might be able to intimidate him.

"Where's my meat?" Adam said.

"You mean the girl?" Zana said. "She's in a safe place. Away from you."

He growled at her.

"You'll be my new meat," Adam said, he spoke like a monstrous Neanderthal.

"The only thing I'll be is your executioner unless you get lost," Zana said.

She finished twirling her blade and pointed it at him.

"Come near me and you die," Zana said.

"No," Adam said. "You die."

He charged her.

She pulled the blade back, holding it like a baseball bat. She was ready to swing it at the deranged zombie and chop his fucking head off.

"You're nothing but meat!" Adam yelled.

And as he yelled that, Zana's mind snapped.

It was no longer Adam charging her.

It was Officer Croc.

"You can't kill me," said the dying policeman, standing up from the bed. "You think Officer Croc can be killed by a worthless bitch like you?"

He faced her.

"You're nothing but meat," he said.

Zana ran for the door. She didn't know how long it took

for the air to get to his heart, but didn't want to be around him during his final moments.

Officer Crocodile pulled out his gun and fired. Zana crouched down as she jumped through the door. The bullet hit only inches above her head.

"How about one more blow job for the road?" he yelled.

He stepped out into the hallway and fired again. Zana ducked around a corner.

The brothel owner's wife stepped out of her room, wondering what the hell was going on.

"What's wrong?" she asked Croc.

"Bitches are getting murdered," said the officer.

He planted a bullet through her forehead, between her stretched eyebrows. Her rock-hard breasts didn't even bounce as her lifeless body hit the floor.

Officer Croc stepped over her and walked on, casually strolling down the hallways, searching for the bitch he needed to see dead before he breathed his last breath.

Zana lowered her sword into Adam's grotesque face, but he did not die. She looked down to see the blade had been stopped by his third arm. The dead hunk of rotting flesh was used like a shield.

"You're dead now, bitch," said Officer Croc through Adam's lips.

He twisted her wrist backward until she let go of the lance and punched her in the stomach. She fell to her knees. The blade was still hanging out of his third arm as he kicked her in the back. A shooting pain went up her spine and she twisted against the ground, jerking like a spastic.

"There you go acting tough again," said Officer Croc inside of Zana's head. "Didn't I tell you strong women don't really exist?"

He kicked her again.

Officer Crocodile walked down the stairs and fired at three of the women standing in the lobby. Two of them ran for safety, but he nailed the third one in the leg. Then he shot down the muscle-bound bouncer by the front door.

The owner of the brothel came out of his office and said, "What are you doing? Have you gone mad?"

Croc shot him twice in the chest.

"I've always been mad," said Croc. "It's part of my endearing charm."

When he saw Zana trying to escape through the back door, he shot the doorknob out of her hand.

"I'll be fucking you one last time," said Croc, raising his pistol. "I've got a hot metal slug just dying to enter you."

Adam grabbed Zana by the hair and pulled her back to her feet. He wrapped his fingers around her throat, crushing her voice box with all his strength.

"Why do you keep haunting me, you bitch?" he yelled in Zana's face.

Zana opened her mouth to speak, but somebody else's voice seemed to come out. Her real voice was confined by his stranglehold.

"Because I love you," she found herself saying.

Then Zana kicked him in the chest, breaking his grip on her neck.

"Come to me," her voice said.

As Adam fell away from her, his third arm whipped through the air. It was as if it had come to life for a brief moment, reaching up to embrace him. The lance that had been skewered into his wife's dead arm snapped free of the rotten flesh. It was driven deep into Adam's chest, between his ribs, through his blackened smoker's lungs.

He landed on his back and wheezed, coughing blood out of his skull-like face. His wife's dead arm hugged his body, pressing the blade deeper into his organs.

"It's time to go," Zana heard herself saying. "There's nothing left for us here."

And the three-armed man closed his eyes, releasing a long, last blood-bubbling breath.

Croc fired the weapon into the floor. His aim faltered as his heart crumpled up inside his chest. He dropped the gun and fell backward.

As the cop lay dying on the floor of the brothel, all the women gathered around him. They stared down at him with blank faces, watching carefully while the life slipped out of his eyes.

"What are you cunts looking at?" Croc said, as his vision went blurry. "You think you're too good for me?"

Zana stood over his body and looked down at him, making sure she was the last thing he'd see before he died.

"You're nothing," said the cop. "The only thing you're good for is filling that stinky hole between your legs."

Zana laughed.

"I'm sorry, did you say something?" she asked. "I was busy thinking about how pathetic you're going to appear once your friends and relatives learn you died of heart failure in a whore house with your dick in your hands."

The cop called her a bitch one last time with his dying breath.

"The scum of the Earth," Zana said to his body and stepped away. "There's no lower life form on this planet than a man like that."

She passed the owner of the brothel on her way back up the stairs.

"I quit," she told him, as he writhed on the ground, trying

to hold the blood inside his body.

The authorities tried to cover up the cop's death as much as they could. They never suspected foul play on Zana's part. They were too busy trying to save face for having one of their senior officers shoot up the local brothel, killing three people and wounding one more.

Zana didn't actually murder him, anyway. It turned out that the whole death by an oxygen-filled syringe is more of a movie myth than a reality. Officer Croc died of a genuine heart attack, caused by his own murderous rampage.

Even though she told her boss she quit, Zana didn't actually stop working at the brothel. The rotten bastard ended up dying in the hospital from his gunshot wounds a few hours after the incident. The brothel was left to his younger brother—a conservative family man who wanted nothing to do with his seedy older brother's whorehouse.

It was actually Yamaya who cut the deal with the brother. She proposed that the women run the brothel for him. The women would do all the work and he would get a cut of the profits. He would never have to step foot in the place again. It was a deal that made everyone happy.

So Zana stayed on as a prostitute and helped Yamaya turn the business into a respectable establishment, one that women would feel safe to work in.

Eventually, Zana's career was much more like the one she originally wanted. She had control over her own life. There were no longer strict rules or fines. She was able to charge whatever she wanted and put much of what she earned into savings. She was able to keep her puppy flowers big and beautiful. She didn't even have to live at the brothel anymore, so she got her own apartment a few miles away, only working a few hours a week.

Every once in a while, she encountered assholes like Officer Crocodile, but she just tried to block out the bad times and focus only on the good.

When Zana's mother finally figured out what her daughter

was doing for a living, she asked her how the hell she could do it and still live with herself.

"You're always getting fucked no matter what job in life you choose," Zana told her. "It's just that with my chosen profession I get fucked literally as well as figuratively."

Then Zana would laugh and cry at exactly the same time.

CHAPTER TWELVE
PIRATE PLANET

Peter ran through the jungle. Three of those creatures were coming after him, including the alpha. No matter how many times he hit those things, they kept getting up and fighting. Their skin was too hard. Their insides were too flexible. He couldn't seem to do much damage to them no matter how hard his punches.

So he gave up and went into the hills to search for Zana. He knew a few of those things had gotten away from him and chased after her. He hoped she was all right.

He called out to her as he ran, but it only lured more of those creatures to him. The sky was getting dark. He didn't have much time.

"I'm not leaving this island without you," he said to the path in front of him. "No matter what."

Peter found the spaceship and some alien corpses impaled by silver beams. The aliens coming after him screeched even louder, as if they smelled their dead family members and believed Peter had something to do with it.

"Which way, Captain Bearbeard?" Peter asked the teddy bear.

Captain Bearbeard pointed at a path off to the left, through the valley. Peter decided to trust his companion and go that way.

"You were right," Peter said to the teddy bear, as he saw Zana up ahead.

She was standing over a dead body.

"Peter?" she asked when she looked up at him.

Peter waved as he came closer.

"We need to get off this island," he said. "Let's go."

She pointed at a pile of fallen timber.

"We need to get Jill," Zana said.

271

"She's still alive?"

They went to her. She was barely conscious. Zana strapped her to his back.

"I told you others were still alive," Peter said with a smile, totally oblivious to the fact the girl was missing her arms and legs.

"Morgan and Adam were still alive as well," she said. She pointed to Adam's body. "Not anymore."

"Let's go," Peter said.

Zana nodded and they went off into the dark jungle toward the beach.

The Acriditoids shrieked as they ran after them. Peter grabbed his sack of extra jelly worm mucus on the way and tied it to Zana's wrist.

"What are you doing?" Zana asked.

Peter saluted her.

"Get to the raft and rub this stuff all over yourselves," Peter said. "We'll hold them off."

"What?" Zana said.

"Get the raft in the water," Peter said. "Use the mucus sacks as shoes when shoving off. Be ready to leave without me if you have to."

"We can't leave without you," she said.

"Just get the raft in the water and stay near the shoreline. If I'm not there in ten minutes I'm probably dead."

"Wait a minute."

But Peter was off, running in the other direction.

He found a good clearing and waited for them. There were more than three now. It sounded like five. The Acriditoids must have bred like rabbits in the caves under this island. Only three were in the ship that crashed here originally, separated from the rest of the fleet on the mainland. They must have had nothing better to do than mate for the past eight decades.

Peter got into a fighting stance, ready to take on the lot of them. Captain Bearbeard was also prepared.

"You ready?" Peter asked the teddy bear.

Captain Bearbeard nodded its fluffy head and focused its beady eyes on the shadows beyond the trees.

"Then let's kick some alien butt," Peter said.

Their red glowing eyes were the first thing Peter saw as they came out of the darkness. They shrieked and opened their mandibles, ready to taste human flesh.

"Now," Peter said.

Peter kicked one in the chest so hard it crashed against a tree. Then he axed one in the throat and daggered one in the side of its abdomen.

Captain Bearbeard did flips through the air and head-butted the one that jumped them from behind.

Peter kneed one in the face. Then he leg-swiped another and elbowed it on the way to the ground.

"The scurvy dogs were no match for us," Peter said.

Four aliens were lying in the dirt beneath them, all knocked unconscious or rolling in pain. Peter gave Captain Bearbeard a pirate salute. The teddy bear gave him a thumbs-up.

Then the alpha appeared in the back, coming out of the shadows. It growled and roared. The thing was the size of a massive gorilla and probably twice as strong.

Captain Bearbeard wiped off his fur and stepped forward, getting into a kung-fu fighting pose. He was planning to drop-kick the monster's head clean off.

"Forget it," Peter said, picking up the teddy bear. "Let's get out of here."

The alpha hissed and gnashed as it tailed them through the jungle onto the beach. As Peter raced across the cocaine-white sand, kicking powder into the air, he saw Zana up ahead. She was still pushing the raft into the sea, worried about the acid splashing onto her legs even though she had a thick coat of mucus covering her.

"Get it in the water," Peter yelled. "Quick."

When Zana saw the alpha coming, the acid didn't seem quite as frightening. She stomped into the water, pushing the inflated raft into the sea and then jumped inside. Jill was in the center, beneath the tarp, inside of a worm skin bag that enveloped all but her face.

When he got to the shoreline, Peter tossed Captain Bearbeard into the boat. Then he turned around. The creature spread out all four of its arms, extending razor sharp claws.

Without protection, Peter jumped into the ocean. His toes splashed a little into the water, but he leapt the rest of the way through the air into the raft. He landed on the edge, dangling off the side. Zana had to pull him in before the next wave knocked him over.

Peter quickly went to the sail and opened it up. A gust of wind grabbed them, pulling them away from the beach.

Zana and Peter looked back.

The alpha didn't stop its pursuit. It entered the water and swam after them.

"It's still coming?" Peter asked.

The thing was even faster in the water than on land. Its four arms pumped like paddles. It was as if it were flying through the water, faster than a shark.

"It's resistant to the acid?" Zana said.

The wind pulled the raft farther away from the beach, but the creature continued pursuing them. It swam harder and faster until it reached the edge of the boat. Only inches away from the side, the thing slipped under the surface. Then it raised a claw out to swipe at them, going for Peter's neck.

But before it could touch anything, the appendage dissolved in the air. Its exoskeleton fell apart, revealing fizzing hollow insides that had already melted away.

"Nope," Peter said. "Guess not."

They watched as its body became liquid beneath the waves. If the thing would have gotten to them a couple of seconds sooner, the creature could have ripped open the inflated raft with its claws and taken all three of them with it. But luck was on Peter's side.

"Quick," Peter said, rubbing mucus all over his body. "Raise the tarp. We're headed into the larger waves."

With the entire raft covered in worm skin and mucus, the acid could not penetrate their protective covering. They were like a giant tapeworm sailing inside of a massive stomach, completely protected by their outer casing.

Once they made it past the breakers, the ocean was calm. Zana was able to peek out of their skin roof and follow the stars.

"We'll be there by morning at the latest," Zana said. "If we don't hit land by then it means we'll be lost at sea for good."

"I'm sure we'll make it," Peter said.

"I wouldn't be so sure," Zana said. "This planet is moving through space. That means the locations of the stars in the sky are moving as well. I might not be able to accurately follow them. They might lead us in the wrong direction."

"Do your best," Peter said. "I'm sure you'll figure it out."

Peter went to check on Jill. She was shaking and trembling. She had a fever and most likely an infection. It was too dark in the raft for Peter to examine her properly, but he was sure Adam didn't sterilize his tools when he severed the limbs from her body. If her fever was from infection then she didn't have a lot of time.

"You think the people at the Citysphere left behind medical supplies?" Peter asked.

Zana shrugged. "I'm sure it would be cheaper just to leave all of the supplies they didn't use than try to transport it all back. There's probably plenty of food, water, and medical equipment left behind."

"And electricity too, right?"

"The place was wave-powered," Zana said. "We'll at least have power for as long as the generators are operable."

"Maybe we'll even be able to contact Earth," Peter said.

Zana nodded. "It's too late for them to come rescue us, but it would be nice to be able to hear from my mom one last time."

Peter agreed. He rubbed Jill's forehead and smiled down on her. Even though she was in such bad shape, he was glad she was still alive.

"You're a hero, you know?" Peter said to Zana.

Zana noticed he was talking about how she saved Jill. She smiled back at him for a second, but then the smile fell from her face. She broke eye contact.

"I'm no hero," she said, looking down at her toes. "I've done horrible things to people. I've done horrible things to you."

Peter's appreciation didn't falter.

"Everyone does horrible things from time to time," he said. "But a true hero will still help people despite the horrible things they've done."

Zana shook her head and breathed her hair out of her face.

The horizon in the direction they traveled was glowing, all lit up. Though they couldn't see it yet, there was light emanating from the glass dome of the Citysphere. It was like a paradise in the middle of a wasteland. A Garden of Eden.

"They left the light on for us," Peter said.

He pointed at the glowing horizon.

"Just keep heading in that direction and we'll be okay," he said.

The closer they came to the mainland, the brighter the sky became and the brighter the smiles glowed on their faces.

Peter hugged Captain Bearbeard to his chest.

"So how'd you enjoy your adventure, Captain Bearbeard?" Peter said to his teddy bear. "Was it full of mysteries and danger? Did you find lots of booty and buried treasure?"

He patted the teddy bear on the head.

"Yeah, me too," Peter said.

Zana looked at him and chuckled.

"You're a weird kid," Zana said. "What's with you anyway?"

"What do you mean?"

"You're always seeing the world in a different way than everyone else," she said. "You're always so positive."

Peter shrugged.

"Everyone else on that island went insane," Zana said. "But not you. No matter what happened, you managed to stay completely sane the entire time, didn't you?"

Peter nodded.

"That's right," he said. "I haven't gone crazy at all."

Then he looked at his teddy bear.

"Neither have I," said Captain Bearbeard.

They both nodded at her.

It might not have seemed like it to anyone else, but the toxic atmosphere affected Peter just as much as it had Zana and Adam. But unlike the two of them, he embraced the madness. His delusions made him happier, stronger.

"I know the treasure is around here somewhere," Peter said several days ago, as he was hiking through the jungle on the island. "Consult the map, Captain Bearbeard."

The teddy bear looked at the map and scanned it with his fluffy paw.

"Over there, me matey," said Captain Bearbeard.

They came to a spot in the sand.

"So who wants to dig first?" Peter asked.

"Arrgh, not me," said Captain Bearbeard. "Me belly's too full of grog."

277

Peter's little brother, Louie, stepped forward.

"I'll do it," Louie said, carrying a shovel over his shoulder.

Peter stared at his little brother as he walked across the cocaine-white sand, his pirate hat too big for his head. Peter just smiled at him, watching his brother pretend to be a pirate as he always used to do.

"Good job, lad," said Captain Bearbeard. "Dig right there."

The teddy bear pointed at the dirt.

"Aye-aye Captain," Louie said, digging into the sand with his shovel.

As they pulled out a chest full of magical gems and jewels, Louie looked up at his brother with a face brighter than Christmas.

"I told you," Peter told his brother. "There's treasure buried everywhere here."

Peter wiped sand from his eyelashes like crusty dried-up tears as he watched his brother stuffing the loot into a sack.

"This is what they call a pirate planet," Peter said. "It's where all the space pirates in the galaxy come to hide their treasure."

"Let's find more!" Louie said.

"Relax, me lad," said Captain Bearbeard. "We have plenty of time to search for booty. For now, let's toast to a job well done."

The teddy bear raised his tiny bottle of rum and took a drink.

"Aye aye, Captain," Louie said.

Peter smiled and raised a pretend bottle of rum.

"Aye aye, Captain," he said.

Then he took a swig of the imaginary liquor. When he lowered his fist, the beach was empty. The teddy bear was lying in the dirt. There was no hole, no shovel, no treasure, no Louie.

But Peter smiled anyway, because he knew he would see his little brother again. It was the fifth time he got to spend time with Louie since he arrived on the island. He hoped the longer he stayed on the planet, the longer he would get to spend time with him.

Picking the teddy bear out of the sand and slipping him into his belt, Peter walked back down the shoreline toward the raft. He still had a long way to go before it was finished. As he walked, Peter whistled a pirate song beneath the sound of the crashing acid waves.

Peter stopped whistling and sang in a deep pirate voice, "Yo ho ho and a bottle of rum."

Then he felt his little brother take him by the hand. When Peter looked, he didn't see anyone standing there with him. So he kept his eyes forward, strolling along the shoreline, pretending he was with his brother until he felt Louie's tiny hand dissipate within his grasp.

They couldn't see the mainland yet, but the light on the horizon was much brighter. It also appeared that morning was coming, even though the sun was not yet in the sky.

"What's that?" Zana asked, pointing up into the clouds.

Peter looked up. There was something in the air.

"Is it a ship of some kind?" Zana said. "It looks like a kite."

When they got closer, Peter could make out what it was.

"It's a cow," Peter said.

Peter pointed and Zana squinted her eyes.

Hovering about sixty feet in the air, there was a cow.

"What's it doing up there?"

It wasn't moving. It seemed frozen in midair.

"It looks like it's see-through," Peter said.

Zana noticed it too. The cow was transparent. She could see through its body to the clouds on the other side. But the closer their raft sailed to it, the less transparent it became.

Once the cow was completely solid, it fell from the sky.

Peter and Zana watched as the cow plummeted. It made a loud *mooooooooooooooooooooooo!* sound on its way down. Then it splashed into the sea.

"What the hell was that?" Zana said.

When they arrived to the cow, it was just a bubbling carcass in the acid. Then the water calmed.

"I think we're going insane," Zana said.

Captain Bearbeard agreed.

Something else caught Peter's attention. It was even stranger than the cow that fell from the sky. It didn't make any sense to him at all. There was a building on a small island in front of them.

"Is that what I think it is?" Peter asked.

Zana looked up at the sign.

"It is," Zana said. "Holy shit. It's a Taco Bell!"

On the small island in front of them, in the middle of the Taco Bell Ocean, was the fast food franchise of the same name.

"Want to go through the drive-thru?" Peter said.

They all laughed. Captain Bearbeard said he wanted a meximelt.

The island was just large enough for the building. It was more of a large rock than an island. They carefully pulled their raft onto the shore and climbed up the steep face toward the entrance of the restaurant.

"Do you think they put it here for promotional reasons?" Peter asked. "Because of the name of the ocean?"

Zana shrugged.

"Maybe tourist groups came by here on hovercrafts," Zana said. "The drive-thru is on the water. Maybe people could even order food here."

Inside, the place was dark and empty. They tried the lights but they didn't turn on.

"No power?" Peter asked. "How did they cook their food with no power?"

"They probably turned the generator off," Zana said.

Peter looked in the back for a generator but there was no sign of one. The place was too dark for him to see properly though. When they opened the large walk-in refrigerator, the place reeked of rancid food. It was still packed with meat and vegetables, but all of it had gone bad already. They closed the door back up again.

The pantry contained a lot of food that was still edible, from slightly stale tortillas to cans of beans.

"We should take all of this stuff with us," Zana said. "Who knows how much we'll need."

They filled milk crates with packaged food and piled them in the center of the dining area by the entrance. Tortillas dangled from Peter's mouth as he worked.

"Maybe we should just stay here for a while," Zana said. "We can rest up, regain our strength. The Citysphere can wait a day or two."

Peter shook his head.

"Maybe the Citysphere can wait," Peter said. "But Jill can't. We need to get her antibiotics immediately."

Zana frowned but completely agreed.

On the way out the door, they heard sounds coming from the dark corners of the Taco Bell. The sound of a crying baby echoed through the deserted building. Peter looked around the room for it, but could find nothing. They could still hear its wails resonating with the wind as they sailed off toward the mainland.

"There it is," Peter said, as the continent came into view. "The biggest piece of land on this planet and it's all ours."

The sun was up and so the light of the Citysphere no longer dominated the sky. They were going to have to search the coastline for it.

"Hang on, Jill," Zana said.

The girl's head was in her lap.

"The waves are going to get bumpy on the way in," Peter said. "Brace yourselves."

"We want to get as close to the Citysphere as possible for Jill's sake," Zana said. "Keep an eye out for it."

"We can't," Peter said, tightening up the skin over their

heads. "It's too dangerous."

"But we could end up miles away from the place," Zana said. "We can't carry Jill that far."

"Maybe we'll get lucky," Peter said.

He rubbed jelly worm slime all over his body and face, and then passed the bag on to Zana. She applied the stuff to Jill first, staring down at the shivering girl with a worried face.

When they took their last look out of the raft before sealing up the tarp, they saw just how large the waves were in front of them. It wasn't the distance from the Citysphere that Zana had to worry about; it was getting their raft flipped over on one of those massive waves of acid.

The waves tossed them back and forth on their way to the rocky shore. The raft hit air on several occasions, tossing them out of their seats, knocking them into each other. The jelly worm skin roof was the only thing keeping them inside.

Zana puked outside of the protective bag she was in. Her half-digested puppy flowers squirmed along the rubber by Peter's feet.

"How close are we?" Zana asked.

A wave shoved them forward.

"It shouldn't be much farther now," Peter said.

Then they hit a rock. The impact was so hard it slammed them all into one corner. There was a loud popping sound. The rock they crashed into had ripped open the raft.

"Abandon ship," Peter said.

They lifted the worm skin tarp and saw they were smashed against the side of a rock face.

"Climb out," Peter said. "Quickly."

Zana put Jill on her back and climbed out of the raft up the rocks. Peter tossed his teddy bear up there, then went for the food. He had to get as much out as he could.

"It's sinking," Zana said. "Get out of there."

"We need the food," Peter said.

"Forget it," she said. "There will be plenty at the Citysphere."

Peter jumped out of the raft and climbed up the rock just as a giant wave smashed into the raft. Once he got to the top and looked down, he saw the wave had swallowed their sailing vessel. It took it away from the rock, flipped it over, and stole all of their supplies.

"Well, at least we don't need it anymore," Peter said, as the raft sank beneath the water.

Zana slapped him on the arm.

"Actually," she told him. "We did."

When Peter turned around, he saw they had yet to make it to the shore. They were only on a large jagged rock, completely surrounded by acid. The coast was still about a hundred yards away.

"How are we going to get over there now?" Zana asked.

"We'd never be able to swim there," Peter said. "We wouldn't last ten yards."

Zana hugged the tumors on her body.

"We were so close," Zana said, her voice crackling as if to cry.

She hugged Peter.

"How are we going to save Jill now?" Zana said. "We're stuck. We'll never get to the Citysphere."

Peter looked in the distance, his eyes scanning the shoreline.

"It doesn't matter," Peter said. "We never would have made it there anyway. Look."

Zana released him and followed his hand as it pointed at the shore. Off in the distance, there was a pillar of smoke. And below it, there was a fire where the Citysphere once stood.

"It's burning down," Peter said.

"What?" Zana said, looking carefully at the distance. "How?"

She couldn't believe it. The Citysphere definitely was burning to the ground.

"Maybe some electrical problem," Peter said. "There was nobody to stop it. I'm sure it was something small that went wild."

A wave crashed against the rock, splashing them on their legs. They didn't know how long the mucus would protect them from the ocean spray.

"I can't dig here," Louie said to Peter, as he tried poking his shovel into the hard surface.

"There's no treasure on this rock," Peter said to Louie.

"Arrgh, he's right, me lad," said Captain Bearbeard, standing on the highest tip of the rock. "We need to get to the shore."

"Can you get us to the shore, Peter?" Louie said.

Peter looked at his little brother and tried to smile.

"I don't know," Peter said. "Our pirate ship has sunk and the ocean water will burn us alive if we try to swim."

Zana saw Peter talking to himself again.

"Maybe the tide will go out far enough to walk to shore," Zana said, sitting close to Jill with her arm around the girl's shoulders.

Peter frowned.

"This planet doesn't have much of a tide," he said. "I don't think that will work."

"Arrrgh, I've got an idea, me hearties," said Captain Bearbeard.

Everyone but Zana looked up at him.

The teddy bear pulled his tiny saber out of its sheath and pointed it at the sky.

"We'll capture the next ship that comes into this harbor," said Captain Bearbeard. "We'll sneak aboard alongside it, fight our way through the team of scallywags, and then make all the crew walk the plank."

"Yeah!" Louie said, clanking his shovel against the rock. "Make the scallywags walk the plank!"

"Then we'll sail their vessel to shore," said Captain Bearbeard. "And loot the mainland of all its treasure!"

Peter smiled.

"Great idea," he said. "But there's not a ship left on this

whole pink planet."

Captain Bearbeard jumped off the tip of the rock and landed in Peter's lap.

"Have a little faith in ye captain," said the teddy bear, pointing his sword at Peter's chin.

"I'm just telling you the truth," Peter said.

"Oh yeah?" said Captain Bearbeard. "What be that then?"

Captain Bearbeard pointed his saber at the coastline. A hovercraft was coming toward them.

Peter stood up, dropping the teddy bear from his lap.

"That's..." Peter began.

Zana saw it too. She stood up.

"Impossible," she said.

"I told ye we'd get ourselves another vessel," said Captain Bearbeard. "Prepare to board!"

As the teddy bear pointed his sword at the coming ship, Peter and Zana jumped up and down. They waved their hands, shouting at the tops of their lungs. But they didn't need to get the attention of those driving the hovercraft. The vessel was coming specifically for them.

"People," Zana said when she saw their faces looking at them through the windows. "There are actually people."

"I guess we're not the only ones left on the planet," Peter said.

He looked back with a big smile on his face, but Louie was no longer there. Captain Bearbeard was lying limp on the rock by his feet.

When the hovercraft pulled up along the side of the rock, a scrawny bald white guy looked out of the window and said, "Any of you know where I can find a good karaoke bar around here?"

Then he laughed at the top of his lungs.

"The name's Chase," said the bald guy as they got into the hovercraft.

Peter shook his hand and introduced himself, but Zana was busy helping two paramedics attend to Jill.

"I'm sure you've got a lot of questions," Chase said. "Lucky for you, I've got plenty of time to answer them."

Peter nodded.

"You're probably wondering why you just appeared out of nowhere on this planet," Chase said, "in the middle of the ocean no less. But there is a reasonable explanation for that, as far-fetched as it seems."

Peter just stared at the bald man.

"Um," Peter said. "I have no idea what you're talking about. We were in a crash. We've been stranded on a deserted island for weeks."

"Huh?" Chase said.

Suddenly he was the one who was confused.

Peter explained his story. He told them about their ship that went down and crashed into the sea. He told them about being on the island and all the people who died there. He explained how they took a raft and sailed miles through the acid sea to get there only to crash onto the rocks within sight of their destination.

Chase knew exactly what flight Peter was talking about. He had a friend on that flight. He was sad to hear he had not survived.

"I'm sorry you were left out there for so long," Chase said. "But the people at the Citysphere have been so busy with other search and rescues there wasn't much time to spare searching every little island."

Peter asked him to explain what he was talking about.

Chase sat him down.

"This planet isn't exactly what it appears to be," Chase said. "We're calling it a *pirate planet*. It was manufactured by some kind of advanced alien race billions of years ago."

Peter smiled at the term *pirate planet* and nodded in complete agreement.

"This planet travels through the galaxy stealing resources from other worlds," Chase said. "As it passed by the Earth, this planet has actually been teleporting random objects from our world onto this one. People, animals, buildings, cars, all sorts of things have been stolen from Earth."

Peter thought back. He told Chase all about the cow that appeared in midair, as well as the magical refrigerator, the two guys in the SUV, the hanged football player, the Taco Bell, even the alien spaceship.

"Yes," Chase said, nodding when he mentioned the ship. "There were quite a few alien vessels that had been stolen from the last civilized system this planet had visited."

The hovercraft pulled into the Citysphere harbor. The docks were lined with a dozen similar ships, with room for a dozen more.

"That's why we're here now," Chase said. "So many people from Earth have been teleported here that there was no way to get them all back home. Most people and objects that get teleported end up landing in the ocean. There's no hope for them. But hundreds of people have been found all over this island alone. Right now, we have search and rescue missions going around the clock. It seems a new person is found every hour."

They stepped out of the ship and onto the metal dock. The paramedics put Jill on a stretcher and rushed her to a small building off the shore. It was an emergency medical station, most likely designed for acid injuries.

"That's why there weren't many resources put into looking for you after your shuttle went down," Chase said. "There are so many people that need help just on the mainland. We don't have the time yet to search all the smaller surrounding islands."

Zana went with Jill and the paramedics, leaving Peter behind. Chase walked with the young man, not at all wondering about his pirate outfit, and took him down a sidewalk toward the Citysphere. The blaze was still going. Smoke poured into the pink sky, raining down ash like snow on them.

"What happened here?" Peter asked. "Why'd it burn down?"

Chase shook his head.

"Despicable," Chase said. "As the last ship was leaving for Earth, riots broke out at the dome. All the people who were being left behind went crazy. There wasn't enough time or resources to return everyone who had been teleported. Many people had to stay here."

"But how could they burn the Citysphere?" Peter said. "Even if they were left behind they'd at least have a place to stay if they didn't burn it down."

Chase nodded. "They weren't thinking. The madness had taken over. You can't blame them, though. Most of them were parents who had been separated from their children. Anyone would go nuts if they had to go through that."

"What about you?" Peter asked. "Were you teleported here as well?"

"No," he said. "I worked at the Citysphere. I volunteered to stay. A lot of people volunteered to stay behind to help those who would be stuck here. There are also a lot of people who came here with the intention of staying. They want to help colonize the planet with us. There are farmers, ranchers, doctors, even religious leaders."

They passed groups of people who were constructing frames for buildings, digging trenches in the ground, carrying lumber.

"The Citysphere might be burning down, but we will rebuild it," Chase said. "We will build a stronger, bigger dome. We will build a society here."

"But I thought human beings couldn't survive on this planet?" Peter asked. "Everything's toxic, even the air."

Chase smiled.

"Everything *was* toxic," Chase said. "But it's a funny thing. This planet also stole a big chunk of the Earth's atmosphere. The toxins in the air have been greatly reduced. And once we grow our own crops, plant our own trees, and process the ground water to be safe to drink—this planet's getting completely terraformed."

Peter looked out across a clearing. There were hundreds of people, working together to create a place they could call home.

"So what do you say, Peter," Chase said, patting him on the back. "Do you want to build a new world with us?"

Peter smiled widely. He just nodded his head.

"It sounds like the biggest adventure we could have possibly imagined," Peter said.

He looked down at Louie. His little brother hugged his legs, smiling up at him.

Peter sat in the dirt, drinking water out of a plastic gallon jug and eating oatmeal from a metal cup. Zana came up behind him and sat down. She was wearing nurse's clothes she had gotten from the medical station. Peter assumed the people in charge didn't want her walking around the place naked like a savage.

"They say Jill's going to make it," Zana said, speaking over the sound of hammering and sawing behind them. "It's going to be hard for her though. Settling an alien planet isn't the life for someone with such a severe disability."

Peter nodded.

"They're serving oatmeal over there," Peter said, pointing at a crowd of people gathered around a table.

Zana decided she didn't want to wait in line. She dipped her finger in his metal cup and scooped out a bite of the thick goop for herself.

"I think everything's going to be exciting from here on out," Peter said.

Zana nodded, sucking the oatmeal off her fingers.

"It won't be our Garden of Eden, though," Zana said.

"It's better than a Garden of Eden," Peter said. "It's an

adventure. A challenge. If this were a paradise, it would have been way too easy."

"Maybe you're right," Zana said.

She took another bite of his oatmeal.

"I signed up for search and rescue," Peter said. "They thought I'd be useful, considering all we've been through."

Zana nodded. "Yeah, I decided to help out at the medical station. I'll probably just be cleaning up crap and keeping out of everyone's way, but I want to be around when Jill regains consciousness."

"Sounds like we're already fitting in," Peter said.

He pulled his cup away and gobbled the last of the oatmeal before Zana could get her finger inside again. She smiled at him. Then she stood up and wiped the dirt from her backside.

"Where are you going?" Peter asked.

"No offense," she said. "But we were on that island alone together for far too long. I think it's about time we see other people."

Peter nodded and saluted her goodbye.

"See you around, pirate boy," she said, waving at him as she walked on toward the people building houses in the distance.

Peter chugged some more water and gazed up at the pink sky.

"It's just us now, Captain Bearbeard," Peter said to the teddy bear. "I know we just got here, but what do you say you and me go on another adventure?"

"What have ye in mind, me lad?" said the teddy bear, coming to life by Peter's feet.

"I say we rally up ourselves a crew, take one of those hovercrafts out to sea, and plunder the Taco Bell that's still loaded with booty. What do you think? Are you up for it?"

"Aye," said the fluffy captain. "That sounds like a fine idea. A fine idea indeed."

Peter stood up and put the teddy bear through his belt loop.

Then he headed back toward the docks where all the search and rescue volunteers were gathered.

Nobody recognized it as he walked, but if somebody would have looked carefully enough, at just the right angle, they would have seen Peter's hand out to his side with his fingers pressed gently together—as if he were leading an excited young child toward a great big grand adventure.

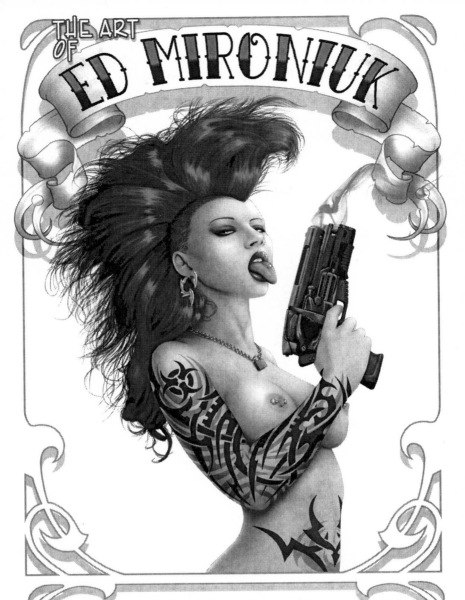

ABOUT THE AUTHOR

Carlton Mellick III is one of the leading authors of the bizarro fiction subgenre. Since 2001, his books have drawn an international cult following, despite the fact that they have been shunned by most libraries and chain bookstores.

He won the Wonderland Book Award for his novel, *Warrior Wolf Women of the Wasteland,* in 2009. His short fiction has appeared in *Vice Magazine, The Year's Best Fantasy and Horror #16, The Magazine of Bizarro Fiction,* and *Zombies: Encounters with the Hungry Dead,* among others. He is also a graduate of Clarion West, where he studied under the likes of Chuck Palahniuk, Connie Willis, and Cory Doctorow.

He lives in Portland, OR, the bizarro fiction mecca.

Visit him online at **www.carltonmellick.com**

BIZARRO BOOKS

CATALOG SPRING 2012

ERASERHEAD
PRESS

Your major resource for the bizarro fiction genre:

WWW.BIZARROCENTRAL.COM

Introduce yourselves to the bizarro fiction genre and all of its authors with the Bizarro Starter Kit series. Each volume features short novels and short stories by ten of the leading bizarro authors, designed to give you a perfect sampling of the genre for only $10.

BB-0X1
"The Bizarro Starter Kit"
(Orange)
Featuring D. Harlan Wilson, Carlton Mellick III, Jeremy Robert Johnson, Kevin L Donihe, Gina Ranalli, Andre Duza, Vincent W. Sakowski, Steve Beard, John Edward Lawson, and Bruce Taylor.
236 pages $10

BB-0X2
"The Bizarro Starter Kit"
(Blue)
Featuring Ray Fracalossy, Jeremy C. Shipp, Jordan Krall, Mykle Hansen, Andersen Prunty, Eckhard Gerdes, Bradley Sands, Steve Aylett, Christian TeBordo, and Tony Rauch. **244 pages $10**

BB-0X2
"The Bizarro Starter Kit"
(Purple)
Featuring Russell Edson, Athena Villaverde, David Agranoff, Matthew Revert, Andrew Goldfarb, Jeff Burk, Garrett Cook, Kris Saknussemm, Cody Goodfellow, and Cameron Pierce **264 pages $10**

BB-001 "The Kafka Effekt" D. Harlan Wilson — A collection of forty-four irreal short stories loosely written in the vein of Franz Kafka, with more than a pinch of William S. Burroughs sprinkled on top. **211 pages $14**

BB-002 "Satan Burger" Carlton Mellick III — The cult novel that put Carlton Mellick III on the map ... Six punks get jobs at a fast food restaurant owned by the devil in a city violently overpopulated by surreal alien cultures. **236 pages $14**

BB-003 "Some Things Are Better Left Unplugged" Vincent Sakwoski — Join The Man and his Nemesis, the obese tabby, for a nightmare roller coaster ride into this postmodern fantasy. **152 pages $10**

BB-004 "Shall We Gather At the Garden?" Kevin L Donihe — Donihe's Debut novel. Midgets take over the world, The Church of Lionel Richie vs. The Church of the Byrds, plant porn and more! **244 pages $14**

BB-005 "Razor Wire Pubic Hair" Carlton Mellick III — A genderless humandildo is purchased by a razor dominatrix and brought into her nightmarish world of bizarre sex and mutilation. **176 pages $11**

BB-006 "Stranger on the Loose" D. Harlan Wilson — The fiction of Wilson's 2nd collection is planted in the soil of normalcy, but what grows out of that soil is a dark, witty, otherworldly jungle... **228 pages $14**

BB-007 "The Baby Jesus Butt Plug" Carlton Mellick III — Using clones of the Baby Jesus for anal sex will be the hip sex fetish of the future. **92 pages $10**

BB-008 "Fishyfleshed" Carlton Mellick III — The world of the past is an illogical flatland lacking in dimension and color, a sick-scape of crispy squid people wandering the desert for no apparent reason. **260 pages $14**

BB-009 "Dead Bitch Army" Andre Duza — Step into a world filled with racist teenagers, cannibals, 100 warped Uncle Sams, automobiles with razor-sharp teeth, living graffiti, and a pissed-off zombie bitch out for revenge. **344 pages $16**

BB-010 "The Menstruating Mall" Carlton Mellick III — "The Breakfast Club meets Chopping Mall as directed by David Lynch." - Brian Keene **212 pages $12**

BB-011 "Angel Dust Apocalypse" Jeremy Robert Johnson — Meth-heads, man-made monsters, and murderous Neo-Nazis. "Seriously amazing short stories..." - Chuck Palahniuk, author of Fight Club **184 pages $11**

BB-012 "Ocean of Lard" Kevin L Donihe / Carlton Mellick III — A parody of those old Choose Your Own Adventure kid's books about some very odd pirates sailing on a sea made of animal fat. **176 pages $12**

BB-015 "Foop!" Chris Genoa — Strange happenings are going on at Dactyl, Inc, the world's first and only time travel tourism company.
"A surreal pie in the face!" - Christopher Moore **300 pages $14**

BB-020 "Punk Land" Carlton Mellick III — In the punk version of Heaven, the anarchist utopia is threatened by corporate fascism and only Goblin, Mortician's sperm, and a blue-mohawked female assassin named Shark Girl can stop them. **284 pages $15**

BB-027 "Siren Promised" Jeremy Robert Johnson & Alan M Clark — Nominated for the Bram Stoker Award. A potent mix of bad drugs, bad dreams, brutal bad guys, and surreal/incredible art by Alan M. Clark. **190 pages $13**

BB-031"Sea of the Patchwork Cats" Carlton Mellick III — A quiet dreamlike tale set in the ashes of the human race. For Mellick enthusiasts who also adore The Twilight Zone. **112 pages $10**

BB-032 **"Extinction Journals" Jeremy Robert Johnson** — An uncanny voyage across a newly nuclear America where one man must confront the problems associated with loneliness, insane dieties, radiation, love, and an ever-evolving cockroach suit with a mind of its own. **104 pages $10**

BB-037 **"The Haunted Vagina" Carlton Mellick III** — It's difficult to love a woman whose vagina is a gateway to the world of the dead. **132 pages $10**

BB-043 **"War Slut" Carlton Mellick III** — Part "1984," part "Waiting for Godot," and part action horror video game adaptation of John Carpenter's "The Thing." **116 pages $10**

BB-047 **"Sausagey Santa" Carlton Mellick III** — A bizarro Christmas tale featuring Santa as a piratey mutant with a body made of sausages. 124 pages $10

BB-048 **"Misadventures in a Thumbnail Universe" Vincent Sakowski** — Dive deep into the surreal and satirical realms of neo-classical Blender Fiction, filled with television shoes and flesh-filled skies. **120 pages $10**

BB-053 **"Ballad of a Slow Poisoner" Andrew Goldfarb** — Millford Mutterwurst sat down on a Tuesday to take his afternoon tea, and made the unpleasant discovery that his elbows were becoming flatter. **128 pages $10**

BB-055 **"Help! A Bear is Eating Me" Mykle Hansen** — The bizarro, heartwarming, magical tale of poor planning, hubris and severe blood loss... **150 pages $11**

BB-056 **"Piecemeal June" Jordan Krall** — A man falls in love with a living sex doll, but with love comes danger when her creator comes after her with crab-squid assassins. **90 pages $9**

BB-058 "The Overwhelming Urge" Andersen Prunty — A collection of bizarro tales by Andersen Prunty. **150 pages $11**

BB-059 "Adolf in Wonderland" Carlton Mellick III — A dreamlike adventure that takes a young descendant of Adolf Hitler's design and sends him down the rabbit hole into a world of imperfection and disorder. **180 pages $11**

BB-061 "Ultra Fuckers" Carlton Mellick III — Absurdist suburban horror about a couple who enter an upper middle class gated community but can't find their way out. **108 pages $9**

BB-062 "House of Houses" Kevin L. Donihe — An odd man wants to marry his house. Unfortunately, all of the houses in the world collapse at the same time in the Great House Holocaust. Now he must travel to House Heaven to find his departed fiancee. **172 pages $11**

BB-064 "Squid Pulp Blues" Jordan Krall — In these three bizarro-noir novellas, the reader is thrown into a world of murderers, drugs made from squid parts, deformed gun-toting veterans, and a mischievous apocalyptic donkey. **204 pages $12**

BB-065 "Jack and Mr. Grin" Andersen Prunty — "When Mr. Grin calls you can hear a smile in his voice. Not a warm and friendly smile, but the kind that seizes your spine in fear. You don't need to pay your phone bill to hear it. That smile is in every line of Prunty's prose." - Tom Bradley. **208 pages $12**

BB-066 "Cybernetrix" Carlton Mellick III — What would you do if your normal everyday world was slowly mutating into the video game world from Tron? **212 pages $12**

BB-072 "Zerostrata" Andersen Prunty — Hansel Nothing lives in a tree house, suffers from memory loss, has a very eccentric family, and falls in love with a woman who runs naked through the woods every night. **144 pages $11**

BB-073 "The Egg Man" Carlton Mellick III — It is a world where humans reproduce like insects. Children are the property of corporations, and having an enormous ten-foot brain implanted into your skull is a grotesque sexual fetish. Mellick's industrial urban dystopia is one of his darkest and grittiest to date. **184 pages $11**

BB-074 "Shark Hunting in Paradise Garden" Cameron Pierce — A group of strange humanoid religious fanatics travel back in time to the Garden of Eden to discover it is invested with hundreds of giant flying maneating sharks. **150 pages $10**

BB-075 "Apeshit" Carlton Mellick III - Friday the 13th meets Visitor Q. Six hipster teens go to a cabin in the woods inhabited by a deformed killer. An incredibly fucked-up parody of B-horror movies with a bizarro slant. **192 pages $12**

BB-076 "Fuckers of Everything on the Crazy Shitting Planet of the Vomit At smosphere" Mykle Hansen - Three bizarro satires. Monster Cocks, Journey to the Center of Agnes Cuddlebottom, and Crazy Shitting Planet. **228 pages $12**

BB-077 "The Kissing Bug" Daniel Scott Buck — In the tradition of Roald Dahl, Tim Burton, and Edward Gorey, comes this bizarro anti-war children's story about a bohemian conenose kissing bug who falls in love with a human woman. **116 pages $10**

BB-078 "MachoPoni" Lotus Rose — It's My Little Pony... *Bizarro* style! A long time ago Poniworld was split in two. On one side of the Jagged Line is the Pastel Kingdom, a magical land of music, parties, and positivity. On the other side of the Jagged Line is Dark Kingdom inhabited by an army of undead ponies. **148 pages $11**

BB-079 "The Faggiest Vampire" Carlton Mellick III — A Roald Dahl-esque children's story about two faggy vampires who partake in a mustache competition to find out which one is truly the faggiest. **104 pages $10**

BB-080 "Sky Tongues" Gina Ranalli — The autobiography of Sky Tongues, the biracial hermaphrodite actress with tongues for fingers. Follow her strange life story as she rises from freak to fame. **204 pages $12**

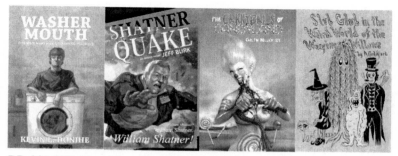

BB-081 **"Washer Mouth" Kevin L. Donihe** - A washing machine becomes human and pursues his dream of meeting his favorite soap opera star. **244 pages $11**

BB-082 **"Shatnerquake" Jeff Burk** - All of the characters ever played by William Shatner are suddenly sucked into our world. Their mission: hunt down and destroy the real William Shatner. **100 pages $10**

BB-083 **"The Cannibals of Candyland" Carlton Mellick III** - There exists a race of cannibals that are made of candy. They live in an underground world made out of candy. One man has dedicated his life to killing them all. **170 pages $11**

BB-084 **"Slub Glub in the Weird World of the Weeping Willows" Andrew Goldfarb** - The charming tale of a blue glob named Slub Glub who helps the weeping willows whose tears are flooding the earth. There are also hyenas, ghosts, and a voodoo priest **100 pages $10**

BB-085 **"Super Fetus" Adam Pepper** - Try to abort this fetus and he'll kick your ass! **104 pages $10**

BB-086 **"Fistful of Feet" Jordan Krall** - A bizarro tribute to spaghetti westerns, featuring Cthulhu-worshipping Indians, a woman with four feet, a crazed gunman who is obsessed with sucking on candy, Syphilis-ridden mutants, sexually transmitted tattoos, and a house devoted to the freakiest fetishes. **228 pages $12**

BB-087 **"Ass Goblins of Auschwitz" Cameron Pierce** - It's Monty Python meets Nazi exploitation in a surreal nightmare as can only be imagined by Bizarro author Cameron Pierce. **104 pages $10**

BB-088 **"Silent Weapons for Quiet Wars" Cody Goodfellow** - "This is high-end psychological surrealist horror meets bottom-feeding low-life crime in a techno-thrilling science fiction world full of Lovecraft and magic..." -John Skipp **212 pages $12**

BB-089 "Warrior Wolf Women of the Wasteland" Carlton Mellick III
— Road Warrior Werewolves versus McDonaldland Mutants...post-apocalyptic fiction has never been quite like this. **316 pages $13**

BB-091 "Super Giant Monster Time" Jeff Burk — A tribute to choose your own adventures and Godzilla movies. Will you escape the giant monsters that are rampaging the fuck out of your city and shit? Or will you join the mob of alien-controlled punk rockers causing chaos in the streets? What happens next depends on you. **188 pages $12**

BB-092 "Perfect Union" Cody Goodfellow — "Cronenberg's THE FLY on a grand scale: human/insect gene-spliced body horror, where the human hive politics are as shocking as the gore." -John Skipp. **272 pages $13**

BB-093 "Sunset with a Beard" Carlton Mellick III — 14 stories of surreal science fiction. **200 pages $12**

BB-094 "My Fake War" Andersen Prunty — The absurd tale of an unlikely soldier forced to fight a war that, quite possibly, does not exist. It's Rambo meets Waiting for Godot in this subversive satire of American values and the scope of the human imagination. **128 pages $11**

BB-095 "Lost in Cat Brain Land" Cameron Pierce — Sad stories from a surreal world. A fascist mustache, the ghost of Franz Kafka, a desert inside a dead cat. Primordial entities mourn the death of their child. The desperate serve tea to mysterious creatures. A hopeless romantic falls in love with a pterodactyl. And much more. **152 pages $11**

BB-096 "The Kobold Wizard's Dildo of Enlightenment +2" Carlton Mellick III — A Dungeons and Dragons parody about a group of people who learn they are only made up characters in an AD&D campaign and must find a way to resist their nerdy teenaged players and retarded dungeon master in order to survive. 232 **pages $12**

BB-098 "A Hundred Horrible Sorrows of Ogner Stump" Andrew Goldfarb — Goldfarb's acclaimed comic series. A magical and weird journey into the horrors of everyday life. **164 pages $11**

BB-099 "Pickled Apocalypse of Pancake Island" Cameron Pierce—A demented fairy tale about a pickle, a pancake, and the apocalypse. **102 pages $8**

BB-100 "Slag Attack" Andersen Prunty— Slag Attack features four visceral, noir stories about the living, crawling apocalypse. A slag is what survivors are calling the slug-like maggots raining from the sky, burrowing inside people, and hollowing out their flesh and their sanity. **148 pages $11**

BB-101 "Slaughterhouse High" Robert Devereaux—A place where schools are built with secret passageways, rebellious teens get zippers installed in their mouths and genitals, and once a year, on that special night, one couple is slaughtered and the bits of their bodies are kept as souvenirs. **304 pages $13**

BB-102 "The Emerald Burrito of Oz" John Skipp & Marc Levinthal —OZ IS REAL! Magic is real! The gate is really in Kansas! And America is finally allowing Earth tourists to visit this weird-ass, mysterious land. But when Gene of Los Angeles heads off for summer vacation in the Emerald City, little does he know that a war is brewing...a war that could destroy both worlds. **280 pages $13**

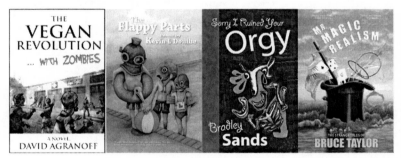

BB-103 "The Vegan Revolution... with Zombies" David Agranoff — When there's no more meat in hell, the vegans will walk the earth. **160 pages $11**

BB-104 "The Flappy Parts" Kevin L Donihe—Poems about bunnies, LSD, and police abuse. You know, things that matter. 132 **pages $11**

BB-105   "Sorry I Ruined Your Orgy" Bradley Sands—Bizarro humorist Bradley Sands returns with one of the strangest, most hilarious collections of the year. **130 pages $11**

BB-106 "Mr. Magic Realism" Bruce Taylor—Like Golden Age science fiction comics written by Freud, *Mr. Magic Realism* is a strange, insightful adventure that spans the furthest reaches of the galaxy, exploring the hidden caverns in the hearts and minds of men, women, aliens, and biomechanical cats. **152 pages $11**

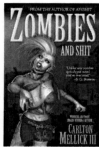   

BB-107 "Zombies and Shit" Carlton Mellick III—"Battle Royale" meets "Return of the Living Dead." Mellick's bizarro tribute to the zombie genre. **308 pages $13**

BB-108 "The Cannibal's Guide to Ethical Living" Mykle Hansen— Over a five star French meal of fine wine, organic vegetables and human flesh, a lunatic delivers a witty, chilling, disturbingly sane argument in favor of eating the rich.. **184 pages $11**

BB-109 "Starfish Girl" Athena Villaverde—In a post-apocalyptic underwater dome society, a girl with a starfish growing from her head and an assassin with sea anenome hair are on the run from a gang of mutant fish men. **160 pages $11**

BB-110 "Lick Your Neighbor" Chris Genoa—Mutant ninjas, a talking whale, kung fu masters, maniacal pilgrims, and an alcoholic clown populate Chris Genoa's surreal, darkly comical and unnerving reimagining of the first Thanksgiving. **303 pages $13**

BB-111 "Night of the Assholes" Kevin L. Donihe—A plague of assholes is infecting the countryside. Normal everyday people are transforming into jerks, snobs, dicks, and douchebags. And they all have only one purpose: to make your life a living hell.. **192 pages $11**

BB-112 "Jimmy Plush, Teddy Bear Detective" Garrett Cook—Hardboiled cases of a private detective trapped within a teddy bear body. **180 pages $11**

BB-113   "The Deadheart Shelters" Forrest Armstrong—The hip hop lovechild of William Burroughs and Dali... **144 pages $11**

BB-114 "Eyeballs Growing All Over Me... Again" Tony Raugh— Absurd, surreal, playful, dream-like, whimsical, and a lot of fun to read. **144 pages $11**

BB-115 "Whargoul" Dave Brockie — From the killing grounds of Stalingrad to the death camps of the holocaust. From torture chambers in Iraq to race riots in the United States, the Whargoul was there, killing and raping. **244 pages $12**

BB-116 "By the Time We Leave Here, We'll Be Friends" J. David Osborne — A David Lynchian nightmare set in a Russian gulag, where its prisoners, guards, traitors, soldiers, lovers, and demons fight for survival and their own rapidly deteriorating humanity. **168 pages $11**

BB-117 "Christmas on Crack" edited by Carlton Mellick III — Perverted Christmas Tales for the whole family! . . . as long as every member of your family is over the age of 18. **168 pages $11**

BB-118 "Crab Town" Carlton Mellick III — Radiation fetishists, balloon people, mutant crabs, sail-bike road warriors, and a love affair between a woman and an H-Bomb. This is one mean asshole of a city. Welcome to Crab Town. **100 pages $8**

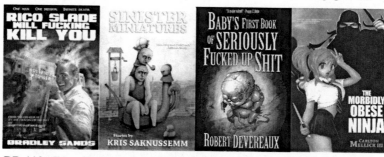

BB-119 "Rico Slade Will Fucking Kill You" Bradley Sands — Rico Slade is an action hero. Rico Slade can rip out a throat with his bare hands. Rico Slade's favorite food is the honey-roasted peanut. Rico Slade will fucking kill everyone. A novel. **122 pages $8**

BB-120 "Sinister Miniatures" Kris Saknussemm — The definitive collection of short fiction by Kris Saknussemm, confirming that he is one of the best, most daring writers of the weird to emerge in the twenty-first century. **180 pages $11**

BB-121 "Baby's First Book of Seriously Fucked up Shit" Robert Devereaux — Ten stories of the strange, the gross, and the just plain fucked up from one of the most original voices in horror. **176 pages $11**

BB-122 "The Morbidly Obese Ninja" Carlton Mellick III — These days, if you want to run a successful company . . . you're going to need a lot of ninjas. **92 pages $8**

BB-123 **"Abortion Arcade" Cameron Pierce** — An intoxicating blend of body horror and midnight movie madness, reminiscent of early David Lynch and the splatterpunks at their most sublime. **172 pages $11**

BB-124 **"Black Hole Blues" Patrick Wensink** — A hilarious double helix of country music and physics. **196 pages $11**

BB-125 **"Barbarian Beast Bitches of the Badlands" Carlton Mellick III** — Three prequels and sequels to *Warrior Wolf Women of the Wasteland*. **284 pages $13**

BB-126 **"The Traveling Dildo Salesman" Kevin L. Donihe** — A nightmare comedy about destiny, faith, and sex toys. Also featuring Donihe's most lurid and infamous short stories: *Milky Agitation, Two-Way Santa, The Helen Mower, Living Room Zombies,* and *Revenge of the Living Masturbation Rag.* **108 pages $8**

BB-127 **"Metamorphosis Blues" Bruce Taylor** — Enter a land of love beasts, intergalactic cowboys, and rock 'n roll. A land where Sears Catalogs are doorways to insanity and men keep mysterious black boxes. Welcome to the monstrous mind of Mr. Magic Realism. **136 pages $11**

BB-128 **"The Driver's Guide to Hitting Pedestrians" Andersen Prunty** — A pocket guide to the twenty-three most painful things in life, written by the most well-adjusted man in the universe. **108 pages $8**

BB-129 **"Island of the Super People" Kevin Shamel** — Four students and their anthropology professor journey to a remote island to study its indigenous population. But this is no ordinary native culture. They're super heroes and villains with flesh costumes and out-landish abilities like self-detonation, musical eyelashes, and microwave hands. **194 pages $11**

BB-130 **"Fantastic Orgy" Carlton Mellick III** — Shark Sex, mutant cats, and strange sexually transmitted diseases. Featuring the stories: *Candy-coated, Ear Cat, Fantastic Orgy, City Hobgoblins,* and *Porno in August.* **136 pages $9**

BB-131 **"Cripple Wolf" Jeff Burk** — Part man. Part wolf. 100% crippled. Also including *Punk Rock Nursing Home, Adrift with Space Badgers, Cook for Your Life, Just Another Day in the Park, Frosty and the Full Monty,* and *House of Cats.* **152 pages $10**

BB-132 **"I Knocked Up Satan's Daughter" Carlton Mellick III** — An adorable, violent, fantastical love story. A romantic comedy for the bizarro fiction reader. **152 pages $10**

BB-133 **"A Town Called Suckhole" David W. Barbee** — Far into the future, in the nuclear bowels of post-apocalyptic Dixie, there is a town. A town of derelict mobile homes, ancient junk, and mutant wildlife. A town of slack jawed rednecks who bask in the splendors of moonshine and mud boggin'. A town dedicated to the bloody and demented legacy of the Old South. A town called Suckhole. **144 pages $10**

BB-134 **"Cthulhu Comes to the Vampire Kingdom" Cameron Pierce** — What you'd get if H. P. Lovecraft wrote a Tim Burton animated film. **148 pages $11**

BB-135 **"I am Genghis Cum" Violet LeVoit** — From the savage Arctic tundra to post-partum mutations to your missing daughter's unmarked grave, join visionary madwoman Violet LeVoit in this non-stop eight-story onslaught of full-tilt Bizarro punk lit thrills. **124 pages $9**

BB-136 **"Haunt" Laura Lee Bahr** — A tripping-balls Los Angeles noir, where a mysterious dame drags you through a time-warping Bizarro hall of mirrors. **316 pages $13**

BB-137 **"Amazing Stories of the Flying Spaghetti Monster" edited by Cameron Pierce** — Like an all-spaghetti evening of Adult Swim, the Flying Spaghetti Monster will show you the many realms of His Noodly Appendage. Learn of those who worship him and the lives he touches in distant, mysterious ways. **228 pages $12**

BB-138 **"Wave of Mutilation" Douglas Lain** — A dream-pop exploration of modern architecture and the American identity, *Wave of Mutilation* is a Zen finger trap for the 21st century. **100 pages $8**

BB-139 **"Hooray for Death!" Mykle Hansen** — Famous Author Mykle Hansen draws unconventional humor from deaths tiny and large, and invites you to laugh while you can. **128 pages $10**

BB-140 **"Hypno-hog's Moonshine Monster Jamboree" Andrew Goldfarb** — Hicks, Hogs, Horror! Goldfarb is back with another strange illustrated tale of backwoods weirdness. **120 pages $9**

BB-141 **"Broken Piano For President" Patrick Wensink** — A comic masterpiece about the fast food industry, booze, and the necessity to choose happiness over work and security. **372 pages $15**

BB-142 **"Please Do Not Shoot Me in the Face" Bradley Sands** — A novel in three parts, *Please Do Not Shoot Me in the Face: A Novel*, is the story of one boy detective, the worst ninja in the world, and the great American fast food wars. It is a novel of loss, destruction, and--incredibly--genuine hope. **224 pages $12**

BB-143 **"Santa Steps Out" Robert Devereaux** — Sex, Death, and Santa Claus ... The ultimate erotic Christmas story is back. **294 pages $13**

BB-144 **"Santa Conquers the Homophobes" Robert Devereaux** — "I wish I could hope to ever attain one-thousandth the perversity of Robert Devereaux's toenail clippings." - Poppy Z. Brite **316 pages $13**

BB-145 **"We Live Inside You" Jeremy Robert Johnson** — "Jeremy Robert Johnson is dancing to a way different drummer. He loves language, he loves the edge, and he loves us people. These stories have range and style and wit. This is entertainment... and literature."- Jack Ketchum **188 pages $11**

BB-146 **"Clockwork Girl" Athena Villaverde** — Urban fairy tales for the weird girl in all of us. Like a combination of Francesca Lia Block, Charles de Lint, Kathe Koja, Tim Burton, and Hayao Miyazaki, her stories are cute, kinky, edgy, magical, provocative, and strange, full of poetic imagery and vicious sexuality. **160 pages $10**

BB-147 **"Armadillo Fists" Carlton Mellick III** — A weird-as-hell gangster story set in a world where people drive giant mechanical dinosaurs instead of cars. **168 pages $11**

BB-148 **"Gargoyle Girls of Spider Island" Cameron Pierce** — Four college seniors venture out into open waters for the tropical party weekend of a lifetime. Instead of a teenage sex fantasy, they find themselves in a nightmare of pirates, sharks, and sex-crazed monsters. **100 pages $8**

BB-149 **"The Handsome Squirm" by Carlton Mellick III** — Like Franz Kafka's *The Trial* meets an erotic body horror version of *The Blob*. **158 pages $11**

BB-150 **"Tentacle Death Trip" Jordan Krall** — It's *Death Race 2000* meets H. P. Lovecraft in bizarro author Jordan Krall's best and most suspenseful work to date. **224 pages $12**

BB-151 **"The Obese" Nick Antosca** — Like Alfred Hitchcock's *The Birds*... but with obese people. **108 pages $10**

BB-152 **"All-Monster Action!" Cody Goodfellow** — The world gave him a blank check and a demand: Create giant monsters to fight our wars. But Dr. Otaku was not satisfied with mere chaos and mass destruction.... **216 pages $12**

BB-153 **"Ugly Heaven" Carlton Mellick III** — Heaven is no longer a paradise. It was once a blissful utopia full of wonders far beyond human comprehension. But the afterlife is now in ruins. It has become an ugly, lonely wasteland populated by strange monstrous beasts, masturbating angels, and sad man-like beings wallowing in the remains of the once-great Kingdom of God. **106 pages $8**

BB-154 **"Space Walrus" Kevin L. Donihe** — Walter is supposed to go where no walrus has ever gone before, but all this astronaut walrus really wants is to take it easy on the intense training, escape the chimpanzee bullies, and win the love of his human trainer Dr. Stephanie. **160 pages $11**

CPSIA information can be obtained at www.ICGtesting.com
Printed in the USA
LVOW06s0244050114

368082LV00001B/101/P